BLACK BLOOD

Also by S.D. Grimm

BLACK BLOOD

CHILDREN OF THE BLOOD MOON

BOOK THREE

S.D. GRIMM

an imprint of
GILEAD PUBLISHING

Black Blood,
Copyright © 2019 by S.D. Grimm

Published by Enclave, an imprint of Gilead Publishing, LLC,
Wheaton, Illinois, USA.
www.gileadpublishing.com
www.enclavepublishing.com

ISBN: 978-1-68370-084-5 (printed softcover)
ISBN: 978-1-68370-085-2 (ebook)

Cover design by Kirk DouPonce, www.DogEaredDesign.com
Interior design by Beth Shagene
Ebook production by Book Genesis, Inc.

Printed in the United States of America.

19 20 21 22 23 24 25 / 5 4 3 2 1

2019-04

This book is dedicated to my children.
I love you more than you know, all the days, forever.

And to Nemo, who is my Westwind.

ACKNOWLEDGMENTS

I started this series nine years ago, with a dream that I would one day be a published author. And now I'm typing "the end" on a nine-year journey with these characters, whom I've grown to love (and hate in the case of some of them); this world that exists as a magical, thriving place in my mind's eye; and this pilgrimage through which I have learned many things about myself. I am blessed to be able to share this story with you and honored that you have read it. In some ways, you have gone through this journey with me, but in other ways you have experienced something all your own through these pages. Such is the magic of a book.

Thank you, dear reader, for making it to the end. I hope this story is a journey you will take again. To revisit old friends, to learn something new about yourself, maybe even to share something you loved with your children someday.

There are so many people who helped make this book—this series —come to life. People who encouraged me when I needed it, who helped make this entire dream a reality, and who gave me the advice and feedback that was necessary.

I want to thank Steve Laube for contracting *Scarlet Moon* a couple years ago, for believing in my story and writing and then making my publishing dreams come true. And Ramona Richards, my editor, who sees the heart of my story and reminds me to keep that intact—and not stray from it. And Julie Gwinn, my agent, who believes in me and my talent. And Kirk DouPonce, who takes my idea for a cover and makes it a masterpiece.

The entire Gilead/Enclave team! Thank you all for doing everything you can to help make this the best book it can be. For your tireless hours helping us authors achieve our dreams. You are much appreciated.

Thank you, my amazing family. Phil, Caleb, Jordan, Mom, Dad, Molly, Shawn, Dale, Linda, you are all amazingly supportive, and I couldn't do this without that from the people I love so dearly. I thank my God every time I remember you.

To my "framily," Jamie and Keanan, Becky and Mike, Heather, and LoriAnn, I owe many thanks. You guys have listened to idea after idea, cheered me up when I needed it, and celebrated with me over every milestone. I am so thankful for our friendship. Form Voltron!

And my team of encouragers, Molly, Cilia, Evie, Lindsay, Avily, and Nadine. Thank you for being there for me when I need it. For being friends I can count on. For sharing laughs and wisdom and memories. I love you all dearly. All the heart-shaped emojis!

I am truly blessed to have so many people in my life who want to see my dreams succeed. Who want to see me continue to dream big. And I have my God to thank for all of that and much, much more. For giving me this talent, this story, this passion. For bringing amazing people into my life. For being the music my words dance to.

And to you, dear reader, thank you again. Your support means the world to me.

Until next time,
Sarah

CHAPTER 1

SO IT BEGINS

The metallic, sulfurous scent of ash and lava permeated the air. From the top of the hill, Logan watched the sun crest the horizon, red and hungry. Like the fire had been, like the lava had been, like the ground had been for blood.

Cracked, broken, and barren, the black chasm from which the dragon had lifted the Mistress's limp form marred the ground.

"The forest smells wounded." Westwind stood beside Logan, staring over the treetops. Trees that Quinn, their Whisperer, had moved with her thoughts. They blocked Logan and his faithful Feravolk army from whatever might come out of the chasm, but injured warriors or not, Logan wanted to get farther away from this place. Some of his army had already left for Moon Over Water, but many remained. Now that the Mistress of Shadows had been freed, she'd attempt to kill the land and all the Feravolk with it unless they could imprison her again. His people were on the battlefront. The Deliverers were their only hope.

He wasn't sure where the black dragon had taken the Mistress, but it had headed south, the direction of the palace. It wouldn't surprise him if the Mistress tried to sink her claws in there first. Control of the palace and its surrounding city of Filgrum would give the Mistress a central stronghold.

"It's dying." Aurora's voice was soft as a mournful howl.

Logan sensed it, too. The Forest of Woes felt sick. Decaying. Unnatural. As if there were no longer memory of animals living here, of trees thriving, of life.

The Mistress's power had done that. To defeat her, he needed Quinn to lead him to the final Deliverer. He already had two of the four—Jayden and his daughter, Serena—but to stop the Mistress and imprison her, he needed all four. First he had to find the third Deliverer and then head to the palace to rescue his son—the fourth Deliverer. A son who had already been in his presence once. His throat tightened.

Logan scanned the camp as his people began to stir in the morning light. Melanie, Gavin, and Ethan—Logan's team of faithful Protectors—slept near Serena, Jayden, and Quinn. His heart throbbed under the weight of knowing that these kids would have to face more evil than he'd seen in his lifetime if they were to save his people—their people.

Westwind's eyes gleamed brilliant yellow against the rust-orange sky. *"Do you think Quinn knows where our Deliverer is? She seems like a young pup."*

"Time to find out." Logan headed toward his army, who were spread out across the hill, the scarlet-red sun lighting his way.

Feravolk who had fought with him—Morgan and her Dissenters as well as those who remained from Island in the Swamp, whom Melanie and her husband, Gavin, had brought—awaited his orders. Those he'd sent ahead to his home camp of Moon Over Water would tell his leader, Alistair, what had happened so they could prepare for the inevitable war with the Mistress. As soon as she regained her strength, he wagered the Mistress would strike with more force than they'd seen even during the Blood Moon wars.

Quinn was asleep, huddled near Ethan, her bedroll pushed aside like a foreign object she'd never been taught to need. She wouldn't leave Ethan's presence. Made sense. He'd rescued her. Ethan didn't seem to mind. His oath to protect the Deliverers extended to Quinn, and he had good instincts. Logan would protect her as well.

Serena and Jayden woke and stretched as Logan approached. Ethan stood, already wearing his sword belt and an expectant expression.

Logan walked over to Quinn. She sat up, and as soon as she saw the wolves, she clutched a handful of her tattered clothes, eyes wide. She tried to hide behind Ethan, who touched Quinn's shoulder and crouched down to her eye level, which seemed slightly higher than the previous night. "Hey, it's okay. They're friends." He nodded to Logan. "What's wrong?"

Logan approached carefully, so as not to scare her. "Quinn, I have something for you. The last Whisperer gave it to me to give to you." He pulled the map book from his bag and held it out to her.

She stared at the book and reached for it, slowly. "Enya told me about this."

"Enya?" Serena knelt near her.

"My phoenix." Quinn's fingers closed around the book, and Logan thought he saw a faint purple flame spark in her eyes. "Yes. This was meant for me." She grinned. It made her look older and younger at the same time. Her eyes met his. "You knew the other Whisperer?"

Logan smiled as he nodded.

She opened the book and flipped through what appeared to be blank pages. "Some of it's locked. The Deliverers will need to touch it for me to open those parts. But these pages are not all—" She shrieked and dropped the book.

"What is it?" Jayden gripped her dagger's hilt.

Quinn trembled. She scooped the book up, and a breeze whispered through it, turning the pages. Then the wind stilled, and Quinn looked at the empty book. "The pages are made from leaves. Dried. Pressed. Their memories are here. New and old. They search to find the ones I need. Look."

Ethan gently touched her shoulder. "I don't think we see what you see, Quinn."

"It's me. When those two women caught me and tied me to the tree."

A picture melted onto the pages. A young girl. A shiver spread through Logan's core. They were burning her.

Westwind growled. *"No wonder she's as skittish as a snared deer."*

Quinn stared at Westwind with her eyes wide and backed away from him. Jayden reached out to touch Westwind's shoulder. Her calming touch soothed the wolf. Logan felt it across the bond.

Jayden turned to Quinn. "There's no need to fear Westwind. He's on our side."

"I'm sorry." She dipped her head and held the book close. "He scares me. The creature that hunted me was wolf-like."

Westwind chuffed then let out a low whine.

"Sorry," she said to him with as little eye contact as possible.

Logan inched closer. "Quinn, to stop the Mistress, we need—"

"To put her back into her prison. I know."

"We can't do that without the Deliverers."

She looked into Logan's eyes. "And our Wielder."

Another puzzle piece entirely. "Can you help us find them?"

Quinn drew up to her full height, which seemed taller than even a moment ago—she was growing before his eyes. The other Whisperer had told him this might happen, but Quinn looked older, too. "I will go ask the trees where the Deliverer is." She even sounded older. Without waiting for a response, she wandered off into a cluster of trees and sat on the ground among them.

"We should get her some new clothes," Serena said. "Those are already too small for her."

"She has grown, hasn't she?" Ethan glanced at Serena. "I thought it was my imagination."

Soft footfalls sounded behind Logan and he turned. Just as he spotted Kara, Westwind growled.

Kara shrugged at the wolf then looked at Logan, her eyes hard as he imagined any assassin's would be. "You think she'll be able to find your missing Deliverer?"

He didn't respond.

"Oh. Cold shoulder?"

"You did try to have us killed." Jayden shot her a frosty stare.

"No. Not killed. When will you see my intention—?"

"Is only for your personal gain. Always has been." Ethan positioned himself in front of Serena and Jayden, between them and Kara. "I don't think we have use for you."

"You do if you're going back to the palace."

Logan held out his hand to dissuade the situation. "I think you've done enough, Kara."

"I've lived in the palace for three years. I know it in and out. You need me on your little extrication mission. Trust me. Or don't. When you go for your son, I'm coming."

"We can't risk her infiltrating your camp, Logan." Ethan glared at Kara as he spoke. "If I remember correctly, that was her heart's desire back at the palace."

"Oh, soldier. I'm touched."

"Don't be. I keep my enemies close. Easier to kill that way."

"Okay." Serena placed her hand against Ethan's arm to keep him from encroaching on Kara even more. "What did she do to you?"

Logan made eye contact with his daughter. Did Serena see something in Kara's heart that made her tell Ethan to stand down? Was the woman trustworthy? Ethan didn't lessen his glare as Jayden promised to fill Serena in. Still, Logan wanted to trust his daughter's judgment, or at least find out what she saw. He shifted his focus to Kara. "Perhaps it's best if we keep an eye on her."

The assassin scoffed and crossed her arms.

"Is there trouble?" Melanie approached them, followed closely by Gavin. Kara pulled out a dagger and pretended to cut her fingernails. Melanie had been the one to bring Kara here, not knowing she was an assassin.

Gavin leaned close to Logan and motioned toward Quinn. She knelt in the copse, her eyes closed. A breeze that touched no one else fluttered her hair around her. "What is she doing?"

"Talking to the trees. It'll help her figure out where the final Deliverer and our Wielder are."

He narrowed his eyes and nodded. "How long will she be . . . like that?"

Logan shrugged. "I don't know, but my hope is that she finds out where the third Deliverer is soon."

Gavin glanced at Logan askance. "What's your plan?"

"I spoke with Reuben this morning. He and Beck are taking the rest of our Feravolk army as well as those from Island in the Swamp to Moon Over Water with a message for Alistair: We are going for the third Deliverer and then for my son." Logan closed his eyes as he thought of how long his son, the fourth Deliverer, had been trapped in the palace. "Alistair needs to be ready to declare war on the Mistress, because when I go for my son, it'll spur her into action no matter how much strength she's regained."

Gavin nodded. "So we move before she has a chance to gather her forces any more than she's already done?"

"Yes."

"And what of the Dissenters and their army?"

"I'll speak to Morgan and see if she wants to stay with us or go with the other Feravolk." He made eye contact with Melanie and then Ethan. "We go for the last Deliverers as soon as Quinn has word."

Kara sat down on a stone to sharpen her knife.

Logan leaned close to Ethan. "If you sense any threats from her—"

"I'll kill her."

Kara eyed Ethan askance, and her lips curled. "I'm hurt, soldier. After all we've been through together?"

"After all you've done to us."

She stood, sauntered closer to him, and traced a finger along his stomach. "After I stitched you up."

He grabbed her wrist and pushed her hand away, but didn't let go. "Kara. I had no idea I had such an effect on your pulse."

She pulled her hand back and smiled. "You have no idea about a lot of things, Ethan."

Gavin cocked his eyebrow and said for Logan's ears alone, "If I hadn't met Kara in Meese, I would think she knew I was bringing her right back to you three."

Logan led him and Melanie back down toward the Feravolk, who were packing up camp. "Who's to say she didn't?" Kara was up to something. The sooner he figured it out, the better. But he knew Ethan would be trying to pry that secret loose from her as well.

Morgan approached. Logan patted Gavin's shoulder and paused as Gavin and Melanie kept walking. Morgan's green eyes made her look old beyond her years. "I wanted to talk to you," she said meekly.

Due to her talent of clairvoyance, he guessed why. "You've seen something."

She opened her mouth slightly, then closed it and looked at the ground. "My sister is in the palace. I want to go with you when you go."

"You've seen me going?"

Her head jerked up and she wore a look of determination. "Yes. And you'll need my help."

"All the Dissenters?"

"Yes, my whole army." Her features softened.

Westwind bristled. *"The look of pity she gives you, Logan. I don't like it."*

"She's burdened, friend. She sees things I wouldn't wish on anyone that young to see."

Westwind chuckled. *"Human emotion looks good on you, when you choose to be heartfelt."*

Logan playfully pushed the wolf's face, then he looked at Morgan's sad eyes. "There's something more."

"Much more, but it's still formulating. I can't trust what isn't nailed down yet, so I don't dwell on it."

His stomach squeezed. "Is it something I can prevent?"

She looked deep into his eyes. "You'll do what's necessary if the time comes."

A pang pulsed over the bond from Westwind. Logan swallowed. "And what is it you have to do besides save your sister?"

"I have to lead the Dissenters to follow you." She smiled. "We will do whatever it takes to save the Feravolk, Logan. We are with you until the end."

The wind picked up. Whispers filtered through the breeze. Words Logan couldn't make out chanted over and over. He knew the sound. He'd heard it before. The trees were talking. Their voices thundered louder. Louder.

Then they hushed and Quinn screamed.

CHAPTER 2

EYES LIKE FIRE

Ethan raced into the copse of trees where Quinn still knelt, his hand clutching the hilt of his borrowed sword. The grooves in the worn leather didn't match up to his fingers. Unfamiliar. Uncomfortable. Like being this close to the erupted volcano—the broken prison of the Mistress of Shadows.

"Quinn?"

She didn't move. Well, she didn't acknowledge him, but she rocked back and forth. Knees to toes. Her eyes remained closed. Like someone who hadn't just screamed. Words escaped her lips, but he couldn't make them out.

He leaned forward and turned his head so his good ear could hear what she said. Still, he couldn't understand her. He approached her slowly. "Hey, Quinn?"

Her head jerked toward him, and she shrank back until her eyes focused on him. She shivered. "It's coming."

"What's coming?" The threat in his chest warmed, and his heart thrummed. "We should get out of here." He called out to his gryphon. *"Zephyr? Where are you?"*

"On my way. I feel a strange danger to you."

Quinn stood, gripping the map book to her chest with one arm and grabbing his hand. Her eyes widened. "The creatures of the dark. The worst ones. Enya warned me about them."

"Tell me about them." Why didn't he hear them? Did his deaf ear prevent him, or was this something unique to Quinn?

"Don't make me." She squeezed his hand tighter.

"Hey, hey, okay. Don't cry. I just need to know how to protect the others." With his borrowed sword. Unfamiliar enemies. Unfamiliar weapons.

She shuddered and, after a good amount of calming breaths, she stared at him, looking at once older and wiser. "Oh, Ethan. I hope someone will protect you." She brushed her fingertips over his cheek as a small child might touch a parent.

He wanted to assure her that he'd be okay, but heat shot through his core, and he stiffened. Stood and pushed her behind him. She was right. Something rode toward them. Something with a thirst for death.

Eeeeethaaaaan.

His name hissed through the wind in a deep, grinding whisper. He pressed hard against the sword hilt's grooves. He didn't care if it felt familiar or not.

"They want your heart," Quinn whispered. "Don't let them get it."

"Not my plan." He swallowed.

The ground trembled.

Smoke rose into the heavens from the other side of the trees—where the chasm sat. The dark clouds choked light from the sky, and the earth split open. Ethan herded Quinn toward Jayden and Serena. Serena's unicorn, Dash, and Jayden's pegasus, Stormcloud, bounded to their sides.

Zephyr landed beside him.

"Get out of here." Ethan waved for the others to run.

Logan raced up next to them. "What's happening?"

A strange glow seeped from the direction of the chasm and bathed the world in a red light. Old, brownish red.

"Blood in the heaven. Blood on the ground." Quinn's small voice grew stronger as she chanted the phrases three times. "We have to run." She buckled over and screamed.

Serena gripped the girl's shoulders, and her wild eyes met Ethan's. "What's wrong with her?"

"You can't tell?" he asked.

Quinn shrieked. "They're killing the trees. The forest is dying!"

Serena stared at her, eyes wide. "I don't know what to do. She feels like she's burning inside, but I can't heal it because it's not truly her pain."

Ethan stared at Quinn's writhing form. If Serena couldn't heal her, who could?

Logan shouted for the Feravolk army to ready themselves for an attack.

"Take her," Ethan whispered and made eye contact with Serena and Jayden. "Get her as far away from here as you can."

Zephyr ruffled his wings. *"That pit. Animals are pouring out of it."* *Eeeeethaaaaan.*

Jayden shuddered. "Did you hear that?"

"It's calling all of you." Quinn straightened. She appeared to shake off whatever had hurt her, and she looked older again. Nearly twelve or thirteen. She started moving away from them. Toward the edge of the hill where the chasm was more visible. It had grown. A stream of black poured up from the ground and out of the pit. Animals and liquid together formed an oozing black mass that spilled out, coating the earth. And the sounds deafened. Howls and groans and shrieks.

The ground quaked.

New cracks split the surface, swallowing trees. The harsh scent of burning soil stung Ethan's nose. Even on the hilltop, the movement sent him sprawling. He tried to keep track of the others as the earth shook and a massive fissure split the hill in two.

Ethan scrambled to his feet and scanned the hillside. Smoke made his eyes water. The girls were all close, but Quinn was nearly on top of the crack. He ran to her. She'd remained unshaken and still moved toward the danger. He grabbed her arm. A flare of heat zapped across Ethan's chest. He had to listen to his talent. "You have to get away from here. Take Serena and Jayden."

"No!" Quinn pushed him aside and stood like a tree with branches outstretched.

"Ethan!" Zephyr sounded panicked.

"Zephyr, help me protect the girls!"

Ethan's talent urged him to defend Quinn, and he raced in front of her, sword ready.

A massive animal sprang out of a new crack in the earth. Heavy paws slammed into him. Pinned him to the ground. His head rattled and he focused to retain consciousness. Eyes, black like pitch with no reflective light, locked onto him. Dark, greasy fur stuck out from its body in clumps that resembled molten lava. The heavy weight shifted as it leaned closer to him. Opened its mouth wider than any normal animal should be able to. And its roar shook Ethan to the core.

He wiggled one arm free, gripped his borrowed weapon tight, and stabbed. His sword went right through the beast's chest. It shrieked. The shriek morphed into a laugh, and it lunged closer, sliding down the blade as if nothing impaled it. Ethan struggled to free the blade as his talent warned him in a burning wave.

The animal's head fell to the ground, and Logan stood over it, holding a reddened sword. "You okay, kid?"

Blood, like coagulated strings of maggots, fell onto Ethan's shirt, and he pushed off the still-standing, headless beast. He jumped up, brushing the remains from his clothes. "Why didn't my sword—" Breathing heavily, he stared at the bloody blade.

Quinn touched his weapon. "You can't fight these creatures with that sword. You need a Wielder-crafted weapon."

Great. He'd lost the Wielder-made one, which Logan had let him borrow, to Scarface. His chest heaved. If this sword wouldn't kill them, he'd have to—

Jayden passed Ethan one of her long daggers. "Don't lose this one." She smiled.

Grateful, he took it. "Thank you. Now run."

Stormcloud bent down, and Jayden and Serena climbed on top of her. Jayden looked at Ethan. "What about you?"

"I protect the Deliverers. Now take Quinn and go."

She nodded, and he turned to face the enemy as Stormcloud's wings beat behind him. Dash and Zephyr stayed, flanking him and Logan. Whatever came out of that chasm carried an evil he could feel. Like oil in the air. He shuddered.

Feravolk warriors flooded up the hill toward them.

Ethan clutched Jayden's weapon tight and glanced at Logan, who stared ahead at the approaching mass of black creatures. Westwind and Aurora joined them.

A shriek pierced the burnt red sky as even more flooded out of the mouth of the chasm. Creatures with eyes like fire rushed toward them through the opening and up the hill.

Liquid, darker than pitch, rose up from the ground, seeped into the trees. When one fell, others moved to take its place. But the trees withered and fell like charred sticks in the wind.

"You have to run, too!"

A jolt of surprise rocked through Ethan at that voice, and he looked over his shoulder. "Quinn? How did you—"

"I couldn't leave you here. If you fight them now, when they are at their most ravenous—the trees cannot hold this many. You will all be killed. Tell Logan. He'll listen to you."

A quiet tug in his talent told him to listen. He didn't want to. It pulled against every protective instinct, but Quinn had remained. He had to get her safe.

Logan touched his shoulder. "She speaks wisdom, kid." He shouted orders for all of them to retreat.

"Ethan!" Quinn screamed.

The fire in his chest caused him to turn.

Smoke that sucked the color out of the air spread out of the mouth of the crack like steam over the surface of water. A huge, canine-like animal stood in the center of the billowing cloud. Its fur glowed like a charred, smoldering log. Ethan stepped in front of Quinn and squared off against the creature. It resembled a massive wolf, rivaling Dash in size. Ethan's eyes locked onto the red flames where the creature should have eyes, and he got pulled into a memory.

He was at the Winking Fox again. Tessa was there—the inn-keeper's daughter, the one who had saved him. Her smile was golden in the evening sun.

Oh no. He knew this night.

The night he'd died.

○

A warm summer breeze filtered through the property out front of the Winking Fox, and Ethan held his sword. A man stood across from him and sneered. Ethan swore he saw flames flicker in the man's eyes, but he shook away the thought.

"Stone Wolf dies tonight." The man's smile seemed evil.

"Dies? It's a friendly sport match." Ethan held out his hands as if to dissuade the man's rising aggression. From time to time, some men forgot the fights were friendly—especially when they found out who he was.

"Not for me." The man's voice took on a deeper tone, almost as if two voices came out of his mouth at once. "Tell me, Stone Wolf, do you believe in Destiny Path?"

Ethan lowered his chin, sword ready. "Nobody chooses my destiny but me."

"Really?"

The man struck the first blow before the fight officially started. Ethan's sword blocked the blade in time. The man was twice as wide as Ethan. His shirt barely contained his muscles, but he couldn't beat Ethan's strength. Ethan's Blood Moon talent made sure of that.

Their swords clashed and Ethan struck again. The man moved back toward the crowd. Ethan kept striking, pushing. His talents worked to show him the threat. His speed fueled him. He felt so alive tonight. On fire. The crowd cheered, and Ethan disarmed the man.

The man fell to the ground, leg nicked. Per the rules, he'd lost and the fight was over.

Ethan held out his hand to help him up. "Good fight."

The man grabbed Ethan's arm, and his iron grip tightened. The fire in Ethan's talent raged, the deepest, hottest warning he'd ever felt. Fear, hot and cold at once, spiked through his blood, and he tugged at his trapped arm. He couldn't break free. It was too late.

The man looked into Ethan's eyes and smirked. "I choose your destiny." His sword pierced Ethan. It stabbed right through his middle. Pressure like he'd never felt speared his stomach and gave way to the burning sting of pain. So much pain.

The man released Ethan's arm, and Ethan stumbled back. Screams muffled all around him as the faces of the crowd grew hazy. Except Tessa's. Crying, she raced toward him. He looked down. His hands curled around the weapon protruding from his stomach. He'd been run through. Blood, bright and spreading, leaked out of him. Stained everything.

Everything hurt.

Even his thoughts.

And he shivered.

Fell to his knees so hard his teeth chattered.

"Ethan!" Tessa's voice cut through the haze. Her face came into focus above him, and he realized he'd fallen onto his back. "Someone help me!" she screamed. A tear clung to her cheek, not dripping off. Sunlight sparkled in the tear, and when Ethan stared at it, he could almost imagine the pain leaking from his body into something else. Not the ground. Not the earth. Somewhere else.

Or he was going somewhere else and leaving the pain behind.

"Ethan, hold on, please."

He wanted to.

Then she was gone. No Tessa. No pain.

Only light.

Bright light that didn't blind him. Then a darkness crept through the corners of the vision and suffocated the light.

Eeeeethaaaaan.

This wasn't how it went that night. He gasped, all at once unable to breathe. Slim fingers covered his eyes, and Ethan sucked in air.

"Don't look. It'll kill you." Quinn's voice. She tugged his arm, and he became fully aware of what was happening around him again. The creatures from the chasm clamored around them. He had to save Quinn. But where was that beast? The one that had caused him to recall his death in vivid detail?

"Don't look for it, Ethan." Quinn tugged his arm. "I sent the trees after it. They won't hold it off forever."

He swallowed and nodded, seeing the wisdom in her words. Together, they mounted Zephyr.

"I thought I'd lost you there," Zephyr said. *"You weren't responding."*

Quinn shivered in his arms. "I don't know how you resisted its pull for so long. It was trying to claim you."

He shuddered. "What was?"

"The barghest. The Mistress has two. She calls them Gnarg and Garmr. And that one wants to claim you."

"You all right, friend?" Zephyr's voice was a calm wind that reached into Ethan's soul.

Ethan clenched his jaw. This barghest's eyes matched the eyes of the man who had killed him that night. So it was true. The creature was coming for him again. It could come at him all it wanted. He wouldn't be so easy to kill this time.

CHAPTER 3

STRIKE THE LAND

Dark, black forms still poured out of the chasm below them, swallowing light from the sky. Jayden clutched Stormcloud's mane tight as the wind whipped her hair around her face. Wild wind. Scared wind. Each blast bit into her skin like a frightened child clawing at her mother's sleeve.

She couldn't calm it.

Serena hugged Jayden's waist as Stormcloud's wings buffeted the wind. "There are so many."

Creatures that looked like fire. And black creatures that moved to reveal folds in their fur that resembled molten lava. Beasts with terrible roars and shattering shrieks. Jayden shook from the inside out. "What are they?"

"Monsters the Mistress created. Their purpose is to hunt the Deliverers and bring them to her."

The way they sniffed the air and looked up into the sky made Jayden squeeze her knees reflexively. Stormcloud moved as if she understood the need to get farther away.

Ethan was down there. Right in the mouth of the battle. Protecting her. She had to do something to help. This was all her fault. She hadn't kept the seeing heart from falling into the volcano. She'd freed the Mistress. "We have to stop them from escaping."

"How?" Serena asked. "We don't know where the Mistress is to put her back. Do we even know how to put her back?"

"Quinn knows." But Quinn had said she'd fly on Zephyr. Jayden scanned the sky. Where was the gryphon?

As Jayden's emotions battled inside of her, Stormcloud stayed above the pit, hovering in the tumultuous wind. *"You are calling the storm. I feel it growing stronger."*

"You're sure?"

"I feel your emotions alive in the air."

Jayden closed her eyes and reached out to the storm with her talent as if it were a person whose emotions she was trying to read. Wind flowed through her like blood. Tossed her hair, wrapped around her heart. This *was* her storm. Her fear pulsed into it. *"I didn't know I could do that."* And it changed everything. "The lightning disabled the firegoat. Do you think it can close the chasm?"

"I think we can try."

Jayden glanced over her shoulder and locked eyes with Serena. Fear pumped through Serena, but that wasn't her strongest emotion. Hope had the strength. It warmed inside her like a beacon. Jayden clung to that warmth.

She didn't want the raging storm to leave, and when she pulsed hope into it, instead of fading, the storm grew stronger. Became easier for her to hold on to. Almost as if a storm born of her fear took more energy than one made from hope.

Serena squeezed Jayden's shoulder. "Look."

More creatures slithered out of the pit—fiery creatures and creatures that looked to be made of smoke. But these took to the sky.

Jayden gripped Stormcloud's mane tight and pulled out her dagger. The storm built inside of her, strong and heavy. A weapon much too large to wield for more than one strike.

Serena touched her shoulder. "I'll hold off the monsters. Do what you can."

But Serena's fear still tickled the back of Jayden's mind. Could she really protect Jayden if she feared being up here in the sky?

"Time to trust us to do our part," Stormcloud's voice whispered into her soul. *"I'll keep you close enough. Strike the land. Strike hard."*

Trust. Jayden breathed deep. Using a storm was one thing. Creating one and filling it with enough charge to strike lightning pulled at her like a tight seam on an outfit she was outgrowing. If she did this, she may not have strength left to fight.

"Dash says Logan ordered them to retreat," Serena said. "All it's done is spurred a hunt from the creatures."

Jayden squinted, trying to see what happened below. Streams of black and fire headed toward fleeing people. A line of defenders stood in the way, letting Feravolk pass as they waited for the never-ending influx of evil to hit them. Her heart clenched. Ethan stood in that line. She couldn't make him out, but she knew he'd be standing there with Logan and Westwind and Dash. She had to do something to limit the number of escaping creatures.

Stormcloud let out a thunderous roar and jostled. "Look out!" Serena pushed Jayden into the back of Stormcloud's neck and slashed her dagger at a creature in the air. Flames licked its streamlined body. Stormcloud shot through the clouds. A firegoat chased them.

"Now, Jayden!" Stormcloud tried to kick the monster and missed. Wind buffeted.

"I feel your fear in the storm. The creatures will feed on it. Call the wind as your friend. Fill it with righteous anger. Save them."

Jayden clung to Stormcloud's words.

Creatures shrieked and flew toward them. Jayden closed her eyes and breathed.

The storm inside her swelled. Holding her breath, she felt the sky congregating for a lightning strike. Electricity bled into her. Made her hair stand on end. Sent a thrill through her.

The creatures in the sky balked, hovering just outside of the storm.

The time was now. Fire in the sky crackled. "Hold on, Serena." She pointed her dagger into the air.

A bolt sent life through her, and she caught the lightning. It filled her weapon and she shot her arm forward. Stared at the angry pit. Pulsed her energy toward it. She released the dagger, and it plummeted to the earth, sending the lightning strike ahead of it.

A crack jolted the earth and sky at the same time. Had it worked? Stormcloud took them higher, out of the electricity's reach.

The sky turned from burnt red to bright yellow. Red melted away, a receding bloodstain, leaving the white of lightning and then a flash of blue. Shrieking animals fled, keeping to the shadows.

The storm receded and light rain sprinkled around them. Cleansing rain. Slowly, red overtook the sky again, but not as dark as before.

Jayden's heart thundered in her chest, and she felt as though she'd just run for an eternity.

Serena gasped and shook Jayden's shoulders. "You did it."

A dark mark covered the ground where the chasm had been. A healing scar. And her dagger protruded from the center. It hadn't closed all of the surface cracks, but the huge hole was covered. The lightning had worked.

Serena squeezed her tight, and Jayden slumped into her embrace, light-headed. Serena touched her temples. "That took a lot of energy out of you."

"I'm certain I couldn't do it again. Not until I've rested."

"Here." Some of Serena's strength poured into her, and Jayden squeezed her arm. This woman, whom she loved like a sister, always had the healing she needed.

"Thank you. I couldn't have done it without you and Stormcloud."

"We all work together. No reason to thank me for that."

Stormcloud fluttered to the ground, and as they slid from her back, Ethan and Logan rushed over.

Dash approached, too, his horn stained with blood. *"I think we got all those hunting us, but we better get out of here. They retreated to the shadows of the Mistress's presence—they are too weak to be far from her. They tore out looking for blood on their way to find her. But as she gets stronger, their reach will extend further."*

Logan was breathless. He looked at Jayden. "Well done. I didn't know you could—"

"I didn't either. Not until yesterday." She smiled at Stormcloud.

Ethan returned her dagger. "You okay?" he whispered and pulled her close.

She hugged him tight. "For now."

Quinn approached them, holding the map book close but no longer clutching it like a scared child. She looked nearly fourteen now.

Jayden felt for Quinn's emotions, and a deep-rooted fear seeped through her. "What's wrong, Quinn?"

"The trees have cut us off from the chasm. The creatures can't get to us for now, but we aren't going to be safe here for long." Quinn hugged her arms around herself and the book. "But it's the prison that worries me."

"What about it?" Logan asked.

"Jayden's dagger is stuck there. She closed it effectively. The oak tree will hold that dagger down with its roots. No one who isn't intended to pluck it from the earth will be able to." She turned to Logan. "But now we won't be able to put the Mistress back."

Jayden's knees weakened, and she sank to the ground. *What have I done?*

"She must be killed," Quinn said. "But we need the Wielder and all four Deliverers."

Logan wiped his hand over his face. "First we need to get away from here. Quinn, did the trees tell you what you needed to know? Do you know who the other Deliverer is?"

"Yes. The fourth Deliverer is in the palace."

Logan bowed his head. "I should have been more specific. I know my son is there. Do you know where the other male Deliverer is?"

"I'm sorry?"

"We have Jayden and Serena. My son, Connor, is at the palace. I need the fourth. It's the child who went to Nivek."

"Oh." Quinn's hazel eyes widened. "I thought you knew."

Something in Jayden's chest squeezed tight and galloped forward at once. She was sensing Logan's emotions. Had the child died? Could they defeat the Mistress without the final Deliverer now that the prison was closed?

Logan swallowed. "Knew what?"

"Ethan is the other Deliverer."

CHAPTER 4

BLACK CHASMS

On four paws, Connor stepped over the cracked earth. Black liquid, as dark and sticky as pitch, bubbled up from the surface. He stooped down and sniffed. It smelled the same as old, decaying blood. A hissing sound, like a swarm of bees, filtered through him. The sky wasn't as dark now, but if it rained today, he would expect it to rain red.

The earth was dying. He felt it like aftershocks from an earthquake. And the ground split wider at the crack. A tree wailed out in pain and fell into a chasm.

Then a creature laughed and rose from the surface. More monsters followed. The dark beasts.

"I knew you'd come." A voice hissed around him. Through him. His fur stood on end.

This was a dream. He was dreaming.

"It's more than a dream."

A vision. Connor turned. A woman stood behind him, separated from him by the chasm. The scarlet sky seemed like a sunset behind her. Auburn hair blew in the wind, and she pierced him with eyes as blue as a clear lake. She was beautiful.

The Mistress.

He bristled and growled. "Step into the light. Let me see how you've decayed."

She shrieked as the vision shifted. Her hair turned stringy, and she smelled of death. Her skin became pale and bony, and her eyes clouded. The sunset dripped like spreading wine. "You know it's you I want. I've always wanted you. I will have you for my husband, or I will kill you."

"Expect to kill me, then. I will destroy you."

She laughed. A horrible sound that cracked the earth. Hounds bayed, and their sounds echoed through the ground.

The hair on his back stood up in a straight line. The abysshounds were calling. They were hunting.

"They search for the Deliverers. I will find all of you. I will take their powers, but I will spare yours. And I will spare you, but I will leave them as dead husks on the ground. Then I will walk over their bodies to my wedding altar. To you, powerful one. Dark one."

A low growl rumbled in his throat. "You cannot have me."

Two tall wolfish forms stepped out from the folds of her dress. Their eyes burned with heat. Eyes too large for their faces. One stepped forward. "Smoke talked of you and your powers. I am an animal, but you don't control me."

Connor froze. No one knew his true powers. Control wasn't the right word, but close enough.

"I am Gnarg. Would you like to see your death?" The creature's canine teeth unfolded—the same as a serpent's fangs—as he opened his mouth wider than natural for any canine. "You know what I am, don't you?"

A blackdog. Death bringer. Barghest. Created by the Mistress of Shadows, Gnarg the male and Garmr the female. They foretold death. Showed it to their victims, then claimed them when the time came. They both used fear to scare their victims to death. Then the Mistress collected those fears to breed new blackdogs. Fears fathered the abysshounds.

Connor shivered. The abysshounds were nothing like him. They may be wolfish, but they stood taller, towered above him. Their fur resembled hot embers, glowing red and black.

"You're afraid," Gnarg said. "You fear that you will become me. A destroyer. You already are."

Connor willed himself to wake. He had to before Gnarg showed him his death and used the vision to destroy him. His eyes opened. He couldn't control his breathing.

"She will find you and have you for her own." Gnarg's final words thundered in Connor's skull. He found himself curled up on the floor in his wolf form.

A strange pull tugged him like another lasso trying to wrap him with a trace spell. The Mistress was looking for him. He wouldn't be able to use his powers. If he did, he'd be a flame and she'd be a very dangerous moth.

Had the chasm only opened last night? Already it felt so strong. He could sense the cursed animals fleeing the confines of their prison, yet he knew they drew closer to where he was. His heart skipped a beat— that meant the Mistress was close. Here in the palace. He trembled. He'd have to stay clear of her or she'd recognize him.

Connor changed into a man and grabbed his clothes. He had to tell Luc and Madison that he was leaving. Remaining here was too dangerous. He still needed to stay away from the other Deliverers, though. He was a lone wolf now. As it should have been all along. His mother, Rebekah, had hoped he'd be able to have a family someday, but she didn't really understand the scope of his powers. It was better this way.

He sighed and sank to the ground, leaned back against his bed, and cupped his head in his hands. This was the danger of getting attached to people. He had one purpose: lock the Mistress away forever. To do that, he'd kill everyone close to him, unless he could avoid using his powers. Because he was a fool if he thought he could keep anyone safe.

He'd just have to meet up with Luc and see if his friend could help Madison escape. The poor Healer. She needed to be freed from Franco's hold.

Something scratched across his spine like the clawing of mice against his wall. He felt the Mistress sniffing.

He shivered. His body tried to shift into wolf form.

Heat.

Skin.

Heat.

Fur.

Emotions toyed with his control. He focused on his human form. He shouldn't need to. Being a human was him; being a wolf was him. Taking on someone else's form took energy from him, as did shifting, but these two forms were his—him. He should have total control over which form to remain in. The anger that made him want to change wasn't his. That anger belonged to his powers. Those weren't his.

Connor focused. Breathed to calm himself. Opened his eyes. They flashed a reflection of light in the mirror across from him: wolf eyes. Human form. His eyes only changed when he took on another person's form. Whether wolf or man, Connor had the same color eyes.

Light flashed into them again. Crackles. His power. The things he could do. He couldn't let his powers manifest. Couldn't let them try to infiltrate him. He had to keep them buried. The memory of a blue porcelain bowl shattering. A mirror cracking. The pond drying like a desert puddle in the sun. Dead animals. Dead trees. So much death when his powers trickled out or escaped.

Rebekah's voice in his ear reminded him: *"Connor, you must hide your power. The things you can do could destroy us all if you're not careful. You are a weapon, my son. A dangerous weapon."*

"But I don't want to destroy you. I don't want to destroy anything."

Her lips were soft on his forehead. *"That's why you must control it. Keep it buried."*

"When I'm angry, it comes out."

She looked into his eyes, her love palpable. "I know, my son. You want to help. To heal. You are noble. You are good. Your power is yours for a reason."

He'd believed her then. When he was young and trusting. But now? He'd dried too many ponds. Watched fish suffocate while he could do nothing to save them. He'd made trees explode. The shards of wood impaled poor animals that died with wide eyes asking him, "Why?" He'd caused a boulder to break and knocked a nest of baby birds to the ground. Life crippled when he used his powers. If this power was his burden, perhaps the best way to help was to stay away from the others.

The man is you.

The thought came softly, a tiny footprint on his heart. Was it his thought? He didn't think so, yet he believed it like it was his own thought, even if it had surprised him. Something Rebekah would say. He might be a wolf, but he was a man. Both. He cared. He was supposed to stick to the mission. It was harder to have a plan when he cared for the people he'd likely be leading to their deaths.

The others, Ethan and Jayden, were they even okay? He should go find them, but that tug in his heart whispered: *stay.*

Why?

The wolf is you.

It was true. The instinct in him had served him flawlessly so far. He'd pushed Rebekah out of the window, trusted the gryphon to catch her, led Ethan to Quinn. He had to help from afar. That's what he was best at. Up close, he was too dangerous. One more thought broke into his head unbidden:

Your power is you.

CHAPTER 5

BELLY OF THE BEAST

A stab of pain pressed into Ryan's side and he jolted awake. His arms wouldn't move the way he wanted, and pins and needles shot through them. The soft, velvety fur of Mist, Belladonna's black lion, rubbed against his cheek. He tried to sit up, but his arms were tied around the creature's neck. He must have fallen asleep on top of it. Belladonna had tied him to it and mounted the black beast behind him.

Of all the things to fall asleep on, a black lion?

"Morning, pet." Belladonna's voice carried to his ear from behind him, and her warm body pressed against his back. "We're home."

Ryan craned his neck at the towering brick wall surrounding the palace. A shudder raced through him, and Belladonna laughed her sultry laugh. He'd been in the belly of this beast before and almost hadn't made it out alive. This time he'd make it his lair. He'd be the dragon that lured Belladonna to her demise.

If only his insides would stop tying into knots.

Belladonna dropped off the creature and cut his ropes. Ryan slid, trying to gain purchase on the slick fur as he forced his sleep-weakened arms to move. His shoulders ached. He grabbed fur. The big cat hissed and the scent resembled sour wine—venom. He knew that smell. Flinching, he let go of his hold and fell to the ground.

Belladonna inched closer. "Don't think about running, or I'll have to heal you of a few arrow wounds to the spine."

Ryan swallowed and looked behind him at the two men accompanying her. Their smiles baited him to run.

Being a dragon was harder than he'd thought. They always appeared so calm until they struck. Running now would be a death wish. But complying would be suicide.

Still, he had to get inside, right? After all, according to Morgan, the pretty brunette he'd met at the Winking Fox, he was supposed to be heading to the palace—if her vision was true. She was counting on him to save her sister, Madison. And to find a key. Infiltrate the king's guard. Something astonishingly stupid like that. She'd also mentioned kissing a blonde, though. So there was that.

Was it wrong to hope that'd be Serena?

Either way, for the plan to work, he had to make Belladonna believe he was her Cain or whatever her old lover's name was. If he didn't run now—like a scared Ryan would—she'd see through his motives.

He'd find that bloody key all right. And he'd free Madison from the clutches of the palace. And the only kissing he'd be doing would be when Serena came for him. *If* she came for him. Thank the Creator that Morgan had seen him kissing a blonde-haired girl and not crazy Belladonna. After being healed from the black lion venom, he'd experienced every sensation as if it were happening for the first time. As if he could feel it fully through every fiber of his being. A new chance. A gift. So he'd save that new first kiss for someone special.

That meant he had one thing to look forward to in the palace.

He could stay strong and stoic for that.

Strong and stoic: the Granden motto. He was a Granden after all. So it had to be in his blood. Even if right now, a couple of arrows in the back scared him to death. It was sure to feel pretty awful.

Honestly, why was this his burden?

What was he, some hero? No. And no one in their right mind would mistake him for one.

"If you seek chivalry, you're on the wrong side, Knight. My pawns are creatures of darkness."

The voice hissed in his head, and he shook it away. Then he looked up at Belladonna's challenging smile to see if she noticed that he was plagued by the voice of a madwoman in his head—a white lion who taunted him. Belladonna dared him to disobey her. So did the voice in his head. He wasn't their pawn. He was a dragon, luring both of them to their doom. He ran.

The sound of a bowstring twang, soft and subtle, vibrated behind him. He'd felt arrows in his flesh before. The pain of this one had most definitely been intensified since the black lion venom.

Mist landed in front of Ryan. Crimson claws extended. Yellow-moon eyes locked onto him. It thrashed its tail and pounced. Fire bled into his palms. He'd killed black lions before. He could kill this one, too.

"Use the fire."

No. He had to get inside.

"That's a good boy."

Wait. The voice wanted him inside? His hands became as cold as a stone covered with dew in the moonlight. Cold as ice on a lake. Cold. So cold.

The black lion hissed.

Belladonna pushed Ryan's shoulder, and he fell onto his back. The arrow broke beneath him, pushed in harder. He screamed as pain ripped through him. He couldn't get up.

"Stupid boy." Belladonna's eyes traced his face. Her dark lips pressed together and her eyes glared. "You have no idea what angering me will do to you."

"I have a pretty good idea."

"I think not." Her hand neared his face, and he expected another harsh smack, then hopefully some healing. She cocked her head and looked into his eyes as if he were nothing more than some beloved pet she was about to punish. That made his insides freeze.

Her fingers touched his ear. A stroke, so strange, like his mother might do to comfort him. Then pain flooded him. Leaked deep into his skin. The arrows from the day he'd saved Jayden seemed to strike him anew. One in his chest, the other in his thigh. He felt every part of them. Felt the venom they'd carried. His blood burned. Boiled. And he screamed so hard his throat turned raw.

While the pain pulsed into him over and over, strong and steady with each heartbeat, Belladonna wrenched the new arrow free, and black spots danced in his vision.

He was going to black out.

Going to fade out.

Going to—she touched him again and everything stopped.

Shaking, chest heaving, and lying in his own sweat, he stared up at her, helpless.

Her dark eyes glimmered. "Every ounce of pain you've ever felt leaves residue in your body like a map through your own personal road of torture. It's a veritable playfield for someone like me to find."

"S-someone like you?"

"A Healer."

"I–I thought you were supposed to help people."

"Only if you don't anger me, pet." Her eyes changed to match the ferocity of the black lion's. Wild and animalistic and crazy. "When you anger me, I can unleash pain in you. Every piece of agony you've ever felt all at once. And don't worry. If you're not afraid of the pain inside you, I can give you plenty more to suffer. I will have you begging for my love."

"Never." *Did I really say that out loud?*

Her hand zipped back, ready to strike his face, but she froze. Her hand remained in the air, waiting like a dog vying to be released for the hunt. He didn't cringe. Didn't flinch. Held his ground. But he didn't want to. He wanted to cry.

"I will break you." The way she said it didn't reveal any anger or persuasion. She believed she'd break him. "Stand up." She motioned for her men to lift him.

He cried out as the pain in his back ripped through him again. Belladonna stood in front of him, the two men still supporting his weight, and pressed her hand against his chest. Warmth flickered into him, not from within him. From her. His wound closed, healed. His legs worked. Then, unbearable heat trickled into him and the ghost of pain spread out from his back. It stopped before his knees buckled.

"It's that easy, pet. I give pain and I take pain. Which you receive depends entirely on you. Now, we're going to meet the king. You will comply, or I'll make you wish you were dead."

He had to get inside. Had to remain the dragon. Dragons were not pets. He faced the gate and clenched his jaw. He had to be a Granden: strong and stoic.

"Good." Belladonna purred. Then she ran her hand along his neck. He flinched. She chuckled. "This is going to be fun."

Hands bound anew and a black lion breathing on his neck, he followed her into the palace. Up the stairs and into the throne room. As soon as the doors opened, a stench Ryan hadn't smelled the last time he'd been there assaulted him.

If he had to name the smell, it would be death. Like dirt. Not fresh dirt. This dirt was old, the kind that sat atop dead-and-buried horses. It matched the awful smell of opening the cellar door to find all of the potatoes had gone rotten—only worse.

Someone in this room smelled dead. He had a pretty good idea who it was, too. The bony, wasted-away form on the throne.

The throne was angled sideways, as if to keep the figure out of direct sunlight. A skeletal hand draped over the armrest. The fingers looked thin and frail. Perhaps it was a woman.

Belladonna approached two men. She called the one with a hooked nose and long fingers Oswell. The other man turned as Belladonna sauntered toward him. A face Ryan would never forget. King Franco. The last time they'd met—for lack of a better word—he'd unleashed a black lion on Ryan and tried to bed Jayden.

She'd left him alive.

It was one of those things he loved about her.

Despite everything that happened, everything Franco had tried to do to her in the palace, Jayden had had the chance to kill him and left him alive. For some reason, that strange act of pity gave Ryan hope. It meant this, whatever it was—fate, destiny path—hadn't tainted her heart fully. One of them might make it out of this unscathed. Untainted by evil. She was still Jayden.

Sure, when backed into a corner, she'd killed to survive. But when given the choice to spare a life, she had. There was still reason to hope for good.

Now that he'd killed someone—killed more than one person—and the venom pulsed in his every heartbeat, he wondered what would become of him. He thought of Belladonna's men—of Cain, now that she'd given him a name—falling off his sword. Lifeless. Scared. Dead.

Dead.

Dead.

"Blood looks good on you. Dried and black."

Ryan shook and crushed his eyes closed.

The wasted form on the throne moved. Her eyes met his. Blue like a sky trying to break through a thin veil of clouds. Cold and depressing. Hopeless.

Her hair was limp and stringy so that her ears—rather large for her head—stuck through the dull strands. Her hair almost looked wet. Not the wet of a rainfall. No, this wet resembled someone who was either just born or had been dead a long time.

By the stench in the room, he guessed the latter.

Her eyebrow cocked. There was no way she'd heard his thoughts, but his heart skittered like a skipping stone that failed to make its last skip. Now a small smile tugged her lips.

Thin, colorless lips.

Belladonna and Franco were talking. About him. He'd heard his name, but his ears wouldn't tune into the conversation within reach. This woman had captured his attention and held it in a vise grip.

"Pet!"

Belladonna's words dragged him slowly out of the reach of that dead-but-alive woman's eyes.

"Yes, it looks as if he's very in-tune with you, Belladonna." The way Franco said her name betrayed his lust for her.

She jerked Ryan's ropes and he stumbled closer. Now his gaze caught something else. A key. That snapped the fog away from wrapping around his brain. Morgan had been right. There was a key, and Franco wore it around his neck.

Franco glared. "I fail to see how he will be of any use."

"He's one of Logan's."

A flicker of heat shot through Franco's eyes, and he rubbed his hands together. "Will Logan come to rescue him?"

Hopefully. Ryan swallowed. He didn't feel very like a dragon right now. Time to stop being caught off-guard.

"Of course he will." Belladonna purred.

"He won't," Ryan said.

Now he had Franco's attention. The man walked closer. "What makes you say that?"

"He doesn't know I'm missing. And he won't until he heads back to the place he left me."

"Kill him."

"Wait." Ryan was surprised to hear Belladonna's protest precede his own. "I made sure the boy's sister got away. Two of my men followed her. She'll run straight to Logan."

"We still don't need him alive."

"He killed my men. I need replacements. Do I have your permission to"—a sly smile slid over her mouth—"train him?"

Franco's eyes narrowed. "In order to receive gifts, you have to have done something worthwhile."

"Oh, I have." She smiled. "I have a link to Logan. Well, not him directly, but that handsome one who runs around with him, protecting the Deliverer."

Ethan? Ryan lost his breath.

"Tell me about this link." Franco drummed his fingers on his biceps. They weren't very impressive. Ryan instinctively flexed his own.

"In order to set the link, I need a spell." She touched the key on Franco's neck, and he watched her with his lust-filled eyes.

It was a key to the spells chamber? *Oh great.* Like he was supposed to be able to get his hands on that? Well, if Belladonna could use it, perhaps he could get it from her. If he played the part of her pet. *Oh, Morgan, what did you see?* Too bad her vision hadn't come with a step-by-boring-step solution.

Franco reluctantly lifted the key from his neck. "Make your spell and train your little soldier. We need those Deliverers." His eyes met Ryan's for an instant, then he turned back to Belladonna. "If he doesn't break, you'll kill him, so don't get attached."

"Don't worry, he'll break." She pushed him toward the door, and Ryan was careful not to look at the key as she placed it over her head and let it rest in the dip of her collarbone. Okay, so he did look, but then he trailed the length of her body so it seemed a little less like he was trying to steal a key and fulfill some not-that-heroic destiny.

Then he caught sight of the bony figure in the chair one last time.

She watched him with her pale eyes. A smile tugged her thin, cracked lips. "I'm the Mistress of Shadows, Ryan. It's nice to finally meet you." And her voice matched the purring one in his head.

CHAPTER 6

LEVELS OF HELL

What? No. Jayden's heart stilled and her hands shook as Quinn's words echoed in her mind. Ethan could not be one of the Deliverers.

Ethan backed away from Quinn, shaking his head. "I'm not a Deliverer, Quinn. I'm one of the Protectors."

Jayden opened her talent and searched his emotions desperately. His pounding heart and denial matched hers.

Quinn's eyes rounded. "Oh, Ethan, I've known you were a Deliverer since we first met."

The sound that came from Logan's throat was a deep growl. He fisted his hands. "How could I have missed it? Anna said the Deliverers would be drawn to me." He stared at Ethan. "There's one way to know for sure." He walked over to his things and pulled out the velvet rolled-up bag.

Jayden knew that bag. It housed the Deliverers' weapons. Her chest tightened.

"No." Ethan backed away from Logan, waving his hands. "You already gave me a sword from there. It didn't mark me."

"Why would being a Deliverer be so bad, Ethan?" Serena touched his shoulder.

He whirled to face her. "I'm supposed to *protect* you. It's my purpose."

His emotions clung to that sentiment. The panic that coursed through him echoed Jayden's. Surpassed it. He *needed* to protect.

Logan offered Ethan the sword, tip down. Jayden stared at the blade as it cut the empty space between her and Ethan.

Stormcloud fluttered her wings. *"Why are you so sad, Jayden?"*

The blade betweem then blurred as she finally let her gaze wander to Ethan. *"Because, Stormcloud, I love him."*

"Not all the Deliverers die."

"If he's a Deliverer, he's my brother."

Logan nudged the sword toward Ethan again.

The cross guard consisted of a pair of wings and the head of a gryphon. A topaz jewel made the gryphon's eye. Her heart clutched. It was his weapon all right, just like the daggers with lightning bolts belonged to her. Her emotions unraveled.

Ethan's hand stopped a hair away from touching the weapon. "If it doesn't glow?"

"You're not the Deliverer. We head to Nivek and search for the Gray family. They adopted the other Deliverer." Logan glanced at Quinn. "Or she remembers something else."

Ethan swallowed. Hesitated. Closed his fist around the grip.

The topaz jewel glowed, and Jayden's hope died. Yellow light wrapped around Ethan's wrist and claimed him. He dropped the sword and it bounced on the ground.

She couldn't tear her eyes from the weapon even as the light in the gem winked out.

"Jayden," Logan said. He wouldn't look up at her. Wouldn't look at either of them. "Meet your brother."

Her heart was speared in two. She couldn't even bring herself to glance at Ethan. How could she have let herself fall for him? She clutched her shirt at the neck in tight fists and willed her feelings to remain locked deep in her heart.

"He could be *my* brother." Serena's soft voice clung to hope. "Ethan, I've always felt that you're my brother. I—"

"Serena, I—I can't do this." He left the weapon and walked away.

"I'm sorry, Ethan." Quinn's voice followed him.

Jayden stood and watched him leave. Her talent hit a wall; he'd closed off his emotions. But he hadn't claimed the sword. He didn't want this either.

Quinn's large eyes filled with confusion. "Doesn't he like Serena?"
Serena patted the Whisperer's shoulder. "Of course he does, Quinn.
He's just feeling overwhelmed right now."

"Then I don't understand." Quinn acted as though her whole world
was imploding. "He should be happy to have you as his betrothed."

"My—?" Serena stepped away from Quinn.

Jayden's chest cracked. "What?" The breathless question came out
unbidden. She didn't really want to hear more.

"The Creator made a special bond between all the Deliverers.
When you meet one another, you will feel the deep kinship of love
even stronger than a three-oath bond. If Ethan is Jayden's brother,
Serena is his intended betrothed. Just like Serena's brother is your
intended betrothed, Jayden."

Air rushed out of Jayden's lungs. Serena? Perfect, beautiful Serena?
The sky wanted to open and pour down rain. Jayden choked all the
feelings inside, turned, and walked away.

"Jayden?" Serena's voice followed.

Jayden walked faster. She wasn't supposed to be angry. Shouldn't
feel heartbroken. In fact it was downright wrong to feel any of those
things. What was she going to be jealous about? That Serena, who
wasn't Ethan's sister, was his betrothed while she was stuck being his
sister?

Someone stepped up next to her, matching her stride, but Jayden
didn't feel like accepting comfort right now. She wanted to strike
something with lightning.

"Bad break, Softheart?"

Jayden's blood heated and she rounded on Kara. "Don't you dare."

"It's nice to see that fire in your eyes, but you don't exactly scare me."

The sky crackled. Thunder rolled and lightning lit up the sky in
fierce zigzags, all congregating above Kara.

She looked up and then back at Jayden. "Impressive."

"I killed Queen Idla and King Franco. You should be scared, Kara."

"Really? Because I know for certain King Franco lives."

The storm died away, leaving Jayden feeling barren and dry as a
desert. Somehow, she knew this to be true. Another hit to her already
shattered heart. "That's impossible."

Kara shrugged. "I would know. I'm bound to him by blood sacrifice. He lives and he's with the Mistress. I'm sure of it. Before you start rousing the sky again, relax. His being alive is good for you for now. He wants what the Mistress does. He'll fight her to get it. Enemy of my enemy and all."

"Franco is not our friend."

"No. We are his."

"Are you insane?" Jayden paused and looked deep into Kara's eyes. Like Thea, she had the uncanny ability to guard her emotions. "What do you know?"

Kara's smile spread across her face. "You're finally asking the right questions. I know Franco's plan to take the power from the Mistress. I also know of Belladonna's plans to take the power from her. So much power and so many people battling for it."

"And you?"

A slice of hatred broke through Kara's eyes and settled like a stab in the heart that Jayden's talent felt. "I want King Franco to suffer for killing my sister."

Jayden resisted the urge to turn off her talent. Feeling Kara's anger soothed her more than anything else right now. "Enemy of my enemy."

"You're smarter than you look." Her wicked smile returned.

"Do you know how to defeat Franco?"

"I have an idea."

"Tell me."

Kara leaned closer. "What's in it for me? See, right now, if Franco dies, I die with him. Such is the unfortunate link to a blood sacrifice. You free me of the link, and I will help you kill him."

"That's why you didn't go to Logan with this information. Does killing you kill Franco?"

Kara crossed her arms. "If it were that easy, I'd have slit my wrists."

"No." Jayden touched Kara's arm, and they both froze. Kara looked into Jayden's eyes, and something warmed Jayden's heart for a beat.

Then it winked out, and Kara pushed Jayden away, laughing. "Softheart, you've got to stop seeing the best in people. Sometimes it just doesn't exist. I gave you a proposition. Now, do we have a blood oath or not?"

"The last time—"

"I kept my end of the bargain and then some. I made sure you all made it out safe. It didn't look like things were going your way at the time, but the oath hand didn't harm me because, like it or not, Thea and I had a better plan than you."

Jayden glanced up the hill to where she'd been standing with the others. Serena was guiding Quinn away—toward the tents—and Logan looked to be deep in conversation with Gavin and Melanie. Ethan was nowhere to be seen.

Whether Jayden wanted to admit it or not, Kara spoke truth. She had upheld her end of the oath.

Jayden turned to the assassin. "What exactly am I promising?"

"Keep Logan from killing me or making me prisoner, and I will help you defeat Franco." Kara took out her dagger and sliced her palm.

She handed the weapon to Jayden, who cut hers as well and shook Kara's hand, wound against wound. Then Jayden let a devious smile light her own face. "Since when does an assassin need my help?"

Kara let out a bitter laugh. "You're more powerful than you think, Softheart, but I'm the better chess player."

She tugged Kara closer. "I think it's time to share with Logan what you know about Franco's plans and how to stop him."

"Lead the way." Kara stole her hand back.

Jayden marched across the hill toward Logan.

As they approached, Serena also towed Quinn to where Logan stood. "You have to tell him."

"What's going on?" Logan asked.

Jayden paused as she watched Ethan crest the hill on the other side. He only glanced at her, and Kara chuckled.

Jayden elbowed the assassin in the gut. That shut her up.

Serena motioned to Quinn. "She knows where all those animals from the chasm have gone."

Logan stared at Quinn expectantly. They all did.

Quinn motioned out. "See the barren land ahead of us? See how the sky turns from red to darker red to near black?"

Logan nodded.

"In the book it's called the borderlands. The Mistress created it when the Creator wanted to talk to her about destroying the abominations she'd made. If you go that way, you will enter the borderlands. Unspeakable evil dwells in there." Her eyelids fluttered. "Here." She pulled out the journal Logan had given her, and flipped out the leaf she used as a bookmark.

The pages appeared blank at first. Then Quinn tapped the page with her finger, and pictures of animals appeared. "The Mistress isn't very strong yet, so she's surrounded herself with her creatures. She wants them all to be free to roam the land, but she's not strong enough to allow that. Neither are they. Her weakness has caused her to lose control of certain creatures already. But as she grows stronger, she will expand her borders, essentially giving her creatures a greater reach."

Jayden leaned closer. "You're saying those animals hunting us are confined by borders?"

Quinn nodded. "They are contained where they are—like a labyrinth of protection to keep us out while the Mistress is at her weakest. She created these beasts that guard her, and she's had a long time to bond with them, if you will. They are loyal to her. And they don't want to be locked up again either. So they help bring the Deliverers to her.

"The way she does this is to set up these levels. There are seven kinds of guards to her prison. The black lions. The kelpies. The abysshounds. The shadow wolves. The maelvargs. The molten bulls. And the firegoats. She'll place them around her so you can't get an army close to her. But each level is designed to let the Deliverers pass through."

"Can I see that?" Logan held his hand out for the book. She passed it to him.

Jayden stood close enough to see. The page depicted a grouping of rings, each level looping around the next, like a target. "Which level are we in now?"

Quinn pointed. "The shadow wolves are here. I think the black lions and kelpies have had free rein for a long time already. They aren't part of this grouping. The abysshounds attacked us already. I think they might be breaking free."

"We have to go through that to get to her?" Gavin asked.

Quinn nodded.

Logan breathed deep. "But she's weak now. Vulnerable."

"Yes." Quinn's hazel eyes filled with hope. "And there is a way through."

"How?" Ethan took the book from Logan.

"I have to get closer to the levels to see it, but the trees will know. They cannot survive in the levels. That's how I knew to read about it. I heard so many voices cry out." A tear escaped her eye, and sadness choked her voice.

Jayden drew closer and touched Quinn's shoulder. Pulsed comfort into her. She could see the book again. The page Ethan stared at was blank. He gave the book back to Quinn, who held it for all to see.

As she touched it, a drawing appeared on the page of a beautiful woman on a throne made of—bones? Her name was written beneath the heads of the two massive, ugly dogs at her feet.

"What's that?" Jayden held out her hand, and Quinn relinquished the book.

"The Mistress of Shadows and her seconds in command, Gnarg and Garmr." She slid her fingers over the next page, and a new picture filled it: an expanse of land like the one they walked toward now. Barren. Sick. Thirsty for life. Jayden shivered. It was almost like the land tried to leak emotion into her, but there was nothing to leak. Just a void of feelings.

Quinn flipped the page again. A picture bled to life as she traced the pressed leaf with her fingers.

Legs like tendrils of smoke led into a body of fog. Dark, black eyes resembling an abyss with red pupils pulsed in the middle of the page. "Those are shadow wolves. They fly." Quinn shuddered. She turned the page and swept her hand over the next blank one. Long front legs led up to a barrel chest. Powerful hind legs and a tail with spikes armored the rear end. A hunched back bore spikes the size of spear tips, and its eyes looked as if they glowed. "Those are maelvargs."

"Maelvargs," Logan repeated with a wince.

"The laughing things with the glowing green eyes?" Ethan asked.

Quinn stared at him. "Y-you've heard of them?"

"In bedtime stories."

The next page showed the beast they'd fought. The wolfish creatures with smoldering fur.

Westwind whined.

Quinn glanced at him. "Does he wonder why they are all canine? They aren't, but many are. The Mistress loves wolves." She shivered.

Logan asked the question Jayden wondered. "How do we defeat these creatures?"

She flipped through blank page after page before she stopped and slid her finger across the thick leaf-paper.

"The shadow wolves are afraid of light. They attack you when you sleep. Prey on your fears. If they bite you, you will never wake of your deepest nightmares. I–I have to keep reading."

Logan nodded. He turned to Gavin. "We need to figure this out. In the meantime, we have to get to the palace for my son."

"And that's where the Mistress is." Kara's nonchalant voice rose up behind Jayden. "Looks like you're headed to the dragon's den. I wonder if you have anyone on your team who knows how to get in undetected."

Logan lunged at her, and, heart racing, Jayden stood between them. "She will help us."

The fire in Logan's eyes seemed more contained, but he glared. "And you trust her?"

"No."

"I will tell you if she lies," Serena said.

"Logan!" Ethan's frantic voice jolted Jayden's heart.

"What is it, kid?" Logan turned toward him.

"Chloe. She's—she's in danger." Ethan looked at Jayden, and at once his regret pulsed into her, so deep and full it squeezed her heart. Then he picked up the sword—the Deliverer's sword. An ache spread through her chest and into her core.

Then all of Ethan's emotions winked out, and he glanced at Logan. "Hurry."

Quinn grabbed Ethan's sleeve. "Wait." Wind rippled her hair and she closed her eyes. "She's this way." She pointed east. "She's with a woman. The trees say the woman rescued her from two attackers, but one of the two men still tracks them. But that's not all." Quinn trembled. "A pack of abysshounds rides on their heels."

Ethan stared at her, his chest heaving. "The levels are closer than they look?"

"Yes." Quinn's voice shook. "But the trees are protecting your friend."

"Westwind smells your abysshounds, Quinn," Logan said.

She shuddered. "They're not mine."

Ethan's frantic gaze locked onto Quinn. "How do we kill them?"

She looked in the book. "Wielder-crafted weapons and fire."

"Lightning?" Jayden asked.

Quinn bit her lip. "The trees say yes."

Logan motioned to Gavin and Melanie. "Get some Dissenters to join us. Chloe and whoever is helping her need our aid. Tell the Dissenters to bring pitch-coated arrows and fire."

Jayden crossed her arms. "I'm going with you."

He looked like he wanted to argue, but he kept his mouth shut and raced the way Quinn had told them to go. Serena and Quinn followed.

Kara smiled. "I'll wait here."

Jayden tugged her sleeve. "You'll come and help."

She didn't need more prodding than that. Perhaps trusting her was a bad idea. Jayden's heart hammered as they raced through the trees.

CHAPTER 7

A FAMILIAR ENEMY

Ethan swallowed his fears as he followed his talent's urging. Ryan. Quinn hadn't said anything about Ryan. If something had happened to his adoptive brother, he'd never forgive himself.

"Wait." Quinn's soft voice stilled him, and he looked over his shoulder at her. He didn't even know she'd come.

"Zephyr—"

"Don't worry, I know protecting them is a part of protecting you." The gryphon stood in front of Quinn, Jayden, and Serena. His ears swiveled. *"Someone is coming."*

The wood flooded with animals and men and women dressed in camouflage cloaks as Gavin caught up to them with the Dissenters. Twigs snapped in the forest ahead of them—at least Zephyr's feathered ears perked that direction.

Westwind nosed the air.

Chloe rushed through the trees, breaking twigs and sticks. Cuts marred her cheek and dried blood stuck to her forehead, but she was alive. Very much alive. She caught sight of Ethan, and her green eyes widened. Thank the Creator his sister was safe. He pressed his finger to his lips and she ran to him, arms extended. She flung her arms around his neck and hugged him tight. "They're chasing me. They're—I've never seen dogs so big. And there's a woman. She showed up and saved me. But the man—he's trying to kill me."

"Hey, hey, you're okay now. Where's Ryan?" His heart rammed into his ribs as Chloe's eyes rounded. "Chloe?" Ethan's voice hitched.

"He—back at One Eye's house and evil woman showed up. Ryan told me to run. I came to get help. But the evil woman took him to the palace."

"What woman?" Jayden asked.

"Her name was Belladonna."

Serena whispered, "No."

Ethan's blood heated. How had Belladonna gotten a hold of Ryan? And what would she do to him? Ethan's mind raced. She had left him alive, perhaps because she recalled seeing him in the palace with Jayden. He could only hope she recognized Ryan and would spare him, too.

Ethan guided Chloe behind him, trying to calm his shaking nerves. "We'll protect you."

She complied, but grabbed his shoulder. "And Ryan?"

He gripped the sword hilt tight. Like it or not, this weapon felt as though it had been made for his hands. "I'm going after him next."

"I knew you'd come for me."

"Always." He raised his sword, waiting for whatever would come through the trees after her.

Chloe grabbed his shirt. "Ethan, we have to run."

"She's right." Quinn trembled.

Logan glanced at the Whisperer then looked at Ethan. "Kid?"

His talent told him to protect the girls. Throbbed in his chest. "If we run, they'll just chase us."

Zephyr bristled and faced the direction Chloe had come.

A man broke through the brush, and Chloe screamed. She ran straight for Jayden and nearly stumbled into her. Westwind and Aurora ambushed the man, and he dropped his weapon, backing into a tree, hands raised.

Ethan stared.

A new flame sparked deep in the pit of his stomach. Not the warning of a threat. The ever-smoldering heat of revenge.

This man bore a scar over his eye. Wore a wooden leg.

Ethan couldn't breathe. This was the same man who had killed his parents.

Zephyr growled. *"Friend, he makes you very angry. You can't protect when you're angry."*

"Yes I can."

"Not . . . not this kind of anger. It blinds you."

Shaking, Ethan stared at the man who had ruined his life. The man looked right at Logan. "You should run if you know what's good for you. We're not all that's chasing her."

"You don't seem afraid," Logan said.

The man laughed. "It's not me they're after. They don't hunt those with black blood."

"And the woman who was helping her?"

The man shrugged. "She got away . . . from me."

A cacophony of howls surrounded them. They shrieked. And the echoes seemed to be above them. Logan sent half of the Dissenters ahead, telling them to rescue the woman if they found her and take out the abysshounds.

Ethan kept his attention on the prisoner. "What do you know of black blood?" Ethan's voice came out darker than he'd expected, but the man finally looked at him. Really looked. His eyes narrowed in what appeared to be recognition.

Thoughts of revenge clawed at the slow burn in Ethan's chest. He nudged Quinn behind him and embraced his talent.

"You can't run fast enough." The man laughed. "They're coming."

Ethan glared at his enemy, the pull of revenge eating away at his heart. "What do you know of the black blood?"

The man just showed his teeth.

Dash stalked stiff-legged to the man and lowered his head. A thunderous growl popped the man's eyes wider. Then Dash thrust his horn into the man's chest.

He screamed.

Serena placed her hand on Dash and looked into the man's eyes. "Help us, and when he takes his horn out of your chest, he won't leave a gaping hole. That's how a sword of noble light works." She glanced over her shoulder. "Ask your questions now, Ethan."

The man didn't wait for Ethan to ask again. "The black blood makes them slaves to the one who controls them."

"Slaves?" Melanie asked.

"Y-yes. They have to do what Belladonna tells them. She uses a ring. It's a powerful tool of compulsion. That's all I know. I swear."

"Why didn't she do it to you?"

He smiled. "She has other ways of making us hers. She wants her 'pets' to obey her out of love. For me, it's gold."

Ethan stepped back, a sick sinking feeling in his stomach. Love? How was that love?

Serena glanced at him and he nodded, his questioning done for now.

Dash removed his horn, and the wound on the man's chest closed. He looked right at Ethan. "She told me to bring her the Deliverers and kill anyone who stands in my way."

Quinn's fingers dug into Ethan's arm.

The burn flaring in Ethan's chest pulsed. If he ducked, Quinn would be hurt.

"Ethan! He's armed!" Chloe screamed.

Zephyr jumped between them, shielding Ethan. "It's okay, Zeph. I won't miss an opportunity to kill him again."

He held the bowstring and drew it back to his cheek, stepping around the gryphon.

The wooden-legged man held up his hands in surrender. His knife thudded to the ground.

Ethan breathed out. His finger started to release the string.

"Ethan. Don't."

Jayden. Didn't she understand what she was asking him to do? His heart trembled. He wanted to listen to her. Wanted to have his revenge. The thoughts warred within him.

"He's surrendered." She touched his arm so gently. "Killing him now would be stooping to his level."

"You would ask me to let *this man* live?"

"I would ask you to do what's right. Please."

He breathed in. Held it. Everything inside of him wanted this man dead. Jayden's grip on his arm pleaded with the small ache inside of him that wanted him to do what was right: Let them take the prisoner.

Be noble. His arm quivered. His aim would fail if he waited much longer.

She squeezed his shoulder. Her calm spirit leaked into him. Lapped over his heart like healing waves. He could listen to his talent now. He could put away thoughts of revenge. She was still rescuing him. Did she even know?

He breathed in and lowered his weapon. Jayden sighed and rubbed his back. He didn't look at her. Instead, he looked toward Quinn. Her wide eyes softened and the smallest smile formed on her mouth and she gave him the tiniest nod. He breathed deep.

Logan sighed. He stepped closer to the prisoner.

But Ethan's talent sparked to life, urging him to take these girls and get them to safety. The abysshounds were getting past the Feravolk. Their snarls sounded closer. Zephyr's huge brown eyes met his, asking what to do. Had only moments passed since this man broke through the trees? "Logan, I have to get them out of here. I—"

"Run, kid. We'll hold these creatures off." Logan motioned at the remaining Dissenters. "Richard, Morgan, stay with the prisoner. The rest of you, let's go help the others." They raced toward the sounds of fighting. Logan started to follow.

"Wait." Chloe grabbed Logan's arm. "Ryan. You saw what Belladonna did to that man. She'll do it to Ryan. You have to send someone to save him. Please."

Logan nodded. "I won't leave him to rot by her hand."

"Thank you."

Logan followed his men, and Ethan nudged Chloe toward camp.

The wooden-legged man chuckled. "Coward. I thought you were dead the night I slit your parents' throats. It's the only reason I left you there. Yet you left me alone. Too much a coward to deal with me then, and too much a coward to deal with me now."

Ethan stopped in his tracks. Revenge tried to take hold of his heart again. He squeezed it away as he fisted his hands and his talent surged.

Jayden gasped. "Ethan. I'm sorry. I had no right to—"

He plucked the knife from his belt and turned. Then he threw it. The blade stuck deep into the man's throat, and he fell against the tree. A vial of purple liquid fell from his hand, and he slumped to the ground. Dead.

"He knew who we are," Ethan said. "And I don't think it's coincidence that a pack of abysshounds is headed this way." He looked at Jayden. "That wasn't for revenge. That was for protection."

"I know." Her voice was a whisper. "Thank you."

He nodded once and turned his attention to Chloe, who stood gaping at him.

"Come on." Ethan grabbed Chloe's hand and pushed her toward the others. "I'm right behind you. Run."

CHAPTER 8

AN UNWANTED TOOL

Another drip of wax hit the table, and Connor still didn't have the answers he was looking for. He flipped to the next page in the huge volume he'd pulled from one of the library's many shelves, and the hair on the back of his neck prickled. The Mistress was on the other side of the palace in the highest room. Every moment, she gained strength. He felt each rush of power as it pulsed through her. So did the ground. It groaned like a man dying in battle.

Someone approached the library, and Connor closed the book and set it at the bottom of his stack. Then he opened another.

The form that filled the doorway stopped.

Stared.

Connor's wolf form clawed inside of him. It wanted to run. It would have been a good idea if he'd already been dressed as a wolf and outside. But he wasn't. Still, he'd managed to avoid Franco until now. Now he'd baited a meeting, and it had worked.

Franco cleared his throat and walked into the library. "There you are."

Connor looked up and feigned surprise. "Oh. Franco. You gave me a start."

"Studying again?" Franco trailed his finger over one of the decoy books Connor had placed on the table. "Study and spar, spar and study. That's all you do." Franco paused, his fingers brushing the spine of the book Connor attempted to hide. "You're much better at the sparring these days."

"I figure those are skills I'll need."

Franco slid into a seat near Connor and set his boots on the table. "General Balton is dead. Captain Jonis is dead. Those other Deliverers are making my life difficult."

"Seems so."

Franco chuckled. "That Healer girl of mine seems attached to you. Do you share her feelings? I rather thought you . . . didn't like women that way."

Franco trailed into friendly conversation, which meant he was setting up his plan. A coiled viper ready to strike. Connor loosened his shoulders and turned in his seat to face Franco. He smiled. "She's beautiful, but I'm afraid she's taken to my friend, Luc."

Franco waved his fingers in the air as if this line of conversation bored him, which likely meant it didn't. "Yes. Smithy. I recall him. He's good with horses. He spars with you often. He's gotten better, too. Didn't he join the Royal Army?"

"Yes. He's one of the best."

"Yet he's still a blacksmith."

Connor shrugged. "I believe that was part of your deal allowing Balton to take him on."

Franco's eyes narrowed. "Right. You seem quite chummy with, what's his name, Luc?"

"Are you asking for my allegiance? Because I think you know you have it. When we reach the four thrones, as your mother called them, I will give my powers to you."

"I know." He lowered his voice. "That's why I want to keep you away from the Mistress. You must know she's here." He placed his boots on the ground and leaned closer to Connor. "You always know what's going on in this palace although you're only ever on the fighting field or in the library. Have you ever even bedded a woman?"

"I've always kept to myself."

"Yes. And now I'm telling you to stay away from the Mistress. I know you can only be found when you wish it." Franco stood as if to leave, then he leaned over Connor's shoulders. "And your trace is missing."

"My wh—? It's missing?"

Franco's chuckle was dark. "Surely you've tested the limits."

"Franco—I'm sorry—Your Majesty—"

He slapped his hand against Connor's back. "No need for formalities unless we're in public. I came here to ask you if you would be my captain. I have an army I need you to lead. A very special army. And there is a way to control them that I think you'll find very interesting."

"Oh?" Connor's heart pounded.

"Yes." Franco pulled a ring—just like the one he wore—out of his pocket. "My mother wanted me to be able to control them. And her general, of course. But Balton is dead, and no one could find the strange bracer she'd given him on his body. Never mind that, though." Franco paused and studied Connor's face.

The bracer. That contraption that had allowed Connor to use compulsion. That had almost killed him. There were other weapons like it?

"These are all forged of the same gold. See, there's only one way to use compulsion to control those with the Blood Moon birthmark. With black blood."

"Black . . ." Connor's words trailed off as his thoughts flipped through pages and pages of books. Then he saw it in his mind's eye. The page with the Black Blood Army on it. Slowly, his brain closed the book so he could read the title.

"Would you like the meet your army?" Franco handed Connor the ring.

Connor smiled. "You trust me?"

"You can't control one wearing another tool of compulsion."

"And there were only the three?"

Franco's eyebrows shot up.

"I just mean, I want to know who else can control my army."

"That's the spirit." Franco slapped his back. "You're going to like this army." Franco led him away from the book that held the key to undoing Franco's bond with Kara and Madison.

The bracer. Rebekah had it. At least he knew where it was.

But black blood. He recalled the title of the book he'd need. The one he'd shelved at the top: *The History of Wielders*. The only one in existence.

He knew what he'd be reading again.

Franco led Connor down into the dank, underground tunnel. Torchlight flickered across the brick walls in a red-orange glow as they walked over the damp, packed dirt. The scent of rats and feces and decay made Connor's queasy stomach roil.

Franco led him a bit farther down the tunnel and knocked on a wooden door. A small shield slid away from the square of cross-hatching at head level, and two blue eyes peered out. Red around the irises. The whites of these eyes looked yellow in the firelight. Or perhaps all the time.

The door opened.

"Welcome to the barracks." Franco smiled.

Bunks lined the walls, two high, and Children of the Blood Moon—those Connor's exact age—lounged on them. The tunnel split in a few directions, and Franco led him past more people. There had to be thousands of Children down here.

"I see you're appraising your army. I assure you, they will defeat your Deliverers. Those with the black blood in their veins will die before they will disobey your orders. The blood makes them stronger, faster, and unafraid to die."

"How do the other men control them?"

Franco shrugged. "Simple really. I tell the army which men to obey and make sure those men obey me. I will pass this over to you now, as you are my captain, and I am your king."

"Yes, Your Majesty."

Franco patted his back. "Very good. Now, what is your first order as captain?"

Connor stared at their empty eyes and his heart ached for them. "I need these men ready. They need sunlight. They need to breathe fresh air or they will not increase their stamina. And they need food. Baths. All of them. Can we move them above ground?"

"You wish to move the barracks?"

"Yes, Your Majesty."

Franco tapped his lower lip. "Very well. Then I expect your training to begin, but, Connor, this compulsion is our little secret. If you tell Madison or that smithy, who I imagine will be your second in command, I will kill them and make you wish you never considered betraying me."

"Of course."

"Good. I'll move them."

"Thank you."

Franco laughed. "And Connor, your humanity is showing. You don't have to waste it on them."

Connor made eye contact with a few of the soldiers. Every single one of them stared at him. Men and women. Ready to kill at the snap of his fingers. He could only hope he could control them without the golden ring—if it had the same effect on him that the bracer had.

Franco squeezed Connor's shoulder. "I'm glad you see the good we will be doing for the land."

"And what's that?"

"Stealing the Creator's power from the Mistress of Shadows." His grin was wicked. "You don't think I'll let her destroy my kingdom just so she can build her own, do you? Oh no. You and I will save Soleden. And when I rule the whole of it, you will be my right hand. Just like we always wanted. Do you think you can convince the other Deliverers to join you?"

"I'll make it happen."

"Good." Franco chuckled. "Belladonna came to me, asking for a spell." He fingered the key on his neck. Access to the Mistress's secrets. Her spells. "She now has a link to the boy who protects them. The thorn I keep stepping on. She says she's certain she'll be able to lure them here within the week—well, if they pass the Mistress's little maze—the one she's created with her army of creatures. Ready your army. We go to war."

Connor placed the ring on his finger, and a small throb behind his temple made him want to retch. The same gold. He wouldn't be able to wear it. Not for that long.

He'd have to get Luc to make him another identical ring. The bracer hadn't hurt Rebekah; perhaps the ring wouldn't hurt Luc.

Commanding this army would kill Connor if he wasn't careful.

CHAPTER 9

STRONG AND STOIC

Two men bullied Ryan down an underground hallway to a thick, wooden door with gray, separating wood. Hands bound behind him, he struggled to keep his balance against their shoving. The sharp prod of Belladonna's knife pricked his back. She'd brought him here to "break him." His stomach squeezed.

Belladonna opened the door. "You boys can wait out here for me," she said to the two other men and ran her fingers along their chests. "Oh." She pulled Ryan's sword from one of the men. "I'll hang onto this." Then she grabbed a lit torch.

"Welcome home, pet." The knife pricked his back again.

Deep in his belly, a fire blazed. *If I wasn't tied up, I'd show her what happens to fools who poke sleeping dragons.* He'd smack the weapon from her hands, grab her wrists, and toss her to the ground. And then he'd stab her through.

Whoa. Wait. Ryan shook his head and breathed deep, trying to clear away those thoughts. *Where did that come from?*

The voice in his head laughed. *"Embracing your anger suits you."*

Jaw clenched, he tried to push the voice deep into his mind where it was muffled. Of course those thoughts came from her—the Mistress of Shadows. They had to have. Because he could not accept it if they'd come from the part of his heart that he alone controlled. He swallowed hard and stepped over the door's threshold. Belladonna's grip on his elbow kept him from continuing ahead of her. Darkness followed the soft click behind him.

"Don't move. There's a staircase in front of you, and I don't want to have to heal your broken bones on the first day."

A bright, yellow light pierced the darkness behind Ryan as Belladonna's torch moved close to his head. The warmth of the fire comforted him. His long shadow descended a staircase he couldn't find the bottom to. A smell he didn't care to identify wafted up, sour and dirty.

The light moved closer and Belladonna's lavender scent surrounded him. "After you, pet."

Lavender was not a scent he could handle. Not after the venom. He shivered. Belladonna wasn't going to make him any fonder of it.

She chuckled. "Scared already? It's just a torch."

Ryan trudged down the staircase, and Belladonna pricked his back if he slowed. At last, the bottom was visible. The terrible scent wafted around the corner, thicker down here. "What is that smell?"

"Ah, get used to it, pet. It's the scent of pain and fear." She breathed in.

Crazy woman.

She led him toward a wide wooden door with iron hinges. The stink grew stronger, recognizable now. Blood. Vomit. Sweat. He focused on being strong and stoic, but his stomach churned.

Belladonna opened the door, and Ryan bent over and dry heaved. She kicked him hard and he slammed to his knees. Stone floor. Of course. He groaned.

"Get up." A deep, rasping voice filled the dank room. Heavy black boots scuffled toward him.

Ryan looked up at the man towering over him. Beefier than One Eye and taller, too. He wore nothing on his hairy chest, but leather straps with steel spikes adorned his neck and arms. Thankfully he wore pants, even if they were black leather. He smelled like sweat and resembled a pig. A sweaty pig made of beef.

Ryan smiled. "Hospitality is your strength. Isn't it?"

Beefy kicked him in the face.

Stunned, flat on his back, Ryan groaned.

Belladonna stepped over him. "Be careful, Butch. This one's mine, and I'd like to keep his face pretty."

The beefy man roared in laughter. "You brought him here to break him, make him a good little pet, didn't you?" He sounded as if he carried too much saliva in his mouth. He grabbed Ryan's shirt in one huge hand and pulled him to standing. Then he grinned, showing off his rotting teeth.

Oh. Good. The other half of the stench identified. Ryan turned away. Strong and stoic. Dragons are strong and stoic. He had to be strong and stoic.

Stone walls surrounded the windowless room. Light came from a few crude torches and a massive fireplace. The flickering flames cast ominous shadows on various weapons adorning the walls. Weapons Ryan had never seen before. Tools for torture.

A wooden bench with leather straps sat in one corner, covered in dried puddles of dark brown, blood that had leeched into the wood. It was rectangular, slightly raised on one side. Near that sat a chair with metal restraints on the armrests. Chains with shackles hung from various places in the ceiling. And a large, bronze bull sat near the fireplace. His eyes moved from that strange contraption to another.

Goosebumps spread over Ryan's skin. His stomach dropped to his weak knees.

Butch let out a roar. "The rack? Want to see what it does?"

Not really.

"Butch, I'd like to start with something different." She patted the whip in her belt.

Butch looked Ryan up and down before he cracked a huge grin. He seemed the truculent type. "Take off his shirt."

Belladonna set Ryan's sword on the ground, and Ryan stared. If he could catch her off guard, he might be able to dash over to it and escape. She faced him and slipped the knife under his shirt. Cut it in half. He staggered, getting closer to his weapon.

"Do you know what I keep in *my* whip?" Butch dangled the ends under Ryan's nose. The long, black snake of a weapon was no ordinary horsewhip. It held shards of something that glittered in the firelight in its three-headed end. "Bone fragments, pieces of metal, and dragon's teeth."

So that was where Belladonna got the idea. Ryan's insides turned like a chicken on a spit.

Butch's eyes narrowed. "Not afraid, farm boy? Next time you come in here, your knees won't stop knocking. That's a promise."

Ryan swallowed. Maybe he'd black out before the punishment process. It couldn't be worse than black lion venom, right?

"Put his arms in the cuffs, dear." Butch smiled at Belladonna.

She cut Ryan's bindings and he swept to the side, dipped down and grabbed for his sword. His fingers grazed the hilt as Belladonna kicked it away. Ryan sprawled after it. A stabbing, ripping pain punctured his side and tore him open clean to his back. He screamed, but wouldn't give up reaching for his weapon. His fingers wrapped around the hilt. Another blow hit him, tearing his already shredded flesh. He curled into a ball as white light clouded his vision in flashes like lightning.

Another blow. He couldn't tell if he still held his weapon.

Something thudded into his chest and pushed him onto his torched back. Belladonna stood above him, his sword at his throat. "That's how you treat a lady?"

Butch's iron grip dragged Ryan to his feet. He caught sight of the whip. Strings of his skin hung from the sharp objects. Butch handed the weapon to Belladonna, then he spun Ryan around and pushed him into the stone wall. Butch's sweaty palms stung Ryan's open wounds. Ryan's cheek pressed against the cold wall as Belladonna and Butch forced Ryan's hands into the cuffs. Butch's acrid breath heated Ryan's face. "Try that again, boy. I dare you."

Oh. He would. He'd try any chance he got.

Butch's iron grip held Ryan's left wrist against the stone wall. "A lefty, huh? Don't see many of those around."

Ryan glared at the man.

Butch smiled. "Now *my* favorite tool." He held up a long stick with a metal orb at the end. "Iron." He stepped back and swung.

Pain shattered Ryan's resolve as the weapon connected with the back of his left hand. Smashed it against the wall. Bones cracked. He wanted to hold it tight to his chest, but the cuffs prevented him from moving. Grated at his tortured bones.

And he screamed.

S.D. GRIMM

"That'll teach you to attack a lady." Butch grinned. Tears formed in Ryan's eyes and Butch laughed. "This will be easy."

The whip struck him again. Smashing him against the wall. Scraping away at his already burning skin.

Another hit. Then another until Ryan sank against the cold manacles, vulnerable, defenseless. His hand throbbed, ached, screamed. All he could do was wait. Another cutting sting ripped into his back, and it took his whole strength to hold in a cry.

Strong.

He writhed as much as he could. Tried to free his hands of the unforgiving metal cuffs when the next blow slapped into him, stealing traces of his flesh as it reluctantly pulled away.

Stoic.

The scream was his. He could hold it in no longer.

He lost count of the number of screams, of the number of scraping lashes he'd endured. He hung there, helpless. The whimper in his throat was his.

He needed to escape. Somehow this had to be a nightmare he could wake from.

Serena. He thought of Serena. Suddenly she stood before him in her pretty blue-green dress. Her hair was pulled up and those dark blue eyes smiled at him. They were at the Winking Fox again, the night he'd told Jayden to let him go. The night Serena had opened up to him.

Her gaze had darted away from him, and pink colored her cheeks.

"What?" he asked her. "You're afraid to tell me?"

"My deepest fear? Of course I am." She smiled bright and beautiful. "You don't tell just anyone your secret fears, you know."

"I do know." He leaned both elbows on the table, wishing he'd chosen to sit next to her instead of across from her.

"Then why ask?"

"You said I could ask you whatever I wanted."

That smile returned. He loved that he could lure it out of her. It made her practically shine. "You're taking that out of context."

"All right. Here's mine: I'm most afraid of being helpless when those I love need me. I want to be able to help them. Rescue them. Protect them.

I don't want to be the one standing there, wishing I could have done more. Been better."

Her eyes softened as she watched him. Slowly, her hand moved across the table, and her fingers laced between his. Every sensation in his fingertips rushed forward. Every sensation made new by his rebirth after the venom. He ached to kiss her.

She squeezed his hand. "That's a noble fear. I believe it will make you try harder than most men to be there for those you love. You're more loyal than you let on, aren't you?"

Yes. He wanted to say yes. Never wanted this moment to end, but the ripping pain in his back tried to steal him away from the memory. He held on. Gripped her hand tighter.

"Ryan?" Serena's voice was fading. "What is it?"

"I—don't go. I–I need you. Serena, I need you."

Her face started to fade. He screamed.

"That's enough." Belladonna's harsh voice pulled him away from Serena. Her face. Her touch. And even as he called her name, he was back in the pit being tortured. He gasped for air as the whip struck him again.

"I said enough!" Belladonna yelled.

Nothing. Ryan dangled there. The metal shackles cutting into his wrists were the only things keeping him upright. His legs had already given out. His left hand had swollen past normal size. And it throbbed. There couldn't be anything left to peel from his burning back. His lungs couldn't force out another scream if he tried.

"It's not enough. Not for him." Butch's raspy voice made Ryan's heart squeeze.

The soft clink of the objects in the whip converged as Butch readied for another blow. Ryan braced himself.

"Butch! *I* have to heal him. *I* say he's done for today."

Ryan hung there, waiting for another round. Instead, the manacles opened. He crumpled to the stone-cold ground. The salt from Belladonna's palms touched his open lacerations. He was too weak to even pull away. He whimpered like a kicked dog.

Butch growled. "Don't be too easy on him."

"I won't heal him completely," she said.

The familiar heating sensation bled through Ryan's body, blending into a welcome cooling. Relief was coming. Torture he could endure if relief would follow.

Weak.

She reduced his wounds to a hundred deep cuts as she moved her hands over them. Deep cuts were nothing compared to what they had been moments before. She took his left hand in hers and eased some of the pain. And he let her.

Broken.

It was his first battle and he'd already lost.

CHAPTER 10

HAUNTED PAST

Logan led his Feravolk deeper into the woods toward the threat amid the snarls and screams of battle. The Feravolk and abysshounds must be deeper in the woods. Perhaps they were causing the enemy to retreat. But he caught no sign of the woman Chloe had said saved her.

Westwind sniffed the air. *"Are you sure this woman who saved Chloe is even alive? Wait, I—"* Westwind skidded to a halt.

Aurora stopped and backed up a few paces, tail tucked. *"No."*

Logan slowed as his friends rushed deeper into the woods, save Melanie and Gavin, who remained with him.

Gavin looked at Logan. "What's wrong?"

Logan faced Aurora. Her tongue darted out between her bared teeth, and she flattened her ears. *"I'm not going. I won't face her."*

Logan crouched near the wolf. "No one will make you do anything you can't. But tell me, Aurora. Who won't you face?" He ran his fingers over the hilt of his sword.

Her golden eyes looked so deep into his. Her pupils were huge and she trembled. *"Rebekah."*

Logan rocked back on his heels and his heart slammed painfully against his ribs. No. Not her. Not now. Anything but this. He could not face his wife again. Not after last time. Someone touched his shoulder and he stood.

"Logan? What's wrong?" Melanie's concern would have been welcome if she didn't sound so much like her sister.

"It's Rebekah. She saved Chloe. My guess is she's trying to find out where Chloe is headed. She wants the Deliverers for Franco, the Mistress, who knows." His voice rose and he hadn't intended for it to.

Melanie backed away from him. "Maybe she—"

"No, Mel. She's gone. I told you what happened in the palace."

Tears welled in Melanie's eyes, and she straightened her spine. "So you're going to let those monsters kill *my* sister? Your *wife?*"

Logan's heart ached. "They won't kill her. She brought them."

Aurora went rigid. *"She's coming."*

Melanie's eyes pleaded with Logan. So she still loved her sister. Logan's jaw tightened. "Maybe you two shouldn't be here."

"I'm staying." Melanie met his gaze, harsh as a mountain lion.

Westwind growled and stood in front of his mate. A woman raced into the clearing, red streaked her arm, a cut marred her cheek. Logan's heart nearly stopped. Her golden hair fluttered in the breeze, caressing her face. Her small stature did not take away from her confidence. The simple gray cloak she wore was not something Logan had seen palace inhabitants wearing. Her dress underneath was a shimmering blue— very much palace apparel. She had the same stunning brown eyes. Just as he remembered them. Her mouth opened as she looked at him, and she nearly stopped running. Then she raced toward him. "Run!"

Logan stood his ground as the other Feravolk raced through the woods, abysshounds on their trail.

Westwind's head shot up. *"Logan?"*

"I can't let any of these beasts get back to the Mistress. We fight them." He glanced at Aurora. *"Aurora, you do not need to stand with me."*

"Yes. I do." Her voice trembled.

At least a dozen wolf-like creatures, as tall as horses and black and red as burning coal broke through the trees after them. The Feravolk who had just come in with Logan raised their weapons and shot flaming arrows as their tired comrades raced behind them. The creatures still stalked forward, even with arrows sticking out of their bodies like flaming quills.

Gavin called for another onslaught of arrows. Finally, one of the creatures reared up and burst into flame. The others hissed and bounded forward.

Rebekah stood next to Logan and braced for the onslaught. "I never expected to see you here." She smiled, but tears coated her eyes. She raised her daggers. "They won't die unless you have a Wielder-crafted weapon or fire."

He nodded but wouldn't look at her. Half of his heart still beat for her. He ignored it. The creatures headed right for the pair of them. Logan readied his weapon, and as he fought alongside his wife, something in his heart wanted this to be the Blood Moon wars again, if only for a moment, if only so he could believe she was still on his side. Still had his back.

His sword punctured one beast's hide, and it snapped at him with jaws. Heat and cold poured out of its mouth like smoke. Rebekah buried her sword in the beast's skull. It turned and bit at her.

Logan slid across the dirt and leaves until he was under the creature. Arrows covered its body, spreading fire over its fur. Logan stood and slammed his blade into the creature's heart. It reared. Snarled. Its paws slammed against the ground, hard, and it turned on Logan, bashing into him with its shoulder. He stumbled back, and that's all the creature needed. It pinned him to the ground.

He tried to free his sword arm to attack another beast that charged him, but a blade sliced deep into the side of its skull.

With a deep moan, the creature toppled over, dead.

Breathing hard, Logan stood and faced Rebekah. She'd saved him. His heart wrenched. That meant she wanted to get close to him for some reason. Could he turn her away? Was he strong enough?

He scanned the area. All the remaining creatures lay dead. Their bodies smoldered in the wind. And at least thirteen Feravolk didn't stand. Something in his chest crumbled.

Thirteen.

And seven of their animals.

How many more lives would they lose?

His warriors started to help take care of the wounded, but Rebekah moved toward them, as if to help. Logan wasn't going to let Rebekah anywhere near his warriors. He motioned toward her and faced one of the young Dissenters. "Take this prisoner back to our camp."

The young man looked at Rebekah. "Sir?"

Rebekah didn't appear to notice what Logan had said. Her eyes were glued on her sister. "Mel."

A tear dripped down Melanie's cheek. Gavin placed his hand on his sword. Melanie shrank behind her husband. Callie, Melanie's mountain lion, paced behind them. Glider, Gavin's eagle, fluttered down and perched atop Gavin's shoulder.

A chill tumbled down Logan's spine when Rebekah's eyes met his. Her cheeks filled with a bit of red despite the cooling autumn air. "Logan?"

This Rebekah was very unlike the one he'd seen in the dark tunnel of the palace. This Rebekah was alive, vibrant, beautiful, everything he remembered.

"Rebekah." He bobbed his head.

She tilted her head to the side. "Rebekah?"

Why did that surprise her? She had to know he wouldn't be running into her arms. "That's your name, isn't it?" He leaned back against a nearby tree, everything in him trembling, fighting against the sanity he barely held on to.

"Of course." Her sparkling eyes searched him, eyelids fluttering. "Did you—did we speak, when you were in the palace?"

"When you tried to kill me?"

"Oh." She stepped closer to him, brows pulling together. Dissenters with swords blocked her path. She pointed at their poised weapons. "What is the meaning of all of this? Am I some traitor that you have to question me? Then get the questioners. I have news for you that cannot wait."

Logan chuckled. "News? So that's your plea? You have news for us?"

"Don't play games, Logan. It was me locked up in the palace for the last seventeen years with no rescue, and I'm treated like a criminal after I escape and find you. Am I so untrustworthy?"

He pushed off the tree and pointed his knife at her. "You tried to kill me. You are nothing but a palace pawn."

"Is that the lie you've been telling yourself? You know me better than that."

"Yes." He walked closer. Swords pulled from his path until he stood directly in front of her, towering over her. "I have some news of my own, *Rebekah*." She flinched. His heart squeezed. "I saw what you did that night."

Behind him, Aurora let out a snarl. The old bond pulled at her. The wolf's heart ached. She hid behind Westwind and whined as if in pain. Westwind lowered his head, staring at Rebekah. Aurora bristled and showed her teeth, but moved away with her tail tucked.

"The night I tried to kill you? I was spelled, Logan. I remember nothing."

"Not that night, Rebekah. The night of the Blood Moon."

Her brows furrowed and she shook her head. "If you saw what I did that night, why are you calling me a traitor? You must have known that I was protecting the Deliverers." Her eyes bored into him, trying to reach the soft side of his heart. "You."

"You expect me to believe you weren't part of Idla's plans? You handed her our son." His throat grew thick. "How could you?"

Trembling, she backed away from him. "Who told you this?"

"Told me? I saw it for myself. You took our son and boarded the queen's carriage. I heard you tell our child he was safe."

Her head shook, her mouth opened, but no words came out. One tear trailed down her cheek. So she understood what he'd seen. There would be no more deception. No more lies.

"It's not what you think," she whispered.

He closed his eyes. "Lies now?" When he met her tearful gaze, he made his glare cold. "The Rebekah I knew was above lies."

"I'm still above lies, Logan." She grabbed his shirt. A sword rose, but Logan put out his hand to stop the man. He looked into the eyes of a desperate liar. Her world of deception unraveled at her feet, and she mourned it instead of coming clean. Was there nothing good left in her heart? He closed his fingers around her wrists and ripped her hands from his shirt.

Unable to bear the way her tearful gaze called to his heart, he turned away from her. He'd never face her again. His last memory of her was made. He looked at the young man again. "Take her to the prisoner's tent. She'll await her punishment."

Westwind had turned with him, but Aurora stared at Rebekah for a beat more. Tears brimmed in Melanie's eyes.

"Logan, wait. Hear me. Please?" Rebekah's voice changed. Sorrow painfully deep filled it, and she sounded like a mourning wolf. "You loved me once!"

Her words grabbed his heart and jerked him to a halt. He balled his hands into fists. He would not turn to see her, not until he was stone again.

"That"—He faced her, surprised at the fury in his steady voice— "was before you took my children from me." He walked toward her, fingernails digging into his palms.

She sank to her knees. Tears streamed down her face.

He would not comfort her. "You handed him to the enemy. You became the enemy."

She spoke in a whisper so small only his wolf hearing picked it up. "What you think happened didn't."

Melanie broke free of Gavin and gripped Logan's sleeve. "Please. Can we hear her side?"

Logan stared at her. He expelled a breath and turned toward Rebekah. She hadn't moved. Her head remained bowed. He knelt next to her. Aurora lay down and crawled closer.

"What happened?" he asked.

Rebekah's delicate hand fingered one of the orange leaves on the forest floor, but she picked up a red one, blood red. "She came to me in my sleep somehow. Queen Idla." She looked at Logan when she said that, but turned her eyes back to the leaf. "She was certain I would have two of the Deliverers. She put a trace spell on me. Told me that if I were to tell you anything she'd kill you, harm my children. She had spies, Logan, and I was scared." Again she brought her tearful eyes up to meet his, but he gave her nothing in return, except a curt nod.

Her eyelids fluttered. "That night you tried to leave me with our son while you took our daughter. I tried to get you to take both babies, but you were afraid someone would catch you. I understood that fear. So I gave you our daughter, with a false letter Idla had drawn up. I knew that would be easy for you to resolve, and that you'd probably figure things out if you saw it. But I knew she would come for me.

"I left the tent right after you. There was so much screaming, so much chaos. Our son was quiet. He knew the secrecy of our mission from the beginning, Logan." She looked up at him with a smile and teary eyes. It vanished when he met her with his cold glare. She dropped her head again. Hurting her was like a knife in his heart, but he couldn't be taken by another lie.

"I ran, knowing that I had to give him to someone," she continued. "As sure as the Creator lives, the opportunity came. A woman I barely knew sat with her baby in her arms, crying for someone to help her. The confusion all around had rendered her helpless. I knelt next to her, putting our son behind me so that she wouldn't see him. She clutched my shoulder, screaming, 'He's not breathing!' I took her baby from her and told her I could help her, but she'd have to calm down. I replaced the dead baby with our son. I rubbed his back to make her think I was reviving her child. Then our boy cried. I hid the dead boy under my cloak and gave her our son instead. So he would be safe."

More tears spilled down her face. "She was so happy. So in love with him. I asked her name. She told me it was Leah Branor. I had heard of the Branors. They were a nice but poor family originally from Nivek. She said she would never forget me, and I told her my name and yours. Then I called for one of the carts taking the mothers away and made sure she got on it.

"I took her boy to the outskirts to be buried, but I knew I was running out of time. I felt the queen's pull. She was coming near. Searching for me.

"Something caught my skirt as I ran. I turned to loosen it, but it was a wolf, Logan. A wolf. She told me I was chosen to take her pup. A dream told her he would be raised in violence and that I would care for him. Five wolf pups circled her paws, and she picked up one of the five—a brown wolf—and set him at my feet. When I touched him, he turned into a human baby and cried.

"The wolf told me she'd bury the Feravolk baby. I left that one and took the wolf baby and raced back to my tent. I had no time for questions, no time for anything. But when I got there, you still weren't back. Idla was there. And there I stood with the baby that the wolf had given me.

"She sent me to her carriage. I went, knowing she would hurt you if I didn't. And yes, Logan, I told the baby he was safe." She looked at him, fresh tears streaming down her cheeks. "What was I supposed to tell him? He needed to know he was safe, that I would never let anyone hurt him." Her eyes accused him, and it was worse than a knife in the heart.

He'd betrayed her.

His own wife.

How could he have trusted Idla over Rebekah? The mirror had showed truth, but Idla had corrupted it with lies. Made him believe what she wanted him to believe.

"Logan?" Rebekah tilted her head. "You do believe me, don't you?"

Of course. The answer had been in her words the whole time: Branor. Leah Branor. How else would Rebekah know the name?

He placed a hand on her shoulder. It fit in his palm, warm and familiar. And that touch reminded him of the ache he still held for her. The scent of red roses surrounded him. "The boy, you said his name was Branor?"

"Yes. Do you know the Branors?" She grabbed his hands in hers. "She named him Ethan. Our son, his name is Ethan. I like the name, Logan." A sparkle lit her eyes.

Logan tried to swallow past the tightening in his throat. How could he have ever doubted her? "I . . ." What could he say? How could he apologize?

He'd wronged her so deeply, and she sat smiling at him through the tears.

Ethan.

Ethan was his son?

His heart wanted to leap, yet pain made it heavy.

A cool nose nudged his arm, and Aurora's muzzle pushed his hand. He let go of Rebekah with one hand to allow the wolf in. *"Logan?"* Aurora's voice interrupted his thoughts. *"May I?"*

He touched her neck. *"You've always been free, my friend."*

"Don't worry. I'll still be able to talk to you."

"Yes, but I'll miss your presence in my thoughts." The bond slipped from him.

Rebekah turned to Aurora, her eyes wide. Aurora nuzzled into Rebekah like a pup. Rebekah buried her face in Aurora's neck and whispered how much she'd missed the wolf.

Then Melanie raced to her sister. Teary-eyed, the two of them hugged so tight for so long.

Logan's throat ached. How could he have left Bekah there? Believed the queen. He'd betrayed his wife, but he'd betrayed Melanie, too. Stolen so much time from all of them.

Westwind sat beside him. *"The pack is as it should be."* He looked up at Logan. *"Don't cry. I don't want to feel your human emotion."* Westwind winked.

"Aurora put up with it."

"Yes. I love that about her."

Logan chuckled sadly.

Westwind narrowed his eyes and showed a few teeth in what resembled a grin. *"Emotion looks good on you."*

"You, too."

Westwind chuffed a laugh.

Rebekah faced Logan again. Her eyes showed so much hope. Hope he'd stripped her of.

She touched his cheek. Wiped away a tear he didn't realize he'd let escape. "Don't cry."

Logan cupped his wife's neck in his hand and tugged her closer. She let him and he kissed her.

She held him fiercely, as though she wanted this, had missed this, as much as he had. She kissed him as though she forgave him, and he hoped she could feel how sorry he was as he held her. Remembered how she felt, tasted. When the kiss ended, she backed away, and her eyes sparkled with the same adoration he'd seen the day he wed her. The taste of her kiss lingered on his lips. It was like he'd stepped back in time. But he hadn't, and he didn't deserve her devotion. "I left you in the palace. I should have gone after you. I—"

Her finger touched his lips. "Logan, you're forgiven. It's over now.

I'm here." She pulled at the chain around her neck. On the end hung her marriage stone. "I never stopped loving you, either."

He closed his eyes. Her soft hands touched the sides of his face. "Logan Laugnahagn, it's all over. We're together again. Nothing short of death can tear us apart. Not this time."

"Not this time." He echoed and pulled her close. "I'm so sor—"

"Please." She cuddled into him. "We all had our parts to play. Mine was in the palace."

CHAPTER 11

A LINK TO DANGER

S erena watched as the dissenters started returning to camp. So many carried dead Feravolk. Her heart dropped. Morgan stopped in front of Ethan. He stood there, nodding and talking. Serena searched with her talent, but she didn't feel pain from Logan. Still, he hadn't returned. Neither had Melanie nor Gavin. What was happening?

Jayden whirled around, as if she felt Serena's sudden worry. "What's wrong?"

"Are they okay? What happened?"

Ethan walked back over to where they stood. "Morgan says Logan and the others are talking to the woman who rescued Chloe. For now, the pack of whatever they were—"

"Abysshounds," Quinn whispered.

Ethan touched Quinn's shoulder, and she immediately leaned into him.

"The trees are tracking everything. They cry out in pain. In fear. They know the Mistress will destroy everything. That's what she does. She brings destruction." She stood tall and shuddered. "Her powers are the opposite of mine—I create life; she destroys it. But her powers have been tainted by greed and evil. So there is no balance between us."

A scraping burn spread across Serena's back as if something ripped her skin off. She cried out and fell forward, dizzy.

Ethan caught her. "Hey, what's wrong?"

She leaned on his arms, shaking. Unable to form words. Unable to do anything but scream as it happened again. Ethan guided her to the ground. His eyes scanned her face, so intense.

"Serena?" Jayden knelt next to her and grabbed her hands.

Serena squeezed. "I think I'm feeling—" her words choked off. "Someone's whipping him."

"Who?" Ethan's voice carried a hint of panic. "Who do I need to rescue?"

"Serena?" Dash raced to her side. He nudged her as a wave of the pain shot through her again.

All at once she felt it. Heard his voice calling to her. For help. *Serena.*

"Ryan," she whispered. "It's Ryan."

Ethan's hold on her stiffened. "He's close?"

"No."

Jayden's eyes glimmered. "Then how . . . ?"

"I–I don't know." Her words were cut off by a strangled scream. Then all the pain ebbed away. "I've never felt anyone's pain like that." She looked at Ethan. "Except yours."

He picked her up, and Jayden led the way to the tent. Everything blurred as Ethan laid her on the bedroll. His and Jayden's voices muffled. Only Dash's rang clear in her head. *"You must care about that boy for your heart to bond to his this way."*

"Is that what makes me feel his pain? A bond I created?" Her thoughts sounded sleepy.

Dash sighed, finally releasing his worry. *"Yes."*

If Quinn was right, she was supposed to be Ethan's betrothed. That didn't feel right. Ryan—he felt right. But that could just be her heart talking.

He'd been quite a gentleman at the Winking Fox—they'd called him the Knight.

The scent of warm bread and a bouquet of women's perfumes swam back as her eyes drifted closed, and she recalled the second time they'd met. That uninhibited smile filled his face. How could someone so confident seem so vulnerable?

He stared at the women who flirted with him, flashed his charming grin, swept them around in a dance, but as soon as his eyes met hers, the smile changed. It melted from his mouth until all that remained was the tiniest curve of his lips. That would have insulted her if not for the way his eyes seemed to capture the rest of his smile. Where they'd been a part of his charming grin in a playful, teasing way, as soon as he looked at her, his eyes expressed intensity that made her feel both desired and respected. Cherished. No one had ever looked at her that way.

At once, he had carved through the crowd and stood in front of her. Instead of the deep, theatrical bow and a show of him sweeping her off her feet as she'd seen him display to the other women, he bowed so that his shoulders dipped slightly, and his eye-contact only broke for a moment.

He held out his hand and took hers in a strong, firm grip. "I wasn't sure I'd see you again."

The way he stared made her blood heat. Like she stood in the center of a consuming fire. Like he stood with her and protected her from the danger of the flames.

"I hoped to see you," she inclined her head, embarrassed by the flush in her cheeks.

"Did you?" His eyebrows rose to hide behind those carefree bangs. Then he grinned. He took her hand and led her out onto the dance floor and guided her through a dance. "It seems Destiny Path was kind then."

The music slowed to a stop, and she hardly noticed.

He chuckled, and it seemed her pause had made him uncomfortable. "Finding everything fascinating again?"

Of course he'd recall that first time they'd met when she couldn't stop taking in the newness of all the city life around her—she'd called everything fascinating. Right now, all she wanted to do was study him. "When you dance with the other girls, it's so effortless. You don't seem to second-guess yourself. With me, you seem unsure. Have I done something?"

Those gray eyes penetrated every thought and his lips parted. "Absolutely."

Truth.

The music played a new song, and he swept his arm around her, drawing her closer. He held out his other hand for her to grasp. She touched it and he smiled. "You've changed everything, Serena."

Everything? He didn't take his eyes off her. He spun her. Dipped her. Led her. And she let him. Unicorns would wear a bridle for no man. But this man could put one on her, and she would trust him completely.

"Ryan?"

"Yes?" The hidden smile in his eyes deepened.

"You said you come here often."

He chuckled, and, for the first time, she lost his eye contact. It stripped her bare. As if she realized how much of herself she'd been putting out there. When he wasn't the one staring, she felt exposed.

"Dancing makes me a better swordfighter."

"Ah. That's why your sister says you dance with all the women."

"She told you that?" He scrunched up one side of his face. "It—it's part of my training. One Eye expects—"

"Do you have to dance with the others tonight?" She wanted to spend every moment that she could with him.

He stopped moving even though the others spun around them. "If you wished it of me, I would never dance with them again."

Truth. Her breath caught. She'd never desired to kiss a man before, and the thought terrified her. Tabitha's voice interrupted the moment as welcome as a whiplash during a daydream: "Men will try to lure you close enough to trap you. They are like dragons in a lair. Once they lure you in, you become theirs. Their treasure. Their prisoners. Never get close enough to be trapped."

She blinked and stepped back.

Ryan's eyebrows pinched together behind his bangs. "Is something wrong?"

"Many things, but it's not your fault. I just need some air."

He released her. "Alone?"

She grabbed his hand. "Would you come with me?"

"Always."

Truth.

Her heart stopped. No matter what Tabitha said, this man was not the dragon she spoke of. He was different.

Serena opened her eyes and jolted from sleep. Her eyes focused on the tent walls, and she inhaled deeply as she sat up.

Ethan scrambled to his feet and raced to her side. "How are you?

How—how's Ryan?" Ethan's eyes were so wide. Yet a hint of rage sparked there.

"How long was I out?"

"A few minutes. Jayden and Quinn went to meet Logan."

"Ryan is alive. I think someone was torturing him."

"Belladonna." Ethan practically growled her name.

"Ethan, if we're to save him—if I'm to heal him—I need to know the extent of my powers." She sat up and glanced at the spot on his stomach where the old wound was. The one she'd felt. "I need you to answer some questions for me."

"Okay."

She sighed. "How did she bring you back from the dead?"

Slowly, Ethan rocked back, pulling away from her as if she spoke insanity. She didn't. She'd felt the wound. It had killed him.

"I hear it's difficult to come back," she prompted.

"It is." His voice cracked. Those brown eyes met hers. "How did you know?"

"I've read the books. Healers don't like to talk about it, but some can bring back the dead. Only with their permission, though. And only one time."

"Per person?"

"Per Healer. As in, Tessa can never do it again. In everything I've read, only one person has ever decided to return. Other Healers have logged many unsuccessful attempts."

Ethan met Serena's stare with wide eyes. "Unsuccessful?"

"Yes. People who die and return to the light rarely wish to come back. What held your heart here?"

Ethan wrapped his fingers around the back of his neck and pulled his head down toward his bent knees.

She gently touched his arm. "I felt your scar, remember?"

His head sprung up. "You felt my—my death?"

"Yes."

"When Tessa brought me back, I was still injured. She didn't heal me."

"When a Healer brings someone back, it usually takes so much energy that they can't fully heal the cause of death. She didn't know she was a Healer. That's why she tended to you the . . . conventional way."

"I suppose it would have been nicer if she'd known then." He offered a strange smile. As if he was trying to make sense out of this. "And I suppose you told her what she is?"

Serena smiled. "Yes, well, not directly. I sent her to be trained by Rochelle."

He chuckled. "So secretive."

"You're one to talk."

"I'm telling you about this, aren't I?"

"Only because I knew enough to ask." Serena rubbed his arm. "Tell me, Ethan. Please."

"It's a risk, isn't it?"

"Yes." Serena's eyes widened. "Healers have died trying and waiting too long to come back."

"Then why should I tell you? So you can die trying to bring some-one back?"

"Ethan, I will take that risk if you or Jayden die. There will be no stopping me. Your answer could help save me."

"It can't."

Truth. Her heart wanted to stall. "Why not?"

"Because Tessa brought me back against my will."

Serena stared at him for so long he buried his face behind his hands. "It's because you're a Deliverer. Your duty is not yet complete and the Creator wants you here." She tapped her finger against her lip. "At least I know Jayden and you would be safe if I need to—"

"Tessa had to tell me she'd die if I stayed. She used her own life to barter with me. She stretched out her hand and told me all I had to do was grab it. I didn't. She grabbed my wrist. That's how, Serena. Please, if I die again, let me stay. When I'm summoned home, I will not fear it."

"Thank you, Ethan, for answering my questions. I know it was hard for you."

"Please don't share—"

"I'll keep the secret as long as I need to."

He frowned but nodded. "We should probably go talk to Logan."

He smiled and stood. She grabbed his hand, but as he pulled her up, he hunched over, pain spreading from his chest. She felt every bit of it. The wound Belladonna had left from the Sword of Black Malice.

Serena touched his back. "What's wrong?"

"Nothing." He straightened.

Lie.

A twinge of pain speared Serena's chest again, but Ethan didn't move except for clenching his jaw. "Nothing?" she asked.

Dash nudged the tent flap and stuck his nose in. *"I felt that."*

"From Ethan?"

Dash just stared at her. *"Belladonna linked with him. Through that sword. Didn't she?"*

Serena clutched her throat. *"She'll find him."*

This time the pull was much harder. Ethan didn't hide the wince, but neither did she. He stared at her. *"You* felt that."

She nodded.

"Is it happening to all of us?"

"No. It's your pain." She unlaced the top of his shirt and stared at the dark scar.

She opened her talent. The tie was there. Belladonna was tugging. "She's coming for you."

"How?"

Serena swallowed. "The wound she healed—she left a way to trace you inside of it."

"The scar?" Ethan stared at her, eyes wide. "She'll find us. I have to go."

"She has Ryan. You're not going without me."

His mouth opened, and he stared at the hand she'd pressed against his chest as another wave of pain pulsed into it. He placed his hand on top of Serena's. She looked into his wide eyes. Ethan scared? She rubbed his shoulder. "I'll find a way to fix this."

She had to.

"Ethan. Serena. Oh."

Both of them turned to see Jayden pop her head into the tent. She stood there with her mouth open.

Serena dropped her hand from Ethan's bare chest.

Jayden motioned over her shoulder. "I was just . . . umm . . . Logan wants to talk to us. I think I'll go."

"Jayden." Ethan laced up his shirt and headed after her.

CHAPTER 12

STEADFAST FEELINGS

Ethan raced out of the tent after Jayden, but slowed his steps. Why muddy the water? What she thought she saw with Serena and him could be explained away because he didn't feel anything for Serena—even though according to Quinn he was supposed to. He shook his head. But Jayden was his sister.

So he didn't have to explain a thing.

He just felt like he should.

This was all too confusing. And wrong. Just very wrong.

Chloe ran down the hill toward him, her green eyes holding more rage than the time he and Ryan had sprung her gryphon trap with a skunk. "You need to do something about this!"

He pointed to himself. "Me?"

"Who else would I be talking to, Ethan Branor?"

He cringed. Chloe, always reminding him that he wasn't truly part of her family. He held up his hands to calm her, even though it never worked. "About what?"

"About Ryan! Logan is up there with his wife, talking about how the child Rebekah took to the palace wasn't her son and that you are. *You* of all people. Do you believe it? Now they aren't going after Ryan." The anger left her face in the form of tears, and he spread his arms to hug her.

Wait. His heart seemed to slow a beat to help him catch up with what she'd just said. Instead of letting him hug her, Chloe pounded her fist into his chest.

He caught her hand, still processing. Logan was his father?

Serena raced by him in a blur.

Logan.

Serena was his sister.

Air left his lungs in a strangled laugh.

"How is this funny?" She slammed her fist into him again, and, at the same time, Belladonna tugged the link.

He buckled over, groaning.

"Oh, Ethan, I'm sorry." Chloe steadied his shoulders. "I didn't mean to hurt you. Not really. I'm just—"

"It's all right, Chloe."

She looked right into his eyes. Tears dripped down her cheeks. Grandens weren't supposed to cry. She wiped them away. "Logan said rescuing Ryan will start a war. It's too dangerous."

Logan didn't know they were torturing Ryan. Surely if he knew . . . .

"You can't make him go, can you?"

He started walking up the hill.

"Ethan?" She ran to keep up with him.

He stopped and faced her. "If he won't go, I will. I have to protect Ryan, Chloe. He's my brother, too."

"I know." She grabbed his shirt in her fists. "You can't go. Not alone."

"Chloe."

"No, Ethan. Please talk to Logan first. We'll save Ryan, but Logan will let us take an army or something. He'll—"

"Okay." He patted her hand. In truth, it didn't matter what Logan would say. Ethan was going after his brother no matter what. If Belladonna could feel where he was, he'd take the fight right to her.

"Don't you dare brush me off, Ethan. I will come with you whether you approve or not."

"I will not lose another sister."

She cocked an eyebrow and tilted her head. "Then it's a good thing I'm not your sister." She stormed ahead of him.

He sighed and followed. Logan stood with a woman who looked very much like Melanie and Serena. She must be Rebekah.

Rebekah's hands flew to her mouth. "Ethan," she whispered.

She recognized him?

Logan followed her. "How could you—?"

"I would know this face anywhere. It's yours, but younger." She smiled at Logan. "With my eyes." She extended her hand toward Ethan.

He tucked his chin, backing away from her. She stopped.

Serena came up beside him. "She tells the truth, Ethan. She's our mother."

Tears dripped from Rebekah's eyes as Serena embraced her.

When Serena stepped back, she smiled and opened her arms for Ethan. Gratefully, he hugged her. His sister. It felt right.

Rebekah moved closer, cautiously. "The last time I held you, you were so small. But never helpless."

Ethan let her hug him. As soon as she did, he wrapped his arms around her, and it felt natural. Ethan glanced at Logan; it would be easy and difficult at the same time to think of him as his own father.

Logan chuckled. "I should have known, kid."

Ethan shrugged.

Logan put a hand on his shoulder, and Ethan caught sight of Jayden, standing beside a tree, listening on the outskirts. Her head tipped up and she stared at him, looking so small and unsure.

Jayden.

He moved toward her, but she practically shrunk behind the tree. Doubt slowed his footsteps. Hadn't she been clear that she loved him? Not exactly. She'd never admitted it. His heartbeat quickened as he remembered their first kiss. She had not been clear about anything.

He reached her and pressed his palm against the tree she hid behind. His hand aware of every feeling, his body aware of the air between them.

Jayden's eyes slowly met his. "You're . . . not my brother?"

He laughed and it sounded foreign to his ear.

All he wanted to do was touch her. Taste her lips on his again. "You're hiding."

"I—I've been thinking a lot."

"About?"

She nodded toward the circle of people still hugging and laughing tearfully, and Chloe standing all alone. He had to find a way to go after Ryan.

"About what Quinn said." Jayden paused, and her gaze darted to the ground.

Ethan placed his finger under her chin. How easily she looked at him. Her eyes were so vulnerable. His heart swelled. If he let her go, would she return to him? "Hey, don't worry. No pressure from me, ever. I don't care about silly traditions. You choose who you want."

"Traditions." She shook her head and closed her eyes. When she opened them, they were the brightest, boldest blue. "Thank you, Ethan."

He swallowed and dropped his hands to his sides. "All I want is for you to be happy."

Her lips parted and she stared at him. Her eyes glistened. She closed the distance between them, and her body heat pressed against him. Gently, she linked her hands behind his neck.

Did they have to be so incredibly soft?

A smile formed on her face. "Ethan, I've loved you since you pledged to protect me."

His heart hitched on a beat. "You . . . ?"

She slid her hand up the back of his neck, sending shivers all over his body. His pulse pounded as she pulled him closer. His arms had somehow made it around her. She tilted her chin up and leaned toward him. His lips met hers. And he tasted her, felt her, breathed her. She hugged him tighter. There wasn't space between them, but she kept nudging his body closer to hers. Did she sigh? Creator in heaven. How he had ever believed Jayden was his sister was beyond him.

"Ethan!"

Chloe's voice snapped him out of everything, and he let go of Jayden reluctantly. She stepped back, as breathless as he, and her lips were bright red. Her cheeks flushed. "You're beautiful," he whispered, and her eyes sparkled.

Chloe tugged his shirt, and he spun to face her, leaning his arm on the tree and hoping she caught his glare.

She stared at him, eyes wide and wounded, and trembled. He softened his expression.

"Ryan." Her voice shook.

He touched her shoulder briefly, then walked past her and toward Logan. Jayden and Chloe followed.

"The Mistress went to the palace," Rebekah said.

"How can you be sure?" Logan asked.

"That's where everything Idla prepared is. The army, the potions, the spells. The Mistress will go there to regain her strength."

"Then we need to stop her before she gets stronger," Ethan said. "We have to go to the palace. We need the Wielder. And we have to rescue Ryan."

Logan held out his hand as if to stop Ethan from rushing into things blind. "We still need the fourth Deliverer."

"Logan, Ryan won't last—"

"Where was he sent?" Rebekah asked at the same moment Ethan started pleading for his brother's life.

Logan placed his hand on Ethan's shoulder, then he turned his attention to Rebekah. "The fourth was sent to Nivek. With the Gray family. Quinn doesn't know—"

"Grays?" Chloe's voice was soft in the open air.

Logan turned to her, his hand on Ethan's shoulder tensing. "You know them?"

Eyes wide, Chloe slid her hand into her dress pocket and retrieved a small journal. The leather binding was barely holding it together. She handed it to Logan.

He took the book, his gaze on Chloe's unwavering expression. He passed his hand over the worn leather cover and opened it. Ethan peered in. The handwriting inside was that of a person not yet familiar with a pen; the letters were large and sloppy.

Chloe's unsteady finger drew his attention to a drawing nestled in the front pocket of the inside cover. "My father handed me my mother's dress when he told me to take my sisters and run. I didn't know it was her dress right away. It was wrapped around the fruits and bread he gave me. But I found that in the pocket."

Logan took the sketch gingerly. And Ethan's heart squeezed. A handsome father and a pretty mother, a babe in her arms, and a young girl, clutching her mother's dress in one hand and her father's finger in the other. A pretty family. A happy family. A family he knew.

"I was five," Chloe said. "I remember holding still for such a long time." Her eyes met Logan's. "Turn it over."

He complied. In a delicate hand, the names were written on the back:

Thomas Gray wife Jane Gray and children Chloe and Ryan.

"It's the only reason I knew what our last name was before father changed it and we moved. He was always changing our last name when we moved." Chloe's voice was soft and dry. "Ryan is the only one without red hair. The only one without green eyes. He's taller than my father ever was." She paused and looked at Ethan. "Father told Ryan to take Jayden and leave. He knew how important both of them were, didn't he?"

Logan handed the journal back to her. He rubbed his hands over his face. "This whole time?" Anger grated his words. "I had all of them! Drawn to their Protectors, she'd said. All the paths were shown to me, and I was blind."

"Ryan?" Jayden stepped closer. "Ryan is my brother?"

"Ryan," Serena said his name softly.

"I had him under my protection, and now he's in the palace!" Logan ran his fingers through his hair. "How am I supposed to get him out of there without starting a war? We're not ready to—"

"Don't stall the war."

Logan turned at the sound of Kara's voice.

The assassin stood there, arms crossed and hip thrust out. "The Mistress has been planning her escape for a long time, and as one of her trusted employees, I know quite a bit about her plans."

Ethan unsheathed his sword and rounded on Kara. She moved on his advance, but Jayden stood between them.

She faced Kara. "Tell us."

"You can't trust her." Rebekah stared at Kara as if she'd seen a ghost.

Kara shot Rebekah a grin. "So quick to trade loyalties?"

"You were never on my side."

"Really? How did you get out of the palace?"

"Connor—"

"Pushed you out a window?"

Rebekah's eyes narrowed.

"That's right." Kara crossed her arms. "Thea told him to do that. You got out because of her. Franco killed my sister. I want him dead."

"I'll tell you if she lies." Serena walked up to Kara and looked into her eyes.

"All right." Logan widened his stance. "Tell us what you know, assassin."

Kara offered a petite smile. "The Mistress gave Idla the power to taint hearts and make an army. They are in the palace. She put poison into their veins and used a potion to bind their blood to the poison. They all bowed to her will because she spelled them and used a tool to control them. Franco has this tool now. He calls them the Black Blood Army and most of them are young. Could you fight them, Logan? Knowing they could be saved?"

"How?" Ethan sheathed his sword.

"The answers to reversing the spell are in the palace." Kara shrugged. "If you want to win, strike now before her power has returned, before her army is at full strength. Go in, get the last Deliverer, and then be ready to strike. You know the prophecies: A sorceress will come with power to destroy all the Creator has built. She'll break the land and the people's hearts and bring death to those who'd oppose her. But hope will be found when the Deliverers rise through fire, through ash, and heal the heart of the land. Through blazing fire and torrent of rain, the forest shall fall and rise again."

Jayden cocked her head. "I didn't know that last part."

Kara smirked. "Maybe you should read more."

A twinge shot through Ethan's chest. "Belladonna will know we're coming."

The burn in his chest wasn't just from Belladonna's scar. Everyone he loved was now in danger.

CHAPTER 13

DESTROYER

Connor stood in the middle of the moonlit meadow in his wolf form and breathed in. His power tainted the air. Zapped beneath his skin. Begged to be set free. To destroy.

His wolf howl had hopefully scared away all the creatures in the area. He bowed his head. Closed his eyes. And felt the force fill him. It trickled into his paws at first, then flooded his senses. Fiery and electric. A rushing wave or a swirling funnel cloud. Too painful to hold in for long.

Still, he held tight until he could hold back no more, then he opened his eyes and stared at the decaying tree on the other side of the meadow.

Force seeped out of him and slammed into the tree. The ground screamed and the tree cried out. Then silence. Nothing but dust and shards of dead bark and the barren meadow. The whole earth between him and the tree was scorched and dry. Dead.

A wasteland.

And he fell to the ground, exhausted.

Two small eyes stared back at him. A tiny creature staggered toward him—young and innocent—and dying.

Oh no. He nuzzled the little fox cub with his nose, and it whimpered as it burrowed into him. Why did they follow him? All the creatures were drawn to him, and when he used his power someone always died. As the last pulse of breath left the kit's lungs, hot tears dripped over Connor's muzzle.

He could never use his full power. Never.

"You should eat something."

Connor didn't look up from the book in his lap as Madison entered his room. She crouched near him, and he smelled fresh bread. And fruit. His stomach begged him to eat. When he didn't reach for the bread, she held it over the book.

It really did smell good.

He took some and looked up at her. "Thank you."

Her eyes opened wide and she sat back.

"What is it?"

She shook her head and stared, mouth agape. "Your eyes . . ."

"What about them?"

"They seem . . . hotter? Is that the right way to put it? They look, reddish. Like heated gold."

He slid the book off his lap slowly, then rushed to the mirror. Red. Not good. Never good. Please not red. He looked in the mirror.

"It's probably lack of sleep. I didn't mean to scare you." Her voice trailed him.

The whites of his eyes were red all right, but Madison wasn't imagining it. She couldn't have been. How would she know? Sure enough, there it was. A sliver of red leaked away from the irises, leaving them golden and peculiar. Nothing that belonged in a normal human being. He slumped against the doorframe, head in his hand. Red eyes meant his power was growing. He didn't have much time.

"Connor, I think you should rest. Maybe get some . . ."

He looked up to where Madison sat on the floor, hands around an open book. The same one he'd just been reading. Her fingers didn't curl around the edges of the cover; her palms were open, as if she wished the book would take free will and jump off of her lap. Yet her eyes remained glued to the pages. What had he been read—oh. *Oh no.*

He stood, remembering the forgotten bread in his hands. It was warm now. Not still warm. Warm again. Because he'd made it warm. Just like he'd let his eyes glow red.

And now Madison was about to put the pieces together.

Her face scrunched up, as if the details on the pages disgusted her.

As if she couldn't imagine anyone being capable of the evil described in that chapter. He closed his eyes. Hot against his eyelids. He breathed. The power crackled below the surface, but he wouldn't be able to unleash its true fury. Not until he'd made contact with the Whisperer.

At first, he'd thought that meant he should stay away from her forever.

A Wielder's powers are his burden.

The book had spoken true, but he could keep the burden small as long as he never touched the Whisperer and completed the circle.

But now? Now he felt that if he didn't touch her soon, his power would rip him apart trying to free itself. The small fits and bursts he'd let out weren't enough anymore. If the circle didn't complete, it would fry him alive.

He opened his eyes, and Madison still leaned over the book. This time her fingers curled around it. Not in ownership, in disbelief. In disagreement that the Creator would make such a creature.

There is a time for peace and a time for war. A time for growth and a time for death. A time to heal and a time to wound.

To wound.

Wound.

Connor crushed his eyes closed and saw the lifeless eyes of that trusting fox. "Madison?" His voice cracked.

"Did you read this?" Her words rushed out on a breath.

He knelt next to her. "Many times."

"Many?" She looked up at him. At his golden eyes.

He saw the rhetorical question on her face: How could the Creator make such a monstrosity? She sat back, and the book thumped onto the floor between them. Her mouth opened.

Breathe. Please.

Air darted into her lungs. "Oh." She pitched forward and hugged him.

Hugged? He wrapped his arms around her.

"You're the Wielder?"

He nodded against her shoulder.

"Connor." She slipped back from him and smiled. "The Creator chose such a kind-hearted person to be his weapon."

Kind-hearted? Kind—? "I'm sorry, what?'

She cocked her head. "You know what a Wielder is capable of, don't you?"

"Destruction." His mouth was so dry. "Death bringer, they called him. Why would you call me kind-hearted? Didn't you read the passage?"

Her hand touched his cheek. "You don't want to use your powers."

He jerked back from her. "Of course not."

"That's why he chose you. He knew the weight it would be on your heart. Don't you see? If he'd chosen someone lesser, someone like Franco, or someone bent on revenge, or—Connor, you were chosen because using the power would break your heart for the people, the land. You won't use them unless you have to."

He stared at her as her words swam in his head. If he had to open the door of death, it would kill everything in its path. Kill. Destroy. Destruction. Desolation. Death. Wielders were rarely forgiven for what they had to do. They burned books about themselves because if the people knew what they were truly capable of, they would hunt them as soon as they were born and kill them.

That was why he had to go through life alone.

Lone wolf.

Wolf without a pack.

A Wielder's burden is his own.

Connor stood. "I think you're right. I could use some air."

"I didn't mean to upset you." She touched his chest.

He swallowed and stared at her . . . hand. Oh no. Not . . . how had he missed that? Typically he could ignore a girl who started batting pretty eyes his way, and that was enough to stop her advances. Madison—he needed her. Heavens, he liked her. She was a friend. A real one. Like Luc. "Madison."

She backed away, blinking. "I should have known."

His skin chilled. "Known what?"

"You're just a genuine, nice person. Aren't you, Connor?"

He tried to deny it. Wanted to apologize for not returning her feelings. Opened his mouth to speak, but all he could do was shake his head in denial.

She giggled, then leaned forward, smiling. "Can you really turn into an animal? What kind? Do the different kinds mean different things?"

"You read more of the chapter than you let on. But you can't lie, Madison. I shouldn't answer you."

"How do you plan to get us out of here?"

"This morning I heard Belladonna saying the Deliverers were headed here. I feel it as well. I plan to go talk to Franco and see if I can't figure out his plan. I know he won't let the Mistress take the Deliverers he wants so badly for himself."

She flinched. "Talk to Franco?"

Connor shrugged. "We all have a part to play."

CHAPTER 14

THE FUTURE IS NEAR

*W*ord *has reached us from Moon Over Water by the wolves, Logan."* Westwind's voice seemed weaker than normal. *"Reuben and Beck and Alistair are on their way toward the palace. They should be within fighting range in four days."*

"Thank you, Westwind." Logan stood at the edge of river separating them from what Quinn called the borderlands: the decaying land that bordered the Mistress's levels. The defense she used to guard her as she sat safely in the palace, regaining her powers.

A defense he'd have to find a way to overcome. Already they'd traveled four days from the chasm.

He listened with all his senses. The forest felt so different. As if it was fighting to stay alive. Starlight punctured through the reddish black hue of the sky tonight. That was a good sign, wasn't it? He wanted to ask Quinn.

Rebekah approached him and wrapped her arms around him, resting her head on his back. "Worrying again? Some things don't change."

He pressed his arms against hers, feeling her warmth. How many nights had he imagined her soft touch while she'd been away? He turned into her, and she didn't break her hold. "I hope this plan works."

"You would have made a wonderful leader for Moon Over Water. I always knew that."

He laughed. "I do not wish to lead anyone, Bekah."

"And yet here you are." She let go of him and held his hand as they headed across the camp to where his trusted leaders had gathered, awaiting his orders.

Morgan and Richard represented the Dissenters.

Gavin and Melanie, Ethan, Jayden, Serena, and Quinn were also present.

"You have news, Morgan?" He turned to her first, hoping that by now she had seen something that would help them.

"Belladonna knows Ethan is approaching. She expects him to rescue Ryan."

Morgan's eyes took on a faraway look. She was likely focusing on something internal—a vision of the future. "As long as we move toward the palace, they will lie in wait for us."

"That means she'll have scouts," Logan said. "Are you sure the Mistress is still weak?"

"I don't see her. I don't know."

"She is." Quinn knelt on the ground and starting drawing something in the dirt with a stick. "Her power moves through the soil, destroying it with poison and pain. The more she destroys, the stronger she'll become."

"Then we don't have much time." Logan's heart hammered. "You're sure Connor will know how to put the Mistress away?"

Quinn nodded. "He has to open the door of death and push her through. The only way he can open the door is if I touch him." She glanced up at Logan, but then resumed her strange drawing.

"All right. We are on the doorstep of our enemy. We have almost all the tools we need to defeat her. We have to strike while she's weak." He glanced at Ethan. "Because she knows we're coming."

"A sorceress will come with power to destroy all the Creator has built. She'll break the land and the people's hearts and bring death to those who'd oppose her. But hope will be found when the Deliverers rise through fire, through ash, and heal the heart of the land. Through blazing fire and torrent of rain, the forest shall fall and rise again." Quinn recited, echoing Kara's earlier words.

Serena knelt beside her. "Do you know what that means?"

She looked up at Serena. "The Wielder does. The trees do. Everything will burn. When she uses her power, everything will burn."

Serena sat back on her heels, glancing up at Logan with her eyebrows pulled together, but an unfelt breeze touched Quinn, and she closed her eyes.

Her stick stilled and she spoke again. "The heart of one, mind of another, the soul of one, and strength of her brother."

"What does that mean, Quinn?" Jayden asked.

Quinn opened her eyes. "She needs the Deliverers to give her these things in order to get the Creator's power. She needs one's heart, one's mind, one's soul, and one's strength. Then she can unlock the power with the keys."

"The keys." Logan crouched near and caught sight of her drawing. It looked like a labyrinth of sorts. A maze in a circular shape. "Is that the key?"

She looked up at him. "This is our map through the levels."

Logan gasped and stared at her. "You know the way in?"

She smiled, so innocent. Oh how he wished war and evil wouldn't rip that innocence from her. "I know the way to the palace. Once we have Ryan and Connor, the six of us can open the door of death and send the Mistress through. The Deliverers must battle the Mistress. Her defeat will make her weak enough to push her through the door of death. And she'll be locked away. The land will heal."

"Wait. You have to be there?" Ethan turned to Quinn, shaking his head.

"Yes." Quinn squared her shoulders.

"No." Ethan held out his hand and glanced at Logan as if asking for help to back him up.

Logan's heart clutched. As much as he wanted to agree, how could he?

Quinn stood. "If I'm not touching Connor when he opens the door of death, then the door of life will remain closed."

"What does that mean?" Logan asked.

Quinn held out the book he'd given her. The pages flitted open. "This shows the doors open." Once she touched the two blank pages, a picture spanned them. Two holes in the sky, one light and one dark. The dark door sucked life toward it. The light door expelled a white cloud that spread over a battlefield. Carnage and dead bodies covered the ground.

"I'm still not sure I understand."

"When the door of death opens, it will claim lives. If I'm touching Connor, the door of life will also open. It will keep many from dying."

"This future is not set in stone," Morgan said. "But Quinn speaks truth. If you are able to do this, the combined power of the Deliverers will defeat her." She paused. "Or make her unbeatable if she is able to take their power."

Logan breathed in. The air was thick. Not just with danger and evil, but with the feeling of apprehension mingled with anticipation: the feel of the eve of battle.

They had to make it through the levels, and Quinn had the map. "Then we go in. We rescue Ryan and Connor. Then we destroy the Mistress before she gains her powers back."

"You have a plan for this rescue?" Melanie asked.

"We split up." Logan drew a diagram in the dirt near Quinn's map. "Half of our army will go with Gavin and Melanie. Half will stay with me. Ethan, we need you to draw Belladonna out, then we'll ambush her. The other half of our army will wait here on the south side while a team infiltrates the palace for the rescue."

"The team?" Gavin raised his eyebrows.

"Me and five other Dissenters. We know the way in. Connor helped us escape," Morgan said. "I know where Ryan and Connor will be. I can get my men there and we can get them out."

"You've seen it?" Jayden asked.

Morgan's eyelashes fluttered. "I've seen so many possibilities that I block it out. But I know where Ryan and Connor will be. And I know when." She looked at Logan. "You will move us closer tomorrow?"

"That's my plan. Half of our army will divert the Mistress's attention while we get the Deliverers in place. We leave early tomorrow and travel hard in this direction." He motioned to Quinn's map. "Once we get here, the team of rescuers can break off."

"What's this?" Ethan leaned down and reached for a long, thin line of liquid that traveled across the ground. He touched it.

"Don't!" Quinn dove for Ethan's hand. He jerked away from the ground as if it stung him. Quinn wiped the moisture off his fingers and cried out. Her body shook. Black lines raised her veins and trailed through her body.

"Quinn!" Ethan caught her form, his eyes wide.

The dark color faded, leaving her clean. She blinked and looked up into Ethan's eyes. "I'm okay now." Her voice seemed small.

"What was that?" Logan asked.

"Black blood. The Mistress sent it forth to destroy the land. The trees are trying to absorb it. That's why they're dying. If you touch it—it's like venom."

Venom. That he understood. "How do we stop it?"

"Send the Mistress to the Afterworld. Her blood will go with it."

"That's her blood?"

"She's had thousands of years to bleed into her prison. This is how she's killing the land and consuming its power. Her blood will travel away, destroying everything. Once it starts flowing back to her, she'll be stronger than—than anything."

"Where is it going?"

"The heart of Soleden. The Forest of Legends. If it kills the heart, the world will stop beating. The Feravolk will cease to be."

CHAPTER 15

OATH HANDS AND WOUNDED HEARTS

Serena curled into a ball on her bedroll and tried to hold back the tears. Scraping pain slammed into her back, then dragged across her skin, leaving a burning trail over her skill. Over and over. Tears dripped down her face. And Ryan's faint voice called her name. Each new ache dulled as quickly as it came, but she knew that wasn't happening for Ryan.

Logan was right to want to plan and wait for Alistair's army from Moon Over Water before striking. But he wasn't right about sending no one to rescue Ryan ahead of time. The Dissenters wouldn't go in until Logan brought them close enough.

That was too late.

If they didn't go soon, Belladonna would break Ryan. His heart was already tainted. She'd sensed the dark scar when she first met him. Belladonna would sense the black lion venom, too. And Belladonna would push him to embrace the taint. The healing walls the scar had created would burst, and the poison would overtake his heart.

Serena held in a sob. Logan might be speaking from wisdom, but if they were too late, Ryan would give his allegiance to the Mistress.

She balled her hands into fists. It was settled. Somehow, someway, she would rescue Ryan herself. And she knew just how to get close enough to the palace.

"Serena?" Someone standing outside the tent whispered her name. "It's Morgan. Can I talk to you?"

She sat up and dried her eyes. Neither Jayden nor Quinn had returned to the tent. They were both likely with Ethan. She swallowed, steadying her voice. "Are you here to talk me out of things?"

"No."

Serena's heart jumped. "Then come in."

Morgan slipped into the tent and closed the flap. She faced Serena and breathed deep. "I know what you're planning."

"You said you wouldn't stop me."

"I won't. Logan and his army won't make it in time. Ryan will be lost."

"And if I go?"

Morgan sighed. "If you go, Ryan has a chance. But you also need the counters book."

"Counters book?"

"Every spell book has one."

"Yes! The hidden book inside." Serena paused. "Do you know how I plan to get to the palace?"

"The woman who gave you that." Morgan motioned to the golden ring Serena wore. "She was Kara's sister."

That was why Kara looked so familiar. "Do you think she will help me?"

Morgan nodded slightly. "And I can help you escape here unseen, but only for the next hour."

Serena grasped Morgan's hands. "Thank you."

Morgan left as quietly as she'd come, and Serena's heart pounded as she stared at the tent's exit. It had to be now, while everything was right. *"Dash?"*

"Yes."

"Could you meet me by the raspberry bushes in a half hour?"

"Yes. Why?"

"I can't tell you . . . yet."

The unicorn's sigh was audible in her thoughts. *"What are you up to?"*

"Trust me? Please?"

"Serena, you know going after that boy alone would be unwise?"

"It's less wise if I don't. We'll lose him, Dash. Morgan has seen it."

Dash paused, thinking.

"A half hour, Dash. I'll see you then."

"Be careful."

She braided her hair and put on her slacks and shirt. She draped her inherited Feravolk cloak over her and pulled up the hood. Her four beautifully crafted daggers were tucked away, two in her black, knee-high boots and two hanging from her belt. Then she bit her lip and glanced over her shoulder as she opened Jayden's bag. She'd seen the small pouch of tangle flower seed in here before. Hoping for forgiveness, she pocketed that, closed Jayden's bag, and stepped out of the tent.

Her soft leather boots hit the soil beneath her like a falling feather as she headed toward one particular tent. When she reached it, she drew a dagger and softly tapped on the door. The taut material gave under her touch.

No one answered.

Carefully lifting the flap, Serena stepped inside. A strong grip curled around her wrist and wrenched her arm behind her. Cool steel pressed against her throat. "Come to kill me in my sleep?"

"Why would I knock?" Serena choked on her words. "Let me go, Kara."

Kara released her, pushing her farther into the tent.

Serena nearly fell forward. She straightened and faced Kara. "Is that how you greet your visitors?"

"*You* came to *my* tent with a dagger drawn."

Serena motioned to Kara's cloak. "Heading out?"

Kara's eyes narrowed and she tucked her knife at the small of her back. "What brings you here, Golden One? Or did you enter the wrong tent?"

"I need your help."

Kara cocked an eyebrow and leaned forward. "It comes at a cost."

"What cost?"

"Depends on the favor."

Serena was losing a battle with time. "If you took me to the palace, could you guarantee me a way out?"

Kara's eyebrows shot up. "Why?"

"I didn't think assassins asked that question."

"I'm curious." Kara smirked.

"Because you hate Franco."

Kara picked up her packed satchel and slung it over her shoulder. "Very well. I'm headed there anyway."

Serena's knees trembled. She felt as if a hummingbird fluttered inside of her. "So you'll take me?"

Kara's stare locked onto Serena, and she stepped closer until she was a breath away. "You would go as my prisoner?" She cocked an eyebrow. "I see your need for secrecy. Logan will search for you."

"I know."

"If he catches us, it could get me killed."

"You're an assassin. You won't let him catch us."

Kara circled Serena, tapping her knife hilt on her open palm. "Logan I can hide from. It's his wolf friends that worry me."

"Let me handle that."

Kara's eyes narrowed.

"It's now or never. And if they catch us, I won't let them kill you."

"Even you can't stop an arrow already released."

"No, but I can heal."

Kara stopped her vulturous circling. "Fair enough."

"I won't discuss my plan until we are away from here."

"If you have a plan." Kara folded her arms. "Why do you trust me?"

"Trust is a strong word. I need you."

"You know I'm going to find a way to kill Franco."

"I wish you luck."

Kara's smile slid across her lips. "You going as my prisoner is all the luck I need."

"I need a blood oath that you will get me inside the palace and equip me with the means I will need to escape—alive."

"And alone?"

"Creator willing, no."

Kara cut her palm with her knife. "You have my word." She handed Serena the knife.

Serena's pulse raced. "If you make an oath with a Healer—"

"I'll die if I break it. Yes, I know."

Serena cut deep so her wound would still be open when Kara clasped her hand. They shook, bloody palm to bloody palm. Serena wiped the red away, her cut already healed.

Kara stared. "Must be nice huh, Golden One?"

"I can heal you." Serena reached for Kara's hand, but Kara pulled away.

"I can hold reins with an oath hand just fine. When do we leave?"

CHAPTER 16

THE TRAP IS BAITED

The sound of metal scraping against stone jolted Ryan from sleep. Dim light from the doorway was like a knife to eyes accustomed to the dark. The lacerations on his back and sides pulled when he moved. At least they felt a few days old thanks to what Belladonna called healing. The memory of fresh pain was enough to make him thankful for what she'd done to ease it.

The silhouette of a woman with a long ponytail and skin-tight pants meant Belladonna had come to retrieve him for his daily torture session with Beefy Butch. Ryan sat up and placed his tortured back against the stone-cold wall of his cell. It stung until he got used to the chill.

He watched Belladonna through the openings between the cross-hatched bars in his prison. Her signature sultry walk brought her closer to him. The sound of diamonds and dragon teeth clinking together like a sick wind chime accompanied her. His stomach squeezed, and he fought to keep her from noticing.

She stopped in front of his cell. "It's time, pet. I've got something special planned today."

He trembled. Of course she did. She always did. Already they'd smashed his sword hand and given him what Butch described "a small taste of the rack," but always they whipped him. Always.

The worst of it was that they never asked him any questions.

There was no point to the torture except for him to endure pain until Belladonna told Butch to stop. Then she pulsed healing into him.

But never fully healing him. Just gave him enough to make him feel grateful, which he always did.

And he hated himself for it.

Nothing he said or did had any bearing on the amount of torture. He was powerless to stop it. He had no control.

He slid off his pallet, strode up to the cell bars, and clutched them in his hands, even though his left still throbbed from being only half healed. She looked at his hand and frowned as she reached her delicate fingers up to touch it. The warm, familiar caress of healing started to soothe him, but he jerked away.

She cocked an eyebrow and narrowed her eyes. "You don't need my healing?"

Ryan glared at her. She made him need her healing. Made him yearn for her touch. It was sick. He stilled the urge to spit in her face.

"Let's see how you fare if you have to spend a whole night without a Healer, *pet.*"

The cell door opened, and Ryan walked out. Struggling was only a waste of energy at this point. The three men in the doorway would make sure of it. The familiar stench of blood and vomit met Ryan at the door to the torture chamber. Heat pulsed through his whole body, making his fingers tingle and his chest tighten. He couldn't breathe. His knees shook.

Meaty hands grabbed him. "Don't fall over." Butch thudded his back, and the sting of pain shot through every gash.

Ryan leaned over, but Butch steadied him. Phlegm gurgled in Butch's throat as he laughed. "This one's almost broken. The light in his eyes has nearly winked out."

Belladonna's whip clicked as she pulled it from her belt.

Ryan trembled. *Focus.* Strong and stoic seemed so far from reach now. Serena's angelic face filled his thoughts. The only thing he could think about that took him away from here.

Ryan sucked in air, able to breathe again. He thought of her sweet-smelling hair and deep blue eyes. He would not dwell on Belladonna. He would not become her Cain.

Fire pulsed through his veins.

Butch pushed him into a chair. Splintered wood pricked against his open wounds. Rank breath heated his face. Ryan turned away as far as he could in the wooden seat.

Belladonna stood on his other side with her arms crossed. "I think it's time for the bronze bull."

"That'll kill him." Butch secured a metal cuff around each of Ryan's wrists, anchoring them to the chair's arms.

"Make sure it doesn't, and I'll heal him."

Ryan glared at her. "I thought you said no healing today."

Belladonna's nostrils flared. Her arm thrust out to her side and a long finger pointed at the bull. "Do it."

Butch shrugged. "I like to hear their screams in that one, but don't expect pretty boy to survive." He strapped Ryan's ankles into metal shackles.

"Good, I'd rather die."

The whites of Belladonna's eyes flashed, and she lunged for Ryan, pressing her hand against his neck and pushing against his throat. "I think it's time for you to understand something, pet."

This time he didn't still the urge. He spit in her face.

"You will pay for that." She glared as she wiped the saliva from her cheek. The dark spark in her eyes sent a shock through Ryan. He struggled to breathe. Her fingers tightened around his neck. "Remember; all the pain you've ever felt is buried in the memory of your body." She tipped her head to the side and released some of her hold. He gulped in air. "Last time I made you feel my power, it was only a slice of the pain I can pulse into you. I'm your worst nightmare."

He tried to move away, pressing his back into the chair, but he was trapped. A whimper escaped his throat as her fingers glided over his cheek.

"That's right. Fear me," she said.

Ryan trembled.

Belladonna gently stroked his ear. Her eyes widened. Her lips parted. Then her smile turned wicked. "My, my, my. It seems you're familiar with something black and . . . venomous already."

Heavy paws pressed against his chest again. He couldn't breathe. Pain slammed into him. The fire flared through every vein. Creator in heaven. It was as though the black lion was attacking him again. He struggled to free his arms and legs to no avail. There was no escape. His back arched and he screamed.

Belladonna chuckled. "And all those whippings?"

No. No, Creator, please. Tears dripped out of his eyes as everything slammed into him. His back seemed to rip open again and again and again all while the venom pulsed in his blood. He screamed so loud he wasn't sure he was still screaming. Black spots covered his vision and then nothing.

Nothing but black and dark and . . . golden hair. Dark blue eyes. *"Hold on, Ryan. I'm coming."*

Hold on? To what? Pain. There was nothing here to hold on to.

Water splashed over his face, and he woke with a start, coughing. He flinched, pulling against the bindings and finding that he was still trapped to that chair. His heart sped and he whimpered, so ashamed of himself.

"Well, that got your attention." Belladonna grabbed his face. She touched the tip of his ear and he braced himself, holding his breath. A trickle of the pain crashed into him again. He writhed as he felt the pain of his back tearing open repeatedly. "Make it stop! Please!"

Her laughter mocked him. And she leaned closer. He braced for her touch. Yearned for the relief. As her hand cupped his cheek, the pain turned off.

"Th-thank you." His voice trembled. He opened his eyes, tears leaking out, to see her wicked grin. Something about it sent a shiver through him.

She laughed and released him. "That's better."

He couldn't get air in his lungs fast enough.

"Now that you know what I can do anywhere, anytime, maybe you'll start behaving like a good pet." She leaned closer. Her lavender scent churning his stomach. "I also have the power to take all your pain away . . . *if* you stop denying my healing."

He nodded.

"What, pet?"

"I'm sorry." His voice cracked.

She stood. "That's better. Butch, I think you're right. The bull may be too much for him today. What else did you have in mind?"

Ryan rested his head against the back of his chair and tried to will moisture back into his mouth. Every exhale shook. Belladonna would kill his resolve if she ever did that again. He'd have to make her believe he was her pet. Fast.

Butch rubbed his hands together, then he strode over to the fireplace. He pulled out a metal rod. It glowed red and orange and bright yellow. "Think he'll scream?"

Ryan's heart melted.

"Oh, Butch." Belladonna clapped her hands together. "We're going to brand him?"

Ryan trembled.

"I was thinking the right side of his chest is the perfect place for the muzzled-dragon seal."

"It's perfect."

Tears leaked out of Ryan's eyes as Butch brought the brand closer. "No. No, don't. Wh-whatever you want—whatever you want, I'll—"

Butch thrust the iron into Ryan's chest. The hard-backed chair didn't yield under Ryan's frantic push. His hands would not free to block him. White-hot iron pressed hard against his skin. It sizzled. Heat warmed his skin. Still Butch held it there. Ryan would be burned clear to his lung. Wait. No scream. He wasn't screaming.

The scent of hot metal—so familiar and comforting—surrounded him. Dull pain pricked his back where the splinters embedded in his skin. He couldn't be dreaming. Yet he wasn't screaming.

Butch pulled the iron away. Where Ryan expected to see his skin dangling from the metal rod, he saw the orange heat of the brand only. He looked down at his chest. There was a raised, red area but that was all. And it faded fast. Belladonna and Butch stared back at him, eyes wide.

Ryan glanced at the indelible scar on his left arm, the one that fire had left when he'd played with the flames as a boy. He'd never been burned by fire again after that night, but he thought it was because he'd been more careful.

Belladonna reached out and touched the iron, lingering no more than a second before she pulled her hand away with a curse. An ugly blister bubbled on her finger, healing fast. Her dark eyes met his. "How did that not hurt you?"

"I told you this boy had thick skin, didn't I?" Butch pointed to him. "I told you I have to whip him harder than any other."

Belladonna nodded slowly. "He is special." She tore her gaze away from Ryan and turned to Butch. "Put him in the bull."

"The Mistress gave me instructions to make sure you don't kill him."

"You will not speak a word of this to her. Put him in the bull."

Butch lumbered over to the fire and placed the metal iron back in.

Ryan stared at the fire. Whatever kind of special gift they thought he had, he didn't. Maybe he should have screamed.

Butch placed hot coals under the huge statue of the bull. "If this kills him, it'll be your head."

"It will be both your heads." A sickly, deep voice filled the room. The Mistress of Shadows.

Ryan shivered as he felt her presence, cold and clammy. He turned his head toward the bony woman. She looked stronger now, but more pale instead of less. She hunched over as she walked near them, and lowered her hood. At least her hair was no longer stringy.

"Your Majesty." Butch and Belladonna bowed.

The Mistress motioned to the bull. "Let's have the demonstration." The same words she spoke aloud echoed in Ryan's head. It was as if she was asking him to give his own demonstration. Of what? These people were crazy!

"Yes, Your Majesty." Butch's meaty hands gripped a shovel. He thrust it into the hot coals of the fireplace and grunted as he heaved out burning embers. He placed them in the tray under the bronze bull.

Knife my bloody heart. Ryan's pulse sped. His hands wouldn't stop sweating. That would kill him. More and more coals piled into the tray. The bull's belly turned a golden color.

Butch wiped sweat from his forehead. "It's ready."

Ryan struggled against Butch and Belladonna as they tied his hands together behind him.

Belladonna laughed. "Got some bite today, pet?"

When his life was on the line, absolutely. Ryan glared at the Mistress, and her voice hissed in his head with a satisfied threat.

He shrugged. "You sure you want to do this? You could lose something very valuable."

"Really?" Her lips spread in a smile. "I know what you are." Her laugh resounded in his skull. *"You are mine as soon as she breaks you. The transformation will be complete. I will bond to you, Deliverer. And I will have your whole heart."*

A shock of heat jolted through Ryan's bloodstream. "I'm not a Deliverer."

"Keep screaming, and I'll know you're alive."

The scent of heated bronze wafted closer as Butch opened the door. Sweltering air poured out. Slammed into his face. Butch and Belladonna's men tossed him inside. The black lion might as well have been suffocating him; this fear felt the same. He closed his eyes, focusing on Serena's face, as the heat consumed him. Pushed against him from all sides, trying to melt his bones. His skin. The air he tried to breathe. Sweat dripped down his face, seeped through his clothes, and heated the ropes around his hands as he lay curled up in the belly of the bull. Strange, the heat comforted him, reminded him of being in the forge back home. Muffled voices outside expressed worry.

"Your Majesty, it'll kill him. He's not screaming."

"Patience, Belladonna. Give him a few more minutes."

Minutes? His heart jolted. Wasn't he supposed to be playing the dragon in a lair? Ryan screamed. He stomped on the bull's side and slammed his elbows into the beast's stomach, all while screaming his throat raw. No one did anything. The voice in his head remained eerily quiet. All at once he stopped and lay still, silent.

"He's dead?" Belladonna's voice sounded strained. Could she actually be worried? Could someone without a heart care? No. She just wanted her leverage. So did he. And it was getting hot in there. If they didn't get him out, he might start screaming for real. The door opened and cool air rushed in, hitting his sweating face and chest. Guards pulled his legs. Ryan kept his eyes closed as they dropped him to the floor. They really could have taken more care with his head.

A hand smoothed his hair. "Pet?"

Fluttering his eyelids for good measure, he looked into Belladonna's face.

Butch towered above him. "He isn't even blistered."

The Mistress studied him with lifeless eyes. *"Think you can outwit me?"* She turned her gaze to Belladonna. "I want him broken by morning."

Belladonna smiled and the sight made his stomach churn. "There is one thing that always has him begging for healing."

Begging? He didn't beg. He screamed. He . . . yes, he closed his eyes. When they whipped, he always screamed. First, he focused on Serena. Eventually, even the memory of her face wasn't strong enough for him to ignore the pain. When he screamed her name, Belladonna whipped him harder. But when he pleaded with Belladonna to stop, to heal him, that's when she let up. If he needed to play that card now, he would. It was time. This dragon would lie and wait until they were close enough to devour. Which meant it was time to play a tame pet.

The guards hauled him to his feet and released his arms. His knees weakened the moment Butch grabbed the whip.

Ryan shook. "Not today. Please, Belladonna." His eyes pleaded with her, and it was less an act than he wanted to admit.

"Remember, I promised you no healing because you denied it earlier."

His heart sped so he thought it might burst. "N-no. I'll do whatever you want."

They placed his shaking hands into the cool, iron shackles.

"Belladonna, please don't do this." His voice quaked.

Belladonna's warm hand touched his back and he flinched. She chuckled. "I think just one more. If you're a good pet."

"I'll be a good pet."

She cocked an eyebrow. The whip clinked like a chime in the wind. A whine escaped his throat. He squeezed his eyes shut. Perhaps he was broken after all. He glanced at the Mistress, not caring if she saw fear in his eyes. *I'm no Deliverer.*

"You are. And your allegiance is almost mine."

For some reason, he believed her. He looked nothing like his father or mother or sisters. His thirst for adventure had always driven him.

And he'd been home with Ethan and Jayden and Serena. Ryan hung with his arms in the metal cuffs as they pulled his arms up to the ceiling. Despite all the fear tugging at his insides, he managed to smile at the Mistress. She could try and break him, but he'd never let her break his friends. That push gave him the strength he needed.

She sneered in return. "I hear you have a delightful scream."

The black-snake of a weapon danced in his periphery. *Strong and stoic.*

The first lash struck him, biting into his skin. He would not scream in front of the Mistress.

"I've heard you scream before."

His body jolted forward again. Weight pulled against his shoulders. Another lash stung him, tore away his flesh. Another. He hung his head, unable to hold in another scream. How long it went on he didn't know. All he knew was he'd never be able to erase the Mistress's smile from the insides of his eyelids.

He'd never be able to forget the sound of his own anguish echoing off the stone walls.

At last Belladonna put the whip away and they lowered him. He wouldn't cry, not in front of the Mistress. Two men picked him off the ground and dragged him to her. He hung in their arms, unable to support himself on his own wobbly legs. Sweat dripped off his nose. Every inch of him groaned at the slightest movement. But he met her gaze.

Her eyes creased in the corners from her satisfied smile. "I think you are ready to serve me."

He kept his voice soft, and his face meek, but his heart pulsed with hate. He locked it away so she wouldn't sense it. "Yes . . . Your Majesty." His own voice scratched his burning throat.

She arched an eyebrow. Maybe she would think he had broken after all. Maybe the dragon would win this round.

CHAPTER 17

DEEP AND SORROWFUL

Cool autumn air brushed Jayden's cheek as she woke to morning light trying to break through the clouds. The steady rise and fall of Ethan's warm chest against her back comforted her. She'd hardly slept. Today they moved closer to the palace. To war.

War.

Something she'd been fighting for months and still wasn't ready to be a part of.

It seemed everything she'd fought for so far, everything she'd lost, was a strange memory. That she'd wake when this was over and see everyone who had died again. That she'd be with those she'd met since and loved now. As much as her heart wanted her to fight for that, it could never happen. When this was over, she didn't know what to expect. Except death.

Thea's warning still haunted her. Ethan wouldn't be able to handle her death.

Jayden stared at the sky. A storm churned. Thick and drenching. Her storm. She swallowed her emotions to keep them from filling the sky. If they all died, it better not be for nothing. She'd make sure the Mistress went down with her.

No more mistakes.

The sun tried to peek out from the clouds but failed. Yet it never stopped shining. Serena would say something about hope shining through—hope Jayden would want to cling to but find herself unable to grasp.

Because war always brought casualties.

Anna had been sure of Jayden's purpose in all of this. Her mother had told her to survive. Was she the right Child? Was she willing to die so the others could live? So they could be free of the Mistress? Of course. Besides, Ethan had told her not to let Thea's prediction claim the time she had left.

Maybe Morgan had seen her death.

Maybe Morgan would tell her she'd survive.

Jayden closed her eyes. If the Creator chose her, would he answer her if she asked for help?

Yes.

She sat up. That voice in her head sounded like a storm. Felt like a strong wind and a bolt of lightning. She breathed deep.

She would persevere. Until the end.

"You okay?" Ethan's soft voice was sun breaking through clouds. He sat up next to her. Hugged her close from behind.

She leaned back into him. She wasn't looking at him, but she opened her talent. Now that she'd bonded to Stormcloud, she didn't need to look at certain people to sense their emotions. Ethan's always lapped against her, unless he was guarding them. And right now he was certainly guarding them.

She pushed to feel them. Love pulsed into her. Warmed her. Then his fear chilled her to the core.

Those emotions battled one another.

She grabbed his hand and squeezed and whispered. "What's wrong?"

He squeezed back, but the wind might have swallowed her words. He didn't respond. Didn't breathe in as if he were about to speak. She turned to look at him. His return smile was soft. Perhaps he didn't want to tell her. He must have sensed her probing because he turned his attention to the river. His hand rubbed her arm. She cuddled into him and kissed his left cheek. The corner of his mouth. Whispered in his ear, "What's wrong?"

He kissed her. Deep and sorrowful.

His touch feather-light on her neck, her jawbone. Then his eyes scanned her face, as if memorizing every detail. A flush warmed her cheeks. She smoothed down her hair, wondering how terrible she looked with it all windblown and slept on. Still he stared at her. She skirted her eyes away from his. "What?"

He shook his head. "Nothing."

"Nothing?"

A small smile tugged the corner of his mouth, and love pulsed stronger than fear. "You're beautiful."

Oh? "Is that all?"

He smiled and then strong arms wrapped around her, pulling her close. Never in all her life had she been so safe. But the worry in him surged so that her own heart ached with it.

"What's wrong?" she whispered into his chest.

Nothing. Yet worry wrestled within him. She looked into his eyes. "Why won't you tell me?"

"Tell you what?" He seemed willing to bare his soul.

She offered a sideways smile. "You're going to sit there and pretend you didn't hear me asking you 'what's wrong?' over and over?"

His lips parted slightly, but surprise flooded him, followed by a spark of worry. She backed away slowly so she could see his whole face. "You're hiding something from me. I keep asking you what's wrong."

"I didn't hear you."

"Really?" She smiled but he didn't, so she lost hers. "Wow, something's got you really worried if Ethan with the magnificent hearing missed something."

"I don't have great hearing, Jayden. And you shouldn't rely on it." He glared and a flare of heat she didn't expect fanned her chest—his anger.

She studied his face. "You want me to leave you alone?"

He paused for a very long time.

"I asked—"

"I heard you . . . that time." He looked at the ground. "I'm a Deliverer now, so Logan's not going to get rid of me. I guess I can tell you." He swallowed. "Besides after I bonded to Zephyr, I can hear better. Just—it's not the same. As it was."

He wasn't making sense.

He looked at her and opened his mouth, closed it. Touched his left ear.

Jayden cupped a hand over his ear. The same one that soldier had punched over and over. Her fingers trembled. "You can't hear out of it."

He shook his head.

She pressed her hand to her mouth. "I'm so sorry, Ethan. I—"

"It's not your fault. I should have told Logan. I just—"

"It's okay." Jayden trailed her hand over his neck. He'd protected her. That was how it happened. "Thank you."

He leaned his forehead against hers. "For what?"

The smile in his voice was beautiful. "For protecting me. You make me feel safe, Ethan."

He stared at her for a moment, then pushed her back gently, keeping his hands on her arms. "Well, I'm not keeping you safe, not as long as Belladonna has a link to me. She can find me. You understand that, don't you?"

"I do. But your talent—"

"I'm not going to take any chances."

She grabbed his hand and clutched it up to her heart. His fear was her fear, too. "Don't you dare do anything stupid."

"There you are." Chloe popped through the trees and stared at them, arms crossed. "Where's Serena?"

Ethan shrugged. "Haven't seen her."

Chloe's hands fell to her sides. "Then she's nowhere."

Ethan's voice became hard. "What do you mean, nowhere?"

"I mean no one has seen her."

"Since when?" Ethan stood.

"Heavens, Ethan. What do you take me for? When I tell you she's missing, I mean Logan has been looking for her."

Stormcloud landed, fluttering her wings into place. Worry pulsed from her. Jayden's heart dropped into her stomach and she rose. "Why didn't I see this?"

Ethan turned to her. "See what?"

Chloe pushed Ethan aside and grabbed Jayden's arms. "She did it, didn't she?"

Ethan's eyes pleaded with Jayden. "Did what?"

Chloe shot him a look over her shoulder. "I wouldn't expect *you* to understand."

"Snare me," he whispered and walked away. A growl rose up from him, and he slammed his fist into a dried tree. The branch splintered and snapped in two.

Jayden stepped back from him.

Chloe didn't. She caught up to him and grabbed his arm before he could throw another punch. "Ethan." He pulled against her grip, but she held tight to his arm. "She did what I would have if Logan hadn't left that wolf guarding my tent last night."

Ethan thrust a finger toward Chloe's face; she didn't flinch. "What she did was stupid."

"Right. I forgot." She slammed her finger into his chest. "Only you can run off in the night without a word."

He clenched his jaw. "This is different."

"Is it? I know you were out here with Jayden all night."

"It was an accident. Nothing . . . happened."

Chloe smirked. "That's not what I mean." For a moment her eyes met Jayden's and filled with pity. Why? Jayden's heart jumped.

Chloe turned back to Ethan. "You meant to say goodbye to her— without truly saying it. You mean to go after Ryan. Alone."

He stood there staring at her.

A cold shiver spread through Jayden's core.

"Tell me you didn't plan to." Chloe put her hands on her hips.

He held out his hands as if to calm her rising temper. "Chloe—"

"Tell me!"

Jayden stepped closer to them both, still too far away to touch him, but his emotions poured into her even so. Regret pulsed strongest. "Ethan? Is it true?" Her voice seemed so fragile in the open air.

His shoulders slumped. "He's my brother."

Jayden's heart sped. "You planned to go after him?"

Chloe's voice rose and tears joined her anger. "Of course he did."

Zephyr landed behind Ethan and tilted his head. Jayden's throat tightened. Was he here to take Ethan away? "Ethan?"

Ethan headed toward the gryphon. "Serena can't be far. And

Belladonna can sense me. If you're with me, you're in danger because of me."

Jayden stood rooted. Her eyes stung with coming tears. "Ethan, please."

Chloe grabbed his sleeve. "Wait. She could be a night away. And the unicorn will be traveling invisible—if she's riding him, you won't see either of them."

"I have to do *something*." He snapped.

"I'm coming with you." Jayden was surprised to hear Chloe say the same thing, only Chloe was still holding Ethan's shirt. Jayden looked down at her leaden feet. Where was she? Standing on the other side of the tree, practically worlds away, all because she hadn't rushed to comfort him when he was angry, and Chloe had. Chloe . . . had.

"Chloe," his voice was soft, and he gently removed her hand from his sleeve. "I'm just going to find Serena."

She shook her head wildly. "You'll join her."

He stared at her.

Tears brimmed in Chloe's eyes. "Ethan, please."

"Please?" His eyes traced her face. "You *want* me to join Serena? I will. I will if—"

"No!" She flung her arms around him so hard he staggered back, but remained in her embrace. "I want you safe. I've already lost one brother to the Mistress's hands."

Shock shot through Ethan like a bolting deer; Jayden felt it in her own heart. He looked at Jayden over Chloe's shaking shoulder and spread up his palms as if to tell her Chloe's behavior confounded him. Jayden could do nothing more than stare at Chloe's back. At the way she buried her face in Ethan's shirt. At the way she hugged him. How could Jayden have missed it? Chloe was . . . she loved Ethan. Not like a brother. She *loved* him. And it looked like Ethan had no idea. He put his arms on her as if to try and see her face. She squeezed him tighter.

"Hey." He rubbed her shoulder. "I'm—all I want to do is protect those I love."

"You always say that." Chloe's voice muffled against his shirt.

"I always mean it."

"That's what scares me." She looked at him, voicing Jayden's thoughts.

"Wait a minute." He shook his head. "You—you're—this whole time you've been trying to keep me here, haven't you? Everything you did was to get Ryan rescued and make sure I had no cause to go after him myself. Wasn't it?"

She turned away from him, her face scrunching up. Jayden opened her talent. Of course love bloomed in Chloe. And fear. And so much pain.

"Chloe?" He tried to turn her head to look at him and she wouldn't. "You were protecting me?" He pulled her close and kissed the top of her head. "Thank you."

Tears spilled out of Chloe's eyes and she wiped them away. Turned and faced him. "You're not mad?"

He smiled. "I didn't say that."

She laughed and pushed his chest, but he didn't let go of her. She sank back into his arms, closing her eyes. "You never let anyone protect *you.*"

A ball formed in Jayden's throat.

He rubbed Chloe's back. "That's not true."

"It is. And *you* need protecting." The love exploded. Jayden's breath caught. *If Ethan knew how Chloe felt, would he?* . . . She blinked her thoughts away. She could not think about this right now. Serena was the first problem. "Take Chloe with you on Zephyr. I'll ride Storm."

Ethan's eyebrows pulled together. "Jayden—"

"If we split up, we have better odds of finding Serena."

He let Chloe go and walked closer to Jayden. "You can't go alone."

"Go where?" Gavin's voice caused Jayden to turn.

"To look for Serena," Chloe answered.

Gavin sighed. "I've already sent Glider. And Kara's gone, too."

"Snare me," Ethan whispered. "Did they leave together?"

Jayden's heart jolted. So Kara had betrayed her again. "She'll give Serena to the Mistress."

Ethan whirled to face her. "I felt no threat for her."

"Meaning?" It was Logan who had found them now. Melanie and Rebekah and Quinn followed close behind.

"Meaning if she left with Kara, Kara wasn't planning any harm to her at the time."

"But if Serena followed Kara?" Logan rubbed his hand over his face. "Westwind can't track the unicorn."

"What about Kara?" Ethan asked.

Logan shook his head. "He can't find her scent. It disappears."

Ethan balled his hand into a fist.

"So they are together," Quinn said. "Dash will hide their tracks, their scent, everything. We won't be able to find them. The trees will not betray a unicorn in hiding. It is against their code."

"Trees have a code?" Ethan practically yelled.

Quinn's eyes widened.

Ethan turned away from her, running his hand over his face. Jayden wanted to calm him, but Stormcloud's thoughts interrupted her.

"Dash and I walked in the woods last night. Together. He seemed to say good-bye to me. I didn't realize he meant this. I thought he meant just in case we didn't . . . make it."

Jayden stared at Stormcloud and felt her friend's sadness. Then she shook all the feelings from her and turned to Logan. "Kara promised to help us defeat Franco. This might be part of her plan."

"Plan?" Ethan's voice sounded harsh. "Kara has a plan all right. She always has a plan. That doesn't mean it's trustworthy. In fact—"

"Let them be." Morgan walked toward their circle. The way she clasped her hands in front of her made her look unsure, which wasn't normal.

Ethan walked right up to her, Chloe in his wake. "What do you see?" Ethan's voice grew quieter, yet harder.

"It's Ryan's best chance of survival if Serena gets into the palace." Morgan held up her hands. "I met Ryan at the Winking Fox one night. I knew this Belladonna you speak of would take him because I'd seen him saving someone. If you go after Serena to stop her, Ryan will give his allegiance to the Mistress. And she will take his portion of the Creator's power and kill him. You have to let Serena go. She's his best chance."

"You knew she would capture my brother?" Chloe screamed and lunged at Morgan, but Ethan caught her and held her back.

Jayden walked over to Chloe and touched her shoulder, letting her talent calm Chloe down.

Chloe breathed in and stopped struggling to get to Morgan.

Then Jayden rubbed her hand over Ethan's arm. He glanced at her and grabbed her hand. Squeezed.

Morgan stepped back, staring at the ground. "I didn't know who Ryan was. Only that I'd seen him before. My sister is in the palace, too. She'll help—"

"Your sister!" Chloe lunged again. "You let him get captured so he'd save your sister?"

Morgan backed up with her arms out.

Jayden swallowed, her throat thick. "Does Ryan survive? In your vision, does he—"

"I don't know."

Ethan gripped Chloe's shoulders, but this time she fell to her knees.

"Their best chance of survival is if we are there, at the palace, waiting to fight off the army that will chase them out." Morgan glanced at Logan and remorse poured out of her.

"Army," Rebekah whispered. "Then the Mistress knows Ryan is a Deliverer."

Exhausted, Jayden lay back on her bedroll and watched the last of the cookfire burn out. Logan had led them fast today. Chloe and Quinn already slept, curled up close to her. Jayden couldn't. Instead, she strained to see any stars breaking though the red haze that grew denser as they neared the northern edge of the borderlands.

They were close to the levels now.

The first level they would face contained monsters called shadow wolves. Strange, strangled cries rode on the wind and sent a shudder through Stormcloud. Jayden felt it over the bond.

"The Whisperer says these creatures fly?"

"Yes." Jayden could only hope the map from Quinn's trees was accurate. It meant they were in a safe spot tonight. And Jayden didn't want to be bitten by something that could take over her mind while she slept. She rolled onto her side to see if Ethan had returned from

talking with Logan. She caught sight of him, but he'd stopped to talk to Morgan. Jayden's stomach tightened. He stood with his right ear tipped subtly toward Morgan.

As she spoke, Ethan bowed his head. Stared at his folded hands as he nodded.

Jayden's heart clutched.

What had Morgan seen now?

Ethan nodded, and their conversation ended, but Morgan glanced at Jayden with a sad look.

Jayden gasped and sat up.

"Not sleeping yet?" Ethan sat next to her. He smiled, but his heart felt heavy to her.

She shook her head. "I've been wanting to talk to you."

"About what?" Ethan faced Jayden and, though he wore a smile, the depths of those brown eyes revealed how much his heart ached. Jayden placed her hand on his arm, and he took her hand in his, rubbing her fingers like a worry stone.

Why hadn't she thought to comfort him before? "Are you okay?"

He looked into her eyes and took a deep breath. "Chloe worries me. I think she'll take off like Serena did and get herself killed."

"You'll keep her safe."

His heart seemed to stop, and he looked at her, his eyes dark, narrowed. And he studied her face. His emotions leeched away from her.

She touched his arm. "No. Don't shut me out. Please."

He looked up at her, brows furrowed. "You feel that?"

"It makes your emotions unreachable to me."

"I'm sorry." Nothing changed, but he dropped her hand and looked at his lap. "I'm not doing it to hide anything from you. I'm doing it for me. It's too overwhelming to feel everything."

She touched his cheek. "Then let me help carry your burden."

That familiar lopsided smile filled his face, and he leaned in and gave her the gentlest kiss. "You help me more than you know."

She rested her head on his shoulder. "Good. I couldn't bear it if I wasn't helping you."

His fingers trailed the length of her arm and stopped at her hand, which he took hold of.

She whispered, "What did Morgan say?"

He remained quiet for too long.

Perhaps he hadn't heard. She looked at him. "Ethan? What did—?"

"I heard you," he said quietly. "I asked her about Ryan, but she said some other things that . . . that I think she meant to say without saying them."

Jayden's throat tightened. "A hint at your future?"

He looked at her and opened his mouth. Love and fear poured into her. "I imagine we're not done losing those we love."

She breathed out and it was painful. Her death. Morgan had seen her death. She touched Ethan's knee and stood. "I'll be right back."

She marched over to Morgan's tent, trying to quell coming tears, and Richard—Morgan's betrothed—stopped her. "Jayden?"

"May I please speak with Morgan?'

He let her pass. She entered the tent and stood in the doorway, hands fisted, trembling. "Did you tell Ethan about my death?"

Morgan's eyes opened wide. "No."

No.

The word echoed in her hollow, empty thoughts.

Not, *I know nothing about your death.*

Not, *what death?*

Just no. Simple. Plain. Inevitable. Jayden's knees weakened and she sat down. Her elbows dug into her thighs, and she cupped her face in her hands. "You've seen it?" Her fingers muffled her shaking words, and she looked at Morgan over them.

She sat across from Jayden, eyes round and sad. "You're young. You look as you do now. The ground is cracked and black and snow falls around you. There's blood dripping from your hairline." Morgan traced an invisible mark on her face. "Your eyes are open and your chest doesn't move. There's a charred and gaping hole in your abdomen."

Jayden couldn't breathe.

She gasped and it squeaked.

Her chest hurt.

Her thoughts hurt.

Her heart screamed in agony.

She sniffed, trying to hold everything inside. Winter was still months away. Months. "Is it set in stone?" Her voice only wavered slightly.

Morgan looked as if she was about to deliver bad news. "It's a vision I see frequently. I was merely telling Ethan that he shouldn't wait to tell those he loves how he feels."

Jayden swallowed and her throat ached. He'd already told her. "I suppose you could say that to everyone." Tears escaped.

"Yes." Morgan touched Jayden's hand. "Richard outlives me."

She blinked away tears and sniffed. "Does he know?"

"No. I think he should be allowed to feel the way he wants just like everyone else. If I tell him, he would try to die for me. I can't allow that. I wouldn't wish seeing your own death on anyone."

Jayden wiped away more tears. "Then why tell me?"

"You asked. And your knowing doesn't change a thing." She sat with Jayden in silence for a few moments. Then she touched Jayden's arm and stood. "Take as much time as you need here." She exited the tent.

Jayden buried her face in her hands, but no more tears would come. She was too hollow for tears. Ethan would love her no matter what, and letting him made her stronger. It was time for her to embrace that truth. And to soak up as much of his love as she could. He deserved to know exactly how she felt. That she wanted to live with him forever.

She fisted her hands and stood. Then, just as she resolved to go out and tell him, screams rent the night.

CHAPTER 18

A DRAGON IN ITS LAIR

Ryan woke from fitful sleep as the door to the dungeon scraped open. Everything hurt too much for him to even lift his head. Stale breeze carried the scent of lavender. Belladonna. Ryan's insides squeezed. "Getting started early today?" The rasp in his voice surprised him.

Footsteps drew closer—she'd brought her guard, of course—and Belladonna crouched into view. The smell of pears joined the lavender. Mock pity shone in her eyes. "If you learned faster, we wouldn't have to continue with this charade, pet."

She stood, but he just lay there, staring at four sets of boots. A clicking sound followed by metal screeching told him she'd opened his cell door.

Half of him shuddered. The other half hoped she'd brought water. Or that she'd heal him.

The threat of coming tears burned his eyes. If she wanted him to beg for healing, he would. He'd grovel. He'd do anything.

A tear slid over the bridge of his nose, and he hated himself for it. For wanting her healing. For not being stronger.

She knelt beside him and stroked his hair. "You look terrible, pet. Will you let me heal you today?"

"Do I have a choice?" He hoped his voice sounded harsh.

"You always do. But how was your night without it?" She reached for him and he closed his eyes. Audibly sighed. Then cursed himself for his willingness.

A dark laugh escaped her. "You do want my healing. Don't you?"

He was supposed to pretend to be broken. Problem was, he wasn't sure how much of it was an act. "Please."

"What was that, pet?"

He swallowed the ache in his throat. "Please heal me. I'll do anything you ask."

"I bet you would. I feel your pain."

He looked up at her. "Y-you do?"

"It's a Healer's curse."

Ryan flexed his broken hand, and Belladonna winced. Maybe she was telling the truth.

"Don't get me wrong." Belladonna trailed a finger along his forearm. "I like that you are strong."

Strong? He laughed. There was no holding that in. Apparently this Healer could lie.

She arched an eyebrow. "You don't think tough women like strong men?"

"What do you want from me?"

"Loyalty. Fealty. Love."

Never. "And you'll heal me?" Why did he have to sound so weak?

Her finger trailed down his left arm to his hand. "I actually take your wounds when I heal you. I experience it as if it's my own pain. Then I heal it." She picked up his left hand, and he braced in fear. This crazy woman could offer relief or more pain, and he was never sure what to expect. She looked at him, pity in her eyes that he wanted to spit at. "Pet, I came here today to heal you if . . ." her dark eyes scanned him. "If you pledge to me your love."

"I pledge it."

She smiled. Her face contorted into a grimace as all the pain ebbed away in his hand. "How you stand the torture I cannot fathom. I've broken other men more quickly than you." She dropped his hand and trailed her fingers up his arm. "You are stronger than anyone I know." Her hand stopped at the top of his shoulder. "You don't let your emotions show your weaknesses."

Right. He turned away from her, his face scrunching up. Tears heated his eyes, but he held them in. As soon as she left his prison at night, she missed her amazing strong man whimpering on the floor of a cage. Strong.

A lie.

Her fingers glided over his back like feathers and every whisper of a touch scorched him. "I can make the hurt go away."

"At a cost to yourself?" His words sounded strangled.

"Yes. But it is worth it, no?" She slammed her hands against his back and he gasped.

Warmth pulsed through him. He released a shaky breath. Cooling followed. The pain started to ebb away. Yes. Yes, it was worth it. Tears choked him and some dripped out of his eyes. He'd lost. He'd let her win. He wasn't strong enough. *Ryan, you weak fool. She's playing you. And winning.*

Was that his own voice?

Her other hand stroked his cheek. He hurried to wipe away any trace of tears. Gently she pulled him to face her. "It is worth it, isn't it?"

He closed his eyes, unwilling to answer her, and sat up. The skin on his back felt tight, as if scars remained. But there was no more pain. He looked into her dark eyes. What had he promised for this?

She laughed. "Of course it is." She pressed her palm against his chest. "Because you can either love my healing—which is my gift to you for your loyalty, fealty, and love—or you can hate it. But if you hate it, I can only assume you love this."

Pain shot through him like a dozen arrows. His back ripped open, his chest burned. He fell to the ground, curled into a ball, breaking connection with her hand, but nothing stopped the pain. The sound of his screaming thundered in his ears.

"Only I can stop it."

"Belladonna . . . p-please . . . make it s-stop."

"That's right." She knelt next to him and smoothed his hair.

It stopped.

He was free of it. All of it. She'd healed everything. Panting on the floor of his cell, he crawled closer to her. He rested his head on her boot. "Th-thank you."

"Thank *you*, for recognizing my power. I so hate to see you writhing like that." She touched under his chin. "Stand. We've got to make you presentable."

For what?

Belladonna narrowed her eyes. "Stand up."

Ryan scrambled to his feet.

"That's better." Her lips slid into a smile. "No torture today. No more torture, unless you step out of line."

No torture? Ryan's knees weakened. Could she be telling him the truth? He feared asking in case she changed her mind.

She placed her hands on the sides of his face. "I hate to see those I love go through torture. And I love you."

Love? His insides churned and he felt sick. How was this love? What was her game now?

The strange pear smell grew stronger as she drew nearer to him. She stood on her tiptoes and pressed her lips against his. He tried to pull away, surprised by her sudden advance.

She was taking his kiss.

The kiss he was saving.

The one he was so sure would be amazing after having been cured from the . . . venom. Venom? What venom? The taste of pear overwhelmed him. Her tongue teased him, parted his lips. He wrapped his arms around her. This was definitely worth waiting for. Could she have been any more . . . her teeth nibbled him. Wait. He shook his head. His stomach roiled and he pushed away from her. Pain throbbed in his temples. This woman was evil. Why was he—?

She pulled him closer, pressed her lips harder against his. Pear exploded on his tongue.

Clouded his thoughts.

Made him feel numb.

She let him go and stepped back licking her lips. "You're good, pet."

Good? He'd show her good. Ryan smiled and leaned one arm on the cell bars. She giggled. She was beautiful. How had he never seen it? "You like it?" He grinned. "Because there's more."

She pressed her finger to his lips. "More later. Right now I've got to get you upstairs."

The room started spinning. Ryan bent over and pressed his hands against his head.

"Uh-oh. Feeling a little dizzy?" Belladonna grabbed his shoulders and propped him up. "I got you, pet." Her warm arms curled around him and she touched his face.

He started at her through narrowed eyes. Perhaps she did love him. He loved her.

CHAPTER 19

WHAT FRIENDS DO

As soon as Franco left him—after another pat on the back—Connor ripped the ring off his finger and placed it on his dresser. His stomach roiled and the pulsing pain in his head, left from that tainted metal, started to recede. He really needed to talk to Luc.

Oh no. A surge of his power shot through his veins, and he clutched the sides of his dresser. He wouldn't look in the mirror in case red eyes stared back.

His powers tried to emerge daily now. With more vengeance than he'd ever felt. He wouldn't be able to contain them forever. Time was running out.

Heat.

Skin.

Heat.

Fur.

He held it together and clutched the dresser ledge tighter until the wave passed through him. Maybe tonight he'd venture into the woods and let out a wave of power. Hopefully he could keep it in until then.

He still needed to find a way to help Madison.

"Must you always forget that some of us are willing to help you?"

That voice was a welcome comfort. Connor smiled as he breathed in a deep, cleansing breath. *"Cliffdiver, I cannot guarantee your safety."*

"I'm a gryphon, master. I live for adventure. Besides, I can think of no nobler cause than helping you."

Connor chuckled. *"Dear friend, please stop calling me 'master.' I would be honored to have your help."*

"You have it."

A knock on his door interrupted his thoughts, and Connor answered it. "Madison? Are you all right?"

She held up a book. "I found this in Franco's room."

Connor stepped aside for her to enter. She rushed to the table in the center of his room and laid the book on it, opening it. "We already know that in order to kill Franco it has to be a beheading with a Wielder-crafted weapon. I don't know where to get one of those, but—"

"I do."

She blinked and looked at him. "Of course."

He nodded. "Luc. The smithy. I know he has some. I gave them to him for safe keeping."

"Well, that's wonderful news!" She bit her lip. "It might be the only wonderful news." She turned back to the book, and Connor joined her at the table. Her finger followed the words as she summarized them. ". . . and the head must be burned. But the willing sacrifice will die, unless another agrees to take her place."

He grabbed Madison's arms. "No. I'm not letting you die for Kara. She—"

"No, that's not my plan." She smiled.

Connor released her and crossed his arms. "Madison, have you been plotting without me?"

"It only seemed fair. That's what you're doing all the time you spend alone, isn't it?"

No. He was out in the woods releasing spurts of his power and trying not to kill anyone.

Her smile softened. "Do you have any friends?"

"Two."

"Me and one other person?"

A small laugh escaped his throat as he looked at the book on the table. "I—three then."

"You weren't counting me as your friend?"

"I thought you meant besides you."

That appeased the mock-hurt look on her face. "Good. Then you should know I'm a trained warrior. I plan to kill Franco and then bring Kara back to life."

That stunned him speechless.

She laughed. "Healers have the ability to bring someone back to life."

"Haven't you already done that for her?"

"Only because of a spell. That was evil and dark. When I brought her back, a piece of her stayed dead. It's not a way to live, Connor. I need to restore that. Heal *her*. It's *my* mission."

"Kara's not here."

"I'm bound to her now. I can find her. And she draws closer daily."

Connor tilted his head. "You came to me for help?" No one ever came to him for help. The thought that she trusted him enough warmed his soul.

"That's what friends do."

"I will help you kill Franco, Madison." In fact, he was sure he'd do anything for her, and that was why having friends was so dangerous for someone like him. Someone who could accidentally kill them.

"Thank you. Now about that weapon?"

"Let's go see Luc. I have another favor to ask him anyway."

Her cheeks colored bright red. "To-together?"

"Unless you'd rather go alone?"

"No!"

He chuckled. "I think you should start sparring with him. It'll keep both of you sharp."

"Really?" She stood now, hugging her stomach as if she were a shy girl being told to ask a young man to dance. "Why?"

"Because when I break out of here, I'm taking the two of you with me." He smiled. "I've got a secret entrance to show you."

She followed him down to the underground floor and outside to the smithy. The closer they got, the more nervous she seemed. Just outside the door she paused. Connor smiled and motioned for her to pass through the doorway first.

"I'll be right with you." Luc's voice rose above the sound of metal hammering metal. The clanking stopped. "Oh. Hello."

Connor followed her in and smiled at the way Luc stood there, holding a red hot sword. He'd known these two would hit it off. It had probably spurred the lie he'd told Franco about the two of them being involved. That and he wanted to know how the king would feel about his Healer being with another man. The bracer had done its job. Franco hadn't cared a bit. "Luc."

"Connor. Is . . . oh . . . are you with him?"

"Madison is a friend."

Luc finally put down the sword and his hammer. "Oh. Good. Um . . . I have something for you."

Connor smiled. "I was hoping."

"The ring?" Madison asked.

Luc's eyebrows darted up behind his bangs. "She knows?"

"Luc, meet Madison."

"How do you do?" He jumped forward and took her hand in his, then he kissed the back, but winced at his black fingers.

"It's very nice to meet you." She smiled and dipped her head.

Connor felt the urge to duck out and leave the two of them alone. He also felt the urge to laugh. Instead, he helped himself to what looked like Luc's forgotten lunch. The apple hadn't even been touched. Connor bit in.

"Right." Luc dropped her hand and pulled out a small drawstring pouch. He gave it to Connor. "It's the perfect duplicate."

Connor fished one ring from the pouch and the other from his pocket. Side-by-side they looked identical. "Amazing."

"You think it'll pass?"

"Absolutely." Connor handed Luc the real ring. "You'll wear this later when we train the soldiers?"

Luc nodded. "If you still wish it of me."

"Luc, I—"

"I'm willing to help you, Connor."

"Doesn't he listen to you, either?" Madison said. They both turned toward her, and she beamed. "I keep telling him the same thing. I *want* to help. It's what friends do."

Luc chuckled. "See, Connor, I've been telling you the same thing."

Apparently he'd have to defend himself. "I know. It's just—"

"You won't ask for help." Luc narrowed his eyes.

Connor had nothing to say to that, but tried to think of something anyway.

Now a grin joined Luc's slitted eyes. "But you have no problem helping yourself to my lunch."

Madison giggled.

"I thought you were done." Connor bit into the apple again and offered a smile.

Luc waved him off. "Right. I think you come down here just to see if I have anything to eat."

Madison winced as she hugged her middle and stumbled back a step.

"You okay?" Luc reached to steady her.

Connor rushed to her side. "Belladonna's at it again?"

Madison nodded. "Someone's being tortured."

A scream resounded from outside. The hair on the back of Connor's neck stood. He smelled Belladonna. And blood. And fear.

"Someone is being whipped," Madison whispered.

"You feel their pain?" Luc asked.

She nodded. "He's there."

Connor exited the smithy, Madison following, and peered around the wall to the outer training fields. Belladonna stood there with three of her men and another young man—shirtless, and his back was shredded. Connor winced. The young man faced another man—a peasant by the looks of his clothes.

Belladonna cracked the whip again, and the shirtless man fell to the ground.

"Get up!" Belladonna pushed him. "Get up and kill him."

No. Connor's power crackled beneath the surface, and he felt the Mistress sniffing. He focused in stilling everything. His powers clawed beneath his skin. Burned inside of him. The young man stood, blood dripping down his back, and he charged the peasant, who stood, dropped his sword, and held his hands up in surrender.

Connor's powers crackled. Pushed against the weak will that bound them.

Belladonna held up her whip. "You heard me, pet."

The young man lifted his sword and ran the peasant through.

Madison gasped.

Connor flinched.

The peasant crumpled.

Belladonna clapped. "Well done, pet."

The young man bowed his head and dropped his weapon. Then he glanced over his shoulder and met Connor's gaze. Connor recognized him. Ryan.

Now Connor understood why Thea had urged him to stay. Ryan was one of the Deliverers, and Belladonna had broken him.

CHAPTER 20

A HEARTWARMING TALE

The morning sun's rays reached through the clouded night, outlining the earth in a golden yellow. Serena slid off of Dash's back and stretched once her feet hit solid ground. Dash staggered a step or two. Serena placed her hand on him. *"Are you okay?"*

"I can no longer cloak Kara and her horse. I'm too tired."

Maybe they shouldn't have stopped to pick up an extra horse. Serena thought it would have been easier with Dash to not carry both of them. She should have helped him cloak the others. *"Dash—"*

"It's all right. We're stopping. We'll see how strong I am after a rest."

Serena glanced at Kara. The woman had managed to ride the whole night without slumping, or showing any outward sign of tiredness, then she dismounted her horse and walked as if she hadn't been bouncing on her bottom for hours. *"Kara is a quiet rider. I think we're far enough from the camp. They won't catch us."*

Kara tied up her horse under a cover of trees. "Your friends will be searching for us by air now that the sun is up. We should hide and rest a few hours so we aren't spotted."

Dash swung his head toward Serena. *"Is she talking?"*

"I believe she is."

Kara had said nothing on the ride thus far. Even when Serena asked her questions or tried to make polite conversation. All she ever did was look at Serena with an unreadable expression and occasionally smirk in a reticent manner. Sometimes, she'd held out her hand to tell Serena to stop moving, then she'd pull out the drawing of what looked like Quinn's map before leading them on again.

That had caused one question to itch in Serena's mind: What had Kara been planning that night Serena had visited her?

They set up their camp in silence, Dash's quiet brooding only detectable through the bond. He swished his tail. *"Make friends with her already, Serena."*

As if she hadn't been trying! Serena let out a frustrated sigh and spread out her bedroll.

"I don't understand you, Golden One."

And that was another thing. *Golden One? Really?* Serena folded her arms. "Well, I don't understand you, either."

Kara shot her a glance as she spread out her bedroll. "Why risk your life like this? What's so important to you?"

Serena flushed. Ryan pulled her like a lure she couldn't ignore. He needed her. That was enough.

Kara crossed her arms. "If I'm to be a part of this, you may as well tell me what your plan is so I can point out the flaws."

"Belladonna has Ryan."

Kara closed her eyes and dropped her head. Her shoulders shook and she laughed. "Ryan?" She laughed harder. "You are going to rescue Charmer? Oh, Golden One. He can take care of himself."

Serena sprang up from her bedroll and fisted her hands. "If he can help himself, he's done a poor job. She will break him. I feel it."

The laughter left Kara's face, but her mockery stayed. "You *feel* it?"

"His pain."

"As in, you're bonded to him?"

"Yes."

Kara's eyes formed slits. "You literally feel his pain?"

"Why do you care?"

"I don't. I'm just curious."

Truth. "I suppose you don't care about any of us."

"You are rather dull. Softheart is so emotional I don't know how soldier puts up with her."

"You could learn a thing or two from both of them, you know."

"Oh?" Kara's amused smile played on her lips. "Like what?"

"Jayden is compassionate—something you lack—and Ethan, well he was consumed by revenge once, too."

Kara's amusement faded. "Oh? And I thought you couldn't understand me." She glared at Serena before she stalked off and started rummaging through her pack.

Dash snorted. *"I said befriend the woman, not turn her off altogether."*

"All I am saying is that there is more to life than revenge."

Dash bit into a mouthful of grass. *"This should be good."*

"Really?" Kara turned on her heel. "And how would you know, Serena? Golden One, blessed, angelic-faced, silly girl who goes riding into the dragon's lair for what? Love?" Kara pulled out a knife and pointed it at Serena and then herself. "You go for love, I go for revenge. Maybe we'll both find our silly little notions, but don't think your rashness is above mine." She sat on her blanket.

Serena sank to her bedroll. Kara's words stung like a slap in the face. "I'm sorry. You're right. I admit, I believed my motives more pure and therefore worthy of rashness. But your motives are no less agonizing. He killed your sister. If he killed Ryan, I think I'd be going to the palace for revenge, too."

Kara shifted on her bedroll and stared.

Serena pulled an apple from her sack and tossed it to Kara. She caught it and cut a deep slice of the fruit. Her eyes never left Serena.

Serena took her own apple. "Tell me about your sister?"

Kara's eyebrows shot up. "Just because I agreed to go to the palace *with* you, doesn't mean I am going *for* you. Let's be clear on that. Also let's be clear on one other thing." Kara pointed her knife at herself then Serena. "*We* aren't friends."

"Just because we aren't friends, which I accept, doesn't mean you can't tell me about your family."

Kara bit into her apple. "Why don't you tell me about your family, Golden One? Then maybe I'll tell you about mine."

"All right." Serena crossed her legs. "I was born the night of the Blood Moon—"

"Weren't we all?" Kara leaned back on her satchel and placed her heels up onto the trunk of the nearest tree. "Don't bore me."

Serena rolled her eyes. "If your story is better—"

Kara's laughter interrupted. "No, go on. I just didn't know you were going to give me the eighteen-year version of Serena's life."

Serena threw her apple at Kara, who caught it and bit in.

"When I was nine, the man I called father sold me to a merchant who sold me to work for the castle court in Meese."

Kara sat up. "Your father sold you?"

"Somehow I thought you might like that part of the story."

"Actually, I'm more intrigued about you working in the castle in Meese. But why did he wait until you were nine?"

"I imagine because I finally started fighting back when he beat me."

Kara stared and Serena fingered her ring. The one that matched the one Kara wore. "Where did you work in the castle?"

"I was a serving girl on kitchen staff, where I made my first friend. Her family was poor and her mother dead. She often told me of her little sister whom she was trying to make sure didn't go hungry. I found out her sister was the same age—another Child of the Blood Moon, but she called me little sister, too. So often I almost believed it. Her hair was blonde and her eyes blue, like mine. She was the first family I ever had. The first person who ever protected me. It was her bravery that I learned from most in all my childhood. I wish I knew what became of her, but I never got to say goodbye."

"Why not?"

"A Healer called Tabitha came for me." Serena ventured a gaze at Kara, who was listening intently, fingering the ring on her hand. Serena shrugged. "I suppose that's all that would interest you of my story."

"Did you ever meet the girl's family?"

"I was purchased by the Healers before that could happen."

"Ah. They were a better home anyway. Right?"

"Many of them were cowards. A few could be swayed to follow me and my . . . rebellious ways."

"Rebellious? Perhaps there's more to the Golden One than meets the eye."

"Perhaps."

"The girl that called you sister, what was her name?"

Serena looked into Kara's eyes. "Thea."

Kara stared at her unblinking, her apple forgotten in her hand. "You recognized the ring. That's why you asked me to come with you?"

"That's why I hoped I could trust you. Thea would have helped me. I loved her."

"She loved you. It doesn't mean I do." Kara got up and fed her apple to the horse before she walked away.

"That went better than expected." Dash snorted.

Serena glanced over her shoulder and rolled her eyes at the unicorn. *"I thought you were resting."*

Dash lay down and sighed. *"Are you going after her?"*

"She won't leave. She's bound by blood oath."

Dash's ears perked and he stood, nose to the wind. *"Do you smell that?"*

Serena sniffed the air and stood. Something in it smelled of a tinge of smoke—not from a cookfire, this scent was stronger—and the breeze suddenly warmer. *"Dragon smoke. Kara's in danger."* She raced after Kara, Dash following. The scent of fire drew closer, and there, on the ground, a dragon sat, red as a fire, with dark, purple scales on her head and piercing green eyes.

Serena's knees shook. The dragon opened its mouth. Serena dashed out of the trees and slammed into Kara. Together they fell to the earth, and Serena covered Kara's body, waiting for the flames.

CHAPTER 21

POLISHED STONE

W hat do you mean?" Madison stared at the ring on Connor's finger. "How can I be part of a plan that I can't know about?"

He sighed and dropped the two books he'd needed from the library onto the table. The Wielder history book he kept beneath the other one. Then he plucked a stone out of his pocket and showed her.

She placed her hands on her hips. "Am I allowed to ask what that's for? And why does it smell like pears?"

Connor tilted his head to the side, impressed that she could smell it. "I don't know about the pear scent. I got this from the spell chamber. The whole room smelled like pears. Franco said something about Belladonna preparing a potion for a lover."

"And you didn't think to ask about that?"

"What do I care what Belladonna does with her lovers?"

Madison leaned on the table. "Maybe it was a spell to make someone her lover. Remember the drink Franco brought me that night you rescued me from him? It smelled like pears."

Connor squeezed his eyes closed. It had. He had to get Ryan out of here. Too many things hinged on this plan working.

Madison's fingers touched the stone. "Connor, you're lost in your thoughts again."

"Sorry."

"What's this for?" She took the polished stone. "Or is that the part you can't tell me?"

Someone knocked on the door. The heavy hand and scent of steel told him it was Luc. "Come in."

Luc opened the door, and Madison hid the stone behind her back. Connor chuckled. "You can show it to him."

"He's here because he gets to know the whole plan?" Her voice held an edge that Connor liked. The palace had stripped her of much of her feisty personality because she feared tripping over some law and landing headfirst on a chopping block.

Well, probably not that extreme. Franco needed her alive. But being chained to his bed was not a long-forgotten threat to her. That her spirit showed signs of revival thrilled him.

Luc's eyes didn't even meet Connor's. He stared at Madison and smiled. He nodded his head toward her. "What are you hiding?" Then his gaze strayed to the table, and his eyes lightened. "You've been to the library?" He strode past Madison.

She tilted her head as her gaze followed him.

Connor's brows met as he watched his friends. This was not good. Not good at all. Could he trust them to keep their heads in the plan if they were going to be this infatuated with one another?

"I do need your help." Connor joined them at the table. He'd been born of wolves, not human parents, for the very reason that if he grew attached to a human being he'd want to spare them. But all his powers did were destroy. He bowed his head. "You know I'm a Death Bringer. It means that if you're close to me, you have a very high chance of dying."

Madison squeezed Connor's hand. "Death is going to happen anyway. You just show it to the path of least destruction."

"Connor?" Luc gripped his shoulder. "I'll help you any way I can."

Connor breathed deep. Time to do this, then. "Will you please give Luc the stone? I need to tell him our plan."

Madison held out the stone.

Luc took it. "Where I come from, we polish marriage stones a lot smoother for this kind of thing." Luc looked into her eyes and she blushed.

She cocked an eyebrow. "Where I come from, a man has to work a lot harder to make a woman notice him."

"Noted," he whispered, and Madison's mouth popped open.

Connor chuckled. "If you need me, I'll be reciting my plan over here." He grabbed a piece of bread from the table.

Madison giggled. "Tell him about the stone. I'll come back later to hear the parts I'm allowed to know." She exited.

Connor shot Luc a grin.

Luc shrugged. "What? You said I might die. I'd like to kiss a girl first."

"I find it hard to believe you've never kissed a girl."

Luc smiled. "What's the stone for?"

Connor looked at the small object in Luc's hand. White like a frozen-over pond. "I put unicorn horn dust on it."

"Oh, Connor."

"I know. I really didn't want Madison to know a dead unicorn fueled its power. It's a cloaking stone. If you touch it to the ring I gave you, concentrate on hiding the ring with these words"—he handed Luc a folded piece of paper—"and then put the stone in your pocket, it should keep anyone from seeing the ring. Then you can wear it, and Franco will never know you're the one actually controlling his Black Blood Army. Franco says the other Deliverers are almost here. The day they come, we'll be ready. Madison says Kara is coming closer, too. I have to think she's with them."

"And then?"

"I'm still working that out. I need to talk to Kara somehow. I'll figure it out."

Luc scratched the back of his neck. "This . . . um . . . plan of yours." He paused, the skin around his eyes tightening in a wince. "You're going to die, aren't you?"

"If all goes as planned, yes."

CHAPTER 22

SHADOW WOLF

*E*than stood at the river's edge, bow in hand. He aimed his arrow at one of those red targets he and Ryan used to paint on the old, moth-eaten potato sacks and tack to hay bales. The target crept farther away as he stared at it. Strange. The circle in the middle was red. Shiny and wet. Ethan lowered his weapon.

Then the circle split in two.

Something didn't feel right.

Black dots filled the center of the circles. They were like red eyes.

The heat of a threat pulsed across Ethan's chest, and he fired his arrow. It missed.

He shot again. Too wide.

The circles drew closer, shrouded in a gray mist like a grounded cloud hovering over the water. His chest burned, and his bow became too heavy to lift. Every arrow he pulled from the quiver at his belt was bent.

Broken.

A laugh echoed on the wind like a growl.

"What are you?" he asked the red circles.

They narrowed like the eyes of a predator. This wasn't right. Nothing made sense. This had to be a dream.

"Come on, Ethan. Wake up!"

Someone grabbed his shirt, and Ethan gripped hold of the attacker's wrists and pushed. The form above him screamed as he flipped her over, rolling with her, and pressed her into the ground. Knee on her chest, he reached for his belt knife. But the girl he'd slammed into to the ground came into clear view. "Quinn?"

The fog shook loose from his head. Chest heaving, he backed up and let her go. "Don't—are you okay?"

She slowly stood, picking up her book from the ground and clutching it tight to her chest as she nodded. Her eyes were wide, and the muscles in her neck pulled taut. Pure fear.

"Quinn, I'm sorry." He held out his hands to calm her. "I—don't wake me up like that, okay?" He wanted to reach out and comfort her, but he didn't want to startle her.

She flung her arms around him and squeezed. "They're coming."

"Who's coming?"

"The shadow wolves. The trees say the levels have expanded. The Mistress is gaining power."

Ethan pried her loose and strapped on his sword belt. "Remind me?"

"They're the ghosts of the afterworld. They howl like the wind and hunt in packs. They can enter your dreams and kill you there."

His heart jolted. "Do they have red eyes?"

"Yes." She trembled.

"Hey." He touched her arm. "Listen. I'm going to keep you safe." He wished he had Jayden's ability to calm others. Sometimes Quinn forgot how powerful she was. She needed to focus on who she was becoming, not who she'd been. "Tell me everything."

"Everyone who is asleep is at risk. You—I think you were—they were attacking you."

Heat exploded across his chest. Whatever they were, they wanted the Deliverers. And Quinn. Ethan raced out of his tent and started shouting a warning. "Sound the alarm!" More people repeated his call until the alarm gong resounded.

Chloe dashed to his side. "What is it?"

He faced her. "Where's Jayden? Something is coming, and whatever it is wants the Deliverers for the Mistress. I really hope Serena is okay."

Chloe raced for the tent while Logan grabbed Ethan's arms. His eyes begged for an explanation. "The shadow wolves. They fly. The level expanded. They can reach us now, and they inhabit dreams. Everyone who is asleep is in danger."

"Can they be killed?" Jayden ran up to where they stood.

Quinn nodded. "By fire or Wielder-crafted weapons."

"And lightning?"

"Let's hope so," Logan said.

White wisps darkened the clouds above. They resembled giant bats with wolfish heads and whips for tails with arrowheads at the end. No shrieks, only the deep, unsettling howl of wind.

The sky rumbled and clouds congregated, blocking the stars. The beasts dove through the cover and dropped close to the earth. Jayden held up her dagger.

Ethan touched her arm. "How many bolts can you call?"

She shook her head. "Maybe one? I–I—" She stared at the sky. "If the wolves were congregated."

"As you wish." Ethan allowed himself a smile, and that fueled him. "Zephyr." He called for his gryphon. As he felt Zephyr drawing closer, he touched Jayden's cheek. "I'll get all those monsters herded into one spot for you."

"Ethan, I—"

He let go and raced toward Zephyr. But he called over his shoulder, "Just don't hit me. I trust you."

Zephyr dropped to the ground, and Ethan touched his friend's shoulder. "We have to get these monsters to chase us. Up for some antagonizing?"

"Always."

"Ethan!" Chloe's voice caused him to turn. She grabbed his arm. "They want you."

"They'll be sorry when the lightning strikes." He jumped onto Zephyr, but Chloe clung to his shirt and jumped, too. "Chloe—"

"You will not win this argument." As the gryphon took flight, she held tight to him. Then she spun around on the gryphon and pulled out her daggers.

"Do *not* fall."

Her smile warmed him. "Don't worry, Ethan Branor. I have your back."

Zephyr zipped through the clouds, closer to the spot where the beasts seemed to be free to maneuver. One of the white beasts dove toward him. Gleaming teeth exposed. Red eyes, the same as the targets from his dream, locked onto him. He slashed, and it shrieked as his blade passed through like a hand through a wisp of smoke. Gone. Blood tainted his blade as clear as water.

Could these things harm people who were awake? They didn't seem substantial enough.

"It's like cutting smoke," Chloe said.

"Yeah. Keep cutting."

"Hold on." Zephyr dove, and Ethan grabbed Chloe's arm.

They headed into a mist, and razor claws sliced at his face from every direction. Zephyr grunted.

"You okay, friend?"

"As long as they don't bite, she'll be fine."

"She?"

"We are impervious to their venom, Ethan. Chloe is not."

Ethan's heart sped. Great. At least he had his talent to help protect her. A creature dove for him, and Chloe's dagger pierced its chest. It puffed away like a cloud of white smoke and vanished. "They're following us."

"You default to this plan often." Chloe glared at him, but there was a smile in it.

"Maybe I like to be chased."

She laughed.

"Incoming."

A group of three more drew too close. Ethan decapitated one and swung to slice through another. No resistance. He'd lose his balance if he wasn't careful.

Chloe killed another. The sky darkened. Thunder rumbled, and everything smelled like rain. He breathed in. "I hope Jayden's ready."

"Here we go. Hang on."

A gust of cool wind followed these creatures. Jayden whirled around. Stormcloud flew above her in the clouds, kicking and fighting each of the animals. They blew away like puffs of smoke, but there were so many.

The Feravolk fought beside Jayden on the ground.

Melanie stayed at her back. "You think you can call a storm in time?"

"There really isn't a choice."

More cold air. And screams followed. They shrieked. Jayden slashed with her dagger, and another puff of mist clamored to fill her lungs with moist air. She looked up. Zephyr dove again, herding the beasts in a chase.

"Here they come."

She braced herself, exposed, but with Melanie and Gavin and Logan protecting her. They dove for her.

Jayden called the storm. Lightning leapt to her command. Filled her every vein. Ready to strike. Ethan passed her. The Creatures gaining on him. Electricity zapped. She told Melanie and the others to run and pointed her dagger at the mass of creatures.

Lightning poured from her blade. Fire crackled and shot into the creatures, right where she directed it. Hundreds of spindly legs of electricity zapped out, lighting up the creatures from the inside and blowing them apart like exploding clouds.

Cheers struck up around her as the Feravolk raced back in to attack the remaining few.

But the shadow wolves knew defeat. With the flutter of an angry wind, they began to fly away.

And she slumped to her knees, exhausted. A tearing rip sent hot pain through her shoulder. She buckled over as the weight of a creature slammed into her.

Blood trickled down her back. Seeped into her clothes.

She spun around and faced the ghost-white creature. Then Logan's sword passed through it, and the monster was nothing but mist.

"Jayden?" Logan grabbed her other shoulder. His blue eyes pierced her, and his worry flooded into her.

"I'm okay." She struggled to her feet. "I'm just tired."

Stormcloud landed beside her, and the skies looked much less full.

Logan's expression turned grim. "You're bleeding. Melanie!"

"You did it!" Melanie touched Jayden's arms. "What happened?"

"It—it scratched me."

"Not a bite?" Quinn asked, eyes wide.

The face of the creature flashed in Jayden's mind. Blood speckled its whiskers, but that could have been anyone's.

"I don't think so."

"If their saliva gets in your bloodstream for too long it can make you have nightmares." Quinn touched her uninjured shoulder. "And they can kill you there."

"I–I feel fine."

CHAPTER 23

VULNERABLE HEART

S erena braced herself for the pain of dragon's fire across her back, but none came. Dash sprung in front of her, but the flames didn't come.

Kara pushed Serena off of her and stood. "What were you thinking?"

"That you were about to die."

"So you jumped in front of an open-mouthed dragon for me? Dragon's fire can hurt Healers. You know that, right?"

Serena stood. "Yes." It surprised her that Kara knew. Dragon's fire could stunt a Healer's power the same way bandy weed could.

Kara had lost her sneer. "Ember wouldn't hurt me. We're bonded."

"Bonded?" Dash stamped his hoof and a shudder of fear rippled over the bond. *"To a dragon? She can lie to you. Get on my back. We're leaving."*

Serena's heart clutched. This could not be happening. *"We can't leave. I have to go after Ryan. And she's my way out."*

"The one person who can deceive us?"

"I didn't know."

"You know now. Let's leave."

"No."

"You would trust her to take you into the palace as a prisoner even now?" Dash faced her, pushed his soft nose into her. *"I won't let that happen."*

Serena looked at the dragon. Ember. Kara had called her Ember.

Kara put out her hand, and the dragon placed its red, scaled chin in her palm. "She's been following me at a distance since I left the Island in the Swamp with your friends Gavin and Melanie." Kara scratched Ember's chin, and the dragon thumped her spiked tail against the ground.

"I thought she'd be larger." Serena marveled at the creature. Maybe she wasn't the color of fire. Maybe it was more like a warm summer sunset. Serena extended a shaking hand. "May I?"

Kara smiled an actual, soft smile and nodded.

With trembling fingers, Serena touched Ember's long neck. The scales were warm and incredibly hard. Ember's eyes flickered to meet Serena's. She opened her talent to feel the dragon's heart. Her probing stalled, and she sensed a heavy door, like thick armor, that she could not break through. Dragons could prevent Healers from reading their hearts. Ember's eye narrowed, but slowly, the door cracked open, exposing the tender heart beneath.

Warmth radiated through Serena's body. The heart felt good. Sensible. Gentle. The door slammed shut.

Serena looked at the dragon. "Thank you."

Ember cocked her head.

"Did you feel it, Dash?"

The unicorn snorted. *"I felt it. Doesn't mean I trust her scaly hide, or the woman to whom she is bonded."*

"It's better than nothing." Serena turned to Dash and stroked him.

"Your hand is warm."

"She will help us." Kara patted Ember's neck. "And promises not to hurt your friends."

Serena turned to the dragon. "Thank you. We'll need all the help we can get."

Half of Kara's face scrunched up. "But . . . she brought a friend."

"What?" Serena gasped as another dragon, slightly larger than Ember but green in color, raised his head and walked closer to them, bending young trees, snapping others. He was slender enough to fit between some. And as he rose, she could see how his colors had rendered him nearly invisible here. Like a grassy hill.

Kara clenched her jaw. "This is Blaze."

"Two dragons?" Dash reared up, flailing his hooves at the beasts. *"No."*

Serena locked eyes with Blaze. Something inside the green eyes seemed soft. Uncertain. Would he be willing to show her a glimpse of his heart? She felt for it. Blaze's eyes narrowed, and he lowered his head, more to her level.

Dash stood between them, swishing his tail.

Smoke poured from Blaze's nostrils.

"He says he doesn't like you, either, horse."

"Horse?" Dash snorted and stamped.

Kara shrugged. "His words. Not mine. But he says something about that vicious sword of noble light."

Serena placed her hand on Dash's shoulder. "Dragons have fire that stunts our abilities. Unicorn horns can cut through dragon scales easily. It's said that only a sword of noble light can kill the evil dragon. But that's not you, is it?" Serena looked at Blaze. "*The* evil dragon is an important distinction."

"What are you talking about now?" Kara crossed her arms.

"A unicorn's horn can kill a dragon, sure. But so can other things. But *the* dragon, the mount of the Mistress, the dragon she created. That dragon must be killed by a unicorn's horn." She looked at Blaze. "If you're on our side, instead of the Mistress's, I think you'll help us."

Blaze tipped his head to the side as if agreeing with her. Serena probed for his heart again. This time, the door opened easily. Loyalty, friendship, and trust lingered there.

Serena smiled at him. "Your heart is pure."

Dash snorted.

Serena let him feel her unease about the situation, too.

She turned to Kara. "Can I trust you?"

"That's up to you." Kara shrugged. "I'm going to the palace regardless."

"I still need you."

Dash's head jerked up. *"Serena?"*

"You can trust me, right? I need you, Dash."

"I trust you, but that is not what will anchor me to this fool's mission.

I will not leave you to die by her hands if I can help it. Just let me be clear. This is stupid."

"I know."

"Reckless."

"I know."

"Dangerous."

"Dash, I am going through with this."

"I know."

Kara held out her palm and sliced it open. Blood pooled in her hand, and she stared at Serena.

Air left Serena's lungs in a rush. "Another blood oath?"

"You must promise that you will never heal me without my permission."

"A Healer can't—"

"Even if I'm unconscious."

"Kara, I can't promise that."

"Then this is as far as I help you."

"Kara! You promised already. You can't break a blood oath with a Healer. You'll die."

"I guess it will be a death at your hands, seeing as you could prevent me from going back on my word." She pushed her hand toward Serena.

"Serena, this is madness."

"What would you have me do, Dash? Let her die?"

"It seems she has a death wish, not wanting you to heal her."

Kara wiggled her fingers. "Now or never, Serena."

Serena slit her palm and sealed her second oath with a dragon.

CHAPTER 24

GIFT FOR A DRAGON

Ryan opened his eyes. A soft down mattress cradled his back. Where was he? He sat up. Crimson, velvet blankets covered him to his waist. Heavens, where was his shirt? His heart sped as he searched the room for any sign of familiarity. Fire crackled in the stone fireplace across from the massive bed he sat in. A large mirror hung on the wall to his left, and an ornate wardrobe fashioned from cherry wood stood against the wall on his right. A table big enough for his whole family to sit at without bumping elbows sat in the center of the room, and draped across one of the chairs was a shirt, breeches, and a vest.

He hopped out of the bed and grabbed the clothes. If anyone walked in on him, he wanted to be decent. At least he was wearing undergarments.

But why was he here? And where was here?

He picked up the pants. The fabric was smooth against his fingers. Whoever laid these clothes out for him had expensive taste. He slipped into the black slacks and grabbed the white shirt. He glanced over his shoulder at the mirror, and air rushed from his lungs. Was that his back? All of those scars were his? He touched one. Numb.

How had—? His head throbbed as he started to remember.

Belladonna. He shook and heat coursed through his blood. She'd left the scars. A constant reminder. His grip around the shirt tightened. Didn't matter. She could scar him all she wanted. She would not break him. Slowly, he started to put the shirt on. Before he had an arm through the sleeve, the door opened, and she entered. His blood turned to ice.

"Pet. I see you've found the clothes."

He wrinkled the shirt in his shaking fist. A dull pain throbbed behind his eyes. Made him want to see how beautiful she was. What in Soleden had spurred that thought? He pushed it away. All he saw were the scars she'd inflicted.

Belladonna walked up to him and trailed a finger down his chest. "Did you sleep well?"

He grabbed her finger and bent it backward.

She pressed her other hand against him, and the feeling of hundreds of lashes knocked into him all at once. Trembling, he buckled over and gripped the chair back. Then all the pain stopped. All but the dull ache behind his eyes. That intensified.

She leaned in and before he knew why, her lips were pressing against his. Everything tasted like pears. Memories flooded back to him. The dungeon. She had kissed him in the dungeon. Why? Oh. Right. Because she loved him.

She looked marvelous. And the headache dissipated. "Where am I?"

"In my quarters." Her eyes sparkled as she stepped toward the wardrobe. "I have a present for you."

He caught her arm. "Where are you going?"

"Don't you want to see your present?"

"Later." He backed toward the bed, pulling her with him.

"Pet, I told you, not until we've seen the Mistress."

Ryan smiled and swung Belladonna toward the mattress. He let go and she bounced on the bed. He pounced on top of her. As he leaned in, her finger pressed against his lips.

"Your eagerness pleases me, pet, but the Mistress will chop off my head if I defile you before she's done with you." She pushed against his chest, and he rolled off of her. "I wish to keep my head." She walked toward the table. Paused at the chair and picked up the white shirt. "Now, get dressed."

The shirt landed on his face, and the leather jerkin slapped against his chest.

"The Mistress does not tolerate tardiness."

Ryan sat up and pulled the shirt on. Looking at himself in the mirror, he almost didn't see a familiar person. He looked so regal. The laced shirt, the dark pants and jerkin. He looked like—like one of the king's personal guards. Not one of the front line guards, but one of the protective men that walked alongside him. Hadn't someone told him he would dress like the king's men? The dizziness hit him again. A tingle started on his forehead and washed over his scalp. He shook his head.

"Feeling all right, pet?"

Ryan opened his eyes to see Belladonna staring back at him in the mirror. Her beauty caused his stomach to flip. He smiled at her. "Can't we just stay here? The view is . . . intoxicating."

Belladonna ran her tongue along her lips. "Like I said, I value my head. She'll take yours, too, once your purpose is complete, so play her little game first, and I might be able to save you."

Ryan walked up to her and touched her smooth cheek with his hand. "I like your head right where it is, too. You want me to play? I'll play. Whatever you wish."

Belladonna's lips parted, then she blinked and shook her head. "Yes. Well, let's meet her then, shall we?" She walked to the door and opened it, motioning for him to follow.

He followed her and, once outside the door, three other men dressed just like him fell in line with them. Belladonna led them down through the back doors and into the private court of the king and his subjects.

Sun hit Ryan's face. When was the last time warmth like that had touched him? How long had he spent in that dungeon? A breeze rippled past, pushing the scent of pears away from him. They passed a training field full of soldiers. A large army. He wondered if Logan might like to know how large—Logan? A splitting pain hit Ryan's head. Who was Logan? And where had that thought come from? Perhaps too much fresh air without any for days was giving him a headache. No. He remembered sunshine. And it was red.

Red.

So much red.

The last time he'd been here, she'd—shaking, he looked at Belladonna's back as she continued toward the courtyard. She'd made him kill people.

He'd killed innocent people.

Ryan stumbled to his knee as he remembered what he'd done. Was it only a day ago? And how had she made him do such horrible things? His head throbbed and he pressed the heel of his hand against his eye.

"Ryan?" Belladonna's voice brought him to his feet. He grabbed his sword—which she was stupid to give him—and before he could swing, her hand touched his shoulder. The pain of a dozen torture sessions slammed into him, and he buckled forward. She steadied him and her lips met his. The scent of pears flooded him. Pain melted away. All his thoughts clouded. He wanted to wrap his arms around her. Her hand on his chest stopped him. "You can't keep forgetting who you are, pet." She glanced at the soldiers practicing in the field. "If you wish to practice with them to stay sharp, I can arrange that."

He didn't take his eyes off her. "I would."

"Good." She grabbed his face and pulled him close, her lips touching his again in that fruit-filled explosion. He shook his head. Thoughts dulled until one remained: he loved Belladonna.

He'd killed those people because she'd asked him to. That was all that mattered.

Because he loved her.

She smiled as her hands slid over his arms. Then she gripped his hand and towed him through the courtyard, past the garden, and into another court. There she dropped his hand and curtseyed.

The Mistress stood in front of him, eyes searching his face. "I got you a gift."

Ryan bowed. The Mistress smiled. Then she snapped her fingers. Two dozen men strode forward carrying heavy chains. On the end of the chains was a massive, charcoal-black dragon. Ryan stepped back, his heartbeat thundering against his ribs. Were they mad? His breathing evened when he noticed the iron muzzle sealing the beast's mouth closed.

The chains held nets that bound the dragon's wings. The creature was trapped, and brooding. As soon as a man got close to its tail, the dragon thrashed. The tail rammed into four men and sent them sprawling. Then it slammed the spiked end of its tail into the man, spearing him through.

Ryan shivered and the cloud in his thoughts cleared. "Wh-why would I want that?"

Belladonna glared at him with that crazy gleam in her eyes that told him to shut up and comply.

The Mistress of Shadows glided closer to him. "They tell me you can tame dragons."

They what? He was sure his eyes had popped out of his head. Whoever gave her that information wanted him dead.

The Mistress's eyes narrowed. "No one else's skin could survive the bull like that with no more than a blistering. So go on. Tame it."

How he was supposed to tame a dragon was beyond him, and suddenly it was his problem. Why were people always expecting more of him than he was capable of? And it was always a woman on the other end of things, too.

"I . . ."

"Do we have a problem, pet?" Belladonna leaned closer and her hand rested on the whip at her belt. Heat flooded through Ryan's core. His pulse raced.

The Mistress narrowed her eyes. "But I have brought all these villagers inside the courtyard to watch the mighty Knight slay the dragon." She motioned behind her where a crowd of wide-eyed faces met him. Women. Children. And every single one of them looked as scared as he felt.

The Mistress smiled. "Release it."

"What?" Ryan staggered back. He tried to calm the shaking in his breaths. "I—I've never even seen a dragon before."

"All the more reason to test your special talents."

"Just try." Belladonna purred in his ear.

Right. She had nothing on the line. For him it was his life.

The soldiers dropped the chains and pulled the contraptions holding the dragon captive free. The dragon spread his black wings and reared onto his hind legs, blocking out the sun. He stretched his long neck—tall like the trees in the Forest of Legends—and Ryan trembled. The villagers screamed, scrambling to find a way out. Quaking soldiers stood their ground, preventing the villagers from leaving. The earth shook as the dragon's front legs thudded against the soil.

Its massive, horned head weaved back and forth as if searching for prey. Men and women scattered from its shadow, screaming. And its amber eyes locked onto Ryan. *"Why aren't you running?"*

Good question. Had Belladonna's whip scared him so much that he feared her over dragon's fire? He cursed himself.

"You don't need to fear him." The Mistress's voice hissed in Ryan's head. *"Tame it."*

The dragon roared, and it sounded like a carriage riding over gravel. The echo of it thundered in Ryan's head. *"You'd be stupid to not fear me."*

It opened its mouth and flame, like the belly of a forge, churned in its gullet. The dragon's voice echoed in Ryan's skull. *"Run."*

But the dragon aimed fire at the innocent villagers and soldiers who were trying to escape. They'd be killed. Ryan ripped his sword free and ran to—to what? Deflect flame with his sword? There. He saw an abandoned shield and scooped it up as he slid across the gravel. The dragon's eyes shifted, and Ryan's heart jolted as he saw where the beast looked. Three children huddled in a cluster in the dragon's sights. The dragon opened his mouth.

Ryan swore and raced in front of the kids, screams resounding in his ears. He curled up behind the circular piece of metal and wood that he knew would do nothing but melt and burn in the fire and held his sword ready. Fire slammed into his shield with a force that pushed him backward. He held tight to the only things protecting those kids as heat encompassed him. Sweat beaded on his forehead and he looked at the kids. They stared back at him, eyes wide, as his shield cut the flames, redirecting the fire around the kids.

As soon as the steam let up, he told the kids to run, and as they raced into the crowd, Ryan peered over the shield at the dragon. "Stop! Please! They set you free! Go."

"Go?" The dragon's chuckle shook the ground. *"But there is so much to torment right here."*

"What do you want?"

Smoke poured from its nose, swirling around Ryan. And the dragon snaked its head closer. *"You're offering me something in exchange for these insignificant lives?"*

Ryan straightened his spine and faced the dragon head on. Who cared if he died saving someone? He didn't have anything to live for now. A life here in the palace was no life.

The dragon's eyes narrowed. *"The shield you carry suits you."*

Ryan glanced down at the warped and charred emblem of the muzzled dragon. *"I'm no dragon tamer, no matter what they say."*

"No. You are the muzzled dragon."

Every muscle in Ryan's body quivered. How dare this beast call him that? He was a dragon in its lair. Waiting. Biding. *"What's your name?"*

Thoughts pulsed into Ryan's mind. A thick, draping smoke cloud rose over him, encompassed him, blinded him, stung his eyes and his nose—it nearly choked him.

"Smoke?"

"Yes. Sssmoke."

"And what do you want?"

"A heart to bond to." One amber eye winked. *"You heart is just where I belong. So dark and comfortable."*

"Dark?" When did that happen? This was a trick, it had to be. Hadn't he been luring the Mistress and Belladonna into a trap? Hadn't he been on the side of right and justice and truth? Hadn't—? The headache stopped him short again and he pressed his palm into his eye.

"Oh yesss. Dark, like the heart of one bitten by a black lion."

Black lion? Snare that stupid creature. Would he ever be free of it?

Rabbit quick, the dragon encircled Ryan with his serpentine neck. His curled horn brushed against Ryan's chin, and Smoke locked his amber gaze on Ryan's face. *"A nice heart to belong to."*

"That isn't who I am." He shuddered.

Smoke's deep chuckle vibrated against him. *"Give it time. You're her vessel now."*

Vessel? *"You deceived me."*

"That's what dragons do."

One sharp clap punctured the still, silent air, and Ryan looked to see the Mistress coming toward him, offering her applause. "Behold your dragon tamer!"

All the townspeople began echoing the applause.

Ryan lowered his sword and shook his head. He pushed against Smoke's hard, black scales. "I'm—"

A flash in Belladonna's eyes told him to stop talking. "You have done well today and pleased the Mistress." She stepped around Smoke's head, drawing closer, pushing Ryan into the dragon's skin. Her lips pressed against his. Why? *Why did she keep . . . oh, that's right.* He loved her.

Smoke laughed.

CHAPTER 25

NIGHT TERRORS

You're sure?" Logan turned to Quinn, who had led them through the decaying land of the shadow wolves for an entire day. She'd stopped and stood with her eyes closed, stating that this was the place.

"Does it seem different to you?" Logan reached out to Westwind.

Westwind tilted his head toward the sky and sniffed. *"It doesn't smell or taste different. But it feels different. Warmer. Fresher."* He nosed Quinn while she stood motionless. *"She is deep in her conversation with them?"*

"The trees? Yes." The trees had led her further into the changing labyrinth.

After a night of fighting and day of travel, exhaustion caused most of Logan's men and women to stumble. They couldn't take much more of this. And Jayden was so weak from calling lightning every few hours to keep the beasts at bay while they tried to find the border to this level. She worried him.

Ethan, too. He wouldn't leave Jayden's side even as she rode on Stormcloud.

Quinn opened her eyes. "We are out of range here. Safe for now. But the maelvargs lie ahead of us." She dropped to the dirt and began to draw another map.

Logan turned to his army. "Set up camp. We rest while we can." He touched Quinn's shoulder. "Thank you."

She looked up at him and smiled. So much older now. She appeared the age of the Deliverers.

Once the others set up camp and half of the troops were resting, Logan took Gavin closer to the red horizon. "Do you think Glider will go ahead and tell us what he sees?"

Gavin crouched down and trailed his finger over the dry ground. "Look. It's cracked."

Logan glanced up at his friend. "Their domain."

"How long before the Mistress gains more power?" Gavin looked out over the barren stretch of land ahead of them. Dead, charred trees littered the ground in what resembled an old battlefield. "Glider says he'll fly over and report what he sees."

"Logan?" Morgan's meek voice interrupted them.

He excused himself from Gavin and joined her. The strange twinge in his chest told him Westwind was listening and feared what Morgan had to say. He loped up beside Logan and walked with him and Morgan. "You have news?"

Her green eyes were pools of sorrow. "There's a monster. You have a wooden coin that a Wielder carved for you?"

The token. The one with two wolf heads on it. Anna had said it marked him as a Protector. "I do."

"It's a key of some sort. It opens a door. And you'll need it if you're to defeat the monster. Her name is Garmr."

Garmr. He knew that name. Quinn had said it. Garmr was one of the Mistress's hounds. "It comes for the Deliverers?"

"Yes. And if you don't defeat this creature, it will take all the Deliverers. Garmr kills with fear. That's how her power works. She latches onto their fears and lets them grow until the fear suffocates her prey. The Mistress will use her to kill the Deliverers once she gets what she needs." Tears glistened unshed in Morgan's eyes. "You will need to go to her realm. You'll be immortal there. And only then can you kill her. In your immortal state."

"What does that mean?"

She shook her head. "I wish I could tell you. That's all I know."

Westwind sat beside Logan, and he realized he'd stopped walking. The way Morgan looked at him made him wonder if defeating this Garmr sealed his fate, but he didn't dare ask. His heart sank like a stone. Then it crumbled. But the pieces seemed to thread back together. It didn't matter if this was his end. He was their Protector. He would do whatever it took.

"Thank you."

She touched his arm gently.

Westwind stood and faced him. His amber eyes soft. *"We will defeat this Garmr."*

"Yes."

"And you will not be alone."

Logan crouched in front of his friend and stroked Westwind's shoulder. *"I know."*

When night came, more fell asleep. Gavin had informed Logan that Glider had seen the strange, spiked monsters from Quinn's book. As soon as she woke, he would ask her how to defeat them. For now, his people needed rest.

Rebekah sat up as he approached her, finally ready to bed down. She traced the worry lines on his face. "They are my worry as well."

"I wonder if I should just lead them back the way we've come. At any moment her power could expand."

"And how would you rescue Ryan and Serena and Connor?"

He sighed. "I would have to go in with a few Dissenters."

"You won't make it."

"Then I go in myself. Stormcloud or Zephyr could take me."

"And how would you bring them all back?"

He rubbed his face in his hands, and Rebekah wrapped her arms around him.

Screams resounded from his men and women. Logan jumped to his feet and rushed toward them. A crowd showed him where to go.

There in the middle of the crowd, on the dry, cracked earth, sat a young girl pressing a blade to Morgan's throat. Bedrolls had been pushed aside in what looked like a struggle.

Westwind jumped into the girl with the weapon, knocking her aside. Morgan scrambled away. The girl, her eyes glazed red, scanned the area, and she snarled at Westwind, holding the knife in front of her.

"She's rabid." Westwind growled back, hackles raised.

"What happened?" Logan asked Morgan.

"I don't know. I was asleep, and the next thing I knew, I woke up to her holding a knife over my bed. She looked so strange. Look at her. It's not normal."

"Did she eat any berries? Show any sign of sickness?"

"One of those nightmare creatures bit her," Quinn said.

Logan looked over his shoulder to find Quinn walking nearer. He held out his hand to stop her from getting too close.

The girl squatted low, snarling at anyone who moved. Black veins began to form around her eyes.

"Logan, she's scared more than anything."

"It's a nightmare. She's trapped in it." A tear slid down Quinn's cheek. "If she doesn't get free, it'll kill her. Once they get the black veins, there's no curing them."

More screams resounded from different areas in the camp.

Quinn looked up at Logan, tears streaming down her face. "They're dying in their sleep."

"And killing others." Logan looked at the girl who still snarled at Westwind. "Melanie said thirty-nine were bitten."

The girl with the knife screamed. "No! Don't eat me! Don't! Get off!"

"She's reliving it!" Quinn pressed her hand over her mouth.

The girl turned her knife against her throat. "I said get off!"

Logan jumped over bedrolls to stop her. Too late. He caught her as her blood dripped warm and red out of her throat. Her red eyes cleared as she looked up at him. Her mouth moved, but no sound came out. She breathed her last.

His heart clutched. He faced Morgan, and she fell to her knees with one hand covering her neck. "I didn't see this coming."

CHAPTER 26

SIMPLE PLANS

Serena stared at the map Kara had drawn in the dirt until her eyes crossed. A piece of bread landed on her lap.

"Eat. Once you're in the castle, you won't know when your next meal will come." Kara bit off a piece of bread and spoke around it. "So what's your marvelous plan for getting out?"

"Yes, Serena, do tell."

She picked up a stick and held one end over Kara's map. "That all depends on whether she's keeping Ryan in these dungeons or these." The stick tip dented the dirt where she'd pointed.

Kara swallowed her bread. "Different prisons, different keys. And a key for the spell room. That's a lot of work once we're inside." She tapped her bottom lip with her finger. "When you get the counters book, don't break any spells inside the castle; Franco might feel something being undone. You won't have time to risk that."

Serena dug in her bag and held up a small drawstring pouch.

Kara's eyes narrowed. "What's that?"

"Tangle flower seed. It'll put the guards to sleep."

Kara narrowed her eyes. "I know what it does."

"You do?"

"I'm an assassin." She held out her hand. "You'll be stripped of your weapons. Let me hold on to that."

Dash's growl was a rumble of thunder as Serena passed the bag over.

Kara glanced at him askance. "I'll make sure she gets it back."

"In your drink, no doubt."

"Dash, please."

"You've felt her heart?"

"Yes. It feels like one tainted by a blood sacrifice. We have to help her get her heart back."

He snorted.

Serena turned to Kara. "Where should we meet once I escape with Ryan and Madison?"

"You needn't wait for me. I'll find you."

"But how will I know—"

"You'll know." Kara arched an eyebrow. Then she held out her hands. "Might as well give me your daggers, too."

Dash's tail snapped as he thrashed it.

"Don't worry. I'll get these back to you as well." She rolled her eyes. "So, your plan?"

"I'll use the tangle flower to get the guards to sleep, steal the keys, and take Ryan and Madison down to the south tunnel that leads out to the stables where Dash will be waiting as a horse. It's simple really."

Kara crossed her arms. "And how are you going to get the guards to take the tangle flower seed? Were you just going to invite them into your *cell* for some tea?"

Serena chewed her bottom lip. "Cell?"

"You thought you'd be free in the palace? You're one of the Deliverers. You'll be a prisoner, remember? *I'll* have to get Ryan and Madison into the same dungeon as you. *I'll* have to get the keys. And *I'll* have to find your counters book. Some simple favor, Serena."

Serena? Not Golden One. This was progress. "Are you sure? The counters book will be hidden. I'm not sure you'll—"

"If I need help, I'll be sure to let you know." Kara's boot scraped over her drawing of the castle grounds. "We have to get moving." She pulled out rope. "Get on your ride. I'll have to tie you to him."

Dash snorted and laid his ears flat.

Kara eyed the unicorn. "Is he going to be a problem?"

"If you keep calling him my 'ride,' yes. Otherwise I'm not entirely sure."

Dash was too quiet as Kara led them closer to the city of Filgrum and the palace housed in the city center. His uneasiness as well as clear distrust of Kara grated on Serena's heart. Perhaps he was right. Perhaps this was a stupid plan.

"It is." His welcome voice broke her thoughts finally as they reached the city gate. *"But I trust you, little one."*

"Thank you." Even in her thoughts, her voice sounded like a choked whisper. It was too late to turn back now.

Serena stared at the majestic stone wall as Kara escorted them inside the city gates. In all the cities she'd visited, she'd never seen anything comparable. The sun rose behind the highest of five towers, letting warm rays glitter against it. Beautiful, but something here smelled dead.

Or at least decaying.

Kara led her mare up to the front gate. Dash followed behind, obsequious for now. The guards stopped her, and she pulled the collar of her shirt aside to reveal a tattoo at the base of her neck. A tattoo? Serena shivered as the guards moved aside for her to enter. She'd never seen anyone tattooed there—except pictures in history books of Healers who were claimed as servants. The tattoos trapped magic inside of them. No one in their right mind would get a tattoo there. Unless . . . Surely Franco knew nothing of the ancient rituals of Healers and tattoos. If he did—her blood ran cold just thinking about it. About what he could make her do.

They passed wagons of fruits and clothes and jewelry in the outer court and entered the inner court. Serena had to tilt her head back to see the massive structure. It had been six years since she'd seen the inside of a palace.

Dash halted and stiffened.

Serena tore her eyes from the building and breath left her lungs. Belladonna.

"Kara." Belladonna's familiar voice sent gooseflesh over Serena's skin. "What have we here?" She strode over, and Dash remained perfectly still. Serena kept her head low and scanned Belladonna's neck for one of the tattoos but found nothing. Only Belladonna's scrutinizing gaze. "Serena." Heat flashed in her pupils. "I should have known." She faced Kara. "What about the other girl?"

Kara shrugged. "She got away."

"With that tagalong boy?" Belladonna grinned. "I can get to him. Between the both of us, we'll get her every single one of them. But of course *you* would target the Healer of the group."

"I have a certain allure to them, I guess."

What did that mean? Serena's throat constricted. Kara wasn't a Healer; Serena would have felt it.

Belladonna's dark eyes lit up. "You going to make her heal you?"

Kara cocked an eyebrow. "You think I waited? Franco should have felt it."

Dash's ears laid flat. *"What's this about?"*

Serena swallowed hard. *"Your guess is as good as mine."*

Belladonna tapped her finger against her cheek. "Now that you mention it, he was rather happy about something the other evening."

"Good." Kara smirked. "Now excuse me, Belladonna, but I have something for the king." Dash used his nose to urge Kara's mare forward.

Serena released a breath as soon as they were out of Belladonna's view. "What was that about?"

"I need one more oath from you." She held out her knife over her hand. Her face was serious. One more blood oath in such a short time would make them sister-kin. "The king has to believe you healed me."

"Kara, I can't lie."

"I know, but your tongue is quick and your mind quicker. He *must* believe you already healed me or he will *make* you heal me, do you understand?"

"I'm afraid I don't."

"I'm his blood sacrifice. In order to kill him, you must kill me and any Healer tied to him." Kara grasped Serena's bound hands and sliced her right palm. "I have kept my side of the bargain, to bring you here and to show you the ways out. I will add helping you get the counters book, but you need to promise this."

Serena stared at the woman's dripping palm. Her own wound slowly closing. Despite Dash's look of warning and the fact that she could sense his thrumming heart, she thrust out her bound hands. Kara squeezed her hand between Serena's and shook, palm to palm.

As Kara's blood met hers again, a bond forged. She could sense Kara's presence. They were connected. They were sister-kin now. Serena had needed no blood to form this bond with Jayden, but it felt the same. She had just bonded herself to a dragon.

Kara stared at her hand as if she felt it, too. She grabbed her reins and spurred her horse toward the stables.

Dash hung his head and ambled along behind Kara's mare. *"I hope you know what you are doing."*

Kara whipped her head around and stared at the unicorn.

Dash lifted his head. *"You can understand me?"*

Kara nodded. "I can tell you things, and you could relay the message to Serena?"

"Yes."

"This could prove useful."

"Indeed."

"We'll need all the help we can get." Kara slid off her horse and helped Serena off Dash. Silently she put both horses into empty stalls.

Serena breathed deep. A sharp grip tightened around her elbow, and Kara leaned close to her ear. "Here is where I am no longer your friend."

Serena's eyes met Dash's. *"Did you hear that Dash? She is my friend."*

"Be careful, Serena." He hid his thoughts so Kara wouldn't hear him.

"Wish me luck."

"Luck? You'll need more than that. The Creator has favor on you, Child. I hope you're truly on your Destiny Path, because if you're not, we're in a great deal of trouble."

Kara pushed her back out into the court, into the palace, and past tapestry upon tapestry until they reached the anteroom. She pulled Serena close again. "Remember, you're my prisoner, so act meek." Kara pushed Serena through the double doors.

The strange, sickly sweet smell of rotting fruit assaulted her, and she saw why. At the end of the room, seated on the throne, and guarded by ten men in black garb and armed with swords, was the Mistress of Shadows. Bright white, deep black, and scarlet red clashed together in the room. Animal skins made up the carpets of black and white, and red interspersed the marble like streaks of blood.

The Mistress's heart knocked on the door of Serena's talent, begging to be read. It was a dark, porous sponge for other people's suffering. Serena cringed.

Belladonna stood near the Mistress's throne on one side and Franco on the other. Serena had never felt so much evil all at once. Her eyes fluttered to the still, silent man who stood beside Belladonna, and her heart nearly missed a beat. Ryan.

He stared ahead, not focusing on anything, but watching everything. No smile graced his face. Emptiness coated his features. And his heart felt dangerous, hardened, hopeless. The sliver of taint he'd once held prisoner in his heart had grown. And instead of being closed and contained, the darkness was an open, pulsating wound. And her chest ached.

What had they done to him? Suddenly it was hard to breathe. Was she too late? No. She would fight for him. She'd get him out of here if it killed her.

His eyes met hers for a brief moment, but no recognition glimmered there.

Kara muscled Serena forward. Her knees gave way and she fell to the floor. Kara grabbed Serena's hair at the base of her scalp and yanked, sending pain through Serena's head. "I've brought you a gift, Mistress."

The Mistress smiled, making Serena's skin crawl. "A Deliverer. Now I have two."

"And I can get you the last two." Belladonna sauntered closer.

"Don't make promises. Just get them."

"The one they call Ethan draws nearer to the palace with the Deliverer as we speak."

"I know. They travel through my maze of creatures." The Mistress looked at Serena while she spoke. It was as if she could hear Serena's pounding pulse. "Yes, my guards let you pass through. They know you by scent. Franco, I trust you will see to it someone makes her comfortable in the dungeons?"

"Yes, Mistress."

"Now, I must retire. After all, I will need my strength very soon." She seemed to look into Serena's mind. "Believe me, by the time your friends show up, they will see that I am more powerful than they imagined." She rose and exited, taking six of the guards with her.

Serena remained with Kara, Belladonna, and Franco, who took the throne. In the absence of the guards, she saw a young woman who looked just like Morgan. Madison. Her heart thrummed in her chest.

Franco rounded on Kara. "Don't just stand there. Make her heal you."

"Your Majesty." Kara bowed humbly. "Didn't you feel it? I have not waited until now. It is already done."

"Done? I felt nothing." He placed long fingers under Serena's chin and craned her neck up uncomfortably. She tried unsuccessfully to cringe away as he leaned closer. "Have you healed Kara?"

Serena glared at the king.

Kara's grip tightened on her hair. "You will answer when you're spoken to."

Franco smiled, and it was wicked and cruel. "A simple yes or no will suffice. Did you heal her?"

Simple? No. Nothing about that was simple. Serena swallowed. A lie would kill her. So would the truth.

CHAPTER 27

SHATTERED DREAMS

*B*lack vines stood out in stark detail against the evening fog. At least, Jayden thought it was evening. Something about all of this was strange. Like a dream. Or the memory of a dream. She shook her head. Where was everyone? And how had she gotten here? She wouldn't just wander into a strange forest alone, would she?

The fog parted, like smoke, and the vines moved. A figure hidden in the shadows glided closer and stood before her. "I wasn't sure you'd come." Her voice echoed inside Jayden's head and fill the void between them.

"Where am I?"

The woman stepped into the misty moonlight. Red moonlight. The color bathed her face. A beautiful face. Pale, blue eyes. Rich, auburn hair. She smiled. "I don't wish to scare you. Not yet."

A dream. She was dreaming. This had to be from the beast. The infection still infiltrated her blood. Her heart raced. The woman before her changed. She looked like death. Pale skin, stringy, dark hair.

"No, don't be scared. I need you. Your mind. I already have the tall one's heart. That's how I will get the Creator's power. The prophecy states I need the heart of one, mind of another, the soul of one, and strength of her brother."

"You can't have my mind!"

The woman changed back into her beautiful form. "My poison already works through you. I need you to bring your friends to me."

"Never. Get out of my head!" Jayden reached for her daggers.

"I can't have you screaming. See this path?" The mist hiding the vines *moved to clear a path. Leaves brushed away from the dirt and dead grass trampled with use. "It leads to the palace. Those escaping to join you have been using it. But I think you'll want to use it as well. I could have someone waiting for you here. If you want. Someone you love."*

Jayden closed her eyes. This was nothing more than a dream. She shook her head. Nothing about this woman felt safe. She smelled like poison. Jayden clutched her head again. "This isn't real."

"Maybe not. But that's the fun part. Taking what isn't real and twisting it until you believe it."

"You can't do that."

"I can if I control your mind." Her smile dripped honey. Honey turned black, like venom.

Venom in the saliva.

Venom in the blood.

Jayden shouted, "You can't have my mind!"

The dream shattered.

Jayden woke to darkness. Sweat covered her, her pulse pounded, and her hands were curled into fists, yet she had no memory of a fitful sleep or a nightmare that would have caused those reactions. A soft nose nuzzled into her, and she patted Stormcloud.

A strange worried look resided in Stormcloud's eyes that matched the mood pulsing over the bond. *"It's the middle of the night. Are you all right?"* Her words seemed innocent enough, but Stormcloud's unspoken question beat through Jayden's every pulse: did she have any nightmares?

Nightmares.

The feeling of claws and teeth digging into her after she'd pulsed lightning at the tree wouldn't leave her alone, but she couldn't recall a single dream.

She felt the hidden wound on the back of her shoulder. Last night it had looked black. Felt hot. When she'd poured water from her waterskin over it, steam sizzled against her arms. Now, burning pain pulsed into her. A stabbing heat.

Stormcloud drew closer. *"Jayden, I feel your worry."*

"I don't think it's anything."

Stormcloud nuzzled her shoulder and Jayden stroked Stormcloud's soft nose and stared up at the stars. She still hadn't been able to talk to Ethan about her impending death. But she'd seen him with Chloe. Maybe her dying wouldn't hurt him so bad if he had Chloe there to comfort him. Sooner or later he'd find out how Chloe felt about him, anyway. Maybe she should just spur the process.

"What makes you so sad?" Stormcloud fluttered her wings.

"My heart is heavy from all we are up against."

Stormcloud pulsed a burst of calming emotion into her, and Jayden smiled. She stood and found Quinn sitting near the base of a tree, the book open in her lap and fire giving her light. With Stormcloud following, Jayden approached Quinn. The Whisperer's eyes were closed, and she looked more Jayden's age now. Wind played with strands of her hair. Jayden wasn't sure she should interrupt whatever Quinn was thinking about, but Quinn opened her eyes and smiled. "Can I help you?"

A weight lifted from Jayden's chest, and she sat beside Quinn. "What does the book say about me?"

"Much."

"When I met Anna, the previous Whisperer, she said the Creator always chooses the right Child."

Quinn didn't respond, just watched Jayden like a captivated listener.

Jayden pulled a stray blade of grass from the ground. "I'm not so sure."

"You don't think you're good enough?"

"I know I'm not. Look how many times I've messed up. And I'm not very strong. I mean, I can strike lightning, but everything has to be lined up right, and I can't do it more than once without resting." And she wasn't strong enough to lose more.

"You know the Mistress feeds on fear and doubt. If she sees yours, she will try and overcome you."

"Then maybe I shouldn't be here." Jayden stared at the ground. A tear spilled out of her eye, but it wasn't from sadness. She fisted a clump of grass, wanted to rip it from the ground and throw it. This was all too hard for her. She couldn't handle it. Everyone expected her to persevere through so much. To pick up the pieces and calm others' nerves and just keep fighting.

Everything she wanted to fight for—every*one* she wanted to fight for—what if they were better off without her mistakes?

Quinn placed a hand on Jayden's back. "I'm sorry you feel so alone."

Alone.

She didn't just feel alone. She *was* alone.

Quinn's hand warmed. "You don't have to carry it all by yourself. We're all here for you. We all have a part to play."

Sunlight bathed the horizon in red. "I'm not sure I can play my part."

Quinn grabbed Jayden's hands. Quinn's hazel eyes looked almost golden in the light. She smiled. "Me either."

"What? You have to. You . . ."

Quinn tilted her head to the side. "I'm scared, too. I'm terrified actually. Of hard things, like knowing which trees' voices to follow to get the right information. Of facing the woman who told those other women to torture me. And of things that seem silly. Like meeting the Wielder."

"The Wielder?"

She nodded. "He's supposed to be my betrothed. I—" Her smile faltered like someone trying not to cry. "I wonder if he'll love me. I see you and Ethan. The way you look at one another. Love one another. And I know that's how it's supposed to be, but I wonder . . ." She pulled up her sleeves to reveal her scarred arms. "I wonder what he'll think of me. If he'll see a Whisperer who lived too long away from others and isn't desirable."

"Oh, Quinn. You don't need to worry. If he doesn't see what the rest of us see, he's not worth it."

Quinn bowed her head and let her hair cover her expression. "I hope I'm doing this right. This Whisperer thing. But I know that it's my purpose. That I may want to doubt myself, but when I doubt myself, I doubt the Creator's purpose. I believe he knows better than I do."

"Why let us go through all of this then? Why not just keep the Mistress confined?"

"I don't think it was the Creator who let her free. I think there are people who have been trying to free her. Perhaps those who don't want to live in a world they can't control. They believe they can get the power and do a better job controlling it themselves."

"With the power."

"Yes."

Jayden sighed. Something about Quinn admitting that she felt inadequate made her more human. More like Jayden. Maybe she wasn't as alone as she thought after all. "That's why we should split the power between four of us? So one of us wouldn't control everything?"

Quinn tilted her head. "Do you want to control everything?"

Jayden looked up at the trees. Felt the breeze. Remembered Morgan's pain as she spoke of the burden of her talent. Jayden breathed the calm air. How could she choose who received what talent? How could she choose to decide which trees grew and which seeds failed? If she was supposed to save the world, she would. But not alone. She had others to help her. Serena. Ryan. Ethan. But also Quinn. And Connor—the Wielder who had helped her once.

"I guess I don't understand everything."

Quinn smiled. "Neither do I."

"But I know I have to do this."

"Do what?"

"Make sure my loved ones have their best chance of survival. Not just to survive, but to thrive."

Quinn squeezed her hand. "When doubt plagues your mind, just remember that."

"I'll try."

"Now rest."

Jayden squeezed back. "You, too."

As she returned to her bedroll, something in her stomach tightened, and the burn on the back of her shoulder seemed to echo it. It was a bite, wasn't it?

A scream split the night. Jayden jolted to a halt. *Another one?* That made seventeen. Melanie was the first to race to the afflicted person, and Jayden clutched her shirt right over her heart.

Ethan ran up to her, eyes wide. "Who is it?"

Jayden shook her head. "I don't know, but if Quinn doesn't find an antidote in that book soon, we're going to lose too many."

He squeezed her shoulder and she flinched. Immediately, his unease pierced her heart like a dagger. He narrowed his eyes. "What's wrong?"

Her eyelashes fluttered.

"Jayden?" His voice hardened.

"One of them scratched me." She pulled down her shirt to show him the mark on her shoulder blade. "It's—"

"You were bitten?" His eyes widened and he grabbed her hand. "We have to tell Logan."

"No. Scratched. And Logan knows." She resisted his pull. "I'm not having nightmares. I'm not screaming." She tugged him back to face her. "Besides, there's no cure yet. Quinn is searching."

He sighed and his breath shook. "You kept this from me?" He backed away from her, chest heaving as his hurt poured into her. "Why?"

"Ethan." She reached for him, but he dodged her touch. "I'm sorry. You had so much to worry about." Her chest squeezed. "I never should have kept this from you."

His emotions started to fade from her perception.

"Ethan! Don't shut me out. Please?" She inched closer to him, and he remained quiet, an incredulous look on his face. "It was wrong of me to hide this from you. I didn't want to burden you with—"

"Burden me?" He shook his head as if trying to understand. "If you don't trust me enough to let me help you carry your burdens—"

"I do!" She grabbed his hands, her knees unsteady. "I'm sorry. Never again."

He stood there, silent, but at least he was no longer trying to actively back away from her. "The moment Quinn finds—"

"You'll be the first person I tell." She looked into his eyes, pleading him to forgive her. "I'm sorry."

He pulled her into him and kissed her hair. Held her close. "I will not lose you to a nightmare."

No. He wouldn't. Jayden's heart clutched and she hugged him back, tighter. Hot tears spilled out. He wouldn't lose her until the snow fell. And she wouldn't be there to comfort him. Did she have to tell him that, too?

Logan lay staring up at the stars. Seven more had died tonight with no cure in sight. That was twenty-four total. Bekah's head rested on his chest, and he ran his fingers through her silky hair. No tents tonight. Tomorrow they moved closer to the palace.

His thoughts wouldn't stop churning on what Morgan had told him.

He heaved a sigh that put the memory away for the time being, and Bekah looked up at him. Her dark eyes searched his face. "You never slept well the night before battle."

"No, but at least you keep me from pacing all night."

She ran her fingers over his ear, his lips, as if memorizing every ridge of his face. "You're older, but you look the same. Have the same expressions."

"And a few more scars."

"Many more scars." She kissed him, long and gentle. "Don't leave me today."

He cupped her head in his hand. "Not today. Not ever. Not as long as you love me."

She cuddled her head onto his chest again. "Then not ever." A warm tear dripped onto his skin.

How many times had he said goodbye to her? During the Blood Moon wars, he'd said it every day. Not the word *goodbye* perhaps— never the word *goodbye*. But the words he'd chosen meant the same thing.

A shrill scream brought Bekah and him to standing. Logan raced out into the camp, searching for the next victim of the shadow wolves. Half the camp clambered to their feet. The scream sounded again, and this time Logan's breath caught. His chest hollowed. Jayden. That was her scream. He scanned the camp for her and found Ethan trying to calm her from thrashing. Stormcloud pressed her nose against Jayden, and Jayden shoved the pegasus away. Logan raced over to them, heartbeat erratic. This could not be happening.

"Nightmare." Logan spoke the admission he most feared.

Ethan looked up at him. He was trembling. "Yes, she—"

"Was bitten." Bekah's words came out in a whisper. She'd followed.

Jayden stood up, daggers in hand, and faced Ethan. He held his hands out, palms open. "Jayden—"

"Get back, monster." She swung her daggers, but he backed up in time.

"Everyone stay back!" Ethan's warning caused everyone to stop moving.

Everyone except Westwind. He raced toward Jayden. *"She has the rabid disease."*

"Westwind!"

"She sleepwalks. She needs to wake up."

"The dream is overcoming her." Quinn covered her mouth with her hands. She jumped in front of Ethan.

Too late.

Jayden swung her daggers.

Ethan pulled Quinn tight to him and whirled her away from Jayden.

The dagger bit into—into nothing. It stayed just above Ethan's back. Zephyr hovered in the air right behind Ethan, his wings beating furiously, creating some sort of shield that kept Jayden from reaching Ethan.

Then vines snaked across the ground and wrapped around Jayden's arm and pulled her hand back.

Logan grabbed Quinn and guided her to Bekah. "Quinn, did you send the vines?"

She nodded. "We have to wake her; it's a nightmare. I–I think the Mistress is using it to steal her mind."

"Keep everyone back." Ethan looked into Logan's eyes. He nodded.

Westwind chuffed and stepped forward. *"I'll not let her stay like this. I—"*

"You can come," Ethan said to Westwind.

Together they approached Jayden. Her eyes were glossed red.

"Jayden?"

"Let me go!" She screamed and pulled hard enough that the vine snapped. She lunged at Ethan, but he dodged her. She circled him, and

Westwind nipped her calf. She turned on him, but he was too quick to be struck.

"Oh no. One of them bit me." She touched her shoulder.

"She's reliving it." Quinn's voice trembled.

Logan's heart chilled.

"She doesn't have the black veins around her eyes," Quinn said. "There's still time to get through to her."

Ethan held out his hands as if to calm Jayden. "Jayden, you have to fight this. You have to wake up."

She snarled. "Don't talk to me, monster."

"It's me. It's Ethan."

She stopped. Her head tilted in an animalistic way that made Logan shiver.

"Hear me, Jayden." Ethan's voice seemed to reach her.

She shook her head. Her shoulders dropped and she lowered her weapon. "Ethan?"

"That's right." He took a step closer. "Wake up. Please."

Someone inched up beside Jayden, slightly behind Ethan on his left side. He encroached too close. Logan recognized him as one of the Dissenters. Likely he wanted to help, but didn't the kid realize how dangerous that would be? Logan reached out to his friend. *Westwind, get that kid out of there.*

"It's working."

"Not Ethan. The one behind—"

"I see him."

So did Jayden. "Look out! It's one of them!" She pushed Ethan aside and threw her dagger.

It thumped into the Dissenter's chest and he fell to the ground.

"No." Ethan tried to catch the falling person.

Logan's heart stalled. *Just a kid!* He raced toward Jayden to stop her from doing that again. Westwind jumped into her, paws slamming into her chest, and she fell to the earth, Westwind licking her face. Jayden shook her head. She sat there, looking stunned. Westwind backed up, whining. Her hands covered her face. Logan raced to her side and touched her shoulder.

"What have I done?" she breathed. "What have I—? Is he dead?"

Logan turned her away from the fallen Feravolk. "Jayden, you're safe now. Look at me."

She pushed against his chest, but her eyes were back. It was her. She clutched his shirt. "Is he dead?"

Ethan approached. "Hey, Jayden?"

"Don't." She pushed Logan away, hugged Westwind, and buried her face into his neck. He sat and wrapped a paw around her back.

Ethan sat with them. He looked up at Logan and nodded. Logan bowed his head. The kid was dead. And Jayden was compromised.

He touched Ethan's shoulder and made eye contact with Westwind. "Don't let her out of your sight. I will not let the Mistress succeed. And I will not let her rip you kids to shreds."

Quinn stood next to him shaking, Bekah beside her. "I know how to make the antidote. We need a plant called firemilk, and we need another called blue weed to fight the maelvargs."

Logan looked at Ethan. "Take Quinn and find them."

Hope filled Ethan's eyes. "Yes, sir."

CHAPTER 28

A FOOL'S FOLLY

Serena stared at Franco's satisfied smile, and her stomach squeezed so tight it hurt. A simple yes or no? He'd trapped her. Either she'd lie and be ripped of her bond with Dash—which would likely kill them both—or betray her blood oath with Kara and die.

Franco's eyes bored into her. "Answer, Healer. Did you heal my assassin? Yes or no?"

She shook. "Yes."

No pain from a bond ripping.

No death.

No lie.

On their journey here, Serena had cracked Kara's tough exterior. Kara had trusted her. So, yes, she'd begun to heal Kara's hardened heart. She breathed deep, shuddering breaths as if air could offer her strength. And relief shot through her like tiny pinpricks through her blood.

Dash's sigh filled Serena's mind. *"Close call, young one. Try and stay out of trouble, will you?"*

"How powerful are you?" Franco's eyes narrowed. "Have you heard that a tattooed Healer can regrow a limb if commanded?"

"It's not true, Serena!" Dash's voice grew frantic.

"It's not true, Your Majesty," Kara said.

Truth.

Serena's heart pounded. Tattooed. He couldn't know, could he? If—if he marked her, she'd be bound to follow his commands to heal whatever he commanded her to. Worse, she'd have to follow his commands if he told her *not* to heal someone.

She trembled. Her hands started to sweat. And she fought hard to remain calm. He couldn't know his threat held weight.

Franco cocked his head. "But it's so ceremonial. A tattoo, then chopping off her hand. As long as I command her not to heal until I place the severed limb back against her body, she'll remain wounded. Right?"

Kara narrowed her eyes and looked Serena over. "You can test a Healer's strength by wounding them to see how fast they heal, Your Majesty. This archaic practice you speak of has not been proven. Would you really risk losing your link with this Healer for that? Or draining her power so you have less life to suck out of her?"

Franco stepped toward her. "My, Kara, haven't you gotten smart? And a little outspoken for my taste." He turned to his guards. "Prepare the ceremony. I will tattoo this Healer. And I will test her power as I choose."

"Are you sure—"

He stuck his finger in Kara's face. "The Mistress will not stake claim on *my* Deliverer, do you understand?"

"Perfectly, Your Majesty."

"Good. I was getting worried that you were switching alliances."

"Never."

"It just so happens that I planned to tattoo Madison, but I think I'll use my potion on the lovely Serena instead." He turned his attention back to Serena and ran his hand along her jawline. She glared at him. "Your neck is so pretty. But lacking something." She pulled away from his touch. He gripped her face tight enough to hurt. "I will make you love me. But first, I'll mark you as mine."

"I'm coming, Serena!"

"Dash, no. You can't. I have to find a way out of this with Ryan." She glanced at Kara, pleading. Her heart quivering.

"I know how to test how fast she heals, Your Majesty." Belladonna's sickly sweet voice halted the guards coming toward her. She raised a whip with three ends. Serena shivered. What was embedded in the leathery ropes? She straightened. It didn't matter. The pain would be temporary, and she'd get out of this.

"Pet, carry her to the torture chamber." Belladonna jiggled her whip.

No hesitation slowed Ryan's steps. He neared Serena, scooped her up, and threw her over his shoulder.

"Ryan," she whispered.

No response.

"Hear me, please?"

Belladonna grabbed her face and dark eyes bored into her. "Don't talk to my pet."

She and Franco led the way out of the room, Ryan carrying her behind them. Madison, Kara, and the soldiers brought up the rear. The whole way down to the torture chambers, Serena's bound hands rubbed against Ryan's back. Ridges from scars covered him. She opened her talent to feel what had happened to him and wanted to scream. Belladonna had done this, and she would pay for it.

At last, the procession entered a dingy room that smelled of blood and waste.

"Is this where they tortured you?" she whispered.

His head flinched her way, then he ignored her again.

"I'm sorry they hurt you. I wish I'd come for you sooner, Ryan." Tears threatened.

"Pet, set her down here and put her hands into the manacles." A slow smirk stretched Belladonna's lips.

He set her down against the wall, and she stood there, not struggling for fear that Belladonna would punish him if he failed. Her heart ached. He loosened the ropes on her hands and grabbed her wrist. She curled her fingers around his hand, and he stilled for a beat, his grip lessening enough for her to slide her hand into his. Palm to palm, she gave him an encouraging squeeze. "Your name is Ryan. Not pet. You're no one's pet."

His gaze met hers. For a moment, the dead haze cleared and those eyes were his. Stormy eyes. And they permeated her soul.

"Ryan?"

The whip clinked together and he shuddered.

"Strap her in, pet." Belladonna growled.

He shook his head and blinked. Only hate and fear shone in his eyes now, and he strapped her in. Metal manacles restricted her movement. She was helpless to defend herself now. A lump in her throat choked her, and she wanted to scream.

Head bowed, Ryan backed away from her.

"Serena? What's happening?" Dash's voice cut into her, frantic.

She breathed in deep. *"Just stay put. Wait for the plan. Please."* Then she cut him out of her thoughts.

Belladonna's smiling face stepped into view, then she walked behind Serena and tore open the back of her shirt. The first lash hit. Serena held in a scream. Her body knitted together. Burning pain receded into cool, healed skin.

"Impressive." Franco chuckled. "Faster than even Madison. Will the tattoo stay?"

Belladonna looked into Serena's eyes and smirked. "We can find out. Do you have the potion?"

Serena's heart stalled. Her soul cried out like a scream at the bottom of a well. She was trapped. She belonged to no one. This unicorn would not be bridled. A fire lit inside of her, and she started to pull at her bound ankles and wrists. What were broken bones that would heal? Missing skin that would regrow? A small price to pay for her soul.

Franco dipped a long, metal stick into a jar of black liquid. *No!* He would not mark her for all eternity!

She screamed.

"Serena?" Dash's voice filled her mind. She tried to block her thoughts from him again. He couldn't save her from this. They'd only take him, too.

Belladonna held her head to the side, and Serena bucked against the chains. A huge man, wearing leather bands with spikes, smashed her into the stone wall. The shackles pulled her wrists, and her shoulders popped from their sockets. "Be still, sprite. Just a dab of bandy weed for you."

No!

He leaned too close and she bit his ear. Ripped.

He roared. "Stupid girl." Then his fist met her face and her vision wavered. Winked out.

She woke with a start and the harsh pain of a needle in her neck. Her heart fell to her stomach. Everything inside of her squeezed. "No!" She was unable to move. "No!" The word drew out in a tearful mourning. And it echoed in the depths of her soul.

Her will would no longer be hers.

And that would make her soul captive to the one who had placed his blood in with the black lion's in that cursed, spelled liquid.

"It's done. You're mine." Franco's breath heated her hair. The burn in her neck cooled. Healed. Sealed the ink into place. Her own talent had made her prisoner. She'd been marked.

Franco's voice grated. "And look, it's healing. Her powers are back."

The beefy man released her, and she fell to the ground.

"It's too late." Even in her thoughts her voice trembled.

"No." Dash's thoughts pulsed pain and agony into her. *"Why didn't you call me?"*

"They knocked me out."

"Now what?" His question felt hopeless at first. Then the fire inside of him ignited. The fire of hope. She could not lose hope.

She clenched her fists. *"Now I get Ryan and Madison, and I figure out how to kill Franco. Because no man will claim me, Dash. Not for long."*

"Good girl."

"Now." Franco rubbed his hands together. "Whip her again. I want to see how this works."

The jagged metal and rock scraped across her skin. Tore it open. Again. Another lash. Another. Again and again they whipped. And her cries echoed off the walls, pounding in her ears, louder and louder until Ryan's head popped up.

His gaze met hers, and she fought to keep from passing out. Another lash pelted her. Another scream.

"Stop healing yourself." Franco's voice cut through her cries.

Something steel seemed to push against her will. Unbreakable. It hurt to draw breath. The tattoo pulsed, and her body stopped healing. "No!" Tears escaped through her closed eyes.

"Now whip her again."

"Please!" The word escaped her mouth. Not for the pain. For mercy. He'd stolen her will to heal.

Another lash.

"Please." It came out as a strangled sob.

Another burning rip across her skin.

With each new cut, her will to heal suffocated. She could feel the hope draining from her. Dash began to kick against his stall.

"Again!"

"Stop!" The sound of a sword being unsheathed made her open her eyes.

Ryan stood in front of her, sword drawn against the king.

She sucked in a breath. He'd be killed. "Ryan!"

He didn't seem to hear her plea. He slashed, and his blade dragged across Franco's exposed chest.

Serena trembled, trying to support the weight of her own head.

Madison cried out and pressed her hands against her chest as Franco's wound healed. Ryan swung again, but Franco's guards sprang to face him.

"Stop. Please!" She begged him, but he wasn't hearing her.

He stabbed one guard through and clashed swords with the next. Men started to surround him. Too many. One stabbed Ryan through, and he fell to his knees. Another pressed a blade to his neck. Serena screamed.

"Stop!" Belladonna yelled. "If you kill him, the Mistress will strike you down where you stand."

The men halted. Ryan looked up from where he hunched over on the ground even as Belladonna pressed her hands against his wound and healed him.

Franco grabbed Serena's hair. "Heal yourself, witch."

Immediately her wounds closed. She spat in his face, and he smacked her. Ryan lunged from the ground, but the guards blocked him.

"Punish him, then put him in the dungeon." Franco turned to Serena. "Put them both in the dungeon." Then he grabbed Belladonna's collar. "Control your pet, or lose him."

Someone else's pain ripped into Serena's side, and she glanced at Kara, who fell to the ground, knife in her gut. Madison staggered away from her.

Franco snarled. "Heal her!"

Madison dropped to her knees and healed Kara.

"What happened?" Franco demanded.

Kara motioned to Madison. "Seems your Healer had a weapon. She stabbed me."

Lie. Serena could hardly breathe. Kara had set everything up. Serena's heart sped so fast she thought she'd never contain it.

"Put her in the dungeon, too." Franco stalked out of the room.

Now everything depended on trusting Kara.

CHAPTER 29

BLUE WEED

Ethan scanned the dismal patch of brown and gray ahead of them, Zephyr and Quinn walking near him. No blue weed in sight—they needed it in order to get through the Mistress's next level. They'd found the firemilk already and sent Zephyr to take it to Melanie. It *had* to work. Zephyr had already returned but had no news of Jayden's condition.

No trace of black veins around her eyes.

Hope shuddered within him, desperately trying to stay alive. A strange whooping laughter echoed over the breeze and made his insides clutch. The sound wanted to cut down his rising hope. He wouldn't let it.

Zephyr bristled next to him. *"They smell you."*

"The maelvargs," Quinn whispered.

"That's what we face in the next level?"

She nodded. "The blue weed keeps them away." She closed her eyes. "I see it. The trees are showing me. It's a slender plant with a long, blue tassel-like flower."

Ethan swallowed. He knew the trees were showing her what to get and where to look, but it took everything to keep from yelling at them to hurry up and give her the message already. "I thought you said the trees would—"

"Hush." Quinn's voice was calm, soft even, but Ethan turned around, ready to slam his fist into anything.

He wanted to know how Jayden was doing. Zephyr had said she appeared fine when he left, but that wasn't enough.

A twig snapped. Quinn spun around, pressing her back against his side and breathing rapidly.

He steadied her. "Hey, you okay?"

She nodded, but it wasn't convincing. The whooping laughter that they'd heard all day drew closer.

Ethan scanned, but saw nothing. "What do you know about these maelvargs?"

She trembled. "They're awful. Armored with spikes on their tails and horrible, sharp teeth."

"These aren't poisonous though, are they?" It seemed everything the Mistress created was.

"She poured poisoned blood into everything she created. Maelvargs' laughs are their poison. They'll look deep into your soul and laugh. If you let yourself stare at them, the laughter can paralyze you."

Great. He offered her a smile. "Stick close then, okay?"

She stared at him and her lips parted. Then her face turned soft in a way that reminded him of Kinsey. "Ethan, you would protect me."

"Of course."

Something about her smile looked older. "I wasn't asking." Her forehead wrinkled, and she stepped closer to him, taller than his chin. So she had grown. She tilted her head, and one corner of her mouth pulled down. "You shouldn't protect me, though. I should protect you."

He couldn't help but chuckle. "I'll protect you, Quinn. No matter what."

"Why would you say that?"

"Because I feel a pull of protection for you." He sighed. "One of my talents is to feel threats for those I love."

"Like family?" Her eyes rounded.

"Exactly. But associated with that is this . . . need to protect." Ethan shook his head. It was hard to put his talent into words. "I feel threats for Logan, you understand?"

She nodded.

He pointed to his chest. "But I don't feel an ache in my very core to protect him." Why was this so hard to say? "When I feel a threat for you, or Jayden, or Serena, or Ryan, I—I have to intervene or I think my heart would beat through my chest."

She touched his arm and her hazel eyes grew wide. "Even if it puts you in danger?"

"Yes."

"So you're telling me I have to stay out of harm's way or you could throw your life away for my sake?"

"I'm saying I would gladly give my life to keep you safe."

"Heavens, Ethan. The Creator must have given you this power for a reason, but I sure hope he gave you enough protection."

"What?" The word came out with a laugh.

She smiled. "You're a Deliverer with the heart of a Protector."

Ethan breathed deep. No response outside of acceptance was adequate. "I think it's time for you to learn a little about sparring. What do you say?"

"Whisperers don't fight, Ethan. We hedge and protect. We heal and grow. We're not supposed to kill. Her eyes met his, and, for the first time, he saw anger there.

"No one is supposed to kill, Quinn."

She glanced away from him. "Yet you do."

Her words broke the wall. The faces of all the men and women he'd killed tried to knock on the door of his being. Too often he brushed them into his peripheral vision. Sometimes he saw them. Dead. Dying. Crying out. A weight he wasn't willing to let crash down on him until this was done. Right now it wasn't done. He could handle it. It wouldn't break his resolve. But the way Quinn looked at him now, that wall started to dissolve.

What he'd done.

It would crush him.

He swallowed, pushing it all back. "I do." His voice cracked. "And I will continue to do so to keep those I love safe."

Her delicate hand touched him and stopped him from walking. "And I love you for it."

A lump caught in his throat as he looked at her. "You . . ."

"I didn't mean to hurt you, Ethan. That might be your path, but it isn't mine. Violence is not mine. I'm sorry it's a burden you must bear."

The air rushed out of his lungs, and he turned away from her, afraid that she might actually be able to see inside of him. Tears fought to form, and he breathed deep, forcing them away. "Me, too."

Her soft fingers brushed against his arm. "We are in the middle of a war. Your strength is the ability to see what others don't in a shard of a moment and make hard decisions out of love. I don't understand it, but I understand you. Your ability to take life or spare it is a strength I do not possess. And I am blessed to have you as my protector."

"She gets you." Zephyr's voice urged him to face Quinn again. He didn't expect to see her smile. He wanted to thank her for understanding him, for not seeing him as a monster. But instead of speaking, he expressed his gratitude with a returned smile. Then something on the ground behind her caught his attention as it rippled in the wind.

"Hey." He pointed to the small, fragile plant. "Isn't that blue weed?"

She spun around and crouched near the small, blue flower. "It is." Her smile was bright, but it faded. "There isn't enough."

"You can grow more."

"I don't know how."

He crouched next to her. "I watched a Whisperer do this once. She started humming and the plant grew until it seeded."

Quinn laced her fingers together and pressed them beneath her chin as she stared at the plant. "Call the life cycle to end to create more life. I have to kill it."

"Kill?" Ethan's voice sounded a bit dry.

"There are consequences for everything we do. Any of us. But you know that already." She looked at him, her eyes brimming with tears, and smiled. "You have to be willing to face them."

"Are you?" he asked, but the question seemed more for himself once he said it. All that life he'd taken. He would have to face it sooner or later.

She started humming, and the blue flower danced in a breeze he couldn't feel.

CHAPTER 30

PROPER PUNISHMENT

Another lash ripped across Ryan's back, and he whimpered, not enough strength left to even scream.

"That's enough." Butch's voice clamored through the ringing in Ryan's ears. Ringing from clamping his jaw so tight.

"It doesn't pay for what he did." Belladonna struck him again.

His vision darkened. He was so tired. No fight left in him. His eyes closed. Blood dripped from his mouth. Sweat from off his nose.

"You'll kill him. He's moments from death." Butch defending him. Now that was funny. If he wasn't so tired, he might actually joke about it.

"He betrayed me for that inferior Healer!" Belladonna's voice screeched.

Inferior Healer?

Serena.

He'd—heavens, where was she? The dungeon. How had he not recognized her the moment they brought her into the palace? How had he stood by and let them hurt her? He wanted to shake his clouded thoughts. Everything inside of him hurt.

You cannot die. That voice gripped him, and he sputtered awake. Was it his? Another lash brought tears to his eyes. *"You and I are bound now. You have to live."*

For her? Never.

But Serena was still in the dungeon. He couldn't leave her there. Not after what he'd let them do to her. That was something to live for.

The door slammed open, and Ryan didn't need to turn to know who ushered the cold air into the room. The Mistress was here. "If you kill my vessel to this land, I will rip your head off, place it back on your body, and rip it off again. Do you hear me?"

Belladonna set down the whip. "Yes, Mistress."

The shackles loosened, and Ryan fell to the ground. More pain shot through him, but he hurt too much to know from where.

"Now heal him . . . but not fully. I can't have him trying to escape."

"Yes, Mistress." Belladonna dropped to her knees beside him as the Mistress's presence left the room. Not his head. She never left his head.

"Pet?"

He tried to answer.

Belladonna pulled him onto her lap, and he whimpered like a dog. "What have I done?" she asked.

"You . . . whipped me."

"You made a mistake. You have to know that's why this happened. If you hadn't made such a terrible mistake, I wouldn't have had to hurt you."

He wanted to spit in her face, to tell her she was crazy, but her healing bled into him. Coursed over the ripped skin. Mended cracked ribs. Replenished his blood. And he gripped that feeling. Let it flow through him. He craved the healing. Needed it. He was her snared pet. "Thank you."

She smiled and leaned closer to him. That familiar taste of pears filled his mouth as she kissed him. And suddenly he never wanted to betray her again.

They tossed him into the dungeon. This cell was smaller and danker, and it carried the heavy scent of death. His back stung with every movement as he lowered himself to the straw and lay on his stomach. Why did she have to leave so many half-healed gashes? If he never had to move again, that would be all right.

"Ryan?" A small voice told him the cell across the room from his was occupied. White light glowed in a small sphere in the person's palm, lighting up her face.

He knew that face. She—a thunderous roar split his head.

"You don't want to know her. She is a Healer. You know what Healers

do to you. Don't you?" Smoke's voice was like a carriage across crushed gravel.

"*They heal.*"

"*They wound.*"

The dragon was right. And Ryan's blood burned. "*They take away my free will. They torture and tease and . . . hurt.*"

"*That's right. The Mistress won't do that to you. She won't make you her pet. She will make you her lover. Fire-bringer.*"

"*Fire?*"

"*You can control the fire, can't you?*"

His palms heated and flame burst in the center. Started the straw on fire. He tamped it out with his hand. Nothing singed him.

Smoke laughed. "*Be careful. That room is full of straw. You will light it on fire.*"

"Can you hear me, Ryan?" The girl across from him leaned closer to her cell bars.

"Why do you keep calling me that?" He sat up, slowly—unable to keep from groaning—and pressed his back against the cold wall. It stung first, then brought some relief.

"She doesn't heal you fully." The white light made a halo around her face. Her beautiful face. Did he know her?

"Too much healing would make me soft."

"I don't think those are your words."

He nodded. They weren't. Fitting. His thoughts weren't his own anymore—why would his words be?

"*Too many voices in your head, Fire-bringer?*" Smoke laughed.

"*Shut up.*"

"*You deny our bond.*"

"*I do.*"

"*You don't because I'm still here.*"

Ryan closed his eyes and pressed his palms against his head.

That sweet angelic voice asked, "What has she done to you? Ryan?"

"Stop calling me that!" As soon as he shouted, he regretted it. Not wanting to see her light anymore—or her sad, hurt, stupidly compassionate expression—he lay on his stomach, buried his face in his arms, and pretended to sleep.

"You should sleep," the Mistress purred.

Why? So she could fill his thoughts with dreams of how she wished to wed him. Her vessel? Was that what she'd called him? What in Soleden did that even mean? If he stayed awake, he could still be himself. Right?

Ryan.

Was that his name?

"Do you remember me, Ryan?" The girl's voice comforted him somehow, but he wouldn't answer.

"I don't think he remembers anyone, Serena." Another soft voice. How many of them were here?

He didn't peek. Didn't want to see more faces bathed in strange, pure light.

He wanted to stay in the darkness.

"What did she do to him?" the first sweet voice asked.

Serena.

"Belladonna broke him, spelled him, and made him bond with the Mistress's dragon. He belongs to the Mistress now."

No. He was no one's. He was a dragon in a lair.

Smoke's hissing chuckle filled his mind, and Ryan pushed the thoughts away. There was a side of his mind where he could be free of Smoke and the Mistress. It was just a difficult maze to find his way back there now.

"Do you feel that, Madison?" Serena asked. "He's using the good side of his heart. He's fighting them."

"I feel it, but half of his heart is hers," Madison answered.

Madison. He saw her face in his mind. He knew her.

Heavens, he knew both of them.

"Keep fighting, Ryan," Serena whispered.

"What should he fight for?" Madison asked.

"Hope. Don't ever lose hope. I came here to rescue you both."

Ryan laughed. "You're in a cell like us." He turned his head so he could see them.

The light still illuminated Serena's face, and something bright burned in her blue eyes. "I'm not here alone." She turned to Madison. "Your sister, Morgan, she sees the future?"

"Yes." Madison's voice seemed lighter.

Morgan. He recalled her, too. He sucked in a painful breath. He was supposed to free Madison, get some bloody key . . . and kiss Serena. Was it possible? Could he still fulfill his promise? He buried his thoughts so those sharing his head wouldn't find them. They still had to believe he was theirs.

"But Franco claimed you for his own. The tattoo. He'll feel your presence. How will you help us escape?" Madison asked.

Ryan popped his head up. Serena's light still illuminated her face. She ran a shaking hand over the tattoo. "If he can feel where I am, then I'll kill him. I won't let anyone control me like that."

"He won't let you kill him," Madison said.

Ryan swallowed. The thought of that man staking claim on Serena burned hotter than dragon's fire. "Then I'll do it."

Her startled look morphed into the most beautiful smile he'd ever seen. "You're back?"

Oh, how he wanted to be. But so much still clouded his thoughts. "Not totally."

"Cling to hope, Ryan. Cling to all that is good. It will help you fight them. *I* will help you fight them."

His heart ached for that to be true.

CHAPTER 31

SPLIT THE PACK

Ethan tossed another pitch-coated arrow into his quiver. A growl at his back sent a shiver down his spine. The maelvargs paced on the edge of their border, their spiked backs arched and drool clinging to their jowls.

Jayden wrapped a hand around his arm. "You ready?"

He faced her and pulled her in for a hug. "The firemilk is working?" He tried to keep the tremble from his voice, but it cracked anyway.

"Yes." She looked up at him, her eyes a beautiful blue that reminded him of the way the sky used to be. "It's better now." She pulled aside her collar and showed him the healing wound. It wasn't the same black, gaping wound as before. Melanie had said all the afflicted who had taken Quinn's cure were faring better, including Jayden. But Ethan still worried.

Her beautiful smile filled her face. "We'll be okay. You'll see."

He curled his fingers around her neck and rubbed his thumb over her jawline.

A tear spilled out of her eye, and she wrapped her arms around his shoulders. Pulled him in and kissed him. He held her, never wanting to let her go. Her body fit so perfectly against his, and her emotions filled him, supporting his fragile hope. He let her feel his fear, and she pulled him closer. Rested her head on his shoulder. "Hold on to hope?"

He kissed the top of her head and spoke through a smile. "Anything for you." He stepped back and waited for her to look into his eyes. "If anything like that happens to you again—"

"I'll tell you. I promise." Her eyes glistened. "I'm sorry I didn't."

"Hey, I forgive you."

She buried her head into his neck, and a tear dripped onto his skin. "Hey, don't cry. You—"

"I killed that boy," she whispered.

Ethan's heart stalled. He closed his eyes and hugged her. "That wasn't you."

"It was me."

"No. That was the Mistress's hand in this. She's trying to take over. We have to fight."

She stepped back, brushing tears from her eyes.

Ethan touched her cheek. He took in every detail of her face. "Just hang on to that hope you were talking about. Okay?" He rubbed his thumb over her skin. A lump in his throat tried to choke him. "Can you do that for me?"

"Anything for you." She sort of smiled.

Those words speared his heart and made him smile all at once. "We'll get through this. You'll see."

The maelvargs whooped. It was like a gurgling, taunting laughter. Ethan stilled the urge to pull out an arrow, light it, and start picking these things off. Problem was, they'd already done that, and all it had done was attract more monsters.

A threat throbbed in his very core, and he froze. He headed closer to where Logan stood with the others. "Logan?"

Logan's eyes widened. "It's about to expand?"

"Stop!" Quinn shouted. She fell to her knees and began to draw one of her maps. Westwind backed up and whined.

This was madness. They were going to walk farther into this maze while the Mistress gained power every moment? Ethan clenched his fists. His best bet would be to mount Zephyr and fly over the whole level. Leave everyone behind. Face Belladonna himself and kill her. Send Ryan and Serena back and wait for Zephyr to come back for him.

He backed up while everyone else kept their attention on Quinn. *Zephyr?*

Morgan grabbed Ethan's arm. She stared at him with her eyes wide. "Don't."

His heart clutched. "It's not like she wants me dead."

"Not yet. But after she uses you, the Mistress will kill you."

"Ethan!" Chloe marched in front of him. "Don't tell me you're thinking of going alone?"

The hurt in Jayden's round eyes cut through him like a knife in his heart.

"No! Jayden, I—" Ethan ripped his arm free of Morgan and glared at her.

"We have to move. Now!" Quinn buckled over and screamed.

"What's wrong with her?" Jayden grabbed Quinn.

"Zeph!" Ethan called and the gryphon bounded to him. He lifted Quinn onto Zephyr's back and looked at Jayden. Then he pointed to Quinn's map. "Look. This part of the level has bridged across our road. We have to get to the other side before these monsters realize their section expanded."

"It might be too late for that." Gavin pulled out a pitch-covered arrow and lit it. Blue flame from the blue weed ignited on the end, and Ethan dipped one of his arrows in the flame. "But it's a good plan. Go with them. Fly to the other side. We'll fight our way through."

"No." Ethan grabbed Chloe's arm and practically pushed her toward Zephyr. Quinn screamed again.

Chloe struggled. "Ethan, no! I'm—"

"Chloe." He gripped both of her arms and pleaded with her. "Take Quinn to the other side. Please."

"But you—"

"I'll take Stormcloud with Jayden. Go."

Tears filled her eyes and she glared at him, then nodded and climbed onto Zephyr. The gryphon took flight.

"Are you really coming with me?" Jayden asked.

"No. Melanie is a Protector. You'll need her over there."

"Ethan." Melanie looked offended.

"The kid's right," Logan said. "Go over and protect them. We don't know if this whole level will expand more."

Blue light pierced the dark. Maelvargs screamed, jumping back from the brightness. Feravolk began shooting arrows and racing through the dead land to find the other side where Quinn's map said they'd be safe.

"You all have to get moving." Melanie jumped onto the pegasus and held out her hand for Jayden. "If this will spur you to safety faster, so be it." The pegasus took flight, and a burning wave raced across Ethan's chest. He looked out to where the Feravolk raced through and maelvargs collided with them in battle.

The whooping laughs turned darker.

Men and women screamed, and Ethan knew what Quinn said was true. The laughter was paralyzing them. "Don't let them look at you!" he shouted to remind them but doubted his words made it to anyone's ears over the laughter and screams.

Maelvargs filtered into the crowd. Their yellow teeth tore into flesh. Spiked tails flailed behind them, stabbing into people as they ran. Ethan pulled back on his bowstring and breathed out. A fiery arrow sailed toward one of the beasts, hitting it in the eye. It screeched.

But the threat warning him was more than that. Quinn. Something had happened to Quinn.

He looked up to see her plummeting through the air, Zephyr fast on her trail.

Ethan pulled out his sword. Logan's strong grip on his arm stopped him.

He stood there, the threat warning him and the look of love and confusion in Logan's eyes detaining him. What was he supposed to do? Stay because it was Logan's job to protect him, or listen to his talent? He pulled his arm free. "I'm sorry. I have to do this."

"Ethan?" The pain in Logan's voice speared him, but he ran toward the center of the bridge, flaming arrow in one hand and blade in the other. Logan, Gavin, and Rebekah ran with him, but he turned on his speed. As Zephyr caught Quinn, a maelvarg jumped and grabbed her dress.

Everything seemed to still while her scream touched his ear. He ran, the creatures moving back from him. Surrounding him and cutting off his way out, as if they wanted to lead him through. Send him straight to the Mistress. He drove his blade into one of the beasts that got too close.

Another lunged, and he chopped into its skull. It fell.

Ahead, Zephyr's wings beat the air, and he clawed at the spiked creatures.

Chloe dove off his back and into the center of three of the creatures.

Ethan screamed and called on more speed. Zephyr dove in where Chloe had gone and came up higher with Quinn limp in his claws. Ethan's stomach dropped. He—he'd hesitated.

"She's alive," Zephyr said.

Ethan waved his arm. *"Take her. Go! Get her safe."*

"But Chloe!"

"I feel her."

"I'll be back for you."

Zephyr's talons punctured another of the beasts, and his hind quarters kicked a third away as he flew higher with Quinn.

Ethan barreled through the creatures surrounding Chloe. She held out her dying blue flame and slashed at their faces. Running as fast as possible, he headed toward the threat. Growls rung up around him. Heavy paws slapped against the dry ground. The threat in his chest burned, and a maelvarg jumped at Chloe from behind. Her scream echoed in his ears. Another landed on top of her. It laughed. She froze. Ethan slid to her, chopping his sword in between the eyes of the creature standing above his sister. It fell, dead.

Heaving, he turned and sliced into another. Blood, black and wet, dripped off his blade.

"Chloe?" Scarlet darkened her clothes. Ethan tried to get her to stand. The creatures hissed at him. Laughed. The sound wrapped around his thoughts. He shook his head and closed his eyes. Free of its spell, he opened his eyes and picked up Chloe. She cried out as he lifted her. "How bad are you hurt?"

Growls vibrated the ground. Glowing green eyes surrounded them. They would herd him to her.

Chloe pushed his shoulder. "Why did you come for me?"

"I have to protect you, I have no choice."

Shouts echoed behind him. Logan, Gavin, and Rebekah raced toward him, killing creatures in their wake. Rebekah stalled for a moment, and Logan killed the beast that had paralyzed her. She shook her head and started moving again.

Whooping laughter drew closer as the circle tightened. Then shrieks filled the air and a couple maelvargs flew, like ragdolls, into the sky. *"This is your friendly rescue service."*

Claws wrapped around Chloe, and Ethan relinquished her to Zephyr. He jumped onto his friend's back and grabbed feathers. Sticky liquid gushed between his fingers. *"Zeph?"*

"I'm all right. And I heal fast."

Zephyr landed on the other side of the borderlands, gently setting Chloe on the ground. Ethan slid off his friend's back. *"Thank you for—"*

"Always."

Finally, the last of them made it through. They'd lost so many. And after the wounded were cared for, Logan walked up to Ethan, with Melanie, Gavin, and Rebekah in his wake. "Why won't you let us protect you?"

Ethan bowed his head, and Logan's question rang in his ear and weighted his heart. It was time. No more getting around it. He lifted his head and looked into Logan's—his father's—eyes. The love there stunned him. "I have to protect them." He explained his talent. His curse. Whatever it was. Gavin rocked back on his heels. Melanie pressed her hand over her heart. Rebekah touched his shoulder.

And Logan's head bowed as he expelled a breath. "Ethan, I wish you'd told me sooner."

He looked up at all of them. This wasn't the disciplinary action he'd expected. He'd thought they'd try to hold him back. Forbid him from running recklessly into danger.

"Son." Logan touched Ethan's other shoulder. "We could have helped you."

"We trust you," Melanie smiled.

Rebekah rubbed his back. "Your talent. It's yours for a reason."

"You're not alone," Logan said. "Let us help you."

Ethan swallowed the rising lump in his throat.

Gavin leaned his arm on Logan's shoulder. "You're a lot like this one." He winked. "But we love you, kid. We'll listen."

"Thank you," Ethan managed.

Rebekah tipped her chin at someone behind him, and Ethan turned to see Morgan.

"Chloe and Quinn are both settled in the healing quarters. They're with Jayden. And they're asking for you," Morgan said, but she walked past Ethan as if asking to talk to Logan.

He glanced at Logan who nodded, so he raced to see his friends. Zephyr's sharp thought stopped him. *"Did you hear her?"*

"No."

"Morgan. She told Logan that her powers seem to be weakening."

"What does that mean?"

"It means she can't see very far into the future anymore."

Ethan's chest squeezed. That meant one thing. They needed to stop the Mistress.

By the time he reached the bedrolls set up for the injured, Chloe and Quinn were both asleep. And Jayden had fallen asleep with Quinn cuddled up to her.

He sat down and leaned his back against one of the few trees that didn't look sick. It was situated next to Chloe's bedroll. Aurora settled next to her, and her shivering stopped.

They'd lost thirty-two today.

Quinn had suffered a bump to the head and a few minor scratches. Otherwise she was going to be fine.

Chloe slept, too. That creature's huge jaws had ripped the skin from her back and chest clean to her shoulder. He could have lost her.

Between Jayden, Quinn, and Chloe, he was stretched too thin. There was no way he could protect all of them. And Belladonna was tracking him. She had to be telling the Mistress where to send these animals. Could he really trust the Protectors to let him do what his talent called for? It was settled; he had to figure out how to sneak away and face that woman himself.

Chloe's eyelids fluttered and she opened them. She moved and grimaced.

"Hey." He wasn't sure where to touch her. "What do you need?"

"You're still here?"

"We haven't rescued Ryan yet, so you're stuck with me." He smiled at her normal biting comments.

She chuckled. Then she tried to sit up and hissed.

"Chloe, just tell me what you need."

"I need to sit up, Ethan Branor." She slunk back onto her bedroll. Not without another grimace.

"What happened to sitting up?"

She shot him a glare. "It's not as comfortable as I thought it would be." She moved the bandage aside and winced.

"Chloe—"

"Does this look all right?"

Ethan leaned closer, trying not to block the soft glow of blue firelight.

She pulled away from him. Her eyes grew huge. "Is it supposed to turn black?"

His heart jumped into his throat. *No.* "Black? Chloe, let me—"

She pulled her blanket up to her mouth and giggled.

Ethan slumped against the tree he'd been leaning on and let out a shaky breath. "Chloe Marie Granden, I—" He breathed again, still shaking, and nervous laughter escaped him. "Snare you." He laughed a little more.

She pushed against his arm. "You should have seen your face."

He shook his head. "Don't you ever do that again."

"I thought your heart stopped beating." She smiled. When was the last time he'd seen her smile?

"*I* thought my heart stopped beating." He took another deep breath. It still came out shaky.

She touched his arm. "I really scared you."

"Of course you did. Don't you remember the black hole in Ryan's chest?"

"I suppose I should have said green." She smirked.

He rolled his eyes. "You feel okay?"

"Thanks to you."

Thanks to him? No. If he'd been doing his job instead of hesitating, he could have spared her injury altogether. His forehead hit his arms. "It's my fault you got hurt."

She touched him. "Hardly. You—you saved my life."

"Zephyr saved your life."

"That gryphon would have been bringing back a dead body if not for you."

He shrugged her hand off his back.

"Ethan, those things were everywhere, there was no way you could have—"

"You need some water?"

"What?"

"I'm asking you if you need a drink."

"No, you're blaming yourself for something that isn't your fault. You did what your gut told you. Looking back is always clearer. That's what my father—well, our father—always said."

Our father? "All right. You're welcome."

She smiled. "You can say that after I thank you for that drink."

"Right." He passed her his waterskin. Her eyelids were already drooping when she handed it back to him. He covered her up, and she drifted back to sleep. Chloe was such a conundrum. He rested his head against the tree, feeling Belladonna's slight tug, testing. Telling herself where he was. How close. He couldn't stay with them any longer.

Jayden stirred. She positioned Quinn and slipped away from her, approaching Ethan. His heart already felt lighter.

She smiled and sat next to him. "You can't stay up all night with her. It's Gavin's watch." She rested her head on his shoulder. Did she know how much he needed that?

"I just think someone should sit here with her."

"I will."

"You will?"

Jayden nodded. "Get some rest." She patted his chest and waved him away.

"Can't I stay here?"

Worry rounded those beautiful blue eyes. "I know you don't want to leave Chloe, but you really should sleep."

"Chloe will be fine."

Her eyebrows scrunched together. "I thought—"

"Don't act like I don't care." He chuckled at the confusion in her eyes. "I want to stay with you." He ran his finger along her soft cheek. "Is that so strange?"

"You need sleep."

Didn't she want him there? His heart did a strange flip, and he pulled his hand back. "You're pushing me away?"

She stared at him a heartbeat too long without answering.

"Jayden?"

"No, Ethan, I never want you to leave." She touched his arm, the worry in her gaze no less intense. "Just promise me you'll take care of yourself?"

"I promise." He slid down and rested his head on her lap. "This okay?"

"Of course." She ran her fingers through his hair, and he closed his eyes.

CHAPTER 32

UNLEASHED

Connor crawled back through the palace tunnels and dressed. Even though he'd just released some, his power still ate at his insides. He'd need to find a way to unleash more of it than he'd been doing.

But more power meant more casualties.

More life lost.

He sighed and pushed himself up through the trap door inside the smithy.

"There you are!" Luc grabbed Connor's arms. "Madison is in the dungeon."

"What?"

"Kara is back. She brought some Healer with her, and when Franco tried to hurt her, Ryan went nuts. He killed a bunch of soldiers before Belladonna could get him back under control."

"Where is he?"

"They're all in the dungeon. Madison, Ryan, and that other Healer. The Mistress called her a Deliverer, too."

"How do you know all of this?"

Luc shrugged. "I have ears, Connor."

Connor swiped his hand through his hair. "I have to get her out."

"What can I do?"

"You can make a key for me." Kara's voice drifted into the smithy ahead of her. "And you can stop talking so loudly." She glanced at Connor. "Wolf. I'm surprised you didn't hear me coming."

Connor fisted his hands. "I'm not helping you, Kara."

"I think you will. I can show you Thea's note to me, but there are parts you really shouldn't see. What with your compassionate heart and all."

"Tell me what you want me to know."

She crossed her arms and leaned against the wall, her smug smile lighting her face. "Wolfy—"

"Don't."

She laughed and pushed off the wall, striding closer to him. "Walk with me."

Connor glanced at Luc, who gave a slight nod and rolled his eyes at Kara. "I swear. The whole palace thinks the two of you are lovers."

"Is that a bad thing?" Kara shrugged.

Connor narrowed his eyes. "I don't believe you have a heart, Kara."

"Oh, Wolf, even I don't have to be a Healer to sense that lie. What's worse: having no heart or not using the one you have?"

He searched her face. Something about her *had* changed. "And do you believe you have a heart, Kara?"

Her lips puckered in a smirk. She held out her arm and he linked their elbows together.

He pulled her close so he could whisper, "If you betray me, you'll regret it."

"I know."

That surprised him. Maybe it shouldn't. "Tell me about this key."

She filled him in as they walked, arm in arm, around the palace grounds. Serena was a Deliverer, and the way to save Ryan from Belladonna and rescue the black blood soldiers from Franco could be found in some hidden counters book. Some book likely only Serena could find because of her Healer powers.

It all hinged on the key Franco wore around his neck.

"How do you plan to get the key?" he asked.

"I have an idea. Belladonna will likely want a stronger potion to give to her 'pet.' Really, she couldn't think of a better nickname?"

Connor paused, his stomach hardening. "Ryan was the one she made a potion for?"

Kara narrowed her eyes. "It makes him think he loves her. But she's looking to make one that's more permanent. She'll want access to the spells chamber. I will simply return the key to Franco for her. Getting the prison key is easy. I already have one of those."

"How much time will I have?"

"A few days. Then it gets tricky. The spell Belladonna plans to use will make Charmer fall in love with her permanently. I need someone to be in his cell." She handed him the prison key.

"Belladonna is aware of what Ryan looks like. How—"

"Thea knew what you're capable of, Wolf. You have to pretend to be Charmer. Then don't let Belladonna spell you."

Right. Because that sounded easy. "What do I do with Ryan?"

"That's up to you." She tapped his fisted palm with the key inside.

"You call that easy?"

"No. You'll actually have to escape, get the stupid counters book, and break Charmer's bond with Smoke. Oh, and Franco will be able to track Serena, so there's that. I hope that army of yours is ready."

Connor swallowed. Did she know everything? He glanced at the ring he wore. The fake one. Luc wore the real one, and he'd ordered the army to follow Connor's instructions. If Connor had to call the army into action to get them out, he would. As long as he didn't have to use his powers yet. "And you're just going to leave us to do this alone?"

"My part isn't with you. After Luc makes the impression of the key and slips it back to me, you're on your own. I'm the enemy, remember?"

He glanced around at the soldiers sparring in the courtyard and then lifted their linked elbows. "You haven't really made that easy to believe."

"You mean easy enough to kill me so you can defeat the king? That's treasonous, Connor."

He drew in a quick breath. *She does know everything.* "That's not—I actually have an idea about that, which doesn't involve killing you . . . permanently."

"Oh, now who's making it difficult to believe I'm the enemy?" She chuckled. "Don't worry. I've always wanted to do this." She slapped the side of his face and jerked away from him. "How dare you!" She whirled away from him and stormed off while he rubbed his cheek.

She'd better tell him when Belladonna was making this potion.

CHAPTER 33

TAINTED

Connor crept on all fours through the secret tunnel to the spells chamber. The note Kara had left on his bed told him to meet her here. He could only imagine the rumors that would be spreading after the maid tidied his room.

The scent of pears and lavender told him Belladonna approached. Two other sets of footsteps echoed down the tunnel with hers. One quiet enough to be Kara. Who was the other? He changed into a mouse. Feeling cramped in the small frame, he knew that he could only hold it for a short time. Belladonna and one of the kitchen cooks ignored him as Belladonna placed the key into the door. Kara, however, glanced over her shoulder and winked. Connor ducked into a small crevice in the wall, suddenly feeling sick. Why would they need a kitchen maid?

The three women entered the spell chamber, but Connor remained outside, shaking his body and changing back into his wolf form. Ears twitching, he waited.

"How long will it take to simmer?" Kara asked, sounding bored.

"A day," Belladonna said.

Kara's laugh was sly. "Soon, he'll be yours."

"Your reward comes from me once the Mistress is defeated."

"When do you leave to collect the other Deliverer? What's her name? Jayden?"

Belladonna practically purred. "That young man who protects her draws closer—I can feel it in the bond I placed inside of him.

But the Mistress seems to think one of her shadow wolves has taken Jayden's mind captive. She has sent her monsters to collect her. I can only hope the young man stays with her. I'll follow his bond and claim the Deliverer before the Mistress has a chance. Then I'll hand Jayden over, like a good little servant, as soon as I get my venom inside of her. We almost have all of them."

Connor rocked back on his haunches. The game Kara played seemed much too dangerous for an ordinary assassin. What was she up to? And did Belladonna really think she could beat the Mistress and Franco to the Creator's power?

"Are you going to let me get the ingredients for my spell, too?" Kara asked.

"The one that will make the Mistress's army turn against her? Turn to me?"

Silence. Connor leaned closer. A chain rattled.

"Very well," Belladonna said. "If Franco doesn't get this key back—"

"I know, I know, you'll kill me. Then him."

"Don't laugh. I know you didn't bind Serena to him."

"I thought you'd like it better that way." Kara's smile was evident in her voice.

Oh. She was good. She knew how to play all her cards. Connor swallowed hard. Kara was certainly playing him, too. At least he suspected it. Belladonna chuckled, but the gurgled scream of a woman drowned it out. The scream cut short. A thump followed. Connor cringed and a shiver made all his fur stand on end. His heart seemed to crumble in his chest. They'd killed her?

"I'll take care of this." Kara dragged the cook's body out into the hall. Then she handed Connor a clay mold of the key. "Don't smash it," she whispered.

He took the mold gently in his teeth, glanced into the cook's lifeless face, and stifled a whine. Kara cocked an eyebrow and motioned for him to flee. He did. But he'd never forget the cook's empty eyes. Even when he didn't use his power, death followed him.

That night, a vision of Madison in a prison, chained beside Serena startled him from sleep every time he closed his eyes. He had to get that key and impersonate Ryan before Belladonna took her spell to him. And he had to stash Ryan somewhere in the meantime. He had the perfect plan. Luc would drag a knocked-out Ryan to the infirmary. Then bring him back.

A zap sizzled through his veins. The power.

It begged to be set free.

Connor gritted his teeth and focused on breathing. He'd have to keep it contained for a little while longer. Just until he played his part this morning. And the Deliverers got free. Then he'd help them the best he could from afar.

Heat.

Skin.

Heat.

Fur.

He had to hang on to himself, as a man. He sucked in a breath. Let it out slow. Slower. Sunlight slit the horizon and he glanced in his mirror. Red eyes stared back. Why today? Why now? Gold returned, slowly, but the hint of red remained.

Daily, his eyes looked more and more like heated gold.

Hopefully he could keep his power contained for a few more hours at least. He dressed in black slacks and a white shirt—just like the king's guard and Belladonna's men—and headed toward the smithy.

He stopped just outside and listened. A strangled plea leaked through the walls. "I don't know what you're talking about." Luc's voice broke through the walls, strained.

"Not good enough. The key!" A gruff voice followed.

Heat spread through Connor's veins. Burned.

"I—" A strangled cry cut off the rest of Luc's sentence.

Connor burst through the door. Two soldiers held Luc down while a third waved a hot branding iron in the air. A threat. To his friend? Not on his watch.

Connor narrowed his eyes. "What are you doing?"

"None of your business. Back away." The soldier nodded toward the door.

Power pulsed in Connor's fingertips. He gritted his teeth.

The solider raised his eyebrows. "Are you leaving, or did you want a turn?" He brandished the hot iron.

Connor clenched his fists and backed out the door. His powers heated inside him, but he didn't need them to free Luc. All he had to do was draw his sword or grab one of the branding irons. The blacksmith's shop was full of weapons. He'd seen where the men stood, where Luc was. He could take them. There was a branding iron right by the door.

"The king saw clay on the key. Now give me the key you made." The soldier's voice had become harsher.

"Fine. Here. Take it," Luc said.

"No," Connor whispered. Now what? Maybe he'd made two. Luc was resourceful.

"I knew you could be reasonable." The soldier chuckled. "Now. Kill him."

Connor slammed the door open and reached for the branding iron stick, but it would be too late. They already held the hot iron near Luc's face.

Heat exploded though Connor in a rush that zapped through every vein. The room swirled with the force of a destructive storm, and Connor pushed his hands against the currents. His power shot forward. Burned inside of him. Blasted out in a wave of heat. Death. Destruction.

The smithy exploded.

The walls blew apart.

Fire scorched the wood.

Screams resounded.

As the debris flew, Connor looked at his palms. What had come over him?

The dust cleared, and Luc stood up. Next to him on the ground lay the three soldiers. Impaled with shards of wood from the walls. Burned with hot coals. The branding iron leaned against the shoulder of one of the dead men. Where the smithy once stood was a barren spot of dusty dirt. All that remained was Luc's chair and the secret trap door it rested atop.

Gone.

Connor stood there, staring at his hands. *No.* He'd used his power.

His knees weakened. He hadn't meant to. Luc rushed up to him as Connor started to stumble.

"Connor?"

He backed away from Luc. Their friendship had sparked this. This was exactly why Wielders needed to work alone.

Cold and consuming, a voice entered his mind. *Wielder.*

It wasn't a question. The Mistress knew he was here.

CHAPTER 34

WELCOME, WIELDER

The cold night air rushed against Connor's face and whipped through his clothes as he rode Cliffdiver through the air. He had to get to Rebekah and her Feravolk camp if he was to tell Logan how to defeat the Mistress.

And he had to make it back before she realized her Wielder was missing.

No. Not *her* Wielder. He'd never be hers.

He shook his head clear of those thoughts, and Cliffdiver turned his white, feathered head and looked at him. *"Master, are you all right?"*

"Please, don't call me master, friend." Connor sighed and looked at his hands, feeling the weight of what he'd unleashed. "I fear I've ruined everything by letting these powers take hold of me."

Cliffdiver flew faster. *"We can only hope there's still time then."*

Not long after, Connor spotted the place his bond had led him to. It was easy to see the Mistress's levels from up here, and all the damage her fiery, poisonous creatures from the abyss had created. Just hours south of the palace, nestled in a safe spot between the maze of the levels, animals gathered near men. The Feravolk. And an eagle flew up beside him.

"Wielder?" the eagle said.

"What's your name?"

"Glider."

"You are bonded?"

"Yes," the eagle said.

"Do you know Logan?"

"He is a friend of mine."

"Good. Please tell him the Wielder wishes to speak to him."

Glider sped off ahead, and Connor breathed in, trying to prepare himself for this moment. "Take us down." Connor pointed.

Tattered and bruised Feravolk men and women moved out of the way as Cliffdiver descended.

Connor jumped off the gryphon's back and caught sight of Rebekah running to greet him. She threw her arms around him, and he hugged her back. "I missed you, Mother."

She touched his cheeks and looked into his eyes. Though hers shimmered with unshed tears, they were more vibrant than he'd ever seen.

"Welcome, Wielder." A man with piercing blue eyes and longer, dark hair extended a hand for Connor to shake.

Connor recognized him. "Logan."

"Please, come to my tent."

Connor stopped and dropped to his knee as two wolves approached him. They were like all the animals who came to him. Apprehensive yet in awe.

"You are the Wielder." The female wolf spoke. She approached more readily and seemed to want to lick his face as if he were a pup.

"Aurora?"

"You know me?" Her tail rose and brushed from one side to the other.

He turned to the other wolf. "You must be Westwind. I've heard so much about both of you."

Westwind lowered his head in a bow.

Connor touched the wolf's shoulder. "Do not bow to me, friend. We are all in this together."

Connor looked up to see so many animals clustering closer. Bowing in reverence. "Friends, I am honored to fight with you." He turned his attention to Logan who regarded him, then motioned for Connor to follow.

Rebekah wrapped her arm around him, and they walked to the only tent in the whole camp. Logan motioned to four people Connor's age and introduced him. Ethan and Jayden. The other two Deliverers. He'd already met Ethan. Jayden studied him.

Then Logan motioned to Morgan. She looked so like Madison.

Connor's heartbeat sped as soon as he saw Quinn. She looked so much older. He'd never seen someone so beautiful. Her eyes were the same. Ageless. Young and innocent as well as wise and weathered.

Ethan was the first to offer a handshake. He pulled Connor closer and slapped his back. "Good to see you."

Connor smiled. "You, too."

Morgan inclined her head in a greeting as did Jayden.

Quinn stared at him, her hazel eyes wide. "You have the same eyes."

He shivered. He could not let her touch him and complete the circle of his power. He was not prepared for that.

Connor caught Jayden staring at him. Her kind, blue eyes seemed to search him. He gravitated closer to her and held out his hand. "May I?"

She put her hand in his palm.

He kissed the back in a proper greeting, but that wasn't the purpose. She was powerful. "You can read my emotions?"

Her eyes widened slightly and she nodded. "You're scared. Resisting something. Hesitant. You can trust us."

He released her hand. "I do."

She smiled. "How did you know what I could do?"

He shrugged. "Wielder."

Connor stared into her eyes. Surely the Creator wanted him to have a pack—a family. But in the presence of all of them, his power still churned inside of him. Brewed like a storm. Would he be able to contain it? Right now all he wanted was to protect everyone in this tent with his life. That meant he'd never stop searching until he found another way. That meant he'd need to see if Quinn had the Whisperer's book and find out what she knew.

The answers to his questions, hopefully.

In his short time here, he needed to learn everything she had to teach him. He didn't realize he'd turned his attention from Jayden to Quinn until he saw her return the tentative gaze. She smiled, and it was so sweet and innocent. Just like a Whisperer should be.

Logan sat on the ground and everyone joined him. He looked right at Connor. "What can you tell us about this Black Blood Army? What do we need to know to stop the Mistress forever now that the door to her prison has been sealed?"

Connor's heart clenched. So it was true.

There was one way.

Opening the door of death.

He could do it.

And everyone would die.

Connor nodded to Quinn across the circle they'd formed. "Quinn, would you please relay for them what the Mistress's powers are and how she'll use them?"

Her eyes popped open. "Should I know this?"

"Isn't it in your book? Do you have the book?"

"Yes. I haven't been able to read all of it yet. It's too dark for me to stomach sometimes."

His heart practically sank and jolted at the same time. *How could she not know?* "Too dark? Quinn, we need the information in that book. You're the only one who can talk to the trees. We need their memories if we're to defeat her." If Quinn knew of no other way to put the Mistress away, what choice would he have left? "You have to read it. Fast. Otherwise we're losing precious time."

Her eyelids fluttered and she opened the book. "Some pages are locked because Ryan, the last Deliverer, has not touched it yet."

"I can help you get Ryan. But you have to read the parts available to you."

"How is he?" Ethan's eyes held desperation.

Connor's chest seemed quiet. "He's . . . it's a good thing Serena showed up when she did."

"Serena made it?" Jayden asked.

Connor nodded. "I will help her and Kara free Ryan." He turned to Morgan, noticing her clasped hands. "And Madison."

"Thank you," Morgan said.

Wind fluttered through the tent, and Quinn's hair whipped around her. She hunched over the book and read.

Connor watched her for a heartbeat, then turned to Logan. "I have the ability to open the door of death. If I can use my powers to open the door, the Mistress can be thrown into the afterworld—as long as she's overpowered. First, I needed to touch all the Deliverers." He glanced at Jayden. "I only have Serena and Ryan left, but I'll get to them soon. Then I'll assess what all of your powers are and have an idea of what we can do to stop her."

"But only you can open this door?" Logan asked.

"No. The Mistress can open it as well. I imagine she's given the same power to Gnarg and Garmr." Because she wanted them to be like him. Because she was obsessed with the Wielder. "If the Mistress gets her hands on the Creator's power and makes it her own, it'll be impossible for us to get her through the door. We should move now. While she's still weak."

"So the four Deliverers need to obtain the Creator's power to be strong enough to push her through the door?" Logan asked.

Connor nodded. "I'm sure you've heard the prophecies? A sorceress will come with power to destroy all the Creator has built. She'll break the land and the people's hearts and bring death to those who'd oppose her. But hope will be found when the Deliverers rise through fire, through ash, and heal the heart of the land.

"Through blazing fire and torrent of rain, the Forest shall fall and rise again. Those who will deliver the land will summon the Creator's power. They will work as one, each having different talents: the heart of one, mind of another, the soul of one, and strength of her brother."

"I've heard most of it." Logan nodded. "Some seems cryptic."

"Basically, the Mistress is looking to control the Deliverers. She wants to control one's heart, one's mind, one's soul, and one's strength. She believes once she has all of that, she will be able to use the keys to unlock the power."

"Good. How do they obtain the power, and where are the thrones and these keys?"

Connor nodded to Quinn. "She should have those answers in her book. There's one more thing." He winced. "The Mistress needs a vessel in order to survive here."

Logan narrowed his eyes.

"She's chosen Ryan. And claimed part of his heart."

Jayden gasped. "Tell me we don't have to kill Ryan."

"No. But the Mistress has a hold on his heart. If Ryan were to die, she'd simply put her heart back inside Smoke until it's time for a new vessel. When it's inside Smoke, she has to remain dormant, but the dragon will keep living. She needs a human vessel to be alive here. She'll just find another."

Ethan breathed deep. "So we have to kill Smoke first?"

Connor looked right at him. "Yes. And if the Mistress taints more than half of Ryan's, when she dies, he will die."

"Then we need to get him out now." Jayden's voice wavered.

"I'm working on that," Connor said. "Tomorrow, with Serena, Kara, and Madison's help, we will free Ryan and bring him back."

"Then we kill the Mistress." Ethan said, his jaw tight.

"Yes."

"What do you need?" Logan asked.

Connor breathed deep and looked to Morgan. "Your powers, are they weakening?"

"Daily."

"Will you tell me what you know?"

"I can't see the battle. But you have an army?"

He nodded. "I know how to kill Franco. And the four of you together will kill the Mistress. I need you to be at the castle's east side in two days."

Logan nodded. "We will be."

"No." Morgan looked at Logan. "You will retreat. Soon. The Deliverers will go on ahead."

Logan's eyebrows pulled together.

"If you take your Feravolk fighters, every single one of them will die."

Connor's heart clutched. So it was true. He would use his power, and they would all die.

Quinn screamed.

Jayden rushed to her side first, but Quinn shook her head. "I have to keep reading."

"She's probably right about the darkness," Connor said quietly. "Quinn?"

A wind kicked up around Quinn and surrounded only her, tossing her hair in all directions, but she clutched the pages of the book tight.

Morgan shook her head. "I don't know if she can hear you."

Connor inched closer. Not too close. "She's likely in a memory. Give her some space."

The wind stopped and Quinn slumped over the book.

"Is she okay?" Jayden asked.

"She took in a lot of information." Connor stepped back. If he touched her, the circle would be complete. He didn't want that arrow in his quiver to be accidentally pulled yet.

"Put her here." Rebekah unrolled her bedroll. Ethan scooped her up and placed her on the bedroll.

Jayden followed with the book, but she paused in front of Connor and whispered, "Don't be too hard on Quinn. She took that all in because you asked her to. She was so worried about meeting you."

"Why?" Was she already afraid of him? What had she read about him?

Jayden's smile resembled more of a frown. "I'll let the two of you discuss that. Just—she's one you'll have to be more gentle with." She touched his arm.

He turned and placed his hand over hers, anchoring it against him. "You're very powerful. You can catch lightning and throw it. You can create a storm with your emotions or someone else's. You're fast. You can feel what I'm feeling and make me feel what you do."

"What?"

"You didn't know?"

"No. In fact, you may want to tell everyone what they can do. I don't think we all know." She started to walk away but paused and looked over her shoulder. "What can you do?"

He backed a step away from her without meaning to. "Terrible things."

She bit her lip and nodded. "It terrifies you."

"As long as I don't touch Quinn—completing the circle—my powers stay suppressed. I'd like to keep it that way for now."

"A Whisperer I used to know would tell me you were given those powers for a reason."

"The reason is putting the Mistress away forever."

Jayden nodded. "Then maybe I was meant to destroy her prison." Then maybe all of them were meant to die.

Jayden bit her bottom lip. "I used to be afraid to love because loss was too hard to deal with. It would have only made me more like Queen Idla."

He nearly flinched at her mention of the dead queen. The queen she'd faced and killed.

She smiled as she walked away from him. And he was left standing beside Morgan.

"Can I talk to you?" she asked.

He nodded toward the tent door, and she followed him out. "You saw something?"

"Yes." She said the word slowly and with a slight lilt that suggested a question, though no question followed. More like she had bad news to deliver and thought lengthening the process or waiting until he was in the right frame of mind might make it better.

Had she seen something about his future? Such was her burden. And he understood burdens.

"Connor, you saved my sister from . . . from unimaginable things. And you're trying to save her still. I wanted to thank you."

"There's no need, Morgan. Your sister is a dear friend." And even as he said it, he knew the weight of that sentiment. She remained quiet for so long his stomach started to squeeze. "You going to tell me what you saw?"

"I saw your death."

That hit him harder than he'd thought. And it surprised him that a piece of him was relieved. Somehow he wondered if it was something dreadful that was going to happen to Quinn. "My death, huh?"

She looked up at him now, intensity in her eyes. "Connor, this is serious."

He chuckled. "I know. It's just—the gravity of what we're up against is something I'm well acquainted with. Is it necessary, or did I mess up?"

Her eyes softened. "To keep the Deliverers alive, it's necessary, but not as effective as you'd like it to be."

So his plan had holes. "Okay. How do I make it effective?"

"I wish I could be of more help. All I know is you have to listen to Quinn."

It all came back to the Whisperer. "Thank you. You're wise, Morgan. Prescient. But you do let your heart get in the way of things sometimes, don't you?"

"We're only human."

He couldn't help but wonder whether or not he was only human.

She paused and faced him. "She can't know you were here. You have to leave now."

CHAPTER 35

BLACK AS PITCH

Jayden filled her quiver with more pitch-covered arrows and stared at the expanse before her. The palace loomed above it like an obsidian tower amidst a volcanic land. They had moved closer, per Connor's orders, two days ago.

When she'd been here last, the grass had been lush, the fruit and vegetables had been the healthiest in the land. Now desolation surrounded the palace. Black earth cracked and lava oozed through.

A storm hung on the horizon like a skittish, unbroken horse. Dangerous when afraid.

It wasn't all her storm, but part of it was. Any wrong move could cause her to snap. If it rained, it'd douse the fire—their only weapon against these creatures. Stormcloud pressed her nose into Jayden's back and a calm strength filled her.

Logan stood on one side of her and Ethan on the other.

She looked into a pool of lava and it moved. Faced her. It wasn't lava at all. The black-and-red creature was one of the molten bulls. No one had reported seeing one; everyone had thought them hidden, but they weren't. Here they were, in the open.

Now that she saw one, she saw others.

The pools of lava: they were the threat.

The bulls lurked in the shadows. In the fire. They were born of bubbling lava, and when she looked at the ground, her heart sped. Sweat broke out on her palms so her hold on her daggers quivered. She held tight to them. These creatures preyed on fear, but as it grew in everyone, hundreds and hundreds of warriors, it bled into her like lava in the cracked earth.

Fear suffocated her.

Wind buffeted everything.

She looked at Quinn. "Are you sure fire works on these monsters?"

One by one, the creatures grew in front of Jayden. Feravolk stood at the edge of the black ground and looked up.

"Your fear feeds them." Quinn's voice seemed so small.

The thunder rumbled.

"You fear killing someone else? Someone you love?" The thought trickled into her like a tiny raindrop. *"Then go with my messenger, and I'll spare your loved ones."*

The heavens broke open. Sizzles met the ground and Stormcloud reared behind Jayden. One of the bulls stepped over the threshold. It tossed its horned head and then roared, showing off a row of jagged teeth.

Jayden stepped back. "How are they doing that?"

Quinn stared at her. "The Mistress just got stronger. She expanded the layer."

"Long live the Feravolk!" Logan's cry spurred the same from others.

Rain poured as they charged forward, their Wielder-crafted weapons leading. She sliced a bull apart. The contact didn't even seem to heat her blade. Stormcloud whirled and kicked. The wind swirled, as if two storms fought one another to remain grounded here. She needed the rain to stop. It doused the fires they desperately needed.

"Jayden!" Ethan fought his way through the beasts, Zephyr behind him. The wind was strong and the storm wouldn't stop. But he'd lost sight of Jayden. The scar Belladonna had left in his chest throbbed and pulled. It fought against the burn that told him how to protect Jayden.

Firegoats, like flying, flaming snakes, shot above them. They dove and killed. Another level had expanded? They were losing and he could do nothing about it.

Ethan breathed deep and listened to his talent. There was one option. He found Logan behind him. "You have to get them to fall back."

"Ethan, we have to get—"

"The only way they survive is if they fall back. Let me protect Jayden; it's what *I'm* supposed to do."

Logan nodded. "Fall back! Fall back!" He grabbed Ethan's shoulder. "You better know what you're doing, kid."

Didn't he know it.

Jayden. There she was. He raced toward her and touched her shoulder. She spun to face him, dagger ready. And her eyes flashed red.

"No." His chest hollowed as all the air left his lungs. He stepped back from her, heart thrumming. "Jayden, it's me. Ethan."

The bulls parted into two snarling rows surrounding Ethan and Jayden, cutting them off from the others, and a dozen abysshounds walked up the path, snarling at the bulls and keeping them in line. The hounds loomed as tall as the bulls, eyes like fire smoldering. But they wouldn't attack. Ethan charged and sliced the head off one of them. Two others snarled and snapped, but wouldn't bite him.

"Return to me, princess." A voice boomed, and Ethan looked down the row of abysshounds to see Franco standing at the end, arms open wide.

And Jayden walked right toward him.

CHAPTER 36

A KEY

The door to the prison slammed open, and Serena sat up. A guard entered, looking frantic and disheveled. He morphed into a different form, someone with dark hair and golden eyes. Serena shrank away from him, but Madison rushed to the bars of her cell. "Connor, what's going on?"

"The Mistress knows I'm here." He looked at Serena. "You must be Serena. Here." He held his hand into the cell. She reached out and he pressed his hand against hers. When he lifted it a key lay in her palm. "I have your daggers waiting in the tunnel. The key is for—"

"The spell chamber," she said. Kara had kept her word.

"This one is for the cell doors."

It was time. Serena sent a thought to her friend. *"Dash, are you ready to escape?"*

"I found a horse to carry the others. I'm about to break out of here, Serena. And it's about time."

"Good. Meet us at the end of those tunnels."

Connor unlocked Ryan's cell door. "Ryan, right? We're here to help you break out of here."

Ryan charged up to the cell door. "I know you, Captain. And I don't trust you."

"Good morning, Belladonna. You're in a pleasant mood." A voice outside the prison door spoke. Serena's blood chilled.

Connor opened Ryan's cell door. Ryan stood in the way, jaw clenched, chest rising and falling faster. Serena sensed the evil part of his heart stretching wider.

Connor glanced over his shoulder at Serena. "This won't work. I don't have time to hide him."

"You have to!" Serena's pulse sped. "Belladonna will make him hers."

Connor closed the cell door, locked it, pocketed the keys, and took off his shirt. Then his face changed. It morphed into a complete likeness of Ryan. "I'm supposed to be him, which means he can't be here."

Serena gasped at Connor's likeness.

Ryan backed up a pace. "I don't look like that!"

Connor spread his arms. "Do you want my help or not?"

Ryan looked at the door like a skittish wolf. "Sh-she'll see me leave. I–I can't—"

"I can hide you," Serena said and hope bloomed in her heart. "Give me a second to concentrate."

Connor grabbed the cell bars, and his eyes pleaded with Serena. "Hurry!"

The door creaked open and Connor's eyes widened. Ryan shrank away.

Serena stared at Ryan. How did Dash hide her when they weren't touching? She used the cloaking feeling she felt when she hid herself and projected it onto Ryan. And his body melted into the air. Gone.

Connor smiled with Ryan's face, but it vanished the moment Belladonna entered, carrying a scent of pear and lavender. Three of her men and Kara followed her. Kara shot a sly smile at Serena and showed her a small glass bottle.

"Good morning, my pet." Belladonna purred as she approached Ryan's cell. "Did you miss me?"

Connor stared. Serena hoped he'd be convincing.

"Good." Belladonna slipped the key into the lock and it clicked open. She strode in, and the sun caught her glistening, wet lips.

Serena wanted to lunge at her. She clenched her fists instead, focusing on keeping Ryan hidden. She could still see him—though he looked hazy. And as Belladonna entered the cell, Ryan cringed. Serena's heart clenched. Then he seemed to realize she couldn't see him, and he backed to the farthest corner of the cell, glancing at Serena. She held a finger to her lips to remind Ryan to stay quiet. He swallowed and nodded once.

"I brought you something." Belladonna moved closer to Connor, and he leaned back slightly. "Shy today, I see." She shot her guards a glance, and they walked toward the door and out of sight.

Kara stayed, however, leaning up against Madison's cell door and crossing her arms. "This should be good."

Belladonna ignored her and turned her attention back to Connor. "Let me fix that." She placed her hands on him and drew her face close to his.

When Connor's lips touched Belladonna's, the stiffness in his body melted away. He let Belladonna draw close. "There, I thought you might remember me." She smiled wickedly.

Oh no. Serena pressed her hands over her mouth, and Madison clutched her cell bars.

"I have to go away for a little while, so you'll stay in here. But hear me." Belladonna put one hand on her heart and one on his bare chest where his heart would beat. "When I return, you and I will be together forever." Then she pulled another vial out of her pocket. "Drink this, my love." She caressed it and handed it to him, stroking his hand as he obediently took the bottle from her.

"As you wish," Connor said, his eyes not even touching the bottle.

Serena's heart sank. Belladonna had claimed the Wielder.

CHAPTER 37

PRECARIOUS PASSAGE

Don't! Don't drink it!" Madison shrieked.

Belladonna flicked her hand, and Madison's body slammed against the wall. Serena's eyes grew wide, and she glanced at Madison, who was shaking her head. When had Belladonna obtained those powers?

Connor continued to tip his head back, but with Madison's distraction, Belladonna had taken her eyes off of him. He winked at Serena and poured the liquid onto the straw behind him.

When Belladonna turned her face back to his, her sickly sweet smile spread unnaturally on her lips. Connor had the empty glass to his mouth, his head tilted back, and he brought it down, handing it to Belladonna.

The woman lit up visibly as she touched his cheek.

Connor wrapped his arms around Belladonna and nipped her ear. She actually giggled. "I have to go. I'll be bringing the Mistress a present that will make me highly favored." She leaned in to kiss him again, and Connor played his part so convincingly that Serena couldn't watch.

She glanced at Ryan instead, who wore the face of someone who had just bitten into rotten fruit by mistake.

"Hurry back," Connor said, and the new coldness of Ryan's voice lingered in his own.

Belladonna smiled seductively before she strode out.

Kara left with her, not even looking Serena's way.

When they were gone, Madison looked down at her hands and opened her palm.

"She gave me this," she said. "It's the bottle. The potion Belladonna puts on her lips before she kisses Ryan."

Kara had switched the potion. Serena looked up as Connor melted back into himself. She let her cloaking talent on Ryan fade, and he bent over, holding his head in his palms.

The headache. Serena pitched forward in her cell. The headaches seemed to plague him worse when he fought the darkness.

Connor took the opportunity to sneak out of the cell. He locked it.

Ryan grabbed the cell bar in one hand and pressed his palm into his eye. "Some help, huh? Leaving me locked in here."

Connor winced, but didn't respond. Instead he opened Serena's cell and then Madison's. He handed Serena the key. "You need to help him break the bond with Smoke. He's bound to the Mistress's dragon. It's made him her vessel. He will remain that even if the bond is broken, but as long as he's bonded to Smoke, anything you say to him isn't safe."

"Vessel?"

Connor nodded. "The Mistress needs a vessel in order to survive here. A human who bonds to her mount—Smoke. She chose Ryan. She needs his heart to survive, otherwise she's bound only to Smoke, but he's not human, so she only survives in a sleeping state."

Serena glanced over at Ryan, who sat on the floor of his cell, back against the stone wall. "If she needs Ryan's heart—if we kill her—"

"She doesn't own more than half of his heart yet, does she?"

"No."

"If she takes over more than half of his heart, I think the only thing that would save him is a link to the Creator's power."

Serena's breath stilled for several heartbeats, and she pushed her cell door open. "How do I get him to break the bond?"

Connor winced and his gaze trailed to Ryan's cell then back to Serena. He touched her shoulder and gave her an encouraging squeeze. "Help him choose to use the other half of his heart." He dropped his hand and turned to leave.

Right. Because that wouldn't be too difficult. Madison grabbed

Connor's sleeve before he could go. "Connor. Good luck. Tell Luc to be careful."

"You, too." Then he turned to Serena. "If you need me, call for me. I'm certain I'll hear you." He offered a grin and morphed into a soldier, put his shirt back on. "Oh." He plucked a pouch from his pocket that Serena recognized. "Tangle flower?" He grinned. "I know just who to give this to. It makes good afternoon tea. After your sorry excuse for a meal is served, you'll have to go. Meet Luc out back—outside the tunnels. Kara said you know where to go."

"I do."

"You have two hours." He glanced at Ryan. "Creator's blessing. I think you'll need it more than I." He left.

"Now what?" Madison asked into the silence. She still held the bottle Kara had given her. There was a paper on it. "A note." She opened it.

> *Golden One, you don't have much time. The battle is brewing outside. You have to get out of here as fast as you can. Get Charmer and the other Healer to the spells chamber. You have two hours.*

She glanced over at Ryan. That wasn't much time to get him ready. She handed Madison the key.

Madison looked up at her. "Where are you going?"

She motioned toward Ryan's cell. "The dragon's lair."

Ryan watched her, like a dog ready to defend his bone, as she moved toward his cell. Opened it. Stepped inside.

She closed the door and sat down on the straw, far enough away that he'd have to move to reach her. "We have to break your bond with Smoke before we can escape. Otherwise . . ."

"The Mistress will have a link to me? She already does."

"Your heart."

He nodded and looked at the ground. He sat there, elbow on one knee, fingering a long piece of straw.

Serena shifted her weight, and Ryan straightened, hands ready to defend. She stilled. "I think her potion wears off. The one she gives you when she kisses you? Your headaches are dying in intensity."

A dark chuckle escaped his throat. "You can feel my pain, too."

Serena ground her teeth. "Whatever Belladonna called herself, she is no Healer."

"No? She healed me enough times." He turned so she could see his scarred back. Her heart ached.

"Ryan, that's not healing. She hurt you." She started to reach for him, but he tucked his chin and pulled away from her. "Do you want to break the bond?"

"Yes." His eyes pleaded with her, and for a moment she thought she saw the real Ryan break through.

"All right. Let me help you. I happen to know a lot about bonds." She smiled, then winced. "It will hurt."

He leaned slightly closer. "Why would you do this for me?"

She fidgeted with the bit of torn lace on her filthy skirts.

His eyes narrowed.

"I—I can feel it taking over." He clutched his chest, his heart. "You can feel it?"

"I can feel people's hearts."

"And mine?"

"Ryan, how much do you remember?"

"The potion is wearing off."

"And?"

"I'm not sure I'm who I used to be anymore."

"No one is who they used to be. But embrace who you are. I feel the good in your heart. It fights. Don't give up." Without thinking, she leaned in to touch his knee.

He caught her hand with a crushing grip. "I don't trust Healers."

Memories of her childhood flared, and she tugged at her hand. Cold sweat. Heartbeats. Faster. Faster. She yanked at her arm. Still stuck. She froze. Shook.

Immediately he released her arm. "I'm sorry."

She looked away, embarrassed that he'd seen her reaction, and willed her pulse to slow. Madison was nearly inside Ryan's cell, but at Serena's nod, she backed away again.

Serena leaned away from him. "I just wish you could trust me."

He closed his eyes. "I'm trying."

"That's all I can ask for."

He looked at her—really looked. "I remember you."

She breathed in. "You do?" Her voice trembled. "Will you let me heal you?"

He stared at her, not saying anything. She rose to her knees and leaned closer. He stayed still. She held out her hand and placed it on his side, and he turned his head, squeezing his eyes shut. He shrank back from her, his breathing quickened. He was unwilling. More than that, he was terrified. Serena dropped her hand from him without healing him, and one of his eyes opened.

"What has she done to you?" she whispered.

He relaxed slightly. "I'll be able to make it out of here. I'm strong enough."

"When you break the bond, it will take a lot out of you. I'm trying to keep it from killing you."

"Can you trust me? I'll tell you if I need healing."

She would earn his trust, even if it took all the time they had left. "I trust you, Ryan. But if you become unconscious, I'm going to heal you."

He smiled, and it was a ghost of the charming grin she remembered. "I remember the night we met."

Her heart stilled as she waited for him to continue.

"I used to think about it every day. You. You're what kept me alive here. Thinking about you. Seeing your face when . . . when she tortured me, kept my hope alive." He winced and touched his chest. It was working. He was breaking it. "And now you're here." He reached for her hand and she grabbed his. "Y-you came to rescue me?"

"Of course."

"Why?" He doubled over, holding tight to her hand.

She stroked his hair. "I came because we couldn't let you rot in the Franco's dungeon, hoping that your charm and wit alone would save you."

He laughed, still fighting the pain.

"I came because . . . because you're one of the Deliverers, and we couldn't let the Mistress get you."

His heart fought—she felt the struggle as if it were in her own chest. Every beat ached. "I came because Ethan wanted to come for you, and someone had to stop him from being stupid and reckless."

"You know my brother well." He winced.

"I wanted that kiss you were too shy to give me."

He bent over and muffled his scream with a fist.

A huge roar burst forth from the courts outside. A dragon's. It was working.

Ryan screamed so loud, she thought his heart might burst. Then he fell, his head landing in her lap. "Is . . . is it over?"

She smoothed his hair. "Yes. You did it. Your heart is free."

"It's still tainted?" He didn't lift his head.

"Yes. But one thing at a time."

He closed his eyes.

"Ryan?"

"Hmmm?"

"You are the strongest person I know."

He didn't respond.

"Is he all right?" Madison clutched the cell bars.

"He's asleep. We'll have to let him rest."

"For how long? We don't have much time."

Serena shook her head. "We have to give him every moment we can spare. Without another dragon we could convince to bond with him, the tear from the ripped bond could kill him."

"If you're going to stay in his cell, at least give me the key to the spell chamber."

"Wait." Ryan's voice rasped.

Serena touched his head. "What is it?"

He sat up slowly. A crooked smile spread across his face. "In Morgan's vision, *I* had the key around my neck. And *you* were with Madison and me when we stormed out of here."

Madison smiled. "Knight, it's good to have you back."

"I'm still not a knight." He looked at Serena and mouthed the words, "Thank you."

CHAPTER 38

THE MESSENGER

Ethan stood in front of Jayden as she took another step toward Franco.

"You're the messenger the woman from my dream sent for me?" Jayden said to him, her eyes glazed red.

No black veins. He had to make sure she didn't become too far gone that he couldn't bring her back.

"Messenger?" Ethan tried to get her to look at him, but she wouldn't.

"You know who I am." Franco smirked.

"Ethan."

What? Ethan's mind raced. "Don't listen to him, Jayden. I'm Ethan." Ethan grabbed her arm. She spun and her dagger headed toward him. He let go and jumped back.

The red in her eyes glinted. "Franco."

"No. You've been poisoned. You're in a nightmare. You—"

She flung her dagger at him, and he ducked, but the weapon fell to the ground before it came close to him. Ethan turned to see Zephyr behind him, whipping his wings to create the shield. *"She's in the dream world again."*

"I have to get her out." Ethan's pulse pounded through his veins.

"She'll kill you."

"She's going to kill you." Chloe dropped off Zephyr's back.

"Chloe? How?"

"Get down!" She pushed him behind her and drew her bow.

She released an arrow, and it sailed right toward Franco. He staggered back as the arrow pierced his skin. Then he looked at Chloe and smiled as he pulled it out.

"You can't kill him." Ethan pushed her behind Zephyr. *"Why would you let her come?"*

"She's quite persuasive."

"Jayden!" Ethan headed toward her again, but a tug in his chest pulled him forward faster, and he fell to his knees. A wave of heat fanned across his chest, but pain accompanied it, and he touched the scar. *Blood? Could the crazy woman actually pull out whatever she'd put inside him?* If that were possible, he'd make her try.

"What's wrong with you, Ethan?" Chloe touched his shoulders.

Five black lions swooped in, landing in a run. They shot toward Ethan and Chloe and bowled into Zephyr. Belladonna rode one. "There you are, pet. I missed you."

He met Belladonna's eyes and looked past her to where Jayden stood. Franco grabbed her arm and pushed her behind him. "What are you waiting for, Belladonna? Let's get out of here."

Her eyes bored into Ethan's. "You're mine."

Ethan drew his sword. "What do you want, Belladonna?"

Her smile stretched unusually red lips. "You."

Thunder rumbled.

Belladonna's black lions circled him.

Ethan and Zephyr might be impervious to the venom, but Chloe wasn't.

Oh, Chloe. Why did she have to come? Now he had two to protect.

But they wouldn't kill Jayden. Not yet. Chloe? What did they care if she lived or died?

Belladonna pointed at him. Then she jerked her arm back. Pain pulled in the old wound at his chest, and he stumbled forward. Zephyr crouched in front of him, growling.

"Kill it."

The black lions lunged toward Zephyr. His claws curled around Ethan. His wings beat against the air, against the storm, and they left the ground.

"Chloe!"

"I'm here. In your creature's claws."

"I wouldn't leave her, friend. But those black beasts are fast."

"You're faster."

Ethan climbed Zephyr's leg and pulled himself onto his back. Then he held his hand down for Chloe.

She looked at it. "You're crazy."

He couldn't help but laugh. "He needs his claws to fight, Chloe. Come on."

She breathed deep and grabbed his hand. He helped pull her up, and she sat in front of him on Zephyr's back. "Maybe you should stop trying to protect me."

"You aren't the only one who gets to protect loved ones, Ethan." She glanced at him over her shoulder.

Belladonna's five black lions barreled toward them. She still rode one, and her dark eyes locked onto him. "You're mine."

An invisible hand clutched his chest and pulled. This time he didn't fight it. He pitched forward. Chloe screamed and grabbed for him. She missed. Air pushed against him, and he fell faster than he thought possible.

Zephyr dove beneath him, and Ethan looked at his friend. *"Save Chloe."*

Zephyr pulled up, and Ethan fell on top of a black lion. He plunged the wooden dagger into the base of its skull and it turned to dust.

Belladonna screeched. This time the creature that caught him was hers. She pulled him close with her invisible grip. "You should be more compliant." She drew the Sword of Black Malice. "Don't worry. I won't kill you. Your little lover just told me a secret. You're one of the Deliverers. You've just put me very far ahead in a game I've been dying to win."

Ethan swallowed. She knew.

She touched the sword to the spot on his chest that had been blackened by that very weapon. "Your strength belongs to me."

What? "You're crazy." He drew his sword and pierced her through. "Where's my brother?"

She laughed. "You can't kill me."

He pulled his sword free of her and aimed for her head. "You want to bet?" He swung, but his sword stopped and his heart raced. Why wasn't it moving?

"I told you." She laughed. "I am your master. Your strength is mine. You cannot kill me."

The black lion swooped close to the ground, to where Franco stood with Jayden. Zephyr slammed into them, and Ethan jumped to the earth. He rolled with the momentum and popped up to his feet. But something in his resolve was shaken. He couldn't kill her?

Belladonna faced him, the Sword of Black Malice in her hands.

Jayden stood compliant next to Franco. He glanced at Belladonna. "Having trouble reeling in your Deliverer? I might be able to help. The Mistress is waiting for her prize."

Belladonna sneered. "I don't need your help."

Franco's eyebrows raised, and he motioned to Ethan. "No? Then I'll take that one, too."

"You have nothing. One of the Deliverers already loves me. The second is in the prison watched by my guards. This one"—she yanked at Ethan's chest anchor, and it jerked him forward no matter how he tried to brace himself—"is bound to me by dark magic. I have three. You only have . . . well as soon as she snaps out of her dream, she'll know who you really are. You won't have her allegiance."

"You forget. The other girl's soul is bound to me by the tattoo."

Serena? Ethan pitched forward. Behind him, Zephyr growled.

"Tell your gryphon to stand down. My black lions will kill him."

"Zeph, are you fast enough to grab Jayden and get out of here?"

"What about you?"

Ethan raised his sword. "I have an ex-Healer to kill."

Belladonna smirked. "I told you—"

"No one controls me." He raced toward her.

She flicked her wrist, and the tug in his chest yanked him off his feet. He slid across the gravel. Stopped. Stood. Shook himself off. "Jayden! Wake up!"

The sky crackled, and Stormcloud flew into the center of the abyss-hounds and bulls. She lifted her back legs and kicked Franco in the head. He fell to the ground and skidded across cracked earth. Slowly, he pushed himself up to his elbows and wiped blood from his face.

And the wounds closed. Healed. A smile snaked across Franco's lips. He stood and spat. "Kill the gryphon and the pegasus."

Stormcloud took flight and the firegoats chased her. She flew straight toward a flash of lightning. Ethan hoped she'd be able to kill them.

Belladonna pointed her sword toward Franco. "Looks like your creatures are occupied. Mine aren't. Kill the gryphon." Zephyr screeched as the four black lions lunged toward him. Chloe's scream stabbed Ethan's heart. He turned. She was still here. Ethan stood in front of her.

Franco stepped closer to Belladonna's sword blade. "You said we were working together to defeat the Mistress."

"I lied."

"You can't kill me."

"With this, I can." She nodded to the Sword of Black Malice. "It creates wounds no Healer can heal, blood sacrifice or not."

Ethan watched the two of them face off. He had to use this to his advantage. If he could get Jayden to snap out of her nightmare, he might just be able to get her to make this storm work for them.

"I have men, too. And they'll take your Deliverer." He gripped Jayden's arm and towed her behind a long line of men.

Belladonna looked at Ethan. "Go get your one true love. Or I'll kill the redhead."

Three black lions pinned Zephyr down. He must have killed one. Still he struggled beneath their claws.

Ethan's heart hammered. He had too many to protect. And the abysshounds kept the other Feravolk from reaching him. He faced Franco's men, and his talent crackled like a flame across his chest. "Jayden, I'm coming for you."

Her head snapped in his direction, and she stared at him. The red in her eyes pulsed. "You'll never claim me, Franco."

Franco chuckled. "That's a nice turn of events. But I can't exactly have her killing you. Good thing I have her. And them." Perhaps a dozen soldiers headed toward the line of abysshounds. "Go ahead, men. Bring him to me."

Ethan focused on his talent. "Chloe, stay away from those black lions, do you hear?"

Lightning cracked across the sky. And Ethan lifted his sword.

Zephyr's struggle tugged at the corner of his mind. *"I've killed another. Keep fighting. I'm coming to help."*

Speed shot into Ethan and his strength grew. The men charged and he fought. His sword met metal. Blades sliced into his skin, but he felt nothing. Jayden was captive, and he wouldn't rest until she was free.

Another body fell to his blade. Another.

A jerk in his chest made him stumble back. Belladonna stood between him and the men. "No, no," she said. "You can't kill him. But you can kill the redhead."

Jayden stood in front of him, and she called lightning. His chest flared. She meant to hit him. Ethan looked into her eyes. *"Jayden, no. Please don't."*

She shook her head. Stormcloud shot through the storm, two fire-goats on her tail.

Ethan dove to the ground as the lightning left her fingertips. Stormcloud flicked her tail to make contact with it. And as she whipped her tail again, the bolt changed direction and sailed straight toward the firegoats.

Shrieking, they fell to the ground.

"Jayden!" He screamed. "Don't doubt my love for you! Please. See me."

She closed her eyes. When she opened them, blue pulsed through the red, dissipating it.

She looked at him and gasped. "Ethan?"

"No." Franco grabbed her wrist.

"Oh, Ethan, aren't you just a thorn in my flesh." Belladonna pulled on the link, and this time, he was ready for it. He resisted. It snapped her arm forward.

She looked at her hand. "How are you doing that?"

His heartbeat sped. It might work. He could be rid of her. He stood strong as she yanked again. His skin ripped open, but he stood there, staring at her. Willing her to see his defiance.

"You're mine!" She screamed and pulled with what looked to be all her might. Ethan stumbled forward and slammed into the ground.

"For that, I'll have to stab you through. You remember what that feels like, don't you?" She charged at him.

The sky lit.

And she threw the sword.

"No!" Chloe knocked him to the ground. Then her body slammed into his with such force he knew. She'd been stabbed. Jayden's scream confirmed it.

"Chloe!"

Her green eyes met his and everything else stopped. Not Chloe. "Sh-she meant to kill you." Crimson dripped over her lips.

Ethan rolled her off of him, careful to catch her and cradle her in his arms. "Ch-Chloe, she can heal with that sword. Sh-she did it for me. You hang on, okay?"

"Ethan?" She touched his cheek and smiled. Her skin was so pale. And her voice so soft.

"What?"

Her eyes moved in and out of focus, but for a moment they focused right on him. "I love you . . . I always . . . have."

"Oh, Chloe, don't—"

"I would have . . . died for you . . . a thousand times over."

He squeezed her hand and pressed it closer to his face. "I love you, too."

Light glimmered for a moment in her eyes, and a smile spread across her face. Then her hand fell. Limp. He curled his body over hers. *Not Chloe. Not another one.*

Ethan fisted his hands and stood. He pulled the Sword of Black Malice from Chloe's lifeless body and stared at Belladonna. "You will pay." His voice was barely above a whisper, but the way her dark eyes flicked to the sword told him she heard every word.

Franco laughed. "Looks like I just gained what you lost."

Ethan ran, sword out, straight at Belladonna. Her eyes opened wide as speed he didn't know he possessed fueled him. Then something fell from her hands. Purple smoke rose up around her. Ethan ran faster.

She would feel this blade. She would feel his wrath. She would die for killing Chloe.

He flung the sword toward the purple mist.

And her scream was silenced.

When the mist dissipated, she was gone.

CHAPTER 39

SIMPLE MISTAKES

Serena watched as her dry bread bounced across her cell floor toward her. Her insides fluttered as the guard stalked away.

"Fifteen minutes," Madison whispered.

Ryan sat up and locked gazes with Serena. "You sure Connor will come through?"

"I am." Madison stood, key in hand.

Truth.

Footsteps stopped in front of the doors. Serena leaned as close to the door as she could, her ears pressing against the cell bars.

"The cook opened a bottle of wine, but His Majesty didn't like it." A feminine voice she didn't recognize sounded out in the hall.

A guard laughed. "Better her head than mine.

"Well, it's not good for wine to go to waste."

"I agree with you, sweetheart." The guard's voice grew husky.

The woman giggled.

Moments later, a bottle crashed against the floor. The door creaked open and Connor entered. "It's done. Is he ready?"

"I'm ready." Ryan stood.

Madison unlocked the door and handed the key to Serena. She fumbled on the lock of Ryan's cell. Connor handed a shirt to Ryan, who smirked before he put it on. "The king's guard, huh?"

"Follow me." Connor stuck his head out into the hall. At last he motioned for them to follow.

Serena's insides tightened. He led them to the winding staircase that would take them down a level. "Kara said she'd meet you. I am going to my troops now. Be careful, sister." He winked. Serena hugged her newfound brother before he slipped silently away.

She continued down the staircase, but Ryan wouldn't let her through the door until he'd checked to see that it was safe. In her head, Serena followed the map that Kara had made her study each night and led them easily to the forbidden room. The spell chamber. Kara appeared from the shadows.

"You made it then." She looked neither surprised nor impressed. "Here." She handed Serena her beautiful daggers and her Feravolk cloak. Serena let the feel of each of her weapons caress her before she put them away. Kara also handed Madison a pair of daggers. Then she turned to Ryan and gave him a sword. "I stole this from Franco's personal weapons. I thought it would be perfect for you.

The stone in the weapon's hilt glowed green, and the light wrapped around Ryan's wrists. He tried to drop it, but it remained in his hands. "What's it doing?"

"It's a Deliverer's sword." Serena looked at the blade as the green light dissipated. Dragon wings made up the cross guard.

Kara touched Serena's arm. "Good luck."

"You're not coming with us?"

"Don't worry about me. I have unfinished business of my own. Be careful, Serena. I think Franco will come looking for you." She tapped the tattoo on Serena's neck. "If he does, I will fight for *him*."

Serena nodded, and Kara pointed to a gray brick on the wall. She pushed. Heavy stone scraped as it moved sideways, stacking behind the wall. There it was. The door to the spell chamber.

"Be fast." Kara melted into the shadows.

Serena faced the door. It was made of up of thick, dark timbers held together by black, twisted iron. The shape was of a long serpentine dragon that snaked along the hinge side, over the top, and down to the keyhole, which it revealed in its parted jaws.

"Of course." Ryan smirked as he touched the dragon mold and slid the key into the lock and turned.

The door opened and Serena stepped inside.

Bottles and books packed aisles and aisles of shelves. A wooden table spread across the floor in front of the shelves, littered with mortars and pestles, wooden, metal, and glass spoons and bowls. A cauldron sat in a quiet fireplace. And in the very front of the room, open on a pedestal for the eye to behold the moment the door opened, sat the book of spells.

Madison stepped into the room. "Here it is."

Serena grabbed her wrist. "Don't touch it." The words came out soft, and she didn't take her eyes off the book. "If it's this easy to find, it's spelled." She released Madison.

Behind them, Ryan unsheathed his sword and stayed by the door "I don't like this."

"How will we get it?" Madison asked.

"Serena," Ryan's voice was low. "Someone's using the back stairs."

Serena met his gaze for a heartbeat. Two heartbeats. "Mirage protects the counters book, but every spell book is bonded to one." She studied the book. "As soon as I touch it, Franco—or whoever is bound to the book—will feel it. And Franco knows just where to find me."

"It's now or never, then." Ryan tipped his head, and his smile warmed her.

She breathed deep. Hovered her hands over the book, testing, feeling. Nothing told her where the counters books hid. She'd have to touch it. The book would be tiny and grow once released. The same unicorn magic she'd used to hide Ryan earlier had been used here. She could sense it.

Her fingers slid over the gold fabric on the front cover, and she closed the book. A loud scraping sound brought her attention to the doorway. Ryan stared wide-eyed as a wall of cinder block began to slide across the entrance. He braced himself against the cement door, keeping it open. "Now would be good."

"Madison, get out of here." She pushed Madison toward the door. Then she faced the book and ran her fingers over the cover. Closed her eyes. Felt through the cloaking magic.

It was dirty. Stolen from a unicorn.

At least she could feel that. Now she needed to find the book.

She touched the back cover.

The spine.

"Serena? I'm not made of metal." Strain etched Ryan's voice.

"Just leave it," Madison said.

"No." This was to save Ryan and all the innocent people the Mistress had spelled. She wasn't leaving it.

Ryan's pain tugged at her. She focused.

"Thieves! Stop, by order of the king!" Voices thundered outside.

Ryan grunted. "Madison, take my sword. I can't fight and hold this door."

"I have my weapons."

Serena's fingers hit something. Her eyes sprang open. She could feel the transparent book inside the back cover. Her fingers found the edge and she pulled.

"Serena!"

The sound of metal clashing metal outside. Soldiers marching.

The strap broke. The book became visible as it was freed. She slipped it into her pocket and ran to the small space Ryan held on to. She jumped over his legs and grabbed his hand, pulling him with her. They landed in a heap on the floor.

The door slid shut, just missing Ryan's boots.

"You okay?" he asked her.

She nodded. They both stood and drew weapons.

Franco rounded the corner with more men. "At least you've come out empty handed."

Kara stood beside the king, daggers drawn.

"I want them alive," Franco said.

All seven guards sprang toward them. Serena turned to Ryan and touched him, filling him with her strength. Then she faced her enemies as they shot toward her.

She stabbed one of the guards in the shoulder. He slammed his arm into her, and she fell to the ground, rolled, and sprang up in time to duck another blow. He was slower. Heavy armor plagued his movement but hindered her from finding a weak spot.

She pulled out a small dagger and threw it as he charged her. It smashed into his face hilt first and stunned him enough for her to move in and slice his exposed throat. He stumbled backward.

When she turned, five men surrounded Ryan. He fell to the ground, injured. She ran toward him.

"Don't heal him," Franco said, and Serena felt the tattoo like a noose around her free will. She shook and stared at Franco, her skin heating with hatred.

"Follow me or he dies."

Kara rounded on Madison and held a sword to the Healer's throat. "I'll chop off her head if you don't follow him back to your cell."

"Well done, Kara." Franco narrowed his eyes. "Heal the Deliverer, Madison." Slowly Kara pushed Madison toward Ryan.

Serena's heart spurted. She could do nothing. And Kara had warned her, but still, this felt too much like betrayal. As she stood there, Franco grabbed her arm and squeezed. How was he so strong? He glared at her, eyes narrowing. Did he know her healing powers weren't connected to him? "I have many Healers." His voice was low. "None as powerful as you. You will learn to obey me."

He tossed Serena to the ground, and she scrambled away from him. Closer to Ryan. As Madison's healing flooded through Ryan, Serena felt it. She glanced at him, but he was looking at Kara. She nodded once and flung Madison aside.

Ryan plucked Madison's dagger from the ground and stabbed Kara through.

"No!" Serena's knees weakened.

Kara fell, hands against her abdomen.

Madison got to her feet and ran. Kara met Serena's gaze as life slipped out of her eyes. "Run."

"Kara, you'll—"

"Knife my heart, Serena. Run." Kara lifted a dart shooter to her lips and started shooting darts at the guards who tried to go past her.

Ryan's strong arm curled around Serena, and he pushed her down the tunnel. *Why? Why would she . . . we were so close to freeing her.*

"Franco won't let her die, Serena. Trust me." Ryan tugged her forward. He was so weak. The ripped bond was reclaiming him.

She pulled her leaden feet from the mud, grabbed Ryan's arm, and ran after Madison. She ran until sunlight spilled onto her face. Then

Ryan stopped and faced the door. "I think three guards made it past Kara." He hunched over, hands on his knees.

"I'll get them. You three need to get out of here." A familiar voice pulled at Serena's memory, and a young man raced toward them from the direction of the stables. He smiled, green eyes sparkling, and held his sword ready.

"Luc!" Madison looked as though she wanted to wrap her arms around him.

"Luc?" Serena recognized him. The fire-eaten boy she'd healed.

He winked. "I said I'd return the favor."

"Luc?" Ryan gripped his shoulder.

Luc touched Ryan's arm. "Good to see you looking better. But you'd better run." He turned toward the door of the tunnel they'd just exited. As the soldiers chasing them came to the doorway, Luc fought them. All three slumped over in the doorway, and Luc cleaned his sword on their clothes before he sheathed it.

"I hope Connor wasn't planning to get out that way," Ryan said.

"He's already out. Follow me." Luc tried to usher them forward, but Serena felt Ryan's strength leave him, and he stumbled to the ground.

A huge, winged beast lowered from the sky and landed behind them. "Blaze." Serena's hope rode on that word as she recognized the dragon. The friend of Kara's bonded dragon.

"It's okay," the dragon said softly. Ryan placed his hands on Blaze's neck, who helped him up. A newfound strength filled Ryan. Blaze's strength. They would share it until Ryan had his own again.

Dash rushed across the dirt-covered earth, sending up billowing clouds in his wake. *"I worried that this moment would never come."*

"Dash!"

"You don't want that horse," Luc said.

Serena smiled. "He's no horse. He's a unicorn."

"Of course! I hadn't recognized him in that disguise." Luc chuckled as a brown stallion with a black mane followed Dash to where they stood. This horse was already bridled and saddled. Luc swung onto the horse's back and held out his hand for Madison.

Serena mounted Dash and looked at Ryan to join her. Dash's nostrils flared. *"He smells like a dragon."*

Ryan hesitated, but Serena held out her hand. Ryan slid from Blaze and crossed to mount Dash behind Serena. "You sure he's okay with me being up here?"

"Yes." Serena looked back at him, and his gaze entrapped her. She couldn't turn away. He was so close to her. His eyes trailed to her lips, and Serena's heart pounded. She wanted to kiss him, but she stayed motionless. Offered him a smile. The look in his eyes intensified, and he leaned in quickly and kissed her, on the cheek.

"For luck," he said and glanced away, hiding a bashful smile.

Hope warmed her insides. "For destiny."

A deep shadow covered them, and they turned as it blocked the sun.

Ryan hugged Serena tight, trembling. "He found me."

She stared up in the sky at the huge, black dragon that made Blaze seem like a baby.

Smoke.

CHAPTER 40

THE BATTLE BREWS

Ryan shielded his eyes as the black dragon rose high into the air above them. Its shadow covered them in its darkness. Its gravelly voice laughed inside Ryan's head and out. *"You dare rip your bond with me? She still has your heart, which means it's still mine."*

"It's not yours."

The dragon's laugh drowned out his plea. Ryan wanted desperately to believe it was true. Every time he felt a piece of himself returning, something beat it away from him.

And right now he was so tired of fighting.

He pitched forward and Serena steadied him. "Hang in there. You're weak from . . . a lot of things. You don't have to do this alone."

Did she know what those words meant to him?

A green form, a tenth of Smoke's mass, stood in between Ryan and the black dragon. Blaze. Fire shot from Smoke's maw, and Ryan pushed Serena forward, into Dash's neck. He covered her the best he could as sparks flooded out around them. Only around them? Ryan looked up to see a purplish haze, like a sphere of violet light shining out from the point in Dash's horn. And through the light, Ryan saw Blaze's body, wings outstretched, shielding them the best he could from the rest of the fire.

"Get cover!" Blaze's voice rang in Ryan's head.

"We need shelter, now!" Ryan said to Serena.

As the stream of fire stopped and Smoke reared his ugly head in what appeared to be another fiery attack, Dash ran out in broad daylight.

But Smoke's head didn't follow them. Instead, the dragon roared. *"Where are you?"*

Ryan covered his ears. "Why doesn't he see us?"

Serena glanced back at him, her eyes round and forehead wrinkled. "Dash is making us invisible."

The unicorn leapt through the castle grounds as Smoke took flight. Blaze streaked across the sky, toward the massive black dragon.

What was he doing?

Blaze hurtled toward Smoke, a stream of fire out ahead of him, blinding Smoke momentarily. It was enough for Blaze to strike with one serpentine-like bite on Smoke's long neck.

Smoke lashed out, and Blaze darted away from the palace. But as Smoke tried to follow, his head whipped back, as if some invisible leash tied him to his spot.

"He's bound to the Mistress. He can't leave her," Serena whispered.

He spouted flames into the air and on the ground, swinging his head around angrily. Ryan watched until a building covered his view.

Dash had brought them around toward the front of the palace and beside a small cottage near the courtyard.

"Are you all right?" Serena faced him.

He nodded. "For now, but—"

Blaze found them from the west. He landed near them. *"The unicorn is right about you not doing this alone."*

"Unicorn?"

Blaze nodded. *"The Healer girl. Dragons call them unicorns."*

"But Smoke still has a hold on me? Why?"

"Your heart has been split nearly in half. Part of it wants me; the other part has been transformed somehow. By her. She's made you her vessel. Thankfully the bigger part wants to remain bonded to me."

Transformed? The word hung in Ryan's ears like a thick fog. Because he'd been made her vessel, just like Smoke had said.

"When the Mistress dies, that part of your heart will die. You know that, don't you?"

"I'll die." He swallowed. *"I don't want to be her vessel."*

"*Then we have to build a wall in your heart, section it off, and fight back against the black blood. If it taints less than half your heart, I think you'll live even if she dies.*"

"*Why would you bond with me if you knew I was such a mess in there?*"

Blaze's red eyes appeared full of the same longing Ryan felt. "*The good in your heart speaks of untold bravery. You would fight for the weak. The helpless. The fatherless. So would I. There was no other heart, half or otherwise, that I would wish to bond with.*"

Ryan's heart squeezed. He didn't deserve such loyalty.

"Thank you." Serena held out her hand, and Blaze leaned his head nearer to her. But Dash whinnied and sidestepped farther from the dragon. Serena sighed. "Well, we aren't out of this yet. We have to take out that beast the Mistress insists on calling a dragon." She smiled at Blaze.

Something in Ryan's heart warmed. "Okay, how do we take it out?"

Serena flinched and touched the tattoo on her neck. "Franco." Her wide eyes met Ryan's. "He's looking for me."

"He won't find you," Ryan insisted.

Luc rounded the corner of the cottage on horseback. Madison still rode with him. He seemed out of breath. "There you are. This horse knew how to find you." He moved his horse closer to them. "I need to take Madison to find Connor."

"Go. Help Connor." Ryan smiled. "We're going to slay a dragon. I don't think that can be done from horseback."

Luc turned his stallion around.

Blaze brought his face close to Ryan. Close enough that he saw the turquoise shimmer in the dragon's scales. "*Now, you do know only a unicorn can slay Smoke, right?*"

"*Let me guess. A horn to its heart?*"

Blaze smiled. "*That's right. That's what the sword of noble light is. Grab your little unicorn friend. We'll take her to the sky, and she can slay a dragon.*"

"*With what horn?*"

"*Her daggers. They work like unicorn horns, do they not?*"

"*I don't know.*"

"*Let's find out.*"

Ryan touched Serena's shoulder. "Would you like to help me slay Smoke?"

Dash stamped his hoof.

"Dash says if we can lure Smoke close enough, we can slay him. He's already weak from the bond ripping."

"Blaze seems to think *you* can slay a dragon. He's much faster than Smoke." Ryan jumped off Dash's back and climbed up onto Blaze. His scales pulsed warmth. He retracted the spikes on his back so Ryan could straddle him. Then Ryan held his hand out to Serena. "Want to take a ride?"

She stared at him with those blue eyes huge. Then she grabbed his hand. "You should know—"

He pulled her onto Blaze's back. She squeezed his middle as if she might otherwise fall off and buried her head in his back as wind swirled around them. "I'm afraid of heights."

A mix of warm and cool. Of dust and air. Of flowers and rain. Everything swirled and whipped, and, as Blaze climbed higher and higher, Ryan wanted to reach into the air. Feel every current on his hands and his face. For the first time since Belladonna had held a dagger to his neck and forced him onto the back of a black lion, he felt free.

Serena's arms around him made him believe he could take on the world. She might be the Healer, a "unicorn," but right now, he was her protector.

Then he saw Smoke, and the weight of reality settled deep and dark into him. His heart screamed to reattach to the black dragon. The source of the Mistress's power. "If we kill him, the Mistress will be weakened. And we can't kill her unless Smoke is dead."

"Good. Let's." Her voice seemed so small up here in the sky.

Blaze flew closer to Smoke.

And the black dragon spotted them. It roared loud enough to shatter the window in the tall tower. Then with one flap of its mighty wings, it jumped to the top of the palace. Roof tiles crumbled beneath its weight, falling to the ground.

"Hang on," Blaze warned.

And Smoke leapt into the air.

Blaze zipped forward, wind pushing into them. Serena squeezed Ryan's waist, and he hung on to Blaze's spike. The wind grew hot and stale as they passed below Smoke's body. Weaved between dragon claws and castle spires. Blaze was fast. Smoke was long.

His tail sailed toward them, and Ryan hunched low. It knocked into him, and he held tight to Blaze's spikes, but Serena's grip tore from him and she fell.

Smoke dove for her.

So did Blaze.

Smoke's claws swiped into Blaze's green scales and sliced through the smaller dragon.

Serena fell straight toward the black dragon's massive jaws. He snapped at her. Fire shot out of him and she screamed.

Flames flooded into the air. Black smoke choked her.

Blaze's body darted beneath her, and Ryan caught her. "I'm sorry. I'm so sorry. I'll never let you fall again. Never." He touched her arm, near her burning skin. "Why aren't you healing?"

"I am. It just takes longer."

Blaze fell unnaturally fast, and his pain pulsed into Serena. She placed her palms against his back, his green scales hot to the touch. And she pumped healing into the dragon.

"Thank you. Now hang on."

She gripped hold of Blaze's spike as a torch of dragon fire headed toward them. Ryan was right; Blaze was fast. He dodged the flame and soared higher. Straight toward the Smoke's chest.

"Pull out a dagger." Ryan clutched her waist and anchored her to him. "You ready?"

She nodded, hands shaking. The last of her scorched skin finally healed.

Smoke's body started to turn, but Blaze changed direction like a leaf riding a wind current. Serena extended her arm as he flew toward the black dragon's chest.

"Serena! Come when you're called, slave. You belong to me now!" A

throb in Serena's neck made her buckle over. Franco called her to heal someone, and she had to obey. If it was Kara, she'd end up dead.

But Smoke's chest was so close.

"Serena? What's wrong?" Ryan hunched over her.

"Franco," she whispered. "He's calling me. I–I have to go."

She tried to stay, tried to hold out her dagger, but her body wouldn't listen. She started to jump off the dragon. She knew where Franco was, but he also knew where she was.

Ryan grabbed her shoulder. She struggled against his grip even though she wanted to hold on to him. "I have to heal—Franco is calling me."

He glared at the mark on her neck, and she covered it up. "Listen, don't jump."

"I have to. He—"

"No. Blaze and I will take you to him."

She stared at him and shook her head. "Ryan, if you—"

He grabbed her hand. "I will not let him hurt you. You understand? I will get your soul back from that monster."

She hoped he could. Tears burned, but she kept them from forming. "Thank you."

Blaze turned in the direction of Franco, and the urge to jump left her.

"Ryan."

"We're in this together, right? That's what you told me." That small smile she remembered returned.

"And I meant it."

CHAPTER 41

STRIKE HARD

Jayden stared at the purple cloud as it dissipated.

Gone.

No Belladonna.

Ethan picked up the Sword of Black Malice and held it. A fire lit his eyes, and then sorrow coursed through him, crushing Jayden. He raced to Chloe and pulled her limp form onto his lap.

Jayden touched his back. Her voice trembled. "Is she . . . ?"

Ethan shoulders shook, and his emotions slammed into her. Pain rippled off him like a volatile storm trembling to become a tornado. Chloe. Chloe was dead.

A laugh cut through everything, and Franco tilted his head to the side in mock pity. Jayden's blood heated. The only way to kill him was to kill Kara and Madison. How could she bring more senseless death? Lightning pulsed into her. She could strike him where he stood, but he wouldn't die.

"You should join me. If you don't, the Mistress will claim you. Neither of us wants that." Franco held out his hand toward her.

Where was Kara now?

Ethan stood in front of Chloe's body, his sword in his left hand, the Sword of Black Malice in his right.

A black horse dashed up the hill, hundreds of soldiers following. Stormcloud landed beside Jayden and reared, but Zephyr stuck close to Ethan as another gryphon—one with a white head—landed near him. Cliffdiver.

The black horse pawed at the ground, and the rider dropped to the earth. She recognized him right away. Connor.

His army surrounded her and Ethan. A storm beat in Jayden's chest. And the sky cracked.

Franco laughed. "Captain, you've brought the army to help me take in two Deliverers."

Connor looked at Ethan. "You don't know what they're capable of, do you, Franco?"

"I have an idea." Franco glanced at the sky, at the soldiers surrounding them, and then smiled at Jayden. "The two of you should surrender now. Between my army and my captain's, you're quite outnumbered."

Connor stepped away from Franco and approached Ethan and Jayden. He placed something into her hands. A note? "We only have one shot at this. Franco has a way to control the army, but after Kara gives you the signal, we have moments." He turned to Ethan and looked at the blackened unicorn horn in his hand. "Is that what I think it is?"

Ethan nodded. "Will it kill him?" His voice was dark. Quiet.

"I–I don't know."

"Belladonna said it would."

Connor shook his head. "I'm not sure."

Ethan handed it over. "Take it. Just in case."

Connor handed Ethan his own sword and sheathed the awful black weapon. "We have one shot at this. You have to save Madison and protect Jayden." He faced her. "Strike him hard." Connor turned. "Men! Kill the king! Protect these two with your life!"

The soldiers raced up the hill.

Franco's wild eyes met Connor's. "I didn't see you as a snake. I did see your cold heart. You send these men to their deaths without a choice."

Connor tried not to flinch. "Are we fighting or talking?"

Franco smiled. "You can't kill me."

Kara raced up the hill, Madison tight to her side with a sword to her neck. "You wanted to talk to me, Wolfy?"

"Idiot!" Franco growled.

Ethan held up his swords as soldiers started up the hill. He angled himself in front of Jayden. "Is that the signal?"

Kara looked at Jayden and nodded. Then she released Madison. "You ready?"

Madison's eyes met Jayden's. "It's okay. But I won't have long. A few minutes at most."

Jayden didn't know what she meant, but Kara's gaze pierced her. "Read the note." Then she swung her sword. Madison's head toppled to the ground and her body crumpled after.

Jayden screamed.

Then Kara slit her own wrist.

"No!" Franco screamed. "You idiot!"

"Now, Jayden!" Connor yelled.

"I–I can kill him." Jayden's pulse beat like lightning through her chest. She could kill Franco.

Jayden pushed Ethan away and held her dagger toward the sky. Franco had to be killed with a Wielder-crafted weapon. Hopefully this counted.

Franco flung his dagger at her, but it didn't matter. Lightning struck her blade, and she slung the bolt at him. It pulsed through her. Into the dagger. Into Franco. She threw the weapon. Just like when she'd killed Idla. Something warm surrounded her. Not even the rain touched her face. She braced herself for the puncture of his weapon. For the end.

Franco stumbled back, his body hitting the ground. His sword splashing down next to him.

His dagger fell. Didn't hit her.

No blood.

Rain touched her again. Franco's dagger dropped to the ground in front of her.

She looked at Ethan who stood there, soaking wet.

He stared at her. "I didn't know I could do that."

"You shielded me. Like Zephyr does."

Franco stood and pulled the dagger from his body, and Jayden shuddered. How? A chill reached her core.

CHAPTER 42

BROKEN BONDS

Connor watched as the men under his control hitched in their steps.

He stood in front of Franco and held up his quarterstaff. Soldiers around them fought one another. One army torn between two leaders —no, two people using compulsion to send them to their graves.

"Captain." Franco spat the word. "Did you think she would be the only one I'd bonded to? Look! Here comes one of my other Healers now."

Above them the form of a dragon descended.

Serena? He couldn't be bonded to her, he . . . had Kara lied? No. There had to be someone else. Kara had said Serena wasn't truly bonded to Franco. They'd just made him believe it. But he'd said Healers. *"Cliffdiver! The Sword of Black Malice? Was it . . . did a Wielder . . . ?"*

Cliffdiver's sorrow flickered over the bond. *"It is a Wielder-crafted weapon. The Mistress tricked him into making it."*

Connor prayed that weapon would be enough to sever Franco's connection with any remaining Healers without killing them. It was said the Sword of Black Malice was built so that whatever wound it created could not be healed by any Healer. That meant it should sever Franco's ties with those he'd bonded to. That meant Connor could kill Franco as long as Kara was dead. He needed enough time to make it to Madison and save her so she could save Kara. Death bringer. His heart clutched.

And he drew the sword.

○

"It didn't work." Jayden unfolded the note.

Softheart, I hope you're not too late. Put her head back on.

Ethan shook his head. "That's the strangest—"
Jayden crumpled the paper. "Madison's a Healer."
"What?"
Jayden raced to where Madison lay on the ground, Zephyr and Stormcloud shielding her and Ethan. She pressed Madison's head up to her body, and the cut on her neck started to heal.

○

"The Sword of Black Malice can break the connection Franco has to the Healers. It is strong enough for that. I've seen it do that before." Cliffdiver's voice raced through Connor's head, and his stomach squeezed.
"Why didn't you tell me?"
"I didn't know the weapon still existed."
He slammed the blade into Franco, and Franco hit the ground. Connor towered over him and stabbed him in the side.

Franco screamed. He stared at the gaping hole in his side. It didn't heal. "What have you done?" He struggled to his feet and launched at Connor with his superior strength. Connor whirled and dodged as Franco's rage fueled him. Strengthened him. Franco was no sword-fighter, but he'd been practicing. And Connor was no match for that kind of strength.

"I severed your connection to them."

Franco roared, and his blade crashed down. Connor's sword clashed against it. But the Sword of Black Malice was tainted magic. And its power ate away at Connor's strength. Begged him to release a wave of destruction. He couldn't use it.

Franco pushed and Connor fell to his knees, head pounding. The sword fell from his grasp, and Franco kicked it away as if it might hurt him again. "You're weak." He sneered. "Prepare to die."

"You first." Connor reached back and grabbed his quarterstaff, the smooth, worn wood familiar in his hands. Its clean power filled him, and he stopped Franco's blow. Stood. Every strike Franco made, Connor thwarted as he pushed Franco backward.

Then he stabbed at Franco with the end of his weapon, sending him sprawling. Connor stood over him. "Ready to die?"

Franco snarled and rolled to his feet. "You can't kill me with that wooden weapon. It has to be a weapon crafted by a—"

"Wielder!" The shout echoed through the clouds like a bolt. "I smell you."

The Mistress was still too weak to summon her full power, but she was preparing for something. He smelled it. A sick storm churned on the wind.

Franco's eyes widened. "You're the Wielder?" He chopped his sword toward Connor's head, and Connor blocked the blow.

"One thing I never showed when we sparred," Franco snarled, "was my true strength!"

Force hit Connor's quarterstaff so hard that his arms ratcheted. The wood cracked. A fiendish light lit Franco's eyes, and he swung again. That blow hit the weakened wood, and Connor's staff broke in two. Franco swung, and his sword blade bit into Connor's flesh, severing bone. Connor's right arm fell to the ground.

He staggered back, dropped to his knees. Held his injured arm close to his body. Everything below the elbow had been cut clean off.

Franco walked closer, his reddened blade stained with Connor's blood. "Your ring is gone. You've lost control of your half of the army, Captain." He lunged and bent to swing his sword at Connor's exposed chest. Connor rolled to standing and lunged forward. He slammed the jagged edge of his quarterstaff into Franco's gut.

Franco dropped his sword and stumbled back. He pulled the staff out of his stomach. The gaping wound stared back at him. Connor picked up the Sword of Black Malice and swung it one-handed at Franco's head. His head fell.

Connor sank to his knees and watched Franco's body fall into a lifeless heap.

The ground rumbled. Power Connor remembered only because the old power in his body had felt it—before it coursed through the earth. Into the sky. The Mistress's power. And she was leaving. Fleeing because she wasn't strong enough to fight the Deliverers at their full strength.

Whoever didn't get out of here when she used her power would die. Surely she didn't want to kill the Deliverers before she got what she craved.

Connor clutched his wounded arm to his chest and screamed, "Fall back!"

Cliffdiver landed in front of him. *"Brace yourself."*

"The Deliverers?" His . . . his friends?

"The other gryphon is with them."

A shriek filled the air—distant, but Ryan covered his ears.

"What is it?" Serena tugged his shoulder.

"The Mistress." He winced. "She's"—he shook his head—"she's going to flee. Blaze, you have to get us out of here."

Blaze tore up higher and higher.

Ryan hugged Serena tight to him to keep her from falling. The Mistress's laugh echoed in his ears as the sky seemed to tear open. A funnel cloud broke from the clouds next to them and hit the earth.

"Jayden, get behind me!" Ethan tugged her arm as the burn pulsed through his chest. Zephyr landed in front of him.

"I need your help to secure all of them," Zephyr said.

"My help?"

"Use the wind to create a shield."

Ethan scanned the hill. Madison's, Kara's, and Chloe's bodies were scattered on the grass around him, and Jayden and Stormcloud stood behind him. Ethan focused on protecting them and something poured into him. Shot out of his hands. Same as when he'd protected Jayden from Franco's dagger. That had come to him by instinct. It wasn't something he knew he was capable of until that moment. This time, he tried to make it stronger. Larger. He screamed as his insides braced for an explosion. Wind buffeted all around him and the Mistress, whatever she was doing, hit hard against his shield. His chest burned, and dirt and earth and trees shot at him. He closed his eyes but dared not move his hands to protect his face. Nothing hit him. He looked up, still holding the strange weight that seemed to pulse out from him like wing beats in the air.

When debris rained down around him in a blood-red cloud, the purple smoke dissipated.

"*Hold it.*" Zephyr's calm voice encouraged him. "*If you let the purple smoke touch you, you will be dragged to wherever the Mistress is going.*"

Ethan ignored his tired muscles and held tight. At last, his talent told him it was safe. He dropped the shield and fell to the ground.

"Ethan?" Jayden's voice warmed his insides. "Are you okay?"

"Exhausted. But I'm okay. You?"

She hugged him. "I'm fine."

The dust cleared, and he saw what was left of the palace. Chloe's body lay on the charred ground that was as desolate as he felt.

Madison stood at his other shoulder. "What happened?"

"You?"

"I'm all right." She smiled.

"So am I. Thanks for asking." Kara sat up.

Ethan shook his head. "How?"

"Look." Jayden's eyes grew round, and she opened her mouth. "She destroyed it. She destroyed it all."

"Where is Connor?" Madison broke free and headed toward the white-headed gryphon. "Connor!"

Ethan and Jayden followed. Jayden gasped. Connor lay on the ground clutching his right arm close to his body. It had been severed right below the elbow. Ethan knelt next to him and winced. He looked at Madison. "Can you—"

A shadow loomed over them, and Ethan stood in front of everyone, sword ready. A green dragon faced him and held its neck low enough for Ethan to see who rode on him. Ryan. A dam inside of him tried to crack. He attempted to call his brother's name, but words failed him.

"Serena!" Jayden raced around him. "Hurry, we need help."

Serena headed straight to Connor and knelt beside him. She grabbed his stump in her hands and held tight. She shook her head. "I can't—I won't be able to bring the severed part back."

Connor nodded.

Ethan decided Connor was taken care of, and he looked back at the dragon. Ryan walked toward him, trailing his hand over the green dragon's scales. Ethan stared at him, throat tightening. "Ry, I'm—"

Ryan reached Ethan and threw his arms around him. Ethan clutched his brother tight.

"You came after me," Ryan said. Then he chuckled. "And you brought an army."

"Hey. I'll always come for you, brother."

"I know." He released Ethan and motioned over his shoulder. "His name's Blaze."

Ethan laughed. "This is Zephyr." He looked over his shoulder to where Serena sat next to Connor. His right hand was still missing, but the wound had been healed.

Ryan opened his mouth but before he could say a word, Jayden rammed into him with a hug that made him close his eyes and smile. Ethan touched his brother's arm and went to check on Serena and Connor. "Hey, are you two okay?"

"Do you see the Sword of Black Malice?" Connor asked. "Please tell me she didn't take it with her storm. Please tell me it's here."

Madison shook her head. "It's gone. Can we still beat her?"

"Of course," Serena said. "She fled from us, didn't she?" She stood and flung her arms around Ethan. "We got Ryan back."

"Thank you for rescuing him."

She looked into Ethan's eyes and spoke softly. "He was bonded to Smoke. His heart is . . . he's sick. He needs us."

Ethan glanced back at his brother. "We need him, too."

She touched his temple. "You feel exhausted."

"Yeah, well, I think we all are. Let's get out of here and make sure Logan is all right."

"I sent Stormcloud to check on them, Ethan." Jayden joined him. "She said the monstrous animals fled when the Mistress left. Logan said there are a lot of wounded, but he's okay. And Quinn."

Ethan turned to Ryan. "Can Blaze take you and Serena?"

"Yes."

"Good." Ethan turned to Connor and offered a hand to help him up. "Will your gryphon take you and Madison?"

Connor took Ethan's hand and stood. "Yes."

"What about Luc?" Madison asked.

"What about Chloe?" Ryan looked into Ethan's eyes, and Ethan's heart broke.

"I–I . . ." He took a shuddering breath. "She didn't make it. I saved her body, Ry."

Ryan looked to where Ethan stared and gaped. A curled-up form with red hair lay on the ground behind Zephyr.

"I'm sorry." Ethan walked toward her. Ryan followed. His feet moved, but he'd forgotten how to cry. He had become too accustomed to keeping pain locked inside. The grief swelled up in him, bubbling to come out like a brand-new emotion.

"I am so sorry, Ryan. The sword that struck her was meant for me." Ethan knelt next to him now. Grief filled his face. "She died in my arms."

"She was your sister, too." A warm tear trickled out of his eye.

A tear? Ryan felt life. If Chloe could choose any place to die, it would have been in Ethan's arms. Ryan tucked his sister's limp form in his arms and bent over her. And he wept. Quietly, but he wept. Emotion seeped through him again—slowly, but he *felt*. The things he'd tucked deep inside while in the palace. Things he wasn't sure he'd ever feel again. Chloe had saved him after all.

Jayden pressed her hand against Ryan's back and looked at Ethan, who was speaking. "We can take her back to camp. Zephyr will help me carry her. I—"

Ryan silenced Ethan with a hug. "Don't apologize anymore." He scooped Chloe's body up in his arms. "Time to go."

"Dash?" Serena raced to the unicorn, who had just appeared. A rider slid off his back, and Jayden's heart stopped.

Madison rushed up to the rider. "Luc." She buried her head in his chest, and he looked over her. His green eyes met Jayden's. Older eyes. Wiser. Pained. Yet happy.

His emotions slammed into her, and she pressed her hands to her face as tears filled her eyes. "Luc?" she whispered his name.

"Jayden?"

She wiped her eyes and ran to her brother as he raced to her. He threw his arms around her and picked her up. Held her so close.

"You're alive." She squeezed him tight. "I thought you were in the barn. You were burning." She looked at his face. He didn't even have a scar.

"Serena healed me."

She turned to her sister-kin. "You healed my brother."

Serena smiled. "I didn't know he was your brother."

Jayden hugged him. She hugged them all. This was her family.

Yes, the Mistress had fled unscathed. So had the vile Belladonna. Yes, they had lost loved ones. Fought battles and faced others. The storms were just building. Not the cleansing storms of water that bring life. No. These were the kind of storms to be feared. The storms of war and bloodshed. The storms that bring death.

But face them she must.

Someone had to be strong enough to deliver the Feravolk. That was why the Creator had chosen her. She was the right one. And she'd prove it. Together they had defeated Franco.

Together they would stop the Mistress.

As they stared to leave, Connor's soft voice stopped them. "One more thing." He looked at the dragon. "I need you to burn something for me." He pointed to something on the ground but closed his eyes and turned away. "Franco's head."

CHAPTER 43

A RED ROSE

Logan had led the remainder of his battered and bruised Feravolk army—including the Dissenters—as far from the palace as he could in a day and a half. They'd followed Westwind and Aurora to the river's edge where grass, a sicker, yellower color than he remembered, covered the ground in patches.

That evening, they mourned the loss of companions.

Logan watched the quiet ripple of waves lap against the raft that carried Chloe's body downstream. Orange, red, yellow, with a blue so dark it looked black, reflected against the water's surface. He stood behind the others, Rebekah next to him.

Jayden stood beside Ryan, her hand on his shoulder. He let her stand close to him, but not Serena. Something kept him at arm's length from her.

Ethan glanced at Jayden often, but she wouldn't even look in his direction. Serena stood beside him instead. An invisible wedge embedded itself between the pairs. The Mistress had planted seeds in that palace.

When he hadn't been there to protect them.

Logan clenched his fists, and Rebekah touched his tight knuckles. Pulled his hand closer to her. Eased the tension. Exactly the kind of comfort these kids needed to be giving to and taking from one another. Yet something stifled it.

Then Quinn and Connor added to the mix. Quinn stood on Ethan's other side, glancing at either Ryan or Connor—perhaps both—with the same fear in her eyes that she held when she looked at Westwind. That wouldn't do, not if these six were to be one unit.

Westwind stood beside Logan. *"It's the whole pack, but something keeps them from being whole."*

"You sense it, too?"

The wolf nosed the air and expelled a breath as if he could catch the scent of their dissonance. *"A good leader knows when his pack is about to quarrel."*

"And does this good leader break it up?"

"Sometimes. When it's necessary. Other times we just nudge them in the right direction."

Logan smiled, but it faded and he looked out over the water. *"Many boats sank today."*

"Yes. Too many. The Mistress isn't done claiming casualties, either."

"No."

Ryan moved first. Jayden's hand dropped from his shoulder, and he turned away from the water. They all disbanded with him, but as Ethan tried to catch Jayden, she quickened her pace and walked beside Ryan. No one said a word as they headed back to camp.

Rebekah stayed close to Logan. "They all grieve differently."

"Yes. But this is more than grief. This . . . this is defeat. The Mistress is pushing them away from one another."

Rebekah touched his back. "Then bring them back together." She kissed his cheek.

Logan watched them all walk back to camp. Connor especially. He noted the kid's severed limb. Healed, sure, but Rebekah had mentioned his weapon of choice was a quarterstaff. Not anymore. The way he carried himself—distant from all the others, yet studying them—confident yet secretive. Logan wasn't sure what to make of him quite yet. "Will Connor be all right?"

Rebekah paused, taking her time forming words. "Connor will talk to me when he's ready."

"He seems to feel out of place here."

"He's a lone wolf, Logan."

"He'll need to accept that he has a pack."

"I hope he will."

Gavin raced down toward the bank from camp, Glider following right after. "Logan, we have visitors."

"What kind?"

Gavin pointed to the trees and Melanie crept out. She waved her hand as if asking someone unseen to follow her. A shiver prickled Logan's arms and raced across his skin as tawny, furry heads poked out of the trees. Mountain lions.

Aurora loped up to Westwind's side and stood beside him. *"I thought cougars traveled alone."*

"They do," Logan answered.

Then more animals appeared. Owls and hawks took to the branches, and coyotes, foxes, lynxes, bears, and more peered out of the woods.

"What happened?" Logan crouched down and reached out to the animals. Three approached him. One, a fox, rubbed into his palm and nipped at his fingers. A coyote crawled in on her belly and Logan eyed Westwind.

Westwind yawned his disapproval but backed up a pace anyway.

"Our bonds started to weaken." The coyote spoke to him.

"You're bonded animals?"

The coyote nodded. *"We all started to . . . feel less human. We forgot our bonds—as if they never were—and wandered away from our camp. Then as we came out from under the dome near the Forest of Woes, we remembered our people and called to them. The bonds worked out here. But the black liquid is spreading. We were sent for help, and we were all drawn here."*

"What would draw you here?"

The coyote's gaze landed on someone behind Logan and he turned. Connor had come closer, eyes on the coyote. He held out his hand, and she rushed to greet him. Connor touched her gently. "Apparently, I drew them here."

"You can understand her."

Connor's wolfish eyes locked onto Logan. "I can understand all of them." He turned his attention to the coyote. "Go and tell your

Feravolk friends that there are others here. Others who haven't been touched by the black blood yet. We have to band together if we are to defeat the Mistress's army. She has bonded people to her animals through her black blood."

Animals started departing. Some in each direction.

Connor stood. "Black liquid is running through the land. Once it takes over the forest's hearts, the Feravolk will lose their communion with nature."

"We'll lose our bonds. Our . . . talents." Melanie's voice was hushed.

"Yes. Your bonded animals will lose what they have gained from you as well. She plans to rip the bonds and then create her own. From the black blood."

"Like what she forced between me and Smoke," Ryan said.

Connor nodded.

Logan faced Connor and stared into his curious eyes. Eyes he'd found familiar and comforting the night Connor, in the form of a wolf, had rescued them from the palace. Had protected them and Rebekah. "Can we still stop her even though we failed this round?"

"Yes." Connor looked at the others. "Unfortunately, she has what she wants. Ryan's heart, Serena's soul, Jayden's mind, and Ethan's strength. But she doesn't have the keys. We have to stop her before she gets powerful enough to demand them."

Logan breathed deep. They had to strike now. "We meet at my tent in one hour. You can tell the rest of us what you know, Wielder." Logan nodded once and turned to face the others, but a quiet voice made him turn back around.

"Please call me Connor."

And just like that, another seed of love grew and blossomed in Logan's heart. He faced the Wielder—just a kid like the Deliverers. Like Quinn, who looked clearly their same age now. He glanced again at Connor's missing limb. A loss he'd taken to protect the same four that Logan's oath and love bound him to protect. Then he breathed deep. "I'd like to call you son."

Connor's mouth opened, but he stood speechless.

Logan squeezed Connor's shoulder and then headed toward camp, a smile on his face and warmth in his heart.

Westwind loped beside him. *"Your heart is large. Even for a human's."*

"Compliment?"

"I think if anyone can bring this pack back together, it's you."

"And why is that? Just because I love all those kids?"

"That. And they're your pack, Logan."

CHAPTER 44

ALLEGIANCE

Whispers from animals pledging allegiance to the Feravolk and their cause still lingered in Connor's ears. As did Logan's profession. He wanted to call him son? Connor shook his head to clear the thoughts and wished he could shake his heart to clear it of attachment just as easily.

As the others left, he strode over to the riverbank. The sinking sun created trails of red through the sky, bleeding into the clouds. He shed his clothes. Time to see how different running like a wolf would be with half an arm.

The quarterstaff would no longer be his weapon, but he'd trained with many other weapons. As long as he could swing a short sword, he could still complete his mission—without the use of his powers. Until he had to open the door of death.

There had to be a way to destroy her without killing the others.

Connor morphed into his wolf form and stood on three legs, getting a sense of balance. He moved. A slight hop accompanied his step now, and his right limb moved—as if it were whole—but he managed.

More than that.

He ran.

Quinn's book had to have the answers he needed. As soon as he was done here, he'd seek her out. That thought also sent shivers through him She no longer looked like the scared girl from the stone. She'd grown into a young woman.

And his Wielder heart pulled toward her the closer they were.

He'd have to keep that bond from taking over his logic. He barely knew her. There was no way he could already have feelings for her. All he had were feelings the bond had created. Those he could ignore. He had to ignore.

Especially since he wouldn't make it out of this alive.

Cliffdiver found him downriver, away from the camp, and sat beside him. *"You seem to be adjusting well."*

Connor glanced at his severed limb. Yes and no. There were things he'd miss, certainly. Things that would be more difficult. But he'd made it out alive, and the Deliverers had killed Franco. Madison still lived. So did Kara. Whatever part Thea intended for her to play, he hoped it was in favor of his people.

"You seek solitude even after a lifetime alone in a palace?" Cliffdiver cocked his white, feathered head.

Connor chuckled. He stood and hopped along the riverbank back toward the camp. *"Sometimes being alone to process new things is needed. Walk with me?"*

"Of course." The gryphon padded next to him. *"What do you wish of me?"*

"As soon as I find out from the Whisperer's tome how to use the map book I smuggled from the library, I will know where the four thrones are. Someone fast will need to go ahead of me and find them in case we fail again when we go after her. Can you recruit those you trust to go on this mission with you?"

"I will." The gryphon flapped his wings and took flight.

Connor reached his pile of clothes. He morphed back into a man and pulled on his breeches. A soft rustle in the trees told him he wasn't alone, but he expected an animal. Not a girl.

Quinn stepped out of the trees, then covered her reddening face and turned back around. "Oh—I–I mean, I didn't know you'd be . . . dressing."

He chuckled and stared at her back as he pulled his shirt over his head. "It's all right. I'm decent."

She turned around, squeezed her eyes closed, and looked away again. "I came to ask if you'd look at the book with me. I think I may have found something. It talks about a map book and folding four corners. I'm not sure I know what it means, but—"

His heart stalled. Could this be what he needed? "I do."

"You know where to find the thrones?" She peered over her shoulder.

"As soon as you show me this passage, I think I will." He needed the book he'd had the prescience to bring when he'd visited the first time. He pulled at his shirt laces in one hand, and tried to grab them with the other, only to realize he couldn't. That would take some getting used to. With Serena's quick healing, it felt as though his right hand was still attached.

"Oh. I—" She stopped and stared at his bare chest. "Oh." She bit her lip. "Do you need help?"

He stepped back from her. She could not touch him. "I'll get it." He pulled one string and anchored it down with the stump of his right arm. Then he looped the other string around it and placed it into his mouth. He pulled with his hand and his teeth and glanced up at Quinn, who stood with her hands clasped under her chin. "Was there something else?" He spoke around the material.

"Yes."

He stopped tying the shirt, and crossed his arms since his bare chest apparently made her uncomfortable. The right hardly wanted to stay crossed, so he settled for gripping his elbow. "What?"

Her hazel eyes grew huge and she shivered. "You should get a new shirt."

He glanced down at the bloodied half-sleeve. "This one was already cut. I—"

She reached toward him and stopped the moment he stiffened. "I can tailor your shirtsleeves for you. Bring them to my tent when you come to see the book."

He froze for a heartbeat. He could not get attached to her. And she was making this very hard. He swallowed. "If you feel so inclined."

"So inclined? Connor, you're the Wielder." She motioned to his shirt. "May I?"

He looked down at the undone ties. "Just—" His voice shook, and he held out the strings so they dangled far enough away from him.

"Don't touch me?" Why did he sound like he regretted those words? Because he actually craved her touch. Not good. Not at all.

She tentatively stepped closer and grabbed them. Something in her eyes looked dulled. Saddened. She probably expected her Wielder to be someone bigger, stronger, possibly handsome. Not this. How weak did he seem to her?

Her slim fingers tied it up, and then she smiled softly and backed away from him. Her gaze landed on his stump, and he suddenly had the desire to hide it from her.

She stared back at him. "Does it hurt?"

"What? No." He rubbed the arm, feeling the strangeness of where it ended but his body thought it kept going.

"Then you just don't like to be touched by me? I only ask because I've seen you touch the others. I've seen them touch you."

How was he supposed to answer that? "I–I, Quinn, it's different with us."

She tilted her head, and her forehead wrinkled. "You're afraid of me?"

A startled chuckle escaped him. "That's one way to put it." He tried to offer a smile, but her eyes rounded. A shiny coating of tears covered them. And he wanted to touch her. Comfort her. But he stopped himself. It was truly better this way.

"I'm sorry." She gripped her left elbow with her right hand and stepped back from him, looking like a timid rabbit. "I'm rather new at this."

"What?"

"Being around other people. Other than Ethan, Serena, and Jayden, I haven't really been around anyone. Anyone nice that is."

Connor wanted to tell her he understood. He'd grown up around people, but other than Rebekah, there was no one he could trust. "There are plenty of nice people around here."

A small smile played on the edges of her mouth, and she bent near the stream. Tickled the water with her fingers. "Some of them still scare me." She looked up at him and smiled her innocent smile. "Like Logan."

"He wouldn't hurt you." He crouched near her—but not too close.

Quinn bit her bottom lip. "I guess, but he scares me a little."

"Why?"

"I think it's the whole wolf thing."

Connor's heart sped. "Wolf thing?"

"Wolves are a little intimidating. Don't you think?"

She was telling him she feared him, too. It was warranted. "Yes, but no more than gryphons. You don't seem to have a problem with them."

She stared at the water. "They look like the barghest and the shadow wolves."

"I hope you don't think wolves are monsters." Didn't she know he'd never want to hurt her? Didn't matter. It was his destiny to hurt everyone he loved. And his Creator-designed bond ached to reach out to her. "They fiercely protect their pack. That's a wolf way of saying family."

"Must be nice to have a family." That sweet, tearful smile would end him.

Yes. Must be. Creator help him. He wanted to touch her.

She looked away again. "I guess we're betrothed to each other."

That was a change in subject. Connor swallowed. His heart throbbed. This could be the moment he freed her. Pushed her away for her own good. "How does that make you feel?"

"It's a bit strange, isn't it? To have someone chosen for you?"

"I grew up in the palace, so I guess it's normal."

Quinn just stared back at him with her hazel eyes wide.

He held out his hand as if to calm her. "But, I would never—I mean if you didn't want to marry me, I wouldn't hold you to it."

"You wouldn't?" The light airiness of her voice cracked his heart.

That hit harder than expected. "Wouldn't you want to wed someone because you love them rather than because of some ancient betrothal?"

"Yes."

"Well, your wish is granted."

She looked down and dried her fingers on her dress. "Thank you."

Maybe for the first time the Wielder and Whisperer wouldn't wed. Maybe they would change history. Perhaps they were meant to. They weren't the best match after all. She was so innocent and he . . . he was a monstrosity. Perhaps her hesitation was for the better. But she shouldn't fear him. "Just so you know, I would never hurt you, Quinn." Unless he killed her. He felt like he'd punched his own gut. Why would he promise such a thing?

Her eyelashes fluttered. "What a strange thing to say."

Of course it was. He was a bloody Wielder. He intended to rub his hand over his face, but it was no longer there. "I mean, my power—I would never intentionally—"

"Connor, you're not making any sense."

"You said you're afraid of wolves. I just thought—"

"Are you bonded to a wolf?"

She didn't know? "Quinn, I—"

"There you are." Westwind loped into the moonlight.

Quinn shrank back from the wolf. "Oh."

Westwind paused at Quinn's reaction and glanced at Connor. *"Logan's looking for you."*

"Thank you," Connor said. And Westwind bowed his head slightly before he loped away. Only then did Quinn's shoulders relax. Connor motioned toward camp. "Logan wants us to head back, I guess."

"See what I mean? A little scary." Quinn smiled.

"You don't like to be sneaked up on?" He stood and thought to offer her his hand but refrained.

"Does anyone?" She gazed into his eyes. "I like your smile." She stepped back and bit her lip. "Is that a normal thing to say? I'm not sure I say the right things around you. You know, like what I'm supposed to say."

"You can say what you want to around me."

She nodded and dipped her head, offering a glance out of the corner of her eye. Her cheeks flushed.

"Quinn, I like your smile, too." Possibly too much.

"Really?"

"Yes. And I'm really sorry about being so hard on you about the book. And for not being the one to rescue you from that island."

"But you did rescue me. You heard me when no one else did. And you sent the others. You really have nothing to apologize for."

Oh, but he did. He needed to apologize for the things he was going to do. The power inside him surged, and it was stronger than ever before. He tried to tamp it down, but it begged to be let out. Slowly, he backed away from Quinn. "I'll meet you at your tent in an hour?"

She offered another shy smile before she walked away.

He turned and faced the stream. The water started to steam. Bubble. And he pushed his power back inside before everything in the cool water died.

CHAPTER 45

TRANSFORMATION

The soft purr vibrated in Ryan's ear. Soft, growing harder.
"The transformation is complete. You can run, but you can never hide. If you destroy me, I will take you down with me. Half your heart is mine. Half is enough for now. You're mine."

A lion looked at him, and Ryan recognized those yellow-moon eyes. But this lion was no longer white. Now it was red. And this time he knew who it was—the Mistress of Shadows. This whole time he'd been anchoring her here. Giving her a way to survive out of her prison. And he couldn't get rid of her. Massive paws pressed against his back. Sharp claws sliced into his shredded skin. He screamed.

"Ryan?"

His entire body shook, and he opened his eyes to see Ethan above him. "Hey, easy." Ethan held out a hand to calm him.

A figure moved behind Ethan. Ryan's heart jumped. Belladonna. He scrambled to grab his sword and held it out as he stood up on his scattered blankets. "Look out."

"Ryan?" Her voice sounded so much like Serena's. Ethan had stepped in front of the blade and blocked Ryan's view of the Healer.

"Ryan? It's Serena."

Serena.

Her form faded. Changed. No longer Belladonna. It *was* Serena. And he wasn't in the dungeon. This was his tent. He dropped his weapon and sank to his knees. "I'm sorry, I—"

Ethan squeezed his shoulder. "You were calling her name, so I brought her in here. I couldn't wake you."

Ryan held in a sob and punched the ground. Not his smartest move. Something in his hand cracked. He stifled the urge to hold it against his chest.

"Hey, you're all right. Now." Ethan's eyes were hard. Ryan understood the look. Ethan's next words confirmed it. "I will kill her for what she did to you."

Serena stood by the tent flap, looking unsure as to whether or not she should be there. "Would you like me to heal you?"

No.

No.

The word echoed in his being like a fearful whisper. No healing. No more healing. Healing made him a prisoner. Prisoner to his own weakness.

His heartbeat seemed to slow as he looked into her eyes. "Why are you asking?"

"Healers have to ask if—if you're conscious that is." She smiled.

"You really need to be at your strongest," Ethan said.

"I think I've had enough healing for a lifetime."

Ethan tilted his head, as if he might protest, but Ryan shook his head.

"I'll take it if I need it," Ryan said.

Ethan nodded. "I'll walk Serena out." He placed his hand on her shoulder, and as soon as they left, Ryan raced out into the blinding sun. *"Blaze?"*

"Dragons heal fast. We don't let unicorns heal us if we don't have to. It's consistent. But you are afraid, friend. She's not your enemy."

Ryan climbed on his friend's back. Warmth flooded through the scales, heating Ryan from the chill in the frosty air. *"I thought of her every time Belladonna tortured me. Serena's face. Her smile. I don't even know why I was so attached to her."*

"She's captivating for a human, I suppose."

Ryan chuckled. *"Yes. But it's more than that. Her heart is different. All she wants to do is take away hurt. Belladonna wanted to give it."* So different. *"Does the Mistress still have a hold on me?"*

"You broke the bond. I have your heart now, but only half of it. You have to be careful not to give more than half back to her. She doesn't own you, but she will try to. You're still her vessel."

"The venom is in me. It makes me dangerous."

"You are dangerous without it."

"But it's not under my control, is it?"

"The venom begs you to listen to it. You can't open that part of yourself or she'll be there waiting. When you sleep, I feel it calling to you. Perhaps there is something you can do to stop it. A potion?"

"I've had enough of potions. Let's just put the Mistress away. Then I can lock up that part of my heart for good."

CHAPTER 46

A WAGER

E than patted Zephyr's feathered chest. "Maybe you should wait here."

"While you approach that dragon? I don't think so."

He eyed his friend askance. *"You sense a threat?"*

"No. I just don't particularly trust dragons."

"Well, that is my brother, and I trust him with my life." Ethan motioned toward Ryan, who leaned against the green dragon's leg.

"I'm coming with you."

Ethan shook his head, smiling, and walked toward Ryan, with Zephyr following. He stared at the dragon's spiked tail, leathery wings, and massive claws. Amazing. Then he stopped in front of Ryan and tipped his chin toward the massive creature.

Ryan gestured toward Zephyr. "A gryphon, huh? I should have expected nothing less."

Ethan chuckled. "A dragon, Ry? I would have put you with a fox or something."

Ryan smiled. "I am rather clever."

"Sly."

"Extremely handsome."

"I wouldn't go that far."

"Charming."

Ethan laughed. His eyes trailed Blaze's massive wings. "You like flying?"

"It's the best. Like jumping off all those cliffs in Nivek when we dove into the lake—and then being able to jump back up. It's amazing."

"Want to see which is faster? Gryphon or dragon?"

Ryan's eyes practically glittered. "You don't stand a chance. Plus, Blaze breathes fire."

"Oh. And you?"

Ryan stared at his hands. His smile left for a moment. He turned his palms over, and a flame ignited in his hand.

"Whoa."

Ryan nodded, staring at the mercurial flame. Then he curled his fingers into a fist and extinguished it. "I thought it was part of the taint inside me. I didn't realize it was a talent. Not until I bonded to Blaze." He paused. "I used it that night in the palace—when Jayden killed Idla. I set a black lion on fire. It almost killed me, and I–I just set it on fire."

"Oh. Ryan, I didn't—"

"I guess we've just been fighting to stay alive. We haven't really had a chance to stop and let our thoughts catch up. At least I haven't."

Ethan crossed his arms. "I'd like to say I'll be glad when this is over, but truth be told, I don't know if I will be. Slowing down will only let all the loss flood in. You know?"

"I do." Ryan squeezed Ethan's shoulder. "Which is why I can't lose you, brother. I can't lose any more."

Ethan's throat felt thick. "Ryan, I'm sorry I lost Chloe. I keep losing them. I—you brought me in when I had no one, and you treated me like family, and this is how I repay you? I—"

"Ethan." Ryan's incredulous look stopped him. "You trying to save *our* sisters in the middle of this war is not repayment. It's because you love them. So don't blame yourself. I don't blame you. I'm mourning *with* you. And you—you're my brother. Always have been. There's no treating you like family. You *are* family." He glanced down at the ground. Then he met Ethan's gaze. "You came for me. I *knew* you would. When I was in that . . . when I need you, you always come for me."

"I always will."

"That's what worries me."

"Hey, we're all in this together. We're stronger together. If we let the Mistress strip us apart, we're weaker. You don't have to do this alone. If you do, you'll probably fail."

Ryan looked at Ethan, and his eyes narrowed as he smiled. "That sounds a little out of character for you."

"He's right." Zephyr chuckled.

Ethan let out a soft laugh as he looked anywhere but at Ryan. "It is." He made eye contact with his brother. "But it's time to start believing it."

Ryan paused. Stared at his hands. "I can't help but feel like I'm the one holding you all back."

"Because you got poisoned? It wasn't your fault. You're one of us."

"Not just that, Ethan." Ryan ran his fingers over Blaze's scales. "The things she . . . Belladonna . . ." His hand curled into a fist, and heat flared in his eyes. The heat of revenge. "Sh-she used her healing to . . . control me. She made me . . ." He paused, steadying the shake in his voice.

Ethan gripped Ryan's shoulder.

Ryan breathed deep. "I believed I loved her. I don't think I can ever let a Healer touch me again." He swallowed. "I'm sorry. Serena . . ."

"Hey." Ethan squeezed Ryan's shoulder, and his chest ached. He needed Belladonna to pay for what she'd done. She deserved a fate worse than death. "Serena will be fine. Okay?"

Ryan nodded.

Ethan tried to gain eye contact. "Do not apologize. What that evil woman did to you is"—he clenched his jaw, tamping down anger—"don't apologize for what she did to you. Serena will understand. And you have time to figure it out."

Ryan still wouldn't look up.

Ethan dropped his hand from his brother's shoulder. "Ryan, I know you feel like you lost a piece of yourself in there. Your self-control."

Ryan's eyes snapped up to meet his.

Ethan clenched his fists. "I want to kill her for hurting you. But you won't get back what you lost by punishing yourself."

"Look at you, growing up." There was an edge to Ryan's voice.

Ethan scoffed.

Ryan shook his head. "I'm sorry. You're right."

"I know." Ethan smiled.

Ryan laughed and smacked Ethan's arm, harder than a typical playful punch. "Idiot."

Ethan held his hands out, palms up, and laughed. "What did I do to deserve that?"

"Jayden said you jumped in front of a sword to save a Healer. A Healer! You really do have a death wish, don't you?" He made to smack Ethan's arm again, but Ethan blocked him.

Ryan cocked an eyebrow.

Ethan smiled. "I said two free hits. You've exceeded your limit."

"Right. Well, let's just get one thing settled."

"What's that?"

Ryan's eyes grew dark. "Belladonna's mine."

Ethan nodded. He'd let Ryan kill her, but he'd be there to make sure Ryan didn't die doing it. "All right, but I'd like to settle something else."

"What's that?"

"Gryphons are faster." He mounted Zephyr, and Ryan jumped on Blaze's back.

"You're on."

CHAPTER 47

FACING FEARS

Cold air pressed against Jayden's face as Stormcloud flew through the clouds. She shivered, but at least it wasn't snowing yet. Snow. Her death would be in snow. Her heart clutched. Maybe she'd die years from now. In the cold snow.

"I think it's time to talk to him." Stormcloud said as she landed and Jayden saw Ethan sparring. Her heart leapt into her throat. What would she say to him? She wanted to help him, but he was—the person he loved died. The moment Chloe had told him she loved him—and he'd reciprocated her love!—she'd died. In his arms.

Those scars were too much for Jayden to handle right now.

Every time he reached out to comfort her, she thought of how she was supposed to die, too, and she didn't want to cause him that kind of heartache. It was time to do what she should have so long ago.

It was time to push him away.

He ended his sparring session and, laughing, sheathed his weapon and took a seat away from the other sparrers. And his sorrow rushed into her like a waterfall. She stared at him, heart ripping more with each beat. And he saw her. Hope rose in him.

Oh, Ethan. He was more important than her feelings. And this was for the best.

She slid off Stormcloud's back and approached him. His warm smile lured her closer than she had planned to sit, but she was still farther than arm's length from him. His brown eyes flicked toward her for a moment, and she caught the pools of sorrow in them. Sorrow he didn't show in his convincing smile.

She didn't dare touch him; too many feelings would open up in her heart if she did. "How are you?"

He breathed deep, as if he wanted to speak and didn't at the same time. Who was she kidding? It didn't really matter how Ethan felt—whether he'd loved Chloe more. Jayden loved him. What he needed mattered most.

She pulled him close, and he wrapped his arms around her. Held her so strong. And he rested his cheek on her head. His emotions rolled over her: pain, sorrow, hurt, anger, and . . . love. He felt loved. By her. She hugged him tighter.

Slowly the love blossomed in his heart. Beat by beat, it surpassed the feelings of hurt and pain. Sorrow remained, but love pulsed beside it.

"I'm so sorry, Ethan," she whispered. "What do you need?"

"Just this."

Her heart fluttered and her throat tightened. Why hadn't she comforted him sooner?

He released his hold and looked deep into her eyes. "How are you holding up?"

"I'm feeling ready to put this witch back where she belongs."

He nodded, the intensity behind his eyes burning her heart with his emotions. "I won't let her take anyone else I love." He grabbed Jayden's hands and shifted so he almost faced her straight on. "Jay—"

"Chloe loved you." Her voice cracked. It wasn't supposed to crack.

His eyebrows rose and he shook his head. "I—I know. I had no idea. Sh-she *loved* me."

"I know."

"You knew?"

"No—well, yes, but only for a few weeks."

"Y-you—why didn't you say something?"

"Should I have?"

He shook his head. "No. It just surprised me."

The strange smile he gave her didn't resemble a look someone gave when they were relieved, but that's what he felt. Relief. And . . . some kind of happiness. He still gripped both of her hands.

"I should have told you. You deserved to know. You could have . . ."

He narrowed his eyes. "Could have what?"

"I don't know." She pulled her hands out of his grip, and he stared at her. Stared. As if her reaction amazed him. *Really?* Was it so amazing that Chloe had loved him? After everything, could he not see it? It had been so obvious. And right there for the taking.

"Jayden," he grabbed her hands again, but she pulled away. He cocked his head. "You thought I was in love with Chloe?"

"You told her—when she was—you admitted it."

"She was dying."

"I'm sorry she's gone. I wanted you to be happy."

He leaned back, and his dark eyes scanned her face. The hint of his lopsided smile spread his lips. "Jayden, are you doubting my love for you?"

That statement bore so much hope.

His eyes squinted as he watched her, as if he expected an answer. She shook her head. "I might have, I guess. A little. I mean—"

This time when he trapped her hands, she didn't resist. He tugged her closer. "The correct answer is 'never.'"

"Never," she repeated without meaning to.

He tilted his head, and one corner of his mouth darted up. "That's right. Now, let me make this absolutely clear." He placed something in her palm. She curled her fingers around the object but didn't tear her gaze from his. Those brown eyes almost sparkled. The object was cool in her hands. Smooth. Except for one side where there were grooves. Grooves on a polished stone. Her heart hammered. She didn't want to look in case this wasn't real. Wasn't what she hoped it was.

He smiled. "Take a look."

Slowly she opened her hand.

Her breathing hitched on her heartbeat. A stone. She couldn't breathe. A marriage stone? There was a picture on it. She'd felt the etchings, but they lay against her palm, and with her hands currently shaking, she feared flipping it over. Wasn't she supposed to be pushing him away?

"Jayden, I pledge my heart to you, if you'll have it."

She sucked in a breath and tears formed. She curled her fingers around the stone and pressed her fist into her forehead as laughter and tears mingled.

He tried to nudge her hand away. "Don't hide. At least look at it. Or say something."

Still clutching the stone tight, she held her fist over her heart. Tears leaked out of her eyes. She couldn't push him away. She was too weak. She loved him too much. "Oh, Ethan. Of course, I accept. I accept and I return your pledge."

He leaned in and kissed her. So deep, she lost every thought. She felt the stone in her hand, felt every touch of his fingers against her neck, her skin. His emotions tapped on her heart. Swirled into her being. And the love there made her ache. Made her want to sing.

How had she ever doubted his love?

He found her hand and uncurled her fingers. "Do you like it?"

It was blue—dark blue—with a crack along one side. She ran her finger over the crack. Lightning. Beneath it reared a horse with wings. How long had it taken him to etch that? "Stormcloud." She looked into his waiting eyes. "I love it."

"That's a relief."

He felt so strangely vulnerable. As if he wasn't sure she'd like it. Confident Ethan feeling unsure? She grabbed his hand. "You know I love you."

Ethan breathed deep and all his walls dropped. True emotion flooded into her as though she'd turned on her talent. And her ears didn't just tingle—her whole body did. He'd never felt so vulnerable and alive at once. The electricity crackled between them. And this kiss shot lightning through her blood. Into her soul. Left her stunned with her eyes closed even after.

He ran his fingers over her cheek, and his breath heated her ear. "Never, ever doubt my love."

She opened her eyes and looked into his. Love pulsed from his—so strong, so pure, and so alive. She brushed her fingers over the side of his face and smiled. "I won't."

Never again.

CHAPTER 48

HIDDEN ANSWERS

Serena sat in her tent and flipped through the pages of the counters book. The way it was set up, she had to actually know the name of the spell to find the counter. But she didn't know which spell had been placed on the Black Blood Army to make the venom pulse through their blood yet not taint their hearts. And she didn't know which spell Belladonna had placed on Ryan to make him love her.

Love.

To think that someone called this fake and forced attachment by the same term as the true and freely given emotion. Well, more than that. Love, real love, was much more than emotion. It was a decision. A powerful force no man could destroy. What Belladonna had taken from Ryan was not love, no matter what she called it.

What Ryan called it.

She sighed and flipped another page. First she had to go through the symptoms listed at the top of each counters spell to find out which one she might need. Finding the counter to Ryan's spell might not be easy, but hopefully finding the black blood counter would be easier. Either way, she was tired of this stupid book and the way the descriptions of these spells made her skin feel oily and gross.

Quinn walked into the tent, her eyes on Serena though her head hung low and defeated.

Serena placed her finger in the page of the book. "What's wrong, sweetheart?"

Quinn folded her hands in her lap and sat cross-legged on the ground near Serena. "I think Connor doesn't want to marry me."

Ah. The betrothals. That heartache weighed heavy on her, too. And Quinn had been so excited and nervous to meet her Wielder. Serena smiled. "Connor is very driven. He might not show his feelings readily."

Quinn nodded, staring at the ground.

Serena bumped her shoulder against Quinn's to try and cheer her. "What did he say? Perhaps I can help you unravel it."

"He said he would rather wed someone because of love than an ancient betrothal."

"That's good."

Quinn's head popped up. "It is?"

"It means he wants you to love him, not feel like you have to marry him."

"How would you get that?"

"Trust me. Betrothals are something that oftentimes both parties don't agree to. I see the way Connor tries not to look at you. He wants you to know you have a choice. If you choose to fall for him, then he'll be willing to let his feelings show."

Quinn stared at her with her mouth open. "Really?"

"Yes. You probably just need to talk to him more."

"About what? I mean, I don't think I'm good at talking to people."

Serena smiled. This was actually a welcome break from all the dark magic in that book. "Well, ask him how he's doing. Have you talked to him about that? Maybe ask him how he's adjusting with his arm?"

Quinn sat silent for a moment, her eyebrows drawn together. "Is Connor bonded to wolves?"

Serena cocked her head. "I'm not sure that's the right term. He's a Wielder, he's bonded to many things. Why do you ask?"

"Because when I told him I was afraid of wolves, he started acting a little funny. If I didn't know better, I'd say he seemed a little hurt."

"Oh, Quinn. Connor *is* a wolf."

"What?"

"He can change his form to be a wolf."

Quinn's eyes rounded. "Oh no. That's why he thinks I don't want to wed him?"

She touched Quinn's shoulder. "Are you afraid of him?"

"No. Maybe I should tell him?"

Serena hoped her grin caused Quinn to let go of her anxiety about this. "It wouldn't hurt."

With a lighter face, Quinn pulled out her book. "Then I will. When he comes by later."

Serena sighed. At least Connor wasn't avoiding Quinn. Ryan, well, he'd been nowhere near her since they returned from the funeral. Perhaps he did hate her now simply because she was a Healer. Didn't seem fair.

She searched in the book until Quinn fell asleep, then she took a break to cover the Whisperer with a blanket.

A few moments later, Connor showed up. "Is Quinn around?"

"Sleeping." Serena met him at the door and invited him inside.

"Do you think she'd mind if I looked at the Whisperer book while she slept?"

"Not at all." She took it from the sleeping Quinn, careful not to disturb her. "You think this has the answers you need?" She handed him the book.

He nodded toward the spell book she carried. "May we both find the answers we need quickly."

There was no arguing with that. She motioned to his severed arm. "I'm sorry I couldn't—"

"No, no." He slid the book under his arm, pinning it to his body, and touched her shoulder with his free hand. "Your healing saved me. Thank you."

That made her feel better. At least it reminded her that not everyone around here hated her power. Just Ryan. She clutched the spell book tight and exited the tent. Connor followed until they parted ways at Logan's tent. Serena found Dash lying in the sunshine beneath the solitude of a tall, lonely tree. She sat and leaned against him, then opened the book again.

"Um, can I join you?"

Serena looked up and stared as Ryan stood in front of her, scratching the back of his neck.

Dash chuckled. "Well, are you going to answer the boy?"

She knew she should stop before he caught her staring, but it was too late. Now he'd entrapped her, and there was nothing she could do. Except stare. And feel her heart pounding.

"Serena?"

"Please." She moved over from Dash to lean against the tree instead. Then she touched the ground beside her, inviting Ryan to lean against the tree, too.

"Are you sure you're okay with this?"

"Yes." She composed herself and straightened her spine, but her insides wanted to melt.

He rubbed the back of his neck again and motioned to the book. "I'd like to help."

"It's a start." Dash's voice cut into her thoughts, but he chuckled. *"You're going to scare him away if you don't stop staring."*

Serena turned her attention back to the book and flipped a few pages. "I really don't know what I'm looking for. It gives names of the spells. Then it gives the counter. I don't know the name for the spell she used. There are lists of symptoms."

He sidled closer to her, and his arm brushed against hers. He didn't move away at the touch. In fact, he seemed to relax. She tried to remain nonchalant about the fact that his contact made her skin flush. Slowly, she turned another page.

He chuckled and the rumble in his chest vibrated into her. "Coon paw? Now that's a strange spell name."

She snatched another look at him and the way the smile lightened his face as he searched the book. It reminded her of that first time they'd met. Her heart fluttered that part of him was still that same Ryan.

He curved his hand into a hook that looked nothing like the rendering of the coon's paw in the book and made a funny face. "I didn't see any inhuman hands, so I don't think this is the one."

Serena laughed at his impression. "Coon's paw is a plant. See?" She motioned to the plant at the same time as he touched the picture and said, "Oh. I see."

Their fingers brushed and they froze. He gripped her hand, and her gaze snapped up to him.

He squeezed her hand and his eyes rounded. "Thank you, Serena. For coming after me. For helping me break the bond. I know I haven't really been—I'm not trying to avoid you. I—well, yes I am, but not for the reasons you think." His fingers trailed across her sensitive skin.

She stayed still and quiet in case he wanted to finish. In case any movement or sound would break this.

He let go of her hand. "I hardly know you. But I feel . . . I feel very close to you."

"The bond created the night we were born does that. I mean, you haven't known Blaze very long, and the two of you are quite close. Bonds are funny things."

A sly smile hit his face and reminded her of the spark in his eyes that had since dulled. "You don't seem to like flying on dragons."

She laughed. "You noticed? It's not the dragon; it's being far above the earth. I didn't realize how terrifying it would be."

"Terrifying and amazing." He caught her in a sideways glance. "At least fascinating."

She smiled at his use of the word she'd overused during their first meeting. And her heart felt lighter. "Definitely fascinating."

"And I don't mind if you have to nearly squeeze me in half to stay on." He looked at her shyly.

"In half? I wasn't *that* scared."

He smirked. "You were pretty scared." The smirk left. Only a small smile remained. And his eyes were the heart of it. "I'm sorry the fact that you're a Healer makes me uncomfortable."

Oh, Ryan. What has that evil woman done to you? "It's understandable. But I'm not like her."

"I know." He whispered and pointed to his head. "I know that here." Then he placed his hand over his heart. "This needs convincing."

Her throat grew thick. "Then I'll do everything I can. Whatever you need."

He looked up at her, his gaze asking if she was serious.

She touched her chest where her heart thrummed. "I can't lie."

"Thank you." Then his gaze fell to the book in her lap. His eyes widened, and his shoulders rose and fell with quick breaths. "Look at this drawing. This is how they looked."

She stared where his fingers traced the page. "What do you see?"

"This trancelike state. This is the army. This is the spell. Look. This is a black lion's wing."

"You're sure."

His voice turned cold. "I'm sure."

"Thank you, Ryan." She opened her arms to hug him, then wasn't sure if she should. But he tucked her in close to him and held her as if he was hugging her for a different reason altogether. The type of healing she couldn't perform with just one touch.

She rubbed her hand over his back and felt ridges of scars beneath her fingers. The pain he still carried because he wouldn't let anyone heal him.

He let go and sprang back, as if he regretted touching her.

Had she offended him? Broken trust? "Ryan?"

His eyes narrowed to slits and he tucked his chin.

"Will you tell me what's wrong?" she asked.

"I can't let you heal me. I—"

"Whatever you need."

He opened his mouth, but fear sparked in his eyes, and he stood. "Should we show Logan what we found?"

She nodded. "He'll want to make the counters potion."

"It said you needed white alor. Do you know where to get that?"

"Yes."

"We're headed back to black lion territory?"

Slowly she touched his shoulder, but he flinched so she pulled her hand back. "You'll have Blaze this time. And if one of them so much as looks at you, I'll absorb the poison."

His eyes widened. "I can't ask you to do that for me."

"You didn't."

CHAPTER 49

TOUCH OF POWER

Connor watched Logan pace the floor of his tent like an agitated wolverine. "You're sure?" Logan asked.

"If I try to search for the Mistress, she will reach out to me. She fell in love with the first Wielder. She has it in her head that I'm like him. The Mistress will call me to her. And she's too weak to hide herself. We need to strike now. But I fear with the leaking of the black blood, everyone's powers are weakening. The Deliverers might not be strong enough unless we unlock the Creator's power."

Rebekah sighed, and Connor glanced at all four of the people in the room with him: the Protectors—Rebekah, Logan, Gavin, and Melanie. Without them, the Deliverers might not make it to the thrones to claim the Creator's power. Whether they knew it or not, their very presence blocked the Mistress from finding them. Except that as she grew stronger and her poison continued to spread, their shield of protection would wane.

"Morgan knows nothing?" Gavin asked.

Connor shook his head. Morgan had been one of the first people he'd talked to here. "She said she's nearly blind to the future. She only has the handful of visions she'd already seen. Nothing new."

"Our powers are dying." Melanie stroked the mountain lion that still sat with her. Even that bond would fade the stronger the Mistress became. The more her black blood infected the land.

Connor straightened. "There might be a way, while she is this weak, without connecting to the Creator's power. Let me talk to Quinn.

Serena is searching for the cure for Belladonna's connection to Ryan. Once that is broken, we need to go after the Mistress."

Logan nodded. "In the morning I want to be away from here. The Mistress knows where she left us. And if she's as weak as you say, we need to finish this now."

Connor swallowed and nodded once before he exited. His mother's voice followed him.

He paused and she touched his shoulder. "How are you?" She rubbed his maimed arm.

"Adjusting."

She nodded. "As a wolf?"

He swallowed. "More as a man."

"You're alive." She hugged him close and kissed his cheek as though he were a little boy. He didn't mind. "I love you."

"I love you, too."

"Good boy." She ruffled his hair and smiled. "I see you're lost in thought again. I'll let you be, but please, do try and trust the others."

"I will."

"Good." Rebekah returned to Logan's tent, and Connor headed to Quinn's.

He knocked and Jayden let him in, but Quinn was asleep. He held up the book he'd borrowed that he'd found practically useless without Quinn's touch. "Do you mind if I wait for her to wake?"

"Of course not." She smiled. "But I'm headed out."

"Oh." Connor froze. He started to follow her. "I probably shouldn't—"

She shrugged. "Wait outside the tent if you want. Quinn will want to know her book is here, though."

"Sure." He stepped out with her and sat down beside the tent, opening the Whisperer book in his lap again. Perhaps he'd missed something the first time. Most of the pages were blank. A few random pages showed horrible things that had happened to Quinn. It was probably better that no one else could see the rest; it kept things secret. But he needed to know if there was another way. A way beyond his powers. A way that wouldn't kill all of them.

He'd saved Luc that day he'd blown up the smithy. But saving one person and saving an army were two different things entirely.

Your power is you.

The thought came unbidden. He wanted to deny it with everything inside of him, but a surge of his power filled him. Thundered in his ears. Begged for release. This came stronger than before, and Connor gritted his teeth.

Something touched his shoulder, and Connor whipped his head around. Quinn hunched over him in the doorway of the tent. Her hazel eyes looked deep into his, and his body started to shift. Change.

Skin.

Fur.

No! Focus. He jerked away from her and stood, letting the book fall to the ground.

She'd . . . she'd touched him.

He swallowed as fire seemed to course through his veins. Warm first, then cool. Then ice. Then blood he could feel pumping through his body vein for vein, warming him up. Sending his power into every part of his being. He was armed now. A deadly weapon. How could he have been so careless?

Quinn stepped one foot out of the tent, hand extended as if she meant to touch him again. "Are you all right?"

"No!" He backed away from her. His heart hammered. "You touched me!" He covered his chest with his right hand, which meant it was still exposed for her to see. Everything inside of him thrummed. It was like electricity in his veins. "How could you?"

He needed to control it. He breathed in, but everything felt hot. Too hot. Like he was going to explode. He needed to leave. To blow something up.

"Was I not supposed to?"

He stumbled back from her, his mind alive with fear. "Get away from me!"

Her eyes rounded, and she backed up toward the tent. "I'm sorry." Her voice was nearly a whisper. But she leaned forward and picked up the book. "I'm sorry," she said again. This time her words sounded choked. She didn't look up at him. Just let her hair cover her face as she backed into the tent, letting the flap close her off from him.

He had to leave.

Connor scrubbed his shaking hand over his face. *What have I done?* He'd scared her off. He squeezed the bridge of his nose. But she'd touched him. Still wasn't a reason to yell at her.

He shook his head and tried to calm his shaking nerves. It didn't work. His wolf form wanted to shift just below the surface. This moment was ripping him apart limb from limb. He didn't even recognize his own body right now. He needed to let the power out. He ran as far away from the Feravolk as he could.

Ran until it was safe to shed his clothes and run in wolf form. And then he caught the scent of Westwind loping toward him.

Connor stopped and turned, his insides vibrating. Burning. He lowered his head and growled. *"If you know what's good for you, you'll get away from me. Far away."*

Westwind halted. *"What's wrong with—?"*

"I command you as the Wielder to run from here!"

Westwind's ears flattened, and his back arched as he lowered his head. Then he fled.

Good. Tears leaked out of Connor's eyes as he raced farther, deeper into the woods.

"Master?" Cliffdiver's voice filled his mind. *"You are—"*

"Stay away! Please! I can't let you get hurt."

"As you wish." Cliffdiver sounded sad, but he'd been through this with Connor enough times. Cliffdiver at least would understand. He hoped. He pushed himself to the limit and ran faster. Until he couldn't contain the raging storm inside any longer. With a roar, he set a blast of his power free.

The explosion rocked through his core—an echo of what he'd felt in his body. Only when the tremors beneath his paws died away did he open his eyes to survey the damage.

Trees surrounding him for at least a hundred meters had shattered.

His power had upturned the earth. Sent birds and squirrels to their deaths. Made the area surrounding him a barren wasteland. He walked amid the disaster he'd created and sat beside what looked like a family of dead squirrels. Then he scanned the area. Dead animals lay every-where in the wreckage he'd created. One by one, he dug a hole and buried their tiny bodies, and then he howled. The mournful sound ripped through his heart and left an ache in his chest.

What had she done to him? He was ruined now.

Ruined. Slowly, Connor stood. He shook his coat and turned back toward the Feravolk camp. Ruined or not, he still needed to find the answers in Quinn's book. He winced. And probably ask her forgiveness for yelling at her.

By the time he'd made it back to Quinn's tent, he was exhausted. That surge had taken everything out of him. He made sure his shirt was as properly tied as he could make it, then called out, "Quinn? Are you in there? It's Connor."

He waited, but no one answered. He turned to leave, but her voice from inside the tent stopped him.

"I'm sorry I touched you." Her words quivered. "I didn't mean to startle you."

He swallowed and faced the tent again. "Quinn, can I . . . can I come in and talk to you?"

"Why would you want to?"

"I need to know if there's anything in that book that'll tell me what I can do to save everyone when I open the door of death."

Shuffling inside the tent told him she was approaching the door. He waited. She pulled the tent flap back and stood there, clutching the book to her chest, using her hair to hide most of her face. But her pink nose and one visible red-rimmed eye made it clear she'd been crying. "I haven't read it all. I—I think it wore me out."

He wanted to comfort her but stepped back instead. When she finally looked into his eyes, the wolf beneath his skin wanted to shift. To run. He forced himself to remain focused.

Heat.

Fur.

Heat.

Skin.

He cleared his throat. "Quinn, I know we don't have a lot of time. I don't want to rush you, but—"

"I know. And I'm sorry." She moved aside. "Please come in."

He took a deep breath and stepped inside, careful not to let any part of him touch her, lest she trigger another outburst of his power.

"I guess I was just a little overwhelmed." She walked past him and over to the bedrolls on the ground, every movement cautious. She sat and looked up at him as if inviting him to join her. "Where did you go?"

He stared at her. How was he supposed to answer that? The images of the massive grave he'd dug today caused his throat to feel thick.

"I'm sorry. I shouldn't have asked." She hid behind her curtain of hair again and set the closed book in front of her.

Connor sat, but not too near.

"I think I found something," she said.

The pages fluttered open, and Connor drew tentatively closer. She pointed. "This looks important. If you can use it to open the door of death, it will magnify your powers."

He reached for the book with his right hand, which wasn't there, then his left, still trying to quiet his simmering thoughts. His shaking soul. "What's on this page?"

"You can't see it, either?" She scooted closer and his body warmed.

Heat.

Fur.

Skin.

He created more distance.

She looked up at him, and her eyebrows pulled together. She shook her head. "I won't hurt you. I won't touch you."

Damage done. "I know—just—please."

She breathed deep. "It's called a Wielder's tool. I think it's some sort of bracer."

The bracer? He needed it? Then why had it made him feel sick? Maybe because it wasn't the whole piece. Did he also need the rings? "Will it kill me?"

"Not if I touch you while you use it."

"If you touch me?" Was that it? He needed a Whisperer to be able to wield it. That made sense. He rubbed his hand over his face. So it was inevitable.

"It's a powerful weapon, and it needs to be handled with someone who is in perfect balance. If you use it, with your power, it could kill you. But if I touch you, the door of life will also open."

The door of life? Then everyone wouldn't have to die. Only half. Half! He rubbed his eyes and growled. Could he do nothing more than that?

She bit her lip and looked at him. "I'm sorry it would come to that."

Sorry? For what? He looked up at her and her big eyes. Oh. She meant because she'd be there. She might die. It was her or him. Half of the team. He swallowed. "I'm sorry, too." Where was the bracer?

"Your mother gave it to me the night she left." Cliffdiver's voice filled his head. *"I placed it in your room. I came looking for you. I . . . saw . . . this was your largest surge of power. Are you all right?"*

Connor's chest squeezed. He was anything but all right. The only way to fix this was to see it through. End it. *"Thank you, friend. I am for now."*

So the bracer had been in the palace when the Mistress destroyed it. His heart sank. He had to find it. "What about the next page?"

Tears trailed down her cheeks. She wiped them away quickly. All of this must be overwhelming to her, too. Or else she knew it would possibly kill her. If he could prevent it, he would. But he couldn't promise her that. Not until he knew for sure. *Creator, take me, not her. Please.*

She sniffed. "Oh. Umm, it says that Whisperers and Wielders complete each other."

"Is that why you touched me?"

"You needed me to in order to get your powers."

A lump formed in his throat. She knew. And she was terrified of him. He ran his hand through his hair. "I needed you to wait. I—"

"It would've overtaken you." Pink colored her nose and cheeks. "Your power won't die off inside you. If I didn't complete the circle, it would have taken over completely. It would have killed you."

Heat.

Skin.

Heat.

Fur.

Skin.

He moved back.

"Here." She pointed and held out the book so he could see. He reached for it with the wrong hand and growled at himself. With his left hand, he tore it from her grasp more harshly than intended.

She shrank away from him.

He wanted to apologize, didn't want her to be afraid of him, but truthfully, he'd be afraid if he were her. He looked at the blank pages. "I–I still can't—" he stopped when he caught sight of her wide eyes and open mouth. "I'm sorry I growled. It wasn't you." He held up his half-arm. "I'm getting used to this—I keep trying to use my right hand."

"Oh." She offered a sad smile. "I'm sorry you're frustrated. I'm sure it doesn't help that I haven't read the whole book and I keep doing things you don't want me to." She looked at her lap and fiddled with the hem of her dress. "I can read more. And I won't touch you unless you're using the bracer."

Now he'd done it. "It's not you, Quinn. I—" Her interactions with people hadn't incited trust, and here he was making her afraid and pushing her to do things and chastising her for . . . heaven's sake . . . for touching him. Whether or not pushing her away was better for her, he needed to apologize. "I'm sorry." He didn't want to scare her again. She must be wondering what kind of a person he was. "Quinn."

She breathed in sharply as she turned toward him. "I'm sorry you're stuck with me."

Damage done. But he needed her to trust him. "I'm not."

"You aren't?" She tucked one leg underneath her and stared at the ground. "I've been alone for most of my life. Sometimes I just get a bit overwhelmed and don't know how to communicate appropriately with others." She offered a sweet smile and swept her hair behind her ear so he could see her whole face. "I bet you didn't ever get lonely in the palace."

He breathed deep. "It's easy to be lonely when no one understands you."

"Even with others around all the time?"

"Especially then."

She shifted her weight, and her arm brushed against his. A tingle rushed through him. His body wanted to shift. Started to shift.

Connor snatched his arm away from her at the same time that she jumped back. "I'm sorry, Connor. I didn't mean to."

He'd done that. She probably thought he hated her. "It's okay."

"It is?"

He sighed. "I have problems communicating appropriately, too."

She looked at him, eyes wide. "But didn't you grow up around people?"

"Yes. And I have a tendency to push them away."

She opened her mouth as if to say "oh," but her expression changed, and she seemed a little sorry for him. "Well, you don't need to push me away."

Those words pierced his soul. If she only knew. "Quinn, can you tell me what you saw about the passage relating to the four thrones? I think it can help me find them."

"Yes." She flipped the pages while he got out his map book.

She sucked in a breath when she saw it. "There are instructions here."

He looked at the pages as the instructions became visible. This was new. Wait. He tilted his head. He'd been looking at the map all wrong. The Deliverers wouldn't need to split up and head to different thrones at the ends of Soleden. He folded the pages as instructed, and the rivers and landscape formed a shape as the folds lined them up. It appeared to be a huge tree.

"The ancient white alor," Quinn said.

"You know it?"

"I was born from it. A seedling that fell into the flaming nest of a phoenix." She smiled. "It's in the middle of the Forest of Legends."

Connor sighed. "We have to tell Logan." He stood and held out his hand for her.

Her eyelashes fluttered and she stared at it. "You're sure?"

"I'm sure."

Her fingers slid over his skin, and he focused on staying human. Then she pulled against him, feather light, and stood. "We're meant to be a team, Connor."

"I know." And he was meant to kill her or die.

CHAPTER 50

DOOR OF HOPE

Logan paced in front of his tent. Even a day and a half away, he was still too close to the shadow of the demolished palace. He couldn't stay here for another moment—wounded warriors or not. The Mistress knew approximately where they were. The stench of death and decay still rode on the wind. Her blood tainted everything. The animals had started fleeing.

Desolation spread. And just a few hours ago, a strange explosion rocked the land.

Connor raced up the hill, Quinn following him. "Logan, call the others. We found the four thrones. I know how to defeat her."

Logan looked at Westwind. *"Please tell me I heard him right."*

Westwind just smiled. *"Your ears already betray you?"*

"Tell me our bond isn't too weak, friend."

"Never."

Quickly, Logan invited the group of his most-trusted members to his tent. The Deliverers, and Connor, Quinn, Morgan, Melanie, Gavin, and Rebekah. As soon as he had all the information he needed, he himself would go to Alistair and tell him the next move.

The moment they were all seated, Logan nodded for Connor to explain everything.

"It's the center of the Forest of Legends," Serena said.

"Have you been there?" Logan asked her.

"Yes. Healers visit the white alor tree there. It's said to guard the heart of the forest. There are ruins there—some kind of old castle. All that's left is the foundation and a few pillars. Everything's covered in vines. There is a secret chamber below the foundation. It used to be a hiding place that was turned into a dungeon of sorts at some point."

"That's where we go." Logan looked at Connor. "And you know how to defeat the Mistress?"

"I have two options," Connor said. "I don't have the bracer, so my power will not be magnified. I will have to be close enough to the Deliverers to use my powers to open the door of death. That's what we have to push the Mistress through. But she'll have to be weak enough first. I'm certain she must be now. The Deliverers can push her through the door." He looked at Ethan. "More specifically, you can push her though with your wind."

"My—I'm sorry?"

Connor smiled. "It seems I'll have to tell you all what your powers are." His smile faded, and he glanced at Logan. "If Quinn is touching me, the door of life will also be opened and her symbiotic power will counteract much of the destruction my power will cause. In other words . . . if she isn't touching me when I open the door, everything will die."

Logan looked at Quinn. Her hazel eyes met his, big and round and innocent. Then he turned his attention back to Connor. "Everything?"

"If I expel that much power, yes. But if she is touching me, it's only half of everything."

"Half?" Melanie's voice was quiet.

"Two of the Deliverers will die. Quinn or I will die. Half of our army will die."

Logan clenched his jaw. He hadn't come this far to let these kids die. To let anything claim them. "All right. We keep Quinn near you at all times."

Quinn gasped.

Logan glanced at her. She'd dropped her hands to her lap and stared at the ground, cheeks blushing. He didn't want to put her in danger, either. But he understood now why Wielders married Whisperers. "What if you have the bracer?"

"My power will reach farther. I will be able to direct the door of death from farther away. That means I won't need to be as close to the Mistress as I would without the bracer."

"But you can do this without the bracer?"

"Only if we get to the thrones before the Mistress's power taints all the land."

"We race time now."

"Or we kill her first," Ryan said. "You said she's weak enough, right? And she's close?"

Connor nodded. "Killing her isn't enough. We have to push her through the door of death."

"She already has the heart, mind, strength, and soul of the Deliverers." Melanie leaned over the table. "If you get close to her while you wield the Creator's power and she gets it, we're done for. Maybe it's meant to stay locked up?"

"How would she unlock it?"

"The keys," Quinn said. She pointed to the book. "See these wooden tokens?"

The tokens Anna had given Logan appeared on the page. "I have those in my possession."

"The Deliverers need them when they approach the thrones. That's how they receive the Creator's power, I think. I don't understand this part about the power being unique gifts they have possessed from the beginning, though. But it's clear that the power is unlocked when all four keys are there together with the Deliverers."

"So the Mistress can't get the power either. Not without these?"

"Well, that's easy enough. We won't give it to her," Jayden said.

Morgan sat up straighter. "I saw something you're not going to like."

"What?" they all asked.

"The bracer. On someone's arm."

"Whose?" Ethan asked.

"Belladonna's."

Ethan touched the black scar on his chest.

"Good." Ryan's voice was dark. "She's someone I've been meaning to kill."

Logan glanced at Ryan and prayed the kid would regain his kind heart. Then he swallowed and turned to Connor. "Can we get the bracer back?"

Morgan closed her eyes. "I see her at the thrones. You're all there."

"Do we get the bracer?"

"My visions aren't as strong as they used to be."

"That's fine," Logan said. His thoughts churned.

"Ryan and I also have news." Serena pushed the counters book to the center of the circle. "I know how to cure the black blood. Idla used a mix of black lion venom and then a spell to stop the damage. Stop it, but keep it knitted into the person's heart. Not so deep it completely taints their hearts. If we cast the cure spell, some of their hearts will be too tainted to survive without making them mad. But in the ones whose hearts are only slightly tainted, that process could be reversed."

"Like Ryan?" Jayden nearly jumped forward to grab Serena's hand.

Ryan stood behind her. He swallowed and wouldn't look in Ethan's direction.

Serena's breath shook. "Ryan's . . . his heart is tainted deep. But he was never spelled. The old Whisperer saved him. The spell is what kept these other soldiers from becoming what—" She paused and looked at Ryan.

He winced and turned away from her.

"Ryan's case is different altogether. Those who were given the spell . . . the venom's just a black ball of hatred inside of their blood. When it pumps through their hearts, the spell guards their hearts."

"So if we undo the spell, we could make them tainted?"

"Yes." Serena nodded at Connor. "So we have to cure them."

"How do we cure them?" Logan asked.

"White alor. But we'd need a lot of it."

"If we get to the white alor tree, Quinn can make more of them grow," Jayden said.

Serena smiled. "Yes." Her bright eyes were back.

"But how do we distribute the cure?" Rebekah asked.

"We can make it like an exploding potion—the kind that you drop in a vial. As the vial breaks, the potion escapes. If we can get close enough to the army, we could save many of them. If we don't free them before we open the door to the Afterworld to defeat the Mistress, they will all die with her."

"Scarface said we had to make the blood run red," Ethan said.

"That's exactly what this will do."

Logan nodded once. "We leave for the Forest of Legends tonight. We get the power and the bracer and wait for the Mistress to show up. Then we defeat her and her Black Blood Army." He looked at Connor. "Or we go to her now when she's at her weakest and end it before she strips us of our powers. Our bonds."

Out of the corner of his eye, he caught sight of a form in the darkness. She hovered near his tent. Kara. What was she up to?

She entered, and Ethan drew his sword, pushing Jayden behind him. Connor stepped in front of Ethan. "Kara?"

"I've come from the Mistress. She is here." Kara walked past Ethan and his sword and slammed a page on the table. A map. Her eyes met Logan's.

"She tells the truth," Serena said.

"Then we leave at dawn. The Mistress is ours."

They began to exit his tent, and Logan turned his wooden token over in his fingers. Morgan's warning came back to him: *"It's a key of some sort. It opens a door. And you'll need it if you're to defeat the monster. Her name is Garmr . . . if you don't defeat this creature, it will take all the Deliverers. Garmr kills with fear. That's how her power works. She latches onto their fears and lets them grow until the fear suffocates her prey. The Mistress will use her to kill the Deliverers once she gets what she needs."*

He would defeat this monster. Face his greatest fear and thrive.

CHAPTER 51

DESTRUCTION

Solitude was something Connor missed. He guessed it was some-thing he got used to. He shifted into his wolf form and loped along the riverbank. The ground under his paws was moist and soft still, but padded with old leaves. Winter would soon be here. Logan had moved them again today, but Connor knew the Mistress would find them. She'd search for him. He had to take the fight to her before she was ready. They needed the Creator's power.

Cliffdiver flew the perimeter on the other side of camp, sorrow filtering over the bond. *"I should be with you for hundreds of years. Not this short time."*

"However short, I am glad to have you for a friend."

"Me too."

Connor stopped and sat just on the outskirt of camp, his tail curl-ing around his haunches. Only the sliver of a moon shone tonight—red reflected across the water. A rustling of leaves announced someone's presence. Connor lifted his nose to the wind. Cherry wood and blos-soms. Quinn. She saw him and stopped still in her tracks. The scent of fear poured off of her. In five hundred years, would he ever be able to make her not fear him? His heart mourned, but he was surprised when a whine escaped his throat.

Quinn took a step nearer to him. "Are you wounded?"

Quaking in fear, she still asked if he was injured. What a sensitive heart she had. His love for her swelled.

"Don't be afraid. I won't hurt you. A friend of mine talks to wolves. If you're wounded, I'm sure he can help you."

"I'm not hurt." He smiled at her before he turned to leave.

"Then what's wrong?"

Connor stopped and faced her. *"You can hear me?"*

"Yes."

"How is that possible? You aren't bonded to wolves."

"No, but I can talk to you." She stepped closer to him.

"Aren't you afraid of me?"

"Should I be?"

Connor limped closer. *"No. But I smell your fear."*

"I am afraid, but maybe I shouldn't be. Are you afraid of me?"

A chill swept through his bones. *"Terrified."*

"Well, you don't need to be. I won't hurt you. I have a friend who is a wolf."

Connor cocked his head.

"He doesn't know that I know, but I made a mistake. I told him I was afraid of wolves. It's true, but I didn't mean I was afraid of him. I thought, maybe if I could have a conversation with one, it would help me to understand him better."

She knew?

She moved closer. "You're hard to see in the dark. Your coat is black?"

"Brown. I—"

"I thought you were limping. Are you sure you're not hurt?"

"I'm all right. Quinn, I—"

"How do you know my name?"

"Quinn?" Serena's voice echoed down toward the water. "Quinn, you've got to come back to the camp. The wolves have spotted danger. There's a monster headed this way."

Connor bristled. *"Monster?"*

The trees swayed. Whispers carried through the breeze. Quinn reached a hand toward Connor. "Come with us. You could be in danger."

Serena stepped closer. "Quinn, who are you—oh."

"I think he's hurt. Wait, the trees say there's more than one monster." She pointed toward the east, just near the river. "There!"

Connor turned—how did he not smell them? A throaty growl heated the air like a crackle of lightning. Connor looked over his shoulder. *"Take Serena and run!"*

Quinn turned. "Run!"

"Connor!" Serena yelled his name.

Quinn spun around. "Where?"

"The wolf, Quinn. It's Connor."

"What?"

"Quinn, please, take Serena and run. She can't get hurt."

Four fiery beasts stepped forward, and the scent of char and heat finally filled the air. Connor's hair stood on end. Creatures of the depths of the underworld. Bulls—huge and fiery. The Mistress had originally created four. One to watch each entrance to her shadow lands. They raced toward the water and rammed their horns into the trees. Quinn screamed as one of the trees ignited and fell across the river. Three of the bulls continued to ram into their trees, but one creature of flame jumped atop the downed trunk. *"The Mistress of Shadows knows you're here, Wielder."*

Connor's powers erupted inside of him like lightning about to strike. He contained them. *"Then why does she send you?"*

It laughed. *"Join her now or die."* The bull raced toward him.

Connor threw back his head and let out a mournful howl as his power crackled beneath his fur. The howl echoed through the trees, and they shifted, as if recognizing his voice. The ground shook. The waters rumbled. One tree uprooted and plummeted toward the bull. His powers exploded into the land. They pulled, wanted to be stronger, and he resisted. Another tree crashed down, bridging the river.

Connor fought the pull of his powers, but the land ached with his indecision.

Quinn had touched him.

He couldn't stop it now.

The other two bulls downed more lit trees, and fire started to spread. He needed to douse it. To save the Feravolk.

His power ripped through him, free.

With a surge this strong, someone would die. He did all he could to target the three remaining beasts headed for him and Serena and Quinn.

Water rose into a long pillar, bleeding the river dry. One bull hit another tree with its horns. It ignited into flame, and fell, spreading more fire through the forest.

Connor unleashed the river. The water fell on the beasts, dousing everything. They screamed and drowned with a hiss. All but one. Black char dripped off of it as it climbed free of the water, and it continued charging at him, hitting everything in its way. Connor leapt forward. His steel-trap jaws enclosed around the creature. Charcoal hooves kicked at his body. His ribs broke. His shoulder cracked. Still he held on. Wind struck up around him as he held on to the creature's throat. And he unleashed another surge of his power into the creature. No blood spilled into his mouth, only dust. So much dust. It choked him. Still he held on until the crackling breaths stopped.

"Let go!" Hands touched his head. Serena was above him. Falling to the ground, he released the beast, and the rest of it blew away in the wind. Both of his sides throbbed, and his left foreleg dangled uselessly. But that was nothing compared to the destruction he'd caused. Most of the water had doused the fire, but the riverbed lay dry. The woods were charred. The valley looked as though it had been without water for decades. Just like the Forest of Death. Just like where that creature had come from.

Death Bringer.

That's what he was.

He tried to drag himself to stand, but pain crushed his insides. He fell to the ground and let out a whine.

"Connor!" Quinn raced to him. "Oh." She touched him and he whimpered.

She ran her fingers along his face. His ear. His neck. He closed his eyes.

"Quinn?"

That was Serena's voice. She . . . why were his thoughts so muddied?

"Oh, look what he's done." Serena stopped and surveyed the landscape.

Now Connor's heart joined in the pain.

Quinn's hand retreated. "The monsters."

"No." Serena dropped to his side. "Connor."

"What?" Quinn's voice was breathless. She backed away from him as Serena leaned over him.

"Hang on, Connor. I got you." Serena placed her hand on him, and he no longer wanted to be healed. When he looked in Quinn's eyes and saw the horror of what he'd done mirrored in them, he wanted to die.

"Connor, if you have no will to live, it makes my job much harder." Serena's voice would have been a comfort if he didn't want to dissolve into nothing.

He thought of his mission to keep the Deliverers safe and his purpose filled him again like a spring. *"Take all the strength you need."*

Serena's healing pulsed through him. Mended everything but the ache in his soul.

Quinn stared at him, her eyes huge. "You—" she stopped and shook her head. "What are you capable of?"

Death.

Destruction.

"My powers are like the Mistress's."

Quinn gasped and pulled away from him, but something deep in Connor's bones rose up like a warning. He looked at Serena. *"She meant to draw me away. The Mistress is here—in the Shadowland. She can access the Shadowland. This was a distraction."*

CHAPTER 52

THE SHADOWS

Logan lay next to his wife while the night grew deeper. Darkness had settled by the time Westwind sent him a warning. Logan sat up, and Rebekah with him.

"What is it?" she asked.

"Westwind sees something strange approaching. I'm going to look into it." He strapped on his weapons, and Rebekah wrapped her arms around him.

"Hurry back." She held him tight.

He pulled her in for a kiss. Then he stepped outside and headed toward the edge of camp. The trees around them shielded the group, but even they looked thinner than before.

The night air was uncommonly cool, but something was off in the breeze. Not just the chill. Not just the lack of moisture in the air. The changing of seasons was always full of new sensations, but this breeze was void of sounds, smells, tastes. A strange light, like a distant fire, gave the night an eerie glow.

"Is your fur on end?" Westwind's voice carried over the bond from where he was—not far west—but the breeze that blew through camp muffled his voice. That shouldn't happen. That was new. It meant the wind belonged to more than the forest.

"Did you sense that?" Logan stopped and felt the air with his fingers. Every speck of dust and sting of cold.

"Something hunts you, friend." Westwind's words came slow and deliberate, as if they waited in the shadows stalking prey. But he was

right. That was the feeling. Something stalked him. A tremor rocked the ground, and Logan turned to the west. Fire sprouted up from the trees near the river. "What is that?"

Westwind's thought slammed into him with the panic his friend felt. *"Connor is battling something made of fire. We need to run. This danger feels dark."*

Logan drew his sword and a deep, brittle laugh—like stepping on frosted grass—skittered over the bond. Not Westwind's laugh. Not their bond. Some different bond. An intrusion.

Rebekah joined him in the wood. "Logan. Aurora said you were in danger."

"It's not here for me."

"It?"

"Whatever it is, it wants the Children."

Rebekah gasped, and the word "no" hung in the middle of her expelled breath.

He tapped into the coldest, most desolate corner in his mind. *"What are you?"*

"I am their worst fear." The reply came as if a whisper on the wind. *"And I've come to claim them."*

"Do not think you can fool me. I know you are no Whisperer."

"No." The voice hissed like water poured onto embers. *"I am in the Shadowland. Come. Join me here."*

"Shadowland?"

"The Mistress's realm. It's how she can send her messengers without them being detected."

Another plane? Logan whirled around to see Ethan, Jayden, and Ryan join him, Ethan with sword drawn. The dragon, gryphon, and pegasus followed. Where was Serena?

"You are her messenger?" he asked the voice in his mind.

"I am more than that. I have her power. I am death."

Logan's sword trembled with the shiver that coursed through him. He looked over his shoulder at the others. Westwind stood behind Rebekah and stared at the void in front of Logan. The others scanned the woods as if trying to find the threat.

If he could fight this creature—the Mistress's barghest—in the

Shadow realm, he could give them all a chance to flee. Morgan had told him this moment would come.

Logan met Westwind's eyes last. *"The bond I shared with you, friend, I now pass to Rebekah."*

"No, Logan, don't. You—"

"When I return, I will take you back, but the cold here is not for you to feel."

"Logan, don't leave me here."

"You have to protect them, Westwind. Now run."

"If you—" His voice cut out and Rebekah gasped.

"Logan?" She started to run to him.

"Logan?" Ethan stepped forward. Jayden screamed his name.

He held up his hand. "No. This fight isn't yours. You cannot follow me here. Listen to me. You have to stick together. You have to work together. Never stop believing that together you can beat her."

Then he stepped into the void and entered the Shadowland.

The trees exploded into expanded pieces of a whole—frozen in time. Shards, brittle and full of ice, shattered all around him, suspended. The creature appeared before him. Razors for teeth. Pitch for eyes. Ears of fire. It looked like no animal. No creature. Nothing that should breathe.

"I don't breathe air. I breathe fear. I am the barghest Garmr, and I have come to claim you."

"Then you will die."

Her laugh was broken in the wind. *"You can't kill death."*

"No?" Logan lifted the token the Whisperer had given him. The one with the wolves on the front. *Anna said I could use this to defeat my biggest fear.* The inability to protect those he loved was his biggest fear. And therefore letting this monster past him counted as that. *"I will."*

It seemed to creep closer but never moved. *"Stupid, noble human."*

"I protect my pack with my life. Die, creature of death. Go into the door of the Afterworld."

"You cannot open that door."

"The Creator gave me a key. See?" He held up the token. *"I carry your greatest fear, Garmr."*

The beast lunged toward Jayden, covering more ground than

natural in the normal realm. She faced it, eyes wide, and screamed. What did she see? Certainly not Garmr. It showed Jayden her greatest fear. Logan rushed to get between the barghest and Jayden and found that he moved as fluidly and fast as the creature had. Morgan had been right. He was immortal here. He had to kill the barghest before it took the lives of those he'd sworn to protect. Those he loved as his own children.

He swung his sword, and Garmr ducked. She turned her attention toward him.

Then something opened like a black void in the Shadowland. A stream of mist pulsed through and took shape as it joined Logan. His pulse pounded. The Mistress of Shadows. Another creature like Garmr followed her. And she stared at Logan. "Oh look. They sent you. One with no powers? This won't be any fun at all." She narrowed her eyes. "Gnarg, Garmr, bring me the Deliverers."

"I am not alone." Logan tossed his wooden token out in front of him, and the two wolves carved into it by the previous Wielder lunged out.

As big as any horse, one black and one white, they stood in front of Logan and lowered their heads. The growls that resounded out of them vibrated the very walls of the Shadowland.

The barghests opened their maws, fangs unfolding like a snake's, and one lunged at the black wolf. The white wolf sprang up and jumped at the Mistress.

The second barghest, Garmr, raced around them and beat Logan to where Jayden stood. She remained in the other realm, and the barghest in this realm. But Garmr closed her jaws on Jayden's head.

Jayden screamed, as something unseen gripped her. While the wolves from the key drove the Mistress and Gnarg back through the opening the Mistress had come through, Logan raced to Garmr. He slammed his body into the creature and buried his sword into Garmr's side. The beast released Jayden and roared.

Garmr turned on him, knocking him to the ground. Logan thrust his sword into the creature's heart. She staggered but still didn't fall.

Behind her, the wolves had almost pushed the Mistress and the other barghest through the hole. The Deliverers were almost safe.

Garmr growled. *"Impossible."* A power rocked the land and Garmr shook. *"No mortal's weapon may pierce me."*

Logan twisted his sword, and Garmr fell, dead. He stood and wiped the blade on her corpse. *"I am immortal in this realm."*

"You will die!" The Mistress's voice echoed through the Shadowland, and Logan looked into her frantic eyes as the hole she'd ripped into this realm began to close her off. But her eyes changed. An evil glow hit them and she said, "No. They will feel my wrath." And she aimed her hand.

Logan looked over his shoulder. Rebekah had rushed to Jayden's side and stood in front of the Deliverers.

No. His heart whispered the word. Whatever the Mistress planned to do would hit them all. He couldn't let that happen.

As a dark string of mist shot through the hole, the wolves drove the Mistress inside, and the hole closed. But the mist split into three sections. The first hit the white wolf, and it shattered into a thousand specks of sunlight. The second hit the black wolf, and it disintegrated into a thousand points of starlight.

And Logan dove in front of the final string of the Mistress's power.

It slammed into him. Light shrouded him, bathed him in a glow of warmth that combated all the cold. At once, the void he stood in exploded. A shock that slammed into him. Shook him until he could no longer keep his eyes open.

Just like Morgan had said. Logan fell. He seemed to fall out of the void and remain inside it simultaneously. Then Jayden grabbed his hand, and a tear fell into his palm. First it was warm and wet, as though his earthly body held it. And then it was crystal and light. It had crossed through the door with him.

One moment he could hear them from both realms. And then, he could only hear them in one. As he breathed his last, he looked up into Rebekah's eyes. He'd saved her. Saved them. Now it was up to them to save the world.

CHAPTER 53

SACRIFICE

Serena's head jerked up as the sky shook. "Did you feel that?" Connor's chest heaved, and he morphed into a man. It was as though he could no longer hold his wolf form. "Someone else died."

"What?" Serena's heart stalled.

"Someone—when I used my powers—someone died."

No wonder he was still so weak. Serena's heart ripped in two. "I have to go make sure it's not one of them!"

"Go. I'll stay with him." Quinn touched Connor's shoulder and handed him his clothes.

Serena whirled around to see Dash running toward her. *"Are you okay?"* he asked.

"I need to find the others." She mounted Dash, and a scream—Jayden's—stopped her cold. Ice seemed to blow over her like the explosion that rocked the world. Dash ran faster. *"I felt it. Did you?"*

"I did. But there was no pain. Only loss." Something inside her chest crumbled. That meant it was too late. Dash brought her to the edge of camp. Rebekah, Jayden, Ethan, Ryan, Westwind, and Aurora all huddled around someone, and Serena's stomach filled with ice. She slid from Dash's back.

Jayden looked over her shoulder to see Serena approaching. Why wouldn't she run? "Hurry! Help us!" Her heart clutched.

Rebekah fell to her knees. "She can't. He's . . ."

"No! He's not!" He couldn't be. Tears blurred Jayden's vision.

Serena knelt beside Logan's still form, and Jayden felt the sob claw up through her core. Serena filled her lungs. "There's no soul here to heal."

"You have to heal him." Ethan gripped her arms. "You said you could go back."

"Go back?" Jayden faced Serena as simultaneous hope and dread pulled within her.

Serena looked into Ethan's red-rimmed eyes and let out a sob. "Once. A Healer can only bring someone back from the dead once, Ethan."

He stared at her as if he didn't understand. Sorrow spread through him in a wave and crashed into Jayden's own sadness.

Serena touched Ethan's arm. "I can't go back for him in case one of you . . ."

Ethan ripped his arm from her touch. "If you can save him, do it!"

Jayden flinched. Then she touched Ethan's back but turned to Serena. "At what cost?"

"It doesn't matter now. This is a power I must save for defeating the Mistress. That's what it's for. Don't you understand?" Her eyes pleaded.

Rebekah wiped away her tears. "Ethan." She touched his shoulder, and he hunched over, shaking. "He did it to kill the barghest. The Mistress sent it here to bring you to her." She looked at Jayden, and the sorrow mingled with so much love it hurt to breathe. "Don't let this divide you." She looked into Serena's eyes. "I understand," she said. "You have to defeat her or we all die. Logan . . . understood."

Something strong tugged Jayden's sleeve. She turned to Westwind and touched his soft, thick fur. "I'm sorry," she whispered.

He nudged her belt knife.

"What is it?"

He nudged the tip and thrust up, trying to remove the weapon. Then he placed his paw on her hand.

"An oath," she whispered.

Rebekah smiled sadly. "You always could understand him well. He wants you to promise that you'll let him protect you."

"Oh, Westwind. Of course I will. I don't need—"

He punched the knife with his muzzle. She took it out and cut her palm. Then he ran his paw over the blade and placed it over her hand.

Then he faced Jayden, and Rebekah spoke for him, tears spilling down her cheeks. "He wants you to promise you'll help him put the Mistress away forever."

"I will."

He sliced his paw a second time, and she repeated the gesture. Then he sat in front of her. His expressive golden eyes speared Jayden's heart. Sadness rolled off of him. And love. And determination. She just wanted to hug him.

He nodded and cut his paw a third time.

"One more." Rebekah's voice wavered and she wiped away tears. Rebekah's voice grew thick. "He wants you to promise you'll . . . you'll . . . never forget Logan."

New tears stung Jayden's eyes. "Of course," she whispered.

Jayden sliced her hand again. Westwind placed his bloody paw in her palm. *"He loved you like a daughter. I know the time for mourning is at hand, but so is the time for war. We keep fighting, we keep going. He did this so you could win. So you would never stop trying. You understand."*

Jayden sucked in a breath and stared into Westwind's eyes. *"I can hear you."*

Westwind pressed his head into her. *"You've always heard me."*

She hugged him close. Buried her face in his fur. And rain fell from the heavens. Drenched them all.

"Build a pyre," Rebekah whispered. "We give him a hero's farewell. We'll need fire."

"That won't be a problem," Ryan said.

No lightning. No thunder. Only rain. Deep, soaking rain. Just like Jayden felt.

Zephyr and Cliffdiver dried the wood, and Blaze set it on fire.

And a piece of Jayden died, then ignited. They sang the Creator's song, and it meant more to her now than ever before. Ethan held her while they sang. And she grabbed Serena's hand and touched Ryan's shoulder. He even allowed Serena to touch him. And as soon as she did, the storm intensified. Filled Jayden to the brim. Ethan kept the fire from getting wet from Jayden's rain with his shield of wind.

Jayden tipped her head up, letting the rain splash on her face. "We're stronger when we're touching."

"I feel that, too," Serena said.

Ethan tightened his grip around Jayden. "Logan's right, we need to stick together."

"No matter what." Jayden looked at the others. They all nodded.

"No matter what," Ryan echoed.

Something in the air changed, fought against Jayden's drenching rain. Ethan gripped her hand. Fear shot through him.

"What's wrong?"

Stormcloud bucked. *"This isn't normal."*

Wind whipped Jayden's hair, and she stared at Ethan. "It's coming fast. Like a—a tornado."

Darkness tainted it. Fed it. And Jayden's skin prickled. "Ethan, she knows where we are."

"I feel it," Ethan said. "It's the Mistress. She's reaching for us."

"That storm is hers."

The storm surged. Dark and angry. Twigs and branches scraped her face. Zephyr stood in front of them and buffeted the wind.

Ethan gripped Jayden's shoulders and pushed her into Zephyr's feathered chest. Lightning crackled and struck a nearby tree. Bark exploded off the trunk, and the wind picked it up. Swirled it around. Ethan's frantic eyes met hers. "It's too strong. I can't shield everyone. Hold on."

Her heart pumped as she tried to listen to the storm. Anger pulsed from it. Hatred so deep and dark the clouds couldn't contain it. The sky couldn't contain it. *"Stormcloud?"*

"I feel it. It's angry. Unnatural. The others are flying. Tell them to follow me to dodge the lightning."

Zephyr lifted them into the sky. Ethan sat behind her and pressed her tight against Zephyr's neck. She clutched the gryphon, feeling Ethan's frantic breathing against her back. What about the others?

The storm dragged them in, hard and fast, and Jayden lost her breath. Dark, windy, filled with dirt and debris that cut into them.

Ethan clutched her, his arms tight around her. "I won't let you go. I—" He paused. His fear pierced her heart.

She looked over her shoulder. "You feel a threat? Ethan, what is it?"

He wouldn't answer. Could he hear her over the storm? He braced himself against her, pressing her deeper into the feathers, his body a protective outer shell. Was he using his shield? What was he saving her from? She wanted to scream, make him tell her. Then she felt it. Lightning was headed at them. Would his shield be strong enough?

He looked right into her eyes. "I love you."

What? No. His face bore the same look her brother Daniel had right before he'd died for her. She grabbed his hand. "Ethan, don't do this!"

He smashed into her with such force that she slammed into Zephyr and saw nothing but darkness.

CHAPTER 54

MUTUAL TRUST

Connor opened his eyes and stood. Quinn's body lay beneath him on the red soil, the burnt orange color of the dirt covered her clothes and face. And dark, wet red spilled out from beneath her in a puddle.

"Quinn?"

She didn't stir.

What had happened? Memories flooded back to him. The Mistress had sent a storm. He'd felt her power in the wind, and it had ripped them all away from one another. Just like she wanted. Everything in him should have told him to protect the Deliverers, but he'd just used up his power to defeat the bulls. He'd been too weak.

Instead, who had he chosen to rescue? Quinn. He'd held her tight, protecting her from the storm, while Cliffdiver wrapped his claws around both of them.

He touched Quinn's forehead and moved hair out of her face. A red scrape marred her forehead and she felt warm. His heart told him finding the Deliverers could wait. His head chastised his heart. Harshly.

"Cliffdiver?"

The gryphon groaned. *"I'm here. Behind you. Is she hurt badly?"*

Connor faced his friend. Red caked Cliffdiver's feathers in more than one place. *"You are."*

"I'll heal."

Connor stared at his friend. *"You—"*

"I'll be fine. How's the girl?"

Connor leaned over her and touched her shoulder. "Quinn?" Something had torn into her leg. The gash trailed from her calf to mid-thigh.

She sucked in air and opened her eyes. As soon as she saw him, she tried to scurry away, but stopped and grimaced as she touched her leg.

He held up his hand to calm her. "It's all right. It's just me."

She scanned her surroundings. "What happened?"

Connor's chest heaved. "Do you remember the storm?"

"Oh. Yes." She looked up at him and her eyes grew wide.

Connor winced. He had an idea of what she was thinking. And he didn't feel like dwelling on that right now—how he'd fallen for the Mistress's distraction and nearly killed Quinn and Serena while trying to save them. And then he'd been completely helpless to fight the Mistress . . . no use dwelling on that. "We'll have to clean that wound. Can you stand?"

She propped herself onto her elbow, moved the material over the wound aside, and breathed in through her teeth.

It looked deep. Connor's stomach clenched. "Let me get something to help you."

What did he have? Only the water strapped to his belt. And his not-exactly-clean shirt. But she was a Whisperer. "If I pour water onto the ground, can you make it grow?"

Her eyelashes fluttered. "I can try."

He unstrapped his waterskin and poured a few drips onto the dry, cracked ground. The red dirt leeched up the moisture before she had a chance to do anything. Not very promising.

"Again." Her hazel eyes bored into him.

He poured some into a tiny divot and she closed her eyes. Laid her head back.

"Quinn." Oh no. He'd asked too much of her. She had to be weak from blood loss. "Hang on. I'm going to take care of you." He just didn't know how.

Something cool and wet lapped against his knee. Water. A whole pool stretched out over the once-cracked dirt. Connor expelled a gasp. This was much more than he'd imagined her capable of. "Quinn, that's incredible! You did it." He looked down at her still form.

A small smile curved her lips, but she didn't open her eyes. "I didn't know I could do that. It feels so . . . amazing." Her eyes opened and she looked up at him.

She was amazing. He knelt beside her and rubbed his hand over her cheek. "You certainly gave me a start."

"Sorry."

He removed his shirt and ripped the sleeve off, accidentally tearing the shirt in the process. Then he placed it in the water. Clear and cool. Pure. Like Quinn. He scrubbed it the best he could and wrung it out. Then he turned to her. "This will sting."

She nodded and closed her eyes again.

The whole time he cleaned and bound her wound—which was harder with one hand—she remained silent. Only her slight winces told him she remained conscious. At last he finished. "Sorry I don't have anything to stitch you up with. It'll leave a pretty big scar, I'm afraid."

Finally she opened her eyes and tried to sit up. He wrapped his arm around her back and helped her. Her eyes widened, and she stared at him, arm draped over his bare shoulders.

She seemed very aware of his closeness, and terrified by it. After what she'd seen him do to the land—demolishing the bulls—it didn't surprise him. "We should probably get out of the open. Can you stand?" Then again, there was nothing for cover here. Except the dead tree Cliffdiver lay beside. He helped her stand. Her warmth pressed into his side, and he felt every shuddering breath she took.

Heat.

Skin.

Heat.

Fur.

He stilled the shift and was surprised when he melted comfortably into his human skin. Perhaps her touch didn't make him shift; maybe it just . . . connected to him on both his wolf and human levels.

"Where are the others?" she asked.

"I don't know. I was hoping you could . . ." His hope died as he looked around for any trees for her to communicate with to try and find the others. Find out if they were okay. Find out where they were and how far everyone was from the thrones.

There was nothing for miles—just cracked orange dirt, a dried-up riverbed, and the dead tree he was taking her to lean against.

"There." Quinn pointed to a clump of brown that seemed to ripple over the dry, flat landscape. "Take me to that bush, and I'll find out where we are. Maybe I can get a location on the others, too."

"I don't know if it's alive."

"I feel its heartbeat."

"Don't make her walk so far on that leg. I'll carry her." Cliffdiver approached and lay down, making it easier for Connor to lift Quinn onto the gryphon's back. But Connor looked at the huge gash in Cliffdiver's shoulder and refused. "No, friend. You rest. I'll carry her. And then you'll let me tend to your wounds."

Quinn touched Cliffdiver's feathered neck. "You're hurt. Maybe I can find a way to help speed up your healing."

Cliffdiver's eyes squinted in what looked like a smile. *"I like this one. Tell her thank you, but gryphons heal fast."*

Connor relayed the message and added, "But he's not carrying you. I will."

Quinn winced as his severed arm slid behind her knees and bent her legs.

He regarded her expression. "You okay?"

"You aren't wearing a shirt." Her skin flushed.

She didn't have to remind him. He scrunched up one side of his face. "I ripped it." That made her laugh.

"You don't need to carry me, I—"

"Too late." He smiled.

Her eyes widened and a pang hit his heart. Poor Quinn. Stuck with the one person who scared her senseless.

They made it to the withered bush, and Connor gently set Quinn down beside it.

She released her hold on him and scooched close enough to touch the bush. Cracked, brown wood nearly the color of Connor's wolf coat made up the plant's thick, gnarled stump. "It's old," Quinn said. "That's good for a long memory." Then she closed her eyes.

Connor tended to Cliffdiver's wounds as he waited. *"This is deep, friend."*

"I'll be fit to travel by morning. Will she?"

Connor glanced over his shoulder at Quinn. Watched while a breeze he wished he could feel tousled strands of her hair like maypole streamers in the wind. All he could do now was hope that this dying bush could help them find the Deliverers and the Forest of Legends fast. Because answers or not, he needed to get out of here by morning.

The sun drew closer to the horizon, so it would be best to let Cliffdiver rest and heal rather than travel a few hours only to have to stop. If they were stuck here for a night, they'd have to find shelter of some sort. Already the sun baked his skin. He stood to have a look around. There. Across from a dry riverbed stood masses of dark, dead trees. And a grouping of toppled stones like the foundation of something big. Connor's heart thundered and he clenched his fists. He knew exactly where he was. And the Mistress likely did, too. Of course she'd send him here. She wanted him to see firsthand the damage a Wielder could create. She wanted him to fear using his powers. On shaky legs, he stood and walked toward the old river.

"Connor?" Quinn's small voice couldn't tear his eyes from the old ruins of destruction. "I know where we are."

"It's called the Forest of Death." His voice cracked.

"How do you know?"

"I've read about it. The Wielder of the fourth age fought a battle here." To save his Whisperer from the clutches of the Mistress. Many had died. The destruction resembled what he'd done while defeating the bulls. Only on a much larger scale.

"Oh. Yes. There was much death here."

He turned to see her limping toward him. "Quinn." He rushed to her and she stumbled. He caught her.

Her hands gripped his arms and he steadied her. Wrapped his left arm around her. She pivoted to face him, regaining her balance. "Sorry."

"No need." He led her to the dead tree on the edge of the old, dried river and helped her sit. She winced as she stretched out her leg. Too bad there was nothing else he could do for her.

"How far is the Forest of Legends from here?" she asked.

"As a gryphon flies? Three days. Will you be ready to travel by morning?"

"Yes."

He didn't expect her to answer so readily, but he was glad of it. "Will the bush be able to get any information on the whereabouts of the others?"

Her hazel eyes rounded. "The bush's roots aren't far-reaching. Talking to other plant life around here will be impossible."

"Then we'll have to go looking for them first thing." He braced himself back on his arm.

Quinn peered toward the dried river. "Would you put some water in it?"

He stared at her. "You can't be serious."

"The heart here still beats, after all this time."

He pulled out his waterskin and headed to the riverbed. Quinn limped after him. "Let me help you." He looped his severed arm around her back.

She leaned into him, and together they walked to the edge. Dry plants—gray like dust—grew up from the bottom. On the sides. He sprinkled water over the edge, and Quinn placed her palms on the ground at the edge. She closed her eyes. Slowly, water trickled into the bottom of the river. Then faster until it lapped against the sides of the river. Gushed forth.

Connor stared as the air in his lungs stalled. "That's incredible."

"You think so?" Her words took his attention from the rushing water and the green grass starting to grow along the river's edge. And her innocent smile melted his heart.

"Absolutely. You're amazing."

She sucked in a breath, then looked away, red coloring her cheeks. "How about some shade?"

He laughed. "There's no shade here."

She beamed, bright and pure, as she pressed her palms to the earth. A sapling burst from the ground and grew until broad, green leaves spread out on full branches above them. He couldn't stop staring at the way they danced in the sunlight. At the beauty she was capable of wielding. Cliffdiver came and lay beside him under the shade. *"She reminds me of my last master's Whisperer. So innocent. She delights in creation."*

Completely opposite from his powers. He looked past the new life she'd restored to the death in its wake. Death a Wielder had created. Absently, he stared at the rushing water.

"It's pretty, isn't it?" Quinn asked.

"Pretty?" Connor spun around, staring at all the green grass and trees and plants Quinn had grown. "It's amazing. Beautiful." He sat down beside her again, in awe. "You're amazing."

Her hazel eyes widened and sparkled.

She was beautiful.

Her eyebrows pulled together, and she glanced at her lap. "I wanted to talk to you about what happened earlier."

Oh. Did she mean the storm? Or the bull? Or his failure to combat the Mistress?

"When the storm came, you shielded me." Her eyes glistened and a tear spilled out. "You were angry with yourself for not protecting the others."

He bowed his head. "Most powerful Wielder in five thousand years, and I can't even combat a stupid storm. It's my responsibility to protect them, and I—" he stopped as the heat of his power rushed into him as if a broken dam had set it free. A growl escaped his throat and Quinn shrank away from him. He breathed, trying to contain the raging waters inside. "You . . . what you can do is beautiful. What I can do—well, you saw it. I don't want you to be afraid of me." Her following silence ripped through him. "What are you thinking?"

Her eyes met his. "I don't know what I'm allowed to say to you."

"Anything."

"Anything?" She stared at him.

"Yes."

"I feel your power clawing inside of you."

Connor sat back. "It's become more difficult to control."

"Then let it out."

"Out?" He scoffed. "Quinn look around you. They call this the

Forest of Death. A Wielder created this lifeless, desolate land with one blast of his power."

"There's a price to great power."

"That's why the Creator hand picks his Wielders, gives them to the world through the animals. So they don't have parents to sway them or . . . loved ones who get in the way of their decision-making. The Wielder who did this fell in love. That's why he used his powers here. To protect a loved one. And look at it."

"It could be healed." She motioned to the water.

"What was left. But what was here, that all died."

She swallowed. "Is that why, after you rescued me from the bulls, you wanted to die?"

He looked into her eyes. "You saw what I did. What I'm capable of."

"Rescuing people?"

He could do nothing more than blink. The words wouldn't come. Emotion flooded through him—the feeling that she perhaps saw the new, green growth in his power, but not the evil. Finally words tumbled out. "Killing, you mean?"

She hugged herself and rubbed her upper arms. "If I could show you that there's more to live for than being afraid of your powers, would you be interested in living for a while longer?"

What was she doing? Reading his soul? "When I used my power last, Logan died. I can't control who lives and who dies. If I protect one, someone else will perish. Quinn, if you insist on touching me when I use my powers, bracer or not, that could be you. I–I can't—"

She leaned forward, eyes wide. "You're worried your power will kill me?"

"Yes. For heaven's sake, yes."

"And the Deliverers?"

He could do nothing to stop the wave of sorrow that shook his shoulders. "Even if the door of life opens, two of them will die. I can't stop that."

She looked around at the quiet stream running through the barren land. Already, green grass grew from the red dirt. "Could you have destroyed this whole place with one blast of power?"

"I could have destroyed more."

She gasped, but said nothing. Her silence ate at him.

He couldn't look at her. "You think I'm dangerous."

"Yes."

That ripped through his heart harsher than he expected. "I wish you could trust me, Quinn."

Her lips parted. "I want you to trust me, too." She moved closer to him. "I want you to know that I won't touch you without your permission again. Okay? I'm sorry about the first time."

"I . . . oh, that was . . . your touch unlocked my power. I didn't mean to scare you with my reaction to that. I'm sorry."

She stared at him as though trying to figure out was he was saying. "I can touch you?"

He laughed nervously.

She offered a small smile. "Trees take in their surroundings through touch. The air, the smells, the water. They touch everything." She ducked her head and smiled shyly. "I thought the phrase how you feel about someone was much more . . . literal."

It made sense now. She wanted to *feel* that she could trust him. Could he let her? Would he be able to hold on to his human form? Either way, it was worth a try to help Quinn trust him.

He scooted closer to her. "I don't want you to be afraid to touch me, Quinn."

Her eyelids fluttered. "You wouldn't mind?"

He shook his head.

Slowly she reached out. Her fingers grazed his shoulder, feather light. Trailed over his upper arm. He sucked in a breath. She slid her hand over his skin and paused where the sword had severed him. She touched the numb scar, then her focus shifted and she pressed her palm to his cheek. Traced his ear. His jawline. A shiver skittered over him and she stopped, eyes wide. "I'm sorry."

He couldn't take his eyes off of her. "Don't be."

Her cheeks flushed, and she dropped her hands to her lap. "When Serena heals, she feels your pain. When Jayden looks at you, she feels your emotions. I feel who you want to be. Who you're growing into."

"You feel that?"

She nodded. "You're afraid of yourself, Connor. You shouldn't be."

The thump in his chest seemed loud enough for her to hear.

She held out her hand for him to touch. "What do you feel?"

Her skin was soft, smooth. He slid his palm over her arm, over the scars he wished he could've rescued her from. "I feel your powers. They're pure and wholesome." He'd felt more than that, though. He'd felt her trepidation, her longing.

"Connor, you're the Wielder for a reason, and that reason is your compassion. You can't keep locking it away. We all know the risk. It won't be your fault."

"Because I already know the risk, allowing you to be there when I use my powers makes it my fault."

She looked away from him, not taking her hand from his grasp. "I disagree. So do the Deliverers."

The Deliverers. "Where did she send them?"

"Don't worry. We'll find them. I'll make sure of it." Of course she would. That was her job. Opening the door of death was his.

The sun turned magenta as it dipped closer to the horizon, and Connor watched it, hoping they'd be able to find a tree tomorrow for Quinn to talk to and locate the Deliverers. She squeezed his hand and then let go and curled up next to Cliffdiver.

Worry kept Connor awake much later.

The next morning, he woke to find Quinn sitting at the water's edge. She stood when he stirred. "Ready?" she asked.

Connor patted Cliffdiver's uninjured shoulder. *"How are you? Are you ready to carry two people and fly?"*

Cliffdiver nodded. *"It's time."*

Quinn stroked his beak. "You're a magnificent animal."

Cliffdiver's eyes crinkled in what looked like a smile. *"I really like this one."*

"Me too." Connor lifted her onto Cliffdiver's back and climbed up behind her. As they took flight, she tipped her head back and spread out her arms to feel the wind.

"Look at the sun!" She pointed as it rose higher above the horizon. "It's beautiful!" She smiled at him over her shoulder. What he didn't expect was her fingers rubbing his arm. "Isn't it?"

His power crackled beneath his skin at her touch, but at her innocent grin, he felt that he could hold on to it. Press it back below the surface. Perhaps she didn't make his power go wild after all.

Cliffdiver carried them as far and fast as he could toward the Forest of Legends, and at every stop, Quinn talked with the trees to try and find the Deliverers. Everywhere they walked, Quinn touched everything, the land, the dead bushes, the tumbleweeds. She even pet each shy animal that approached him, swearing fealty to the Wielder. And each creature, each plant, even the ground thrived with her touch. Connor marveled at her. And he hoped this battle wouldn't strip her of that innocence.

That evening, Cliffdiver landed in a place that resembled the first barren wasteland. Old power resided here. Wielder magic had destroyed this place as well. It fared better—but all the trees here were dead. The stream that had once been here was nothing but a hollow snake carved in the dirt. Nothing to relay Quinn's messages.

Quinn grabbed Connor's hand. "You're sad?"

"No, I'm . . ." He looked into her eyes and found himself unable to lie to her. "Yes."

"Come with me." She tugged his arm and limped toward the dried up riverbed. Cliffdiver followed. Quinn stopped on the bank. "Look at it."

"There's nothing to see, Quinn. It's dried up."

She tilted her head, as though she felt sorry for him. "Listen."

His powers surged into him, and he stepped away from her. It was almost as though she'd called them. His heartbeat sped. "What are you doing?"

She gripped her elbows, hugging herself. "I'll show you how to use your powers."

"No."

"If you let me, I can bring new life to this barren wasteland." Her eyes practically glittered like the fresh water in a stream.

His heart thundered, and the power inside of him begged to be released. "No, Quinn." He tried to tamp it down.

"I think you should listen to her." Cliffdiver's voice interrupted his concentration. *"She calms you. She pours into everything she creates. Everything she touches. Look at you. Her innocence—"*

"I can't control it!" Connor whirled around to face Cliffdiver, fist clenched. His power clawed to be set free. Not again. Not now. He needed to shift. To run. To make something explode.

Quinn touched his shoulder softly, and he spun around, chest heaving. Did she understand nothing?

"Connor, please?" She reached out and grabbed his hand.

And his power became a calm sea inside him. A sea, powerful and massive, ready to strike but calm enough to wait. He stared at her hand. "H-how are you doing that?"

His gaze trailed up to meet hers. She rubbed his arm slowly and moved closer to him. "You can control it. You just need to trust."

He swallowed, shaking. He pointed to himself with his missing arm, and then was glad that Quinn didn't seem to notice.

"Do you trust me?" She held out her hands. He didn't back away as she grabbed his hand and the stump of his right arm.

He trembled.

She cocked her head. "Are you all right?"

"Yes."

"No. You're worried about something."

"A great many things, Quinn."

"Tell me." Her pretty eyes rounded, and he suddenly wanted nothing more than to bare his soul to her. That scared him. Deep into his core.

He swallowed. "If you help me when we face the Mistress, if you're there to open the door of life, one of us will die. I'll try to make sure it's me, but—"

She gasped. "Connor! Why would you say such a thing?"

A pang spread through his chest and pulsed with each heartbeat. "You didn't know?"

"So easily you accept this?" Her voice was a whisper.

"Easily? No. I don't want you to die. I'll make sure it's me—"

"Why?"

"I've made mistake after mistake as a Wielder. I deserve to die."

"Oh. That's your burden." She looked up at him with glistening eyes. "You think because you've made mistakes and your power is destructive that you deserve death. You stay true to your mission because it's some kind of atonement for the death you've caused. You *will* cause."

His heart melted in his chest. He backed away from her, slipping through her fingers, shaking his head. But he couldn't deny it.

She limped closer. "You fear happiness. Closeness. Companionship."

"Quinn, it's best if—"

Nearer still. "How many people are blessed to be able to spend such precious time with those they love before they die?" She was so close now that she joined her hands around the back of his neck. "Could you love me?"

He looked into those compassionate eyes. Eyes he never wanted to lie to. "I already do."

"You do?" So much hope registered in her gaze. "You're willing to deny your heart's desire because you are devoted to your cause?"

"I have to be."

"No, you don't. It's noble, Connor. You don't deserve to die. I am not as noble as you. I don't want to let you go because I want my heart's desire."

His throat seemed thick. His pulse raced. And he wanted nothing more than to crush her close to him and kiss her. "Quinn, that's a dangerous thing to say."

"I will forgo my heart's desire for you."

He shook his head, unwilling to accept this gift. "I don't deserve someone like you."

"Yes. You do."

His heart ached that she would believe that about him.

She closed her eyes, and her shoulders rose and dropped steadily as she breathed deep. When her eyes opened, so much compassion filled them that his heart wanted to burst from longing. "You are afraid to use your powers because you haven't seen what we can do together. I want to show you. Have hope. I'll be there with you, at the end. I'll open the door of life, and I'll make sure your powers don't claim either of us. Understand?"

He nodded, wishing he could believe it. But she did. Perhaps that was enough for both of them. She held out her right hand, palm up. "Trust me."

"I do."

She wiggled her fingers and smiled. "Then take my hand."

He gripped her slim fingers in his rough, calloused ones.

She closed her eyes. "Now use your powers."

"Quinn, no." He pulled his hand back, but her grip was much too strong for him to break free of. He stared at his trapped hand. At her face.

She cracked one eye open. "Trust." She closed her eye again, and that sweet smile didn't waver.

He wouldn't. Too much would die. She didn't understand.

A strange, warming sensation trickled into his hand, as if he were basking in the sun. Then it cooled. Not too cold, just refreshing cold, as if someone splashed water on him after a long day of sparring. Then his heart jumped. She was feeding his powers.

No.

"Quinn."

"Trust."

His powers crackled and her touch infused them with strength. He trembled. Destruction. Death. He couldn't risk hurting her.

"Don't break the connection now, Connor. I need to be touching you."

She was right. And now he was strong enough to pull from her grasp. Now, when his powers beat just below the surface. Pounded to be set free. She'd called enough to make an explosion.

The power flooded through him. Zapped through his being, and he targeted the barren, charred trees across the river, hoping the wreckage that would follow wouldn't hurt her or Cliffdiver.

And the power gushed out of him, breaking his heart to pieces. A torrent of wind and dust hit the ground on the other side of the river and exploded, left a crater. Trees toppled. Wind—harsh and biting—ripped over the land, touched them. Tussled their hair. And Quinn stood unmoving, eyes closed, through it all.

He wanted to cry as he watched the dust begin to settle, but then he sucked in a breath and stared. As the cloud of brown, stirred-up earth cleared, he could see that lush and vibrant greenery covered every surface.

Trees grew and huge, leafy tops expanded above them. Sheltered the earth. No longer cracked and barren. And the crater had filled with water. Sparkling, clear water that flowed into the stream.

She opened her eyes, and a look of wonder overtook her face. "It's even more beautiful than I imagined."

His heart raced. "H-how did—"

"You destroyed the dead parts, Connor. I simply used the residue of your power to make the unfertilized seeds grow."

He looked around, and for miles all he saw was green. The dead things had been destroyed, and the new life had sprouted. "You did that?"

"*We* did." That determined look overtook her features again. He gazed deep into those awestruck, hazel eyes. "You mean to tell me that, if you're touching me when I use my powers, you can turn the destruction I cause into . . . paradise?"

"Will you trust me now?"

He gripped her hand tighter. His power flickered below the surface, and he pushed it back down. It obeyed. Connor gasped and stared at Quinn. "Your touch gives me control?"

She smiled so that her nose crinkled. "I knew you'd figure it out."

His shoulders shook with laughter, and he tugged her into him. "I don't deserve you."

"You do. And one day, I hope you'll figure that out as well." She hopped on her tiptoes and kissed him.

He stared at her for a moment as the shock of that small gesture seeped into him. Warmed his very core. Her eyes widened, her mouth open as if she realized she shouldn't have done that. But just as she started to back away, he caught her. Lowered his head. She stood frozen, waiting. Her eyes closed, and she tipped her head toward him. And he kissed her back. She pulled his power from him, and he released it this time. No holding back. He trusted her completely. As it surged through him, hot and dangerous and strong, hers pushed into him, cooling and calm and stable. They whirled around each other as she spread her fingers into his hair and trailed them along his shoulders. His neck.

Everything seemed suddenly alive.

And he stared into her eyes.

She beamed. "You opened up to me."

"Yes." He was breathless.

"Look." She turned in a slow circle and he followed her gaze. The land around them had become, if possible, more beautiful. The trees thicker and larger, the green more lush, the water more serene.

"Connor?" she said, the wind making her hair dance around her face.

"Yes?"

"Your love makes me stronger."

His breath snagged in his tightening throat. "And yours"—he looked into her eyes and smoothed her hair from her face—"heals me."

She buried her head in his chest and held him. "You are powerful."

"So are you."

"Now, let's save the world."

With her, he suddenly felt as though he could.

CHAPTER 55

BROKEN AND MENDED

Ryan opened his eyes. Something about the world being utterly dark unsettled him. He groped for any memory that might tell him where he was or how he got here. A steady *drip, drip* told him he was back in his prison cell at the palace. A cold sweat broke out on his skin, and he jolted to a sitting position. His back didn't ache from healing whip wounds. His heart stalled. Someone had healed him.

Belladonna.

"Yesss. She healed you again. She wounds. She heals."

"You're awake."

That shaky voice sounded too sweet to be Belladonna's. It was like Serena's. Was Belladonna so jealous of Serena that she tried to sound like her now?

His breathing quickened. "Too afraid to show yourself?" he asked the darkness.

"I'm not afraid of you, Ryan."

"Of course you're not."

"Don't move. We're surrounded by black leather vines. They've made this dome around us, but they're feeding on the tree."

Tree? That didn't make sense. He was in the prison cell. Wasn't he? He wracked his brain, trying to remember anything that would make sense.

"She lies to you. You know where you are."

"Ryan? Your heart is fighting her hold on you. The Mistress is trying to find you. Don't let her."

He shook his head, trying to clear his vision. This was Belladonna using Serena against him. Her new trick. It had to be.

Slowly his eyes adjusted, and he scanned the small area. She sat on the ground across from him. He stood, and the weight of a weapon tapped his leg. His sword? She'd given him his sword? That was a mistake. She'd pay now. "I am not your pet." He pulled the weapon from its scabbard and swung it at her.

She screamed and dodged. "Ryan!"

His sword bit into whatever was behind her. It shrieked, and sunlight leaked through the crack.

The light dissolved what he thought was the wall of his prison. And through his squinting, he made out black leather vine. That didn't make sense.

He glanced left, to where Belladonna had run. But it wasn't Belladonna standing there, daggers drawn. His throat went dry. "Serena?"

"Look out!" She stepped in front of a thick, black vine that shot toward him. It wrapped around her middle and squeezed. She screamed.

"Serena!" His heart pounded like a hammer on an anvil. He'd almost hurt her. He'd thought she was Belladonna. The voice chuckled in his head, and he locked it away in the dark part of his heart as he cut through the vine holding Serena captive.

She fell to the ground and untangled herself. "Hurry. I think together we can open it enough to get out."

She cut at the wall with her daggers. His blade sliced through the same vine. It screeched with each hack. Another vine snaked toward Serena, and he pushed her behind him, cutting it in two. Then he grabbed her arm, pulled her into him, and jumped through the opening they'd created. On the other side, they dashed to their feet, but the vine followed. It curled around Ryan's ankle. Barbs, thick and long, punctured his skin. Deep. Deeper. He cut the vine and rolled out of the way, watching it shrivel in the sun and retreat.

He sat there, heaving as everything flooded back to him. The last thing he remembered was the storm Jayden had warned them the Mistress was sending. He'd heard the Mistress's voice on the wind and in his head. He remembered flinging his body on top of Serena so the debris didn't hit her, and Blaze grabbing both of them in his claws.

Where was Blaze? Where was Jayden? "Where are the others?" he asked.

Serena paused near him, hands on her knees as she gasped for air. "Don't you remember the storm?"

"I do now," he said quietly. Then he stood, wincing at the pain in his ankle. Stupid vine. Ryan slumped against a brittle, willowy tree and checked the wound. Purple snaked up the veins beneath his skin, and heavens it burned. That could not be good.

Serena started walking.

"Where are we going?" he tried to catch up to her, pain with every stride.

"Closer to Dash. He found Blaze and healed him. They're resting. They should find us soon."

"Healed?" Ryan's chest constricted and he stopped, leaning against another tree. "What happened? And how do you know?"

"The bond."

Right. The bond. Ryan tried to communicate with his dragon, but heard nothing back. Didn't even feel him. "I can't hear him."

"Someone tried to kill Blaze with arrows that puncture dragon hide. He's asleep. You'll hear him soon enough."

"How did we end up in the vines?"

"We were knocked from Blaze." She stopped and faced him. "When I woke up, we were surrounded. I'm sorry I fell asleep. I used a lot of energy healing you."

A lump formed in his throat. "You healed me without permission?"

Her eyebrows pulled together, and she approached him, arms crossed. "If you're unconscious, I don't need your permission. Not according to Healer custom."

"I don't appreciate being healed without my permission."

"It's against my moral code to just let you die."

Oh. He stared at his clothes. Blood spattered his pants at the thigh. His shirt. He pulled his collar aside and the whole back seemed to be covered in blood. "That bad, huh?" His voice was quiet.

She shrugged, and a faint smile played on her lips. "Getting you to keep up with bone sticking out of your leg and that blow to your skull would have been unbearable, believe me."

He steadied himself against the tree as he sank to the ground. "I'm sorry I snapped at you."

She sighed and joined him on the ground. "Let me see that wound." She leaned forward tentatively, as if he were a dragon with fire loaded in his gullet.

Then he remembered thinking she was Belladonna. "I'm sorry." His voice nearly stuck in his throat. "For nearly . . . I could've killed . . ." His throat tightened. "I didn't realize it was you. I—"

Why was it so hard to squeeze the words out?

"Two apologies? What am I going to expect of you next?" Her smile was radiant. Mostly because it said that she forgave him and felt sorry for him. She reached toward his wounded ankle and stopped when he flinched.

Her hand stayed suspended for that brief moment. "Will you let me heal your leg? The vine's poison will make you sick."

He trembled and then closed his eyes in shame.

"Am I so terrifying?" Her voice was soft.

Yes. She was still a Healer with the same powers as Belladonna. The same touch. "No."

Her eyebrows rose. "Why do you flinch away from me?"

When Belladonna healed him, he lost control of what he felt. Of his dignity. He closed his eyes, knowing nothing he'd say about the haunting dreams or the fear that Belladonna paralyzed him with would be adequate to explain what kind of terror overtook him.

"Okay." She sat back. "How about more traditional methods? Perhaps I'd be less formidable if I tended to you like a Wise Woman?"

"Healers practice traditional methods?"

"Yes. Many of us are drawn to helping people, and with the scarcity of our powers in the old days, it was often better to be in hiding. Still, many Healers became Wise Women. And the knowledge has been a part of our education for centuries. I'd just need some bandy root. It gets rid of the burn, fights any type of abscess, and begins healing quicker."

Burn. It did burn. "Where does the stuff grow?"

"Damp places." She rose, soundlessly and gracefully. "Places like this."

"You're not going off alone?" He stood to follow her, sending a burning pain up his leg.

She glanced over her shoulder at him. "I'm used to being alone. Besides, you might want to stay off that—"

"I'll be fine."

She rolled her eyes. He followed her anyway, looking for a plant that she'd said had broad, oval leaves, with a thick stem and magenta blossom. He'd never find it before dark at this rate. And she'd wandered so far ahead of him by now. He tripped over a tree root, sending a shock of pain through his ankle, and caught himself on a tree. *Knife my heart, that stings.*

But there it was, at the mossy base of the tree. "Serena! Is this what you're looking for?"

She bounded over to him. "Yes!" She plucked the plant and told him to sit.

He had no complaints at that order. He watched her as she squeezed the nectar from the blossom onto a cloth from her satchel. "Ready?"

Letting her care for him in a way that didn't involve spells or magic put him at ease. She didn't even look into his eyes once as she worked. Of course she didn't. Here she was, a Healer, and he'd forced her to take care of him this way, so he could what? Protect himself from the terrible powers of Healers? Stupid. He should've just let her heal him.

"There." She sat back and sighed.

"Thank you. Serena, I—"

"Don't complain."

"I'm not com—"

"If you do, I'll heal you with my powers." She yawned and slumped against him, head on his shoulder. "This is unexpected."

It certainly was. "Serena?"

Her eyes closed.

"Do you think we should sleep here?" It wasn't even dark. Had she stayed up all night?

"Sleep sounds nice." Her words slurred.

He nudged her and she didn't move. "Serena? I don't know where Dash and Blaze are. Serena?"

"You think you can hide from me? Foolish boy."

The Mistress's voice thundered in his head, and a shiver pulsed through him. His skin turned cold and he started sweating. "Serena?" He shook her shoulder. Nothing. Something was very wrong. He had to get as far away from that voice as possible. He scooped Serena in his arms and carried her until the forest changed. Thick, dark trees became thin. Woody, instead of covered with protective bark. Bare. Smooth. Strange.

Still he kept going. The pain in his ankle was a dull ache thanks to her medicine, but he wished he could move faster. At last, the voice didn't resound in his head. He couldn't even feel the slight nudge of the Mistress's power. Then he fell to his knees and set Serena down beside him. He moved her hair off of her beautiful face. A sliver of a cut on her cheek bled, and he wiped the red away. She must have gotten it when he'd gone through the dense underbrush. More blood trickled from the cut, and he dabbed it with his shirt.

Wait. Blood?

He shook Serena's shoulders and called her name, aware how frantic he sounded. Finally, she yawned and pushed off the ground. Her eyelids fluttered open. "Oh no, did I fall asleep?" She touched her cheek and the dried spot of blood. "Where are we?"

His stomach twisted in knots. "I'm not exactly sure. All I know is we're farther away from the Mistress now."

"Oh." She paused and looked at him. "You carried me?"

"You wouldn't wake up. And you're not healing."

She rubbed the cut beneath her eye. "I didn't expect it to have such a strong effect."

"What do you mean?"

"The bandy weed. It stops my healing powers."

"What?" He didn't mean to yell. "How could you let me . . . why would you—"

"I wanted to be sure you'd let me care for that wound. I didn't think I'd be able to drag you around the woods."

He clenched his jaw and slumped next to her. She was right, of course. And he was acting like a child. A stupid child.

Something stirred in the forest, and Ryan jumped to his feet, placing his body between the noise and Serena. His fists heated and fire sparked in his palms.

"Ryan, what's—"

He held up his hand to warn her to be quiet.

A tiny squirrel zipped out of the tree and chattered at Ryan as it climbed up the thick bark to look down on him.

Serena laughed. "He certainly had you scared."

Ryan looked back at her and her pretty smile. The way her eyes sparkled when she laughed. But he couldn't join in. His knees were water. He sank to the ground next to her again. "The Mistress knows where I am. Smoke knows where I am."

"Oh." Her eyes rounded. "Dash is close. He'll feel Smoke's evil approaching. Just keep that part of your heart sealed until he and Blaze get here."

"I don't think I can."

She stared at him a moment, tilting her head. "I wonder . . ." She splayed her palms against the mossy earth and closed her eyes. "Unicorns have a connection to a forest's heart. We can feel if it's sick. This one is. That's probably why your bond with Blaze is straining so much. Half of your heart is—"

"Darker than a blacksmith's fingers."

She looked up at him, eyes boring into him with such compassion and determination. "Ryan, I will help you fix your heart once we've healed the land and I get my full powers back. I promise you." She didn't wait for him to respond. She just motioned deeper into a darker part of the wood. "Dash is this way. Come on."

Something about that part of the forest felt off. Ryan reached out and grabbed her arm. She swung around to face him, a dagger against his wrist. He let go. "What's wrong with you?"

She exhaled and sheathed her weapon. "I wasn't sure if you were . . . in your right mind."

Oh. Right. He grimaced. "That part of the wood isn't safe." Ryan looked up at the towering trees as the golden glow of sunset descended beneath the top of the world. The trunks were a sickly gray color, and the scent was more of a dragon's lair, leftover smoke and coals, but it looked as if no fire had touched the place in a long time. What made a shiver run down his spine was that this place lured him. He felt the pull beckoning the tainted part of his heart.

No way he'd head that direction. Not if he had any hope of keeping the barrier in his heart intact. "I'm not going that way."

"I'm sorry."

That was a surprise. "For what?"

"I should have been more sensitive to the fact that you wouldn't want to approach the darker, more tainted areas." Serena's eyes scanned him. "What do you feel?"

"What do you mean?" he whispered while staring at the spot of the wood he was sure would birth something evil.

"Do you feel something threatening?"

"Yes."

"Your instincts are good." She adjusted the straps on her pack and replaced one dagger. "Hold my hand."

He stared at her offered hand.

"I think I can make both of us invisible, but only if you're touching me. I haven't mastered covering two people yet. She disappeared. Ryan felt her hand close around his wrist. "You'll have to be quiet."

He could see her now, but she was fuzzy.

Something that swallowed light emerged from the deep part of the forest. It sniffed the air. Ryan's blood became ice. A black lion. Fear chained his mouth shut and glued his boots to the ground.

Eyes like a scarlet moon locked onto him. *"I sense you."* The voice growled.

Something sparked in Ryan's blood, and the fire wanted to spring forth from his hands. But he kept it contained.

"Oh, pet?" A voice shattered Ryan's world and nearly brought him to his knees. "Mist can smell you. I know you're here." Belladonna stepped out from the trees and locked eyes with him.

"Ryan, please, you're burning me." Serena's whisper trembled.

He couldn't control it.

Belladonna grinned. "Be a good pet and obey me."

He started to let go of Serena's hand. "I–I have to go."

She grabbed his wrist. "No, stay with me. What are you seeing?"

"C-can she see us?"

Serena stood in front of him, desperate to keep him grounded, but Belladonna's gaze entrapped him.

"Ryan." Serena's voice broke into his thoughts but didn't shatter them. They still held him captive. "It's an abysshound. It's showing you your worst fear. The fear isn't real."

Belladonna looked real.

"She can feel me." He trembled. He wanted to sink to his knees and beg Belladonna for forgiveness.

"I know you're hiding here." Belladonna pulled out the whip at her waist, and Ryan's knees turned to water. He was stuck. He couldn't breathe. She'd come back to whip him. She was going to break him for good. His heart beat faster. The venom within pulsed in every beat, breaking those fragile bindings that held it into place. He could stand it no longer. He tried to squeeze from Serena's grip. He could surrender himself and save her at least, and maybe Belladonna would be less harsh on him.

"Hear me," Serena whispered. "Close your eyes." Her voice was a soothing dream, and it snapped his attention from Belladonna. Courage started to return.

"Come with me." She pushed him backward. And then what he thought was Belladonna chasing him changed.

It was a massive hound made of lava with a gaping maw, viper-like fangs, and hot coals for eyes. Most of him wanted to run in fear, but a small part of him was intensely curious.

Its fiery hair stood out wildly all along its body, and its four large paws padded closer without a sound. It sniffed the air, weaving its head back and forth, trying to locate them, and then it stopped. Its red eyes locked onto them.

"It smells us." Serena quivered.

The growl it issued was unlike anything Ryan had ever heard. The shriek actually hurt his bones.

"Don't look into its eyes." Serena tugged his arm. "If it sees you, it will show you your death and claim you. It's not an abysshound. It's Gnarg."

The creature jumped, fluid like smoke, and landed in front of them. Ryan slashed with his sword and nearly sliced its leg, the creature looked right into his eyes, and he froze.

"Run!" Serena pulled and ripped his gaze from the beast's. He followed her, but the creature took two bounds and caught up to them.

Heat ignited in Ryan's palms.

"Dragon's breath will not help you here, young scaly one. But how you are keeping hidden is a secret I wish you'd share." The voice that came from Gnarg was unnatural, a scraping in the wind, as if the clouds were made of ice that ripped into one another. "I sense you."

Its laugh was even worse. It sounded as if it were choking on blood. Ryan tried to calm the fire in his hands.

"Ryan, please. You're burning me."

He couldn't stop it! He started to remove his hand from hers, and she held tighter.

"I have to be touching you."

Gnarg stepped forward, and Ryan raised his hand and released a stream of fire from his palm. Gnarg screamed and shrank back, shaking its smoldering head. Only when it backed away did he still his fire.

"Good hit." Serena tugged his arm. "Now run."

No need to tell him again. Ryan ran, towing Serena along. Gnarg feebly jumped after them like a wolf losing interest in the hunt.

They ran until it no longer chased them.

Until they no longer saw it.

Until its stench didn't ride on the wind.

The forest smelled different, and Ryan knew immediately what he had smelled under the smoke at the other place. Death.

Serena fell to the ground.

"Serena?" He crouched beside her.

"Sorry, I'm tired."

"You're not back to normal, are you?"

She looked at her hand. "I am. The burns healed. Making us invisible just drains me. And my powers don't feel as strong as they used to."

Burns? Burns. Breath squeezed painfully from his lungs. "I hurt you?" He reached for her and she pulled back.

"It's okay. You didn't know." She offered a sad smile.

"Okay? How was that okay?"

She blinked as if surprised. "It wasn't—that creature really got to you. What did you see?"

"Belladonna." Her name came out as a whisper. Here he was, supposed to protect Serena, and he'd been ready to give himself over to Belladonna—the woman who scared him like no other.

Serena's hand glided over his back. His numb, scarred back. He elbowed her away even though he didn't want to. What kind of man was he? A weak one. He couldn't face Belladonna because she'd hurt him.

"I'm sorry." Her voice was so small.

She sat with her elbows on her knees and her hands drawn into her, cupped together under her chin.

He pointed to himself. "No, I'm sorry." His voice cracked. Why did he push her away?

"Belladonna is your biggest fear." Serena's quiet words slayed his soul. "She deserves death for what she did to you."

He could do nothing more than stare for fear that his voice would betray the depth of his brokenness.

"I can help you if you let me," she said. "But I am afraid to offer you anything. Each time I do, you pull away from me."

There it was. "I don't want to pull away from you, Serena."

"Then what do you want?"

He wanted to not be afraid to let her touch him. He wanted to understand what Belladonna had done to him that made him act this way. He wanted to see her—them—free of all that had happened in the past. But when she touched his back, he felt nothing. That numbness reminded him of the scars. Of his desire for Belladonna's healing. Of all the ways he'd failed. How he always needed to be rescued and never managed to save anyone. And Serena's face was associated with his worst torture—because he'd thought of her to try and free himself from the pain. All of that complicated everything.

He clenched his fists and realized they were hot.

She stared at his hands. "You need to learn to control your anger. It activates your talent somehow."

"You can tell I'm angry?" He looked up at her. "Because you can see my heart?" His tainted, dark heart.

She sort of chuckled and covered her mouth. "Sorry. I could see your heart before, but you keep it locked up now. I can tell you're angry because it's obvious."

Idiot. He almost laughed. Then he focused on something else she'd said. Locked up? What did that mean?

"It has to do with not trusting her." Blaze's voice was a comfort that Ryan needed right then. Hope rising, he stood as Blaze descended into the woods and landed near them.

"You are all right?" Ryan raced up to his friend. *"What happened?"*

Blaze actually laughed. *"A unicorn healed me. Can you believe it?"*

"Yes." He looked at Serena. *"One healed me, too."*

Serena walked up to Blaze and placed her hand on his scaled neck. "Dash said you were injured with arrows meant to piece dragon hide?"

"Yes." His voice was serious.

"You can hear him?" Ryan asked.

"Due to my sister-kin bond with Kara." She frowned.

"Something wrong?"

She looked at him as if deciding whether or not to answer. "I can't understand why she left. She ripped a page from the counters book and left."

"Which page?"

"The one for the white alor potion."

His stomach squeezed. "We need that."

"Well, I did write it out. It helps me memorize things."

"That's fortunate." He leaned back against Blaze as the dragon lay down behind him. "I'm sure Kara has her reasons. I just hope they're to our benefit." They probably weren't.

"You don't trust her?"

Ryan shook his head. "I only trust people who have earned it."

Serena narrowed her eyes.

"How far away is Dash?" He desperately needed to change the subject.

"He will follow us toward the Forest of Legends if Blaze will take us." She glanced shyly at the dragon.

Ryan smirked at her uneasiness. "I thought you were afraid of heights."

Her eyes widened. He chuckled softly and held out his hand to help her climb onto the dragon, bowing for added flourish. "Milady."

That got her to laugh. But she stared at his outstretched hand for a beat too long. He couldn't blame her. What a fool. He'd just burned her, and now he was asking her to touch him. He'd become the monster they all feared. And the only person who healed him inside was afraid to be near him. Her patience. Her grace. Her compassion leaked into his soul. Even when she didn't touch him, she reached into his broken places and healed him.

With a pang in his heart, he started to retract his hand, but she grabbed it right before he could.

Her smile was radiant. "You have a strange sense of humor, Knight."

He couldn't contain his shocked laugh. "I'm no knight."

She paused, hand in his, and drew closer to him. "You are to me."

And as he stood there speechless, she climbed onto Blaze.

"You coming?" She scooted back to make room, and he mounted the dragon in front of her, still trying to hold tight to her words. She wrapped her arms around his middle, sending a shiver through him. She was comforting in a way that broke him and mended him all at once. He closed his eyes and just felt her. This was real. Not a dream he'd created to escape the pain. And she didn't deserve to be treated like someone he feared.

But he did.

He feared not being able to open himself to her fully. He feared making himself vulnerable. Then he'd lose control. And he could never lose control again. He had today with the barghest. When he'd thought she was Belladonna. "I'm sorry," he said over his shoulder.

"For what?"

"You're afraid of me. Aren't you?"

"I think you're the one who's afraid of me."

Of course she'd see right through him. "You must think me weak."

She paused for so long, he stopped expecting an answer. At last, she spoke into his ear. "Ryan, you are the strongest person I know. I know of no one else who could fight that much darkness daily and win."

"I would rather die than be a tool of the Mistress or a slave to Belladonna."

She hugged him and rested her head on his back. "I would rather die than let either of those things happen to you."

The truth of her words filled him with hope. He gripped her hand in his and held it against his heart. He'd face his biggest fears for Serena. And he'd do it to keep her safe. To keep her from being tainted by evil. If that meant facing Belladonna, he would. And he'd find a way to kill her for good this time. "Can Healers die?"

She paused again. "Yes."

"Then I could kill her?" His chest ached after he uttered that thought, and his palms heated.

"I think *we* can. Together."

Good. Because she'd probably be at the Forest of Legends waiting for him.

CHAPTER 56

PAST SINS

Serena held tight to Ryan as they flew toward the Forest of Legends. Cool air kissed her face and chilled her arms. Clouds dissipated around them. She wanted to reach out and touch them. Slowly, she separated her hands, trying to call on her courage. Ryan clutched her arm to him.

"What's wrong?" She held him tightly again.

"Nothing. Your grip loosened. I thought you fell asleep."

She smiled against his back, and he chuckled. It sounded deep and full in her ear. And she loved it. "I just wanted to touch a cloud."

"Why didn't you say so?"

Blaze soared higher. White enveloped them. She lifted her head and slowly reached out with one hand. Her fingers chilled. The clouds were cold and wet and beautiful.

"You like it?"

She swirled the white with her fingers, but the dampness settled into her skin. "It's fascinating."

He looked over his shoulder and caught her gaze. That small smile curved his lips.

She let go of his waist and placed her hands against his hips. "You won't let me fall?"

"Never again."

She breathed deep, held it. Her hands let go, and she raised them into the air. Exhaled. Ryan's arms anchored her legs, and Blaze dove lower. A squeal escaped her throat and she laughed. Her stomach dropped, but she resisted grabbing him again.

"And?" he asked.

"That was thrilling and terrifying and amazing."

He chuckled. "Isn't it?"

Blaze descended through a low cloud, and she reached out to touch it, less fear in her stomach. She didn't even need to hold tight to Ryan anymore. She reached up, fingertips skimming the cool white. "It's beautiful up here."

He glanced at her over his shoulder. "The view is fascinating."

Blaze burst out of the clouds, and a golden-red line of disappearing sunlight pierced the horizon. She shivered in the open air, her clothes slightly damp.

Blaze's warm scales weren't enough to keep her from being cold now. She cuddled closer to Ryan and shivered. Heat pulsed through his shirt. "Better?" he asked.

"You can do that?"

He shrugged. "I thought I'd try."

She pressed her cold hands against his back. Ridges of scars met her touch, and Ryan stiffened. When she pulled her hands off of him and wrapped them around his middle, he relaxed a bit. He'd said Belladonna touched his back to heal him. She pressed her cheek against the ridges and held him. It wasn't healing, no matter what Belladonna had called it.

"We'll be landing soon." Ryan's deep voice rumbled in her ear. "Blaze found a spot to rest for the night."

"Can you feel Jayden or Ethan?" She hadn't sensed their bonds yet, but held out hope that the closer they got to the Forest of Legends she would.

"I don't check. I don't know if *she'll* feel it."

"That's probably best."

They'd been traveling two days with no sign of anyone else yet, but they would all know to reach the Forest of Legends, too.

Blaze started to descend, and Serena clutched Ryan. He laughed. "You really don't like this?"

"I do. It also scares me."

"Sometimes the best things in life are a little scary."

Truth.

Serena remained quiet until they landed. Blaze warmed a spot on the ground then lay down. Ryan leaned against the dragon, and Serena sat beside him, Blaze's scales warming her back. She picked up a stick and etched a groove in the dirt. "I knew her before. Belladonna." She ventured to look at Ryan. "I'm nothing like her."

"I know," he said quietly, avoiding her gaze.

"She's not a Healer, Ryan."

His throat bobbed. "I see that now. Is she more powerful than you?"

"Yes and no. As a Healer, no, but Belladonna has made a deal with the Mistress. She chose a black lion to bond with. She was given a venomous heart."

Ryan sucked in a breath. "Like mine?" An icy chill filled the air around them. And Ryan trembled.

"You're nothing like her. She gave herself to evil. You fight it." She looked into his eyes.

His bowed head was close to hers. "I could become like her. If I let it take over?" His voice cracked.

"In theory, but in theory so could I."

"And you think we can kill her?"

"Yes."

His eyes met hers, and hope burst through them. "You're with me? In spite of who I am?"

"I'm with you *because* of who you are." She wanted to say because she loved him, but she stumbled over the words, for many reasons.

"Thank you." His smile seemed so sad.

"Ryan." She moved closer to him. He didn't say anything, just released a shaky breath. "Listen to me." She grabbed his hand and waited for him to look at her. "When we fell from Blaze, I was conscious for the whole thing. You shielded me."

"I should hope so."

She smiled and her own emotions made the corners of her mouth waver. "I wasn't hurt when we fell. Because of you."

He shook his head. "Good. I would hate it if—"

"You don't understand. I'm a Healer. No one protects Healers."

He looked at her as though that was the strangest thing he'd ever heard. "Everyone needs rescuing at one point or another."

Tears stung her eyes and her voice quavered. "Thank you."

Ryan winced and hung his head. "It isn't fair for me to compare you to Belladonna; she isn't you. She's nothing like you. But the Healing, it—it scares me, Serena."

"I know, and I—"

"When I was bloody and whimpering on the floor like a beaten dog, all I wanted was Belladonna. Don't you see? I wanted the enemy to touch me, to soothe me because I felt relief. She made me need her. Her healing made me grovel at her feet. I wanted it so badly that I believed I loved her."

Serena fought hard to stay strong as Ryan's eyes filled with tears. She hugged him close. He squeezed back.

"You have every right to be ashamed of me," he said softly.

"I'm not ashamed of you, Ryan. I promise you, I will help you kill that woman."

"It won't be pretty. She terrifies me. I have never been more afraid of anything in my life."

"Then I will do my best to make sure she never hurts you again."

He looked into her eyes and squeezed her hands tight. "I can't ask you to do that."

"You didn't."

"I can't let you."

"Why not?"

"Because I would never forgive myself if she hurt you. She hates you."

"She's always hated me," Serena said.

"No. I've heard her secret desires. She would kill you simply because I love you."

Serena stared, dropping his hands and leaning away. Her eyes were glued open, she was sure. Had she really heard him right?

He grimaced. "I know it hasn't been obvious."

"It's not that." She was surprised at how airy her voice sounded. She wanted to say she loved him, too, but the words stuck. "No one has ever said that to me before. Ever."

"That they love you?"

She nodded, unable to find words.

"Serena, that's the saddest thing I've ever—I love you."

"Please."

"You deserve to hear it, and truthfully. You kept me alive. You kept my heart from becoming fully tainted. You saved me. Then you came back for me. You showed me kindness when I was unlovable. You never lost hope in me. I love you. I love you so much my heart wants to burst from it." He wrapped her in his arms.

Serena shook as the tears poured out of her relentlessly. He held her close, as her emotional dam broke. Yet she knew she was safe, even if she still felt vulnerable. She wanted to say she returned his love. But that thought terrified her.

She was just like him, wasn't she? Damaged with no desire to let someone love her. Afraid that no one could.

He ran his fingers through her hair. "Thank you. For not giving up on me. For coming after me. For rescuing me."

"Of course." She smiled. A warmth flooded her heart and she nestled closer to him. Whether she was afraid or not, he deserved to know. "I love you."

His chest heaved under her head. "You don't have to say it because I did. I understand if you don't."

"I can't lie."

His breathing hitched. "You—?" His chest shook. "I'm a monster."

Serena pulled back and looked at his face. "Prove it."

"What?"

"Let me see your heart."

He looked right into her eyes like he'd do anything she asked. "How?"

"Trust me." She touched his cheek.

The veil lifted.

He had opened his heart to her. It thundered in her ears. The pure part, the tainted part. It ached. For her. From fear. He was broken in there, but alive. So alive. And fighting the darkness.

It was such a beautiful heart. Compassion and love blossomed there. Even though a huge chunk of darkness covered part of it, he kept it contained. No one should be able to fight the pull of the dark so hard. But he did.

She looked into his eyes. "You have the most beautiful heart I've ever felt."

He stared at her. "You can't be serious."

"I love you."

A smile covered his face, one that reminded her of the first time they met. "I love you more."

Truth.

Her heart soared. It might not be *the* truth, but it was his truth. His hands slid up her back, and he pulled her closer. She didn't resist. She placed her hand over his chest and felt his heartbeat. Looked into his eyes. Stormy gray eyes that searched her face. Her lips. She leaned in and kissed him. And he crushed her close. His heart beat strong and pure, and the pure part seemed to pulse harder than the darkness. She wrapped her arms around him, and his heart squeezed against the darkness harder. Pushed it away as strongly as he pulled her close. Closer. And she never wanted him to let go.

When morning broke, Serena found herself huddled on the ground, and Ryan sat not far from her, cooking what looked like a rabbit over a fire. He flit his fingers through the flames without getting hurt. The dancing fire mesmerized him as much as watching him did her. "Where's Blaze?"

He looked up at her, snapping out of a deep thought. "He found a dead dragon near here. He's checking it out. The same arrows that shot him are embedded in this one."

"That's terrible." Serena stood.

"And quite far away from where he was when Dash found him."

"Which makes you think what?"

She felt for Dash, let him tap into their conversation. He'd already left for the day to try and meet them at their next place. *"Someone isn't just hunting dragons. They're hunting you."*

"I agree." She crouched near Ryan. "Do you feel the Mistress?"

He nodded, looking at the fire again. "She's always in the back of my mind like a leech I can't get rid of."

Something cracked like a stick snapping. Ryan stopped still. He pressed his finger to his lips. Serena scanned the wood for movement. Froze. Looked out beyond the cliff on the other side for anything in the air. Slowly, she grabbed Ryan's hand. He flinched.

"I'll hide you," she whispered.

He nodded and drew his sword.

Everything grew unnaturally dark. The scent of lavender permeated the air. Ryan's hand warmed. "Black lions." He spoke her fear aloud.

Someone moved through the wood like a cat on the hunt, and her skin chilled. Belladonna. Five black lions surrounded her, and they sniffed the air.

Ryan shuddered. Hot flame pulsed into his hand. Serena almost screamed. "Ryan."

She wasn't getting his attention. She grabbed his elbow with her other hand.

His hands cooled and he looked at her. "Let me go."

"No!" Her whisper turned harsh, and a black lion turned its yellow gaze onto them.

Ryan gasped. "It's talking to me. She knows I'm here."

Serena pulled him back farther away from Belladonna. How was that even possible? He couldn't be bonded to that.

"It smells us." Ryan's voice trembled.

"We've got to run."

"You run. Keep yourself cloaked and run."

She strengthened her grip around his hand. "We stay together."

"I can't risk her getting her hands on you."

"We'll hide."

His eyes softened. "How do you think she keeps finding us? It has to be the taint." His eyes scanned her face. Serena's breath hitched. The warmth of him, soft this time, like a fire meant to bring comfort and keep off the chill, drew her in.

"Serena," he whispered. "I love you, more than life itself."

Truth.

Then he released her. Cold enveloped her, crushed her. Ryan stood there, exposed. The black lion crouched, whipping its tail back and forth. A purr escaped its throat.

No.

She reached for him, and that look of love covered his face again as he stepped away.

Please, Ryan.

The black lions encircled him. "Pet?" Belladonna walked nearer, a wide smile on her face. "How fortunate to have found you here. Now where's that wretched Healer?"

Ryan tipped his head toward her. "Belladonna."

Serena held her tears in, her sobs clawed at her stomach begging to be set free. Sorrow choked her. Belladonna placed her hand on the black lion. "She said she smelled something, but I should have her skinned for not telling me it was you." Her smile snaked across her lips. "I knew you couldn't stay away from me."

Ryan closed his eyes. "Your pull is strong."

"I know. But I wasn't tracking you, so this is a pleasant surprise."

Ryan sucked in a breath. "You . . ."

"It surprises you? It shouldn't. I placed my links where I could. When you killed Franco, you gave me a lot of power. He'd blood-willed all his power to me." She pulled out a knife and walked closer to Ryan. The scent of pears clung to her. The black lions kept a tight circle around them both. "That means I have her soul."

Serena's heart stopped. She touched the tattoo on the base of her neck. *No.*

Belladonna slashed the knife and cut into Ryan's arm as he placed his hands up to block her strike. Blood seeped onto his sleeve. Serena felt his pain, and Belladonna looked right where Serena stood hidden. "Heal him, slave."

Serena's legs disobeyed her. They moved forward and took her right up to the black lions. Tails thrashing, they moved aside so she could walk between them. Right up to Ryan. She knew, by the way his eyes met hers, that she was no longer hidden. She was exposed. And controlled.

She reached toward his arm. "I'm sorry."

"No *sorrys*. You didn't know." He offered his arm for her to heal. She sealed the wound, but not before her tear dripped inside.

"Isn't this nice?" Belladonna pulled out her whip, and Ryan cringed.

He pushed Serena behind him. "You have us now. There's no reason to use force."

"No?" She laughed. Then her expression darkened. "There's always reason. You would protect her from me, pet? You're supposed to hand her over."

Ryan turned to Serena and whispered. "Blaze is fast. We both have fire. There's a way out of this."

The hope in her heart blossomed, and Serena clung to it. He pushed her down and dove on top of her as heat sprayed above them. Fire so hot, it scorched the air. Serena buried herself in his protective arms. The black lions screeched. *Blaze!* He'd come to their rescue.

Belladonna's strange, strangled laugh rose above all the noise.

The fire stopped.

"Heal them!" Belladonna commanded.

Serena rose. Where was Blaze? She looked out over the cliff to watch him falling.

Belladonna stood holding a crossbow and glared at Ryan. "You thought your dragon was strong enough to combat me, pet. Really? Could you have bonded to anything smaller? Have you forgotten that I studied under the great wizard Rubius? Have you forgotten that *I* killed him?"

Serena gasped and Belladonna chuckled. Her dark eyes locked onto Serena. "See, even your Healer knows what that means. His powers are now mine. And the two of you will help me get the Creator's power and destroy the Mistress."

Ryan grabbed Serena's arm.

"Don't stop me, please," she said. "It'll tear me apart. I have to do this."

The land had been blackened, and two mounds of ash told the deaths of two black lions. The others were injured. Serena moved toward the first. It hissed at her. She couldn't stop moving toward it anyway.

Serena healed the black lions, even as they hissed and growled.

Ryan took his protective stance in front of her again. "You have a few powers. So do I." He shot fire from his hands at Belladonna.

She held up her hand, and his flames winked out. "You have to try harder than that. How do you think I got close enough to your dragon to shoot it?"

He blasted fire in a steady stream at two of the black lions. The third lunged at them. Belladonna aimed her arrow.

"Ryan, look out!"

The arrow sailed right for him and speared through his stomach. He fell. But he'd taken out two of the black lions. One remained. Serena bent to heal Ryan.

"Stop." Belladonna's voice was quiet.

Serena's hands froze. The warring needs inside of her nearly tore her apart. She wanted to heal him and the tattoo wouldn't let her. "Ryan, I—"

"It's okay."

It wasn't okay. A clicking sound resounded in the breeze, and Ryan wrapped a bloodied hand around her wrist. "Go."

"No."

"Please."

Belladonna towered over them.

Serena looked up at her. At the whip dangling in the crazy woman's hand. "He's dying!"

"It's a small price to pay for his disobedience." She put her boot on Ryan's shoulder and pressed. Serena took out her daggers and sliced deep into Belladonna's calf.

Her wild, crazy eyes locked onto Serena. "You dare?" The whip curled around Serena's dagger, and Belladonna wrenched it from Serena's grip. Serena pulled out another dagger and threw it. The blade sunk deep into Belladonna's chest. Belladonna yanked it out and tossed it away. "You're more foolish than I thought."

"You can't have him!" Tears raced down Serena's cheeks.

"I already do. And I have you, too."

A black lion pinned Serena to the ground, face first. She struggled to free her other dagger. The animal moved back, keeping weight on

Serena's legs. Stinging slices ripped into her back and sharp, cutting objects shredded her skin.

"Do not heal." Belladonna's voice remained placid as Serena screamed.

Again Belladonna whipped her.

And again.

"Leave her alone!" Ryan shouted.

Then Belladonna stopped. She stooped over Ryan's form. "She can't heal you unless I let her." She ripped the arrow from him, and his cries seemed to shake the trees.

Serena tried to move the heavy weight of the lion, but claws pricked her skin. Held her there. Where was Dash?

He felt closer. Running, but not fast enough. By the time he got here, they'd be gone.

Belladonna coursed healing into Ryan's wound. "Stand up, pet. Groveling will do you no good." She reached out to place her hand on Ryan's heart. His hands balled into fists, he jerked his head away from her and squeezed his eyes shut. A small whimper escaped his throat. Belladonna stopped, her palm inches from him. "You fear my touch?"

He said nothing.

"I scare you." Her smile grew. "Good. Because I don't want you to make the mistake of leaving, ever again." She stroked his ear and Ryan screamed. He crashed to his knees, writhing on the ground.

"Stop!" Serena wriggled beneath the black lion.

The toe of a boot bashed into Serena's head. "You do not control anything here. See? Your powers are mine."

The boot hit her again. Ryan's screams filled her ears. The pounding crushed against her skull. Blood flowed from her nose, from her head, from her ear. Her mind filled with memories of her father standing in front of her laughing. "Does this hurt?" he laughed over and over in her head.

She gritted her teeth and pulled one arm free. When Belladonna's boot came forward, Serena caught it. Something in her hand snapped, but she didn't care. Belladonna lost her balance, and the black lion fluttered its wings to catch her. Weight lifted, and Serena rolled out from beneath the monster. She stood and pulled out her dagger as she raced to Ryan.

Sweat soaked him and he shivered, still writhing. "Turn it off. Please. I'll do anything you say. Just turn it off."

Belladonna crouched low over Ryan. "What do you think, pet?"

"I'm s-sorry."

No. He'd done nothing wrong.

"P-please. Make it s-stop."

"That's a good boy." She stroked his ear and kissed him. Immediately his thrashing ended. He curled into a tight ball and tears leaked from his eyes. "Now. We can't kill Serena, but we can beat her and keep her from healing until we get to the four thrones." She pulled a little vial of purple liquid from her pocket. "You are familiar with this, aren't you?"

Serena shivered.

Belladonna slid Ryan's sword from its scabbard and placed it in his hand, blade first. Then she looked at Serena. "You should heal yourself for this, slave. I don't want anything to go wrong."

Serena's bones and tendons mended. Her wounds closed. But no relief rushed through her. She didn't control her talent.

"Stand, pet. And face your enemy."

Ryan stood, unsteady on his feet. His eyes bored into Serena, the same eyes she'd seen in the palace. Dull. Dead. Broken.

Her breath shook. "Ryan?"

"Don't call me that."

Belladonna stroked his neck. "See, he's mine. Now, pet, you won't technically be killing her. Just making her less of a problem." Belladonna smiled. "Go ahead, I can guarantee she won't hurt you. Cut off her head or bring me her heart."

Ryan's sword tip dragged in the dirt as he took two steps toward her.

Serena backed up.

Belladonna shook her finger and her head. "No, no. That way leads to the cliffs."

Serena gasped. Her feet pulled her backward. The trees around her parted. A misty fog hung over her. She turned. What would have been a magnificent view of a giant chasm chilled her to the bone.

"On second thought, go ahead." Belladonna shrugged. "A fall like that could take you days to heal from. We'll have your decapitated body in the wagon before you're able to run should you choose the easy way out. Or, my black lion will catch you before you hit the ground and bring you right back."

Serena looked into Ryan's eyes, pleading for him to snap out of whatever spell she had him under. "Ryan, you don't have to do this."

He chuckled. "You should've run."

"I won't hurt you."

"Then lower your weapons and let me take your head."

What?

He nodded, none of the love in his face remaining. His smile matched Belladonna's.

Serena sheathed her weapon and turned, leaving her back unguarded. She moved her hair over her shoulder to show Ryan her exposed neck. She almost laughed at her inability to show him vulnerability earlier. But if she didn't let him do this, what would Belladonna do to him? His warmth pressed against her, parting the misty fog around her.

His head drew close to her ear. "Do you trust me?"

Her heart jumped, but she dared not look at him. "I'd rather you cut out my heart than take my head."

His breathing hitched. "I don't think I could do either."

Her heart stuttered.

"Forgive me." Then he said louder, "My heart only has room for one, Belladonna."

Ryan raced toward Belladonna and grabbed her arm. Then he looked over his shoulder at Serena, showed her the vial of purple liquid, and tossed it to the ground.

No!

She ran toward them, but the purple mist disappeared. Belladonna was gone. The black lion was gone.

And Ryan was gone.

CHAPTER 57

LINKED

The wind slammed into Cliffdiver, and he faltered. Connor's heart froze as Quinn clutched him from behind. "The storm. That's her storm. It feels the same."

Out of the storm rode the Mistress of Shadows on Smoke's back. Three riders on firegoats flanked them. Smoke opened his mouth, and a fireball propelled toward them.

"Hang on!" Cliffdiver dove to avoid the streak of fire as it careened through the clouds.

"Smoke." Connor held tight to Cliffdiver with his one hand. "She's come for us!"

"She knows we're strong. We can beat her."

Another gale ripped into them, and Cliffdiver shrieked in pain. It was too much for him. Connor looked over his shoulder at Quinn. "Hold on to him."

He let go, held out his hand, and unleashed his power at the storm.

A boom rocked the earth. Shattered the sky.

The storm stilled.

And a deep, dark laugh came from the other side of him. "Wielder, you killed my firegoats and their riders. I shouldn't be pleased, but I am. Your power is much greater than I thought it would be."

Quinn looked over her shoulder. "Connor! She's behind us."

Connor turned toward the voice to see the Mistress of Shadows on her mount.

Smoke laughed, like gravel crunching. And then the dragon opened its maw. Fire billowed in his gullet.

"Cliffdiver!"

"Hold tight!" The gryphon dove, but four black lions flew beneath him. As the gryphon descended, the black lions swarmed them.

Connor guided Quinn's hand to Cliffdiver's feathers and again told her to hold tight. *"Cliffdiver, take Quinn and get out of here. Find the Deliverers and keep them from getting caught."*

Then he slid out of Quinn's arms and stood up on the gryphon's back. And as Smoke dove beneath them, Connor jumped. He slammed into the hard scales.

The Mistress towered over him, her lips curled in an evil grin. "And now you're mine."

Quinn's body landed beside him, and Connor caught her before she could fall off the dragon. Not Quinn. His heart ached. Why had she followed?

"Cliffdiver, go! Warn the Deliverers!"

The Mistress waved her hand and a gust of wind ripped Quinn from his grip and off of Smoke's back.

"No!" Connor shouted and looked over the edge of the dragon.

"Catch her!" The Mistress yelled. Her eyes narrowed as she stared at Connor. "You care for her? Then I have leverage. I never expected to have that against you, Wielder."

Connor fisted his hand, and his power sparked in him.

"Go ahead. Use it. It won't harm me. But you already know that, don't you? Only the Deliverers have the power to destroy me. But you . . . you have the power to bring them to me. To lead me to the thrones."

A black lion caught up to them, Belladonna riding it, and Connor gasped when he saw Ryan behind her. "You have the Whisperer?" Belladonna purred. And Connor saw Quinn sitting on the back of one of the lions

"Good. Land, Smoke." The Mistress grinned. Then she waved her hand dismissively, and Connor felt as though a tree branch slammed into the side of his head. He saw nothing more.

Connor jolted awake. He found himself tied to a tree with cord strong enough to hold him.

Ryan sat, stoking a fire with a stick.

"Ryan?"

He turned, and the dark, empty look in his eyes made Connor shake. Belladonna had claimed him again.

"Pet." Belladonna approached. She cocked her eyebrow at Connor. "You're awake."

The fire popped, and Connor saw Quinn slumped against another tree beyond the flames. "What have you done to her?"

"Nothing. I care not for her. Though I'm surprised her screaming didn't wake you."

He struggled against his bindings, but his half an arm was tied tight. If he were to shift into a creature small enough, he could get free. His heart hammered.

Quinn suddenly opened her eyes and cried out as if someone were torturing her, but no one touched her. What was happening to her?

"Quinn!"

She didn't answer.

Connor glared at Belladonna. "What's wrong with her?"

"Who knows?" Belladonna shrugged and walked away from him. She'd been blocking his line of sight to the Mistress. She sat atop her dragon. As soon as he made eye contact with her, she slid off of the dragon and strode over. And beyond her, he saw hundreds of tents spread out in the forest, surrounded by dying trees. His stomach tightened into a ball.

The Mistress sneered. "She feels the trees dying. She takes in their pain. Soon, when the forest dies, she will succumb. It will be a pleasure to watch her writhe." She dragged her finger across Connor's jawline. Over his bare chest. "Your punishment for falling for someone other than me." She scraped his chin.

He flinched. His glare met hers. "You haven't won yet."

"I know. I need the Creator's power first." She faced Belladonna. "You can get me the others?"

Belladonna smirked. Connor knew how she would find them. She had a link to Serena from Franco's blood-will. The tattoo Serena wore was in her power now. And Ethan's scar. If he was with Jayden, she would have them all. She sauntered away from the Mistress. "I have a link to two of them. And they grow nearer to each other. I can find them fast."

"Good. Get them."

Belladonna called her black lion. Then she turned to Ryan. "Come on, pet."

"He stays with me."

Belladonna's eyebrow rose. "Then how will I lure in the Deliverers? They'll want to rescue him."

The Mistress's eyes narrowed. "Then take Kara with you as well. I want to make sure they come back to *me*."

Kara? Connor scanned the woods for her. He spotted her only when the assassin dropped out of a tree. She didn't say a word. Didn't even smile. Whose side was she on truly?

She strode past him close. "Wait for the distraction, Wolf."

Distraction?

She paused and whispered, "Which is stronger? A mouse or a black lion?" Then she sauntered to join Belladonna and Ryan before he could ask her to clarify. But as Ryan and Kara left with Belladonna, Connor started to plan his escape. He couldn't turn into a black lion—those were beasts created by the Mistress. But he could become a mouse. And he could become a gryphon.

Quinn shrieked and crumpled to the ground.

The Mistress laughed. "The black blood eats away at her."

Connor's heart wanted to break.

CHAPTER 58

SHADOWLANDS

*Y*ou are mine. Come to me."
Jayden spun around as she tried to find the source of the voice. Her knees weakened. She'd heard that voice before. In her head after the shadow wolves had bitten her. A sinking feeling settled in her stomach. This place, the wood, the mist, she'd been here before. It reminded her of the forest where Franco had taken her. The place she'd seen Smoke.

Franco was dead. This was a dream.

She fisted her hands and closed her eyes, willing herself to wake up. To remember what had been happening before the dream.

The storm! The Mistress had separated them all! Jayden had to get out of here. She had to get back to Ethan.

"You are mine." The voice hissed her head.

"Stop saying that!" Jayden stared at the crimson clouds as lightning flashed within them. A storm she couldn't feel in her veins. It wasn't hers. Could she even call her own storm anymore? Did she have any powers left? Already, her talents felt weaker.

"I have reached the Forest of Legends, and I am killing its beating heart. By the time you get there, you will be mine. And you will help me get a hold of your lover as well."

Ethan? "No! Never! You can't have him!"

"You say that as though you have the power to stop me. Listen carefully, because you will not remember this when you wake. You will come to the

Forest of Legends, and you will bring your friends to the trap I have set. Understand?"

"You don't control me."

"You need more venom in your brain? I will send my hounds to hunt you."

Venom? Jayden shook. *Was that how the Mistress was controlling her still? Venom continued to pulse through her veins?* Jayden pulled out her daggers and breathed in. Tried to reach out to the clouds and make them churn. Her powers filled her, but they were harder to reach this time. Still, she was able to feel a small amount of lightning at her disposal. "You can't have me! And you can't have Ethan!"

Ethan sat up and rubbed his head. The sky cracked and boomed, and Jayden screamed his name. She lay sleeping not far from him, and he moved over to her, trying to remember where they were. How they got here. Where was Zephyr? Heavens, where were they?

And the storm the Mistress had sent rushed back to him.

Jayden had tried to stop it while he'd held on to his shield to protect them, but she'd gone limp in his arms.

She screamed his name again, and he shook her shoulders. "Jayden? Jayden!"

She sucked in a breath and scrambled away from him, eyes wide and red.

No. Not again. "Jayden?" His heart thundered.

She stood and drew her daggers, and he backed away from her, palms open in surrender.

"Hey, Jayden? It's me. You're okay. It was a dream.""A dream?" She watched him and circled him slowly, daggers still aimed at him. Her eyes flickered red. "Who are you?"

"Who am . . . ?" His lungs squeezed so tight they hurt. Not again. He stood, slowly, arms still out, and created more distance between them. "Jayden, it's Ethan."

"No." She shook her head tentatively at first and then more wildly. "No! You're not Ethan. What have you done with him?" He felt the warning of her attack through his talent a few moments before she jumped at him, and he was able to sidestep and grab her arm, pinning it behind her. That didn't stop her though. She still had another dagger, and she leaned forward while thrusting her arm back. The sting of her blade cut his forearm just barely, but he had to release her to avoid being stabbed.

"Ethan would never hurt me!"

"I don't want to hurt you." He tried to plead with her. *"Zephyr? Where are you?"* Something trickled back over to the bond, and it felt more like confusion.

A low growl from the trees stopped both of them, and the gryphon stepped out. He thrashed his tail and lowered his head. The look in his eyes was strangely feral. And when Ethan looked at him, Zephyr took one step forward. But Jayden lifted her arm to throw a dagger.

"Jayden, no!" Ethan jumped at her and pushed her arm down before she could hurt Zephyr.

"You are friend?" Zephyr's voice crackled in Ethan's mind.

"Friend. Yes." Something sad weighted his heart. He knew it was Zephyr's feelings. The bond was fading. Ethan pressed Jayden's arm to her side, feeling her struggle with all her might. *"Where is the Forest of Legends?"* If the bond was breaking, he needed to know where to head.

Zephyr tilted his head in a very birdlike manner. Then he spread his wings and flew off. Wind eddied around them, tossing twigs and leaves into their faces. Jayden's struggle stopped momentarily as the gryphon took flight. And then Ethan flinched as something inside of him that was open suddenly closed.

A communication shut off.

A piece of himself missing.

He gasped for breath. *"Zeph? Zephyr!"*

Nothing.

Ethan breathed deep as a warming sensation spread over his chest. His talent, and it felt strange. Weaker.

Then Jayden's wrath jerked back to life, and she spun toward him. That was close! And confirmation that his talents were definitely weakening.

Ethan let go, spinning away from her. "Calm down! I'm not going to hurt you."

The red in her eyes pulsed brighter, and she raced straight at him. Just then, a screech sounded above them and Zephyr dove at them, claws extended. What was the gryphon doing? Without communication, Ethan had no idea. But Jayden was about to try and stab Zephyr, so Ethan did the only thing he could think to. He jumped into her and pushed her down, landing on top of her. Zephyr screeched again and flew off. And Ethan's talent warned him. Too late for him to react.

Jayden's dagger pierced through his clothes, and she stabbed him in the gut. Twisted the blade. "Get off me!" She pushed against him.

His thoughts spun.

Pictures flooded his mind. Feelings overwhelmed him and then stilled so that he could take in every small detail of the moment.

The pain crushing his insides.

He hit the ground hard and then remembered to breathe.

Since when was breathing something he had to think about doing? "Jayden?" It took everything in him to force out her name.

She stared at her dagger blade. At the red that dripped off and splashed to the ground in slow motion. As it hit the dirt, the pain in Ethan's gut slammed into him full force, and he pressed his hands against his stomach and screamed.

"Tell me what you did to Ethan!" She charged him again, and he knew this was it. She was going to kill him. And he was powerless to stop her.

"Drop your weapon." A voice behind him sounded out hard and cold.

Part of him felt as though he remembered it; part of him felt as though this could be a dream. A hazy, rippling dream. He felt so cold all of a sudden. It looked like dozens of women in white stepped out of the trees, holding loaded bows. They headed for Jayden.

He wanted to yell at them to not hurt her, but nothing came out of his mouth except blood. And then everything turned hazy. Then dark.

"Ethan?"

A voice filled his mind. He blinked. And realized he lay on his back.

"Ethan?"

Sharper now. He knew that voice. He sat up and sucked in a breath. "Tessa?"

The young barmaid from the Winking Fox—his dear friend—wrapped him in a hug, and the first thing he realized was that nothing hurt. Was he alive? Ethan looked down to see that blood covered his shirt, but there was no wound. His heart raced. "Jayden?"

Tessa's eyes softened. "She's—well, she's not in her right mind, but no harm has come to her."

"How did you—?"

"Serena sent me here. To meet the Healers."

"Ethan!" Someone came running toward him, and he stood in time to catch Rochelle as she launched herself into him for a hug. "It's so good to see you!" She stepped back and her sweet smile hadn't changed despite the dirt smudge on her cheek and tangles in her hair. "The Healers recognized you. Ruth healed you. We have no idea what's wrong with Jayden though. It's almost like there's a block in her brain, and—oh! I wish I had another shirt for you, but I know how you hate those white ones. Did—"

"Slow down." He chuckled and placed his hands on her arms.

She smiled. "Sorry. There's a lot to catch you up on. Where's Serena?"

"Where are we?"

"The Forest of Legends. We had to abandon the Tree of Wisdom. A huge storm came, and lightning struck it. The Healers scattered. I am rounding up those who are willing to fight in our cause. Serena sent Tessa with a message that you would need help."

"Yes. The Mistress is on her way here to try and defeat us. We're headed to the white alor tree in the center of the wood."

Rochelle's eyes widened. "I know that tree. We will come to your aid. We are seventeen strong in this group, but I know of others not far from here."

"Will you find them and bring them back to the white alor? Will you fight with us?"

"We will." A new voice caused Ethan to turn. Ruth, the Healer who had tried to have him killed what seemed like lifetimes ago, approached.

"Thank you. And"—he picked up the bloody edge of his shirt—"thank you."

She smiled, but worry weathered her features. "Jayden has been shadow touched."

"Yes. A shadow wolf bit her. She—"

"The Mistress holds her mind. I believe she's trapped in the dream world. She's not . . . herself."

Ethan swallowed. How would he get her out of it? "C-can I see her?"

"Brace yourself." Ruth held out her hand to show Ethan the way to Jayden, then she walked with him. As they drew closer, he could hear Jayden yelling at the Healers to let her go. Her voice was rough and harsh. And the words she used were nothing Jayden would say.

Ethan flinched internally and breathed deep. He would not lose her to this. He loved her. And that wouldn't break so easily. But that wasn't all. They had to defeat the Mistress, and without Jayden's storm, they didn't stand a chance.

"Be careful." Tessa touched his shoulder. He placed his on top of hers and squeezed. Then he walked forward to where Jayden sat tied to a tree.

Her head whipped in his direction as he approached, and she glared. A burning wave shot through his whole being, and his heart crumbled to pieces. Her eyes were dark red, and black veins surrounded them, making her face look cracked. No. He'd—he'd lost her?

She sneered. "You again? Good. These other fools won't listen to me. But I know you will." The voice that came out of her wasn't Jayden's. In fact, it sounded deeper. Harsher. Almost like a roar accompanied her words.

He stepped back.

She laughed, and it grated his nerves.

He would not lose her like this. There had to be a way to reach her. He would find a way.

"Jayden?" There was nowhere she could go that he wouldn't follow. And if she needed him, he would be there. He inched closer and sank to his knees so he could face her. "Can you hear me?"

"I'm right here. Of course I can hear you!" She lurched toward him, straining against her bonds.

His throat ached. "I know you're trapped in there. I need you to fight it. To fight her. She doesn't own you."

She laughed again. "Own me? What are you talk—"

"Hear me. Please? You know who I am. Can't you feel me?"

"Are you listening to me, fool?"

Ethan breathed deep and focused on the small glimmer in Jayden's eyes that read like hope. She could hear him! She was trapped in there somewhere, and he knew he could get through to her. He held up his hand, the one with the reminder of his oath, two scars deep. "We're bound. Remember?"

A hiss accompanied her next words, but he wasn't listening. He reached inside his thoughts, his heart, and felt the bond he still had— the one linked to Jayden—and he poured everything he had into that. *"Remember when I said I'd do anything for you?"*

"Anything?" Her small voice came back, vulnerable and unsure. But it was hers. His chest squeezed and he let her words drown out the voice that screamed at him from her mouth. The voice that wasn't her. Instead, he listened to the quiet words that touched his heart.

Holding tight to the bond, he focused on hearing her. Speaking to her. *"Don't ever doubt my love."*

"I won't! Ethan, I won't! You can hear me? Where are you?"

"You're in the dream world." He grabbed Jayden's hand. She struggled against his touch. Hissed in his face. He closed his eyes and concentrated. *"Hold on to me. Find your way back to me. I'm right here. I haven't left you."*

"You found me?" Her voice seemed a small whimper in his mind, but then he felt her courage fill her. She would fight. She would never give up.

"Always. You can do this. I'm right here."

Ethan's encouragement echoed in her mind: *You can do this.*

But how? Firegoats surrounded her, circling, and the Mistress descended out of the storm cloud that she'd commandeered Jayden's power to make.

"Let me out!" Jayden screamed.

The Mistress laughed. *"There is no out for you. This is your mind. You are trapped."*

Jayden clenched her fists. *"Ethan?"*

"Take my hand, Jayden! Please?" His voice was strong.

Jayden shouted at the Mistress. "This isn't real!" Then she fell to her knees and bowed her head. *"Where are you, Ethan?"*

"I'm right here. Take my hand."

His hand? None of this was real, but Ethan was. She just had to find him. Jayden trusted his voice. Leaned on it. Closed her eyes and reached out.

"No!" The Mistress shrieked.

Jayden kept reaching. A warm, strong grip held her hand and she felt the scars. Familiar scars that spoke of Ethan's love for her. He had come for her! She clutched his hand. "You found me?" Her voice sounded tearful.

"Yes! I'm right here. Open your eyes."

She obeyed. She didn't know what she expected to see, but Ethan sat in front of her, hand in hers, head bowed, and eyes closed. "Ethan?"

His head snapped up, and he looked at her. At once he moved closer and pressed his palms against her cheeks. "Jayden? It's you?"

"It's me!" She wanted to touch him, but her arms were pinned down by rope. Then she watched as Healers, some whose faces she recognized, raced to her and started untying the rope as Ethan kept repeating, "It's her, it's her. Set her free."

All the while, he continued looking deep into her eyes, and his hands never left her cheeks. Even as her tears spilled out.

As soon as she was free, she propelled herself into his arms, and he held her. His strength, her armor. Her shield. Her support.

"I thought I was lost in there forever." Her voice cracked." You found me. You brought me back."

"Wherever you go, I will go with you."

She breathed in his strength and looked up at him. At his reddened shirt. The huge blood stain was dry, but a hole told her he'd been stabbed. "What happened?" She gripped the material in shaking fingers.

He covered her hand with his and looked deep into her eyes. It seemed an eternity before he finally said, "The Mistress attacked me."

Her blood chilled. "The Mist—you mean me?"

"No." Nothing wavered the conviction in his words. "It wasn't you. It was her. And there's one way to make sure you're free of her forever."

Jayden set her jaw and fisted her hands. "Let's take her out. For good."

He nodded, solemn, then his eyes softened. "Together."

"Always."

He paused, oath hand pressed against her cheek again, with those familiar ridges offering so much comfort. "Jayden."

"Yes?"

"Don't go where I can't follow." He smiled that lopsided grin, and she leaned close. Closed her eyes. He kissed her, and everything but this moment melted away. Her hands trailed over his skin, and his firm grip kept her close. The fissure in her heart mended, and she kissed him with her all. With her heart. With her emotions. Tears and joy, sadness and pain, all of it flooded through her veins and fueled her kiss. Overwhelming love for the man who had said he'd be honored to die for her, who would take her place. He was her protector. Her hero. Her Ethan.

Ethan and Jayden had taken Rochelle, Ruth, and Tessa aside and explained that they needed to get to the four thrones. As suspected, Ruth knew of what Ethan spoke. For three days, they traveled in secret, but Ethan thought the travel too slow for his taste. Both Zephyr and Stormcloud had left, and already—with the loss of their bonds—Ethan felt his talents draining.

He approached Ruth, keeping his voice low. "Are you sure you know where these thrones are?

"Yes. They're supposedly by the white alor tree." Her voice was solemn. "We are getting closer, but it will be good to travel in secret."

"You mean fewer numbers?" Ethan motioned to the others.

"Yes." Ruth's eyes were sad. She turned to Rochelle. "Gather the other Healers. Meet us back by the alor tree once you have everyone. There's no telling when the Mistress will arrive."

The next morning, most of the Healers left to search for reinforcements. Jayden strapped on her pack, ready to get the Creator's power and stop the Mistress forever.

Though the air blew cooler, there was no threat of snow. Today was not the day she'd die. She could at least hold on to that.

Ethan grabbed her hand, and she clutched his and looked up into his eyes. He smiled softly.

Then Ruth stepped out in front of them. "This way." They traveled deeper into the forest together, following Ruth for two days.

The next morning was colder, but still not cold enough for snow. And Ruth led them deeper into the wood. At last she stopped, but she placed her finger to her lips. "Someone is coming."

Ethan touched his sword but didn't draw it. "I feel no threat."

A unicorn Jayden recognized broke through the trees, and Serena walked beside him. Melanie and Gavin were close behind her.

"Serena!" Jayden raced to her sister-kin. Ethan did, too, and the three of them embraced. Jayden took in the serious look on Serena's face. "You still have Dash." She marveled at the unicorn and shook her head. "I can't feel Stormcloud, and Ethan said Zephyr left him."

Serena grabbed her hands. "I felt you. My bond is weakening, but I felt you both."

Ethan's unease slammed into Jayden, and his words speared her. "Where's Ryan?"

She looked at Jayden, and her heart seemed to crumble. "He surrendered to Belladonna to save me."

"What?" Ethan gripped the hilt of his sword.

"Belladonna has him again," Jayden whispered and her knees weakened. "What will that do to his heart?"

Serena shook her head and wrapped her arms around herself. "I don't know." Her eyelashes fluttered. "She's turning him into her slave. She's tortured him. I can feel his pain already."

The ground trembled, and a sound like the groaning trees, only stronger, longer, and sadder, filled the air.

"What's happening?" Melanie asked.

S.D. GRIMM

"Dash says the forest is trying to absorb the poison, but it can't anymore." Serena shook her head.

Ruth looked at Melanie with that same sorrow in her eyes. "The Mistress's blood is killing everything. Soon, even we will lose our bonds. Our Feravolk talents. Everything. Many of the unicorns have already given their lives to help the forest remain alive longer. We don't have much time. Her blood has spread to the Forest of Legends. If we don't defeat her before it takes over this forest's heart, the Feravolk will cease to be."

Serena fell to her knees and buckled over in what looked like pain. "She's breaking him."

Melanie pressed her hand to Serena's back. "Can you tell where they are?"

Serena closed her eyes. "He's close."

Jayden clasped her hands together, the ache in her heart throbbing. "If we go to the thrones and defeat the Mistress now, before we lose our powers, will we have time to save him?"

"Jayden." Serena's hurt flooded into her. "I want to save Ryan, too. But he's the Mistress's vessel. If Belladonna is trying to make his heart blacker, don't you think we have to kill the Mistress before she can? Otherwise, won't Ryan die when the Mistress does? Didn't Connor say the only way to save Ryan from the Mistress was to kill her?"

"That or cut out his heart." Kara's voice came from the trees, and the assassin faced them and smirked. "We meet again."

CHAPTER 59

ENEMY OF MY ENEMY

Serena's fingernails dug deep into her palms as Kara pushed her shoulder off the tree she leaned against and strode forward.

Five black lions followed her, padding out of hiding. Belladonna rode one.

Ryan rode another.

And the dark look in his eyes, void of hope, void of heat, was the same look Serena had seen in the palace. The hint of pears rode on the stale wind. He was back under Belladonna's spell.

Serena wanted to crumble to her knees. Where was the hope now? Their powers were slipping. The bonds breaking.

Belladonna's black lion walked closest to them, and she held out her hand, palm facing them. All the huge, black, winged beasts stopped.

"How is she still bonded?" Jayden's voice seemed so small. Fragile. Hopeless.

"Ryan?" Serena said his name.

He looked her way, and his eyes narrowed, but his words were for Belladonna. "She's trying to reach me, as you said she would."

Serena fought the urge to scream his name as a sob shattered in her chest. "Oh, Ryan." She barely had air in her lungs to push the words out. What had Belladonna done?

Belladonna glared at Serena, then pointed the Sword of Black Malice at Melanie and Gavin and Ruth. "Kill them. Bring me the Deliverers. My lions will feed on the corpse of your unicorn."

"*No.*" The word echoed in Serena's chest. "*If they're all injured, I don't think I have enough power left to heal them. Does Ruth?*"

Dash turned to her.

She could tell he was speaking, but she heard nothing. Dread crept over her heart like a curtain. He whickered and stamped his hoof. Then he nuzzled her. When they touched, she could hear him. "*The bonds are breaking.*" He sounded as if he were in pain. "*Serena, you must kill Smoke so the Mistress has nowhere to store her heart. Only a unicorn can kill that dragon. Your daggers. They are swords of noble light.*" His outline melted into the trees surrounding them, but Serena could still see him at her side.

"*Why does it sound like you're saying goodbye to me? Dash, are you losing your powers too?*"

A single tear dripped from his eye. A plant grew at the source of the splash. Then the ground sizzled, like tree sap boiling out of a heated green log. The small plant withered at his hooves. His mane had lost all its luster.

Around her, the black lions sprang forward as if they had been unleashed. She heard muffled screams as if the din of the oncoming fight was shielded from her ears so she could hear Dash.

"*Do you trust me?*" he asked.

She stroked his soft nose. "*Of course.*"

Tears dripped from his eyes, and he thrust his horn into her chest. Her knees wanted to buckle.

Someone screamed. Ethan jumped between her and the lions. The fleeting thought that Kara had betrayed her throbbed in her heart beside the physical pain.

Belladonna's eyes grew wide, but she stopped her creatures from moving toward them. "What does that unicorn think it's doing?"

Dash's horn had pierced her heart. It still beat around the horn. When he removed his horn, he could heal her. Her trust in him didn't waver. Dash would not kill her. He needed to tell her how to defeat the dragon, and this would make sure she didn't miss a word. Pain she could withstand now if their bond would be restored later.

"*When the forest dies, I will also die. I won't live on like the other animals, Serena. I will melt into the wood. I am born of it, and I die into it. Our bond can never be restored, even after this is done. This is the only way I will live."*

He tilted his horn to the side, ripping her chest open more. Then she saw the gaping hole in his own chest. It took the form of light. A ray of hope inside of him. As he closed his eyes, that light poured from his chest into hers through his horn. The sword of noble light. Of course. *"Now you will have your powers for longer because I have given you everything I have left: my heart. When I remove my horn from you, I will die. But my heart will beat inside you. It will give you all that's left of my powers. You will always have me with you now. I love you, little one. Save the forest. Bring the unicorns back."*

A different ache speared her chest. No. *"Dash, don't go. I need you. I can't defeat Smoke. I'm—"*

"You are a unicorn. Always have been. More depends on you than you know. You have to survive."

He removed his horn and her chest sealed. Healed. But Dash faded away like dust motes sparkling in the sun. And it tore Serena apart. She wanted to fall to her knees, but as if her ears were opened, the sounds of swords clashing and creatures shrieking slammed into her.

Ethan pushed her behind him as the black lions herded them farther from their friends. She didn't even have time to mourn. She—her eyes filled with tears, and she pulled her daggers free.

A black lion spread its wings and jumped at her. Ethan plunged a wooden sword into its heart. It dissipated like smoke on the wind.

Jayden's scream woke her from her stupor.

And Belladonna made eye contact with Jayden. "I almost have all of you." She held her hand in the air and made a fist. Then she pulled.

Ethan cried out and stumbled forward. A black lion pounced on him.

Serena and Jayden both raced forward to attack the beast.

Belladonna continued walking toward them, and Serena caught sight of Gavin fighting with Ryan. Trying not to hurt him. A black lion jumped onto Gavin's back, and blood-red claws ripped out his throat.

He fell, dead.

Serena trembled where she stood, momentarily frozen. She wanted to race to him, but the loss of feeling his pain stopped her. There was no soul left alive in him. No one to heal.

Her heart could take no more.

She turned to see Belladonna stab Ruth through with the Sword of Black Malice.

Melanie raced in front of Belladonna, the only person left to stand between the evil woman and Serena and Jayden.

Melanie looked over her shoulder. "Run! Get to the thrones! Go!"

Serena grabbed Jayden's sleeve.

"No!" Jayden raced back toward Ethan to try and free him.

Serena ran at Belladonna, and Melanie glanced back at her—and the dark sword speared her through. Belladonna pulled the blade out, and Melanie crumpled to the ground. Dead, a gaping wound in her stomach.

Jayden cried out in agony as she fell to her knees.

Belladonna snapped her fingers and the four remaining black lions flocked around her. Surrounded all of them.

Ryan walked to her side. The scent of pears made Serena's stomach churn. Kara flanked her other side. Ethan jumped to his feet, but Belladonna jerked her fist, and he stumbled to his knees.

"Now." Belladonna sneered at Serena. "I will have the Creator's power. You will give it to me."

Jayden spit at her.

Belladonna chuckled at Jayden. "You are the last one for me to claim. But the Mistress made my job easier. She already has your mind. Doesn't she?" Belladonna smiled wickedly at Kara. "You put bandy root on one of those dart shooters, right?"

Kara glanced at Belladonna as if she was insulted. "I don't make mistakes." Then she pressed a dart shooter to her lips and blew. Jayden fell to the ground. Serena wanted to scream. Kara had betrayed them again, and then Serena felt a prick in her neck. All trace of her healing powers seeped from her veins because of the bandy root. And then tangle flower took hold. As she fell next to Jayden's limp form, she tried desperately to cling to hope.

CHAPTER 60

BROTHER AGAINST BROTHER

E than jerked his head up, all his thoughts spinning. Where was he? Not where he'd been moments ago. Actually, he didn't even know if it was moments ago. How long had he been out? He tried to move his arms, and his blood turned to ice. He was standing, arms and legs chained to a wooden pole, his arms extended above his head. The pole scratched his skin as he peered around at his surroundings. The chilly room—if anyone would call it that—smelled dank and rancid, with the strangest hint of pears. Moist brick lined the walls, and the yellow flames of torches cast a sickly glow on everyone's skin. Were they underground?

Some of the corners remained in shadow, and beams from floor to ceiling supported the room at various spots. He squinted, eyes adjusting. What was in that back corner? Old food storage baskets? A cell that the door had rusted off of? What was this place?

Jayden and Serena were bound in rickety chairs too far away for him to reach. And a woman with crazy eyes stepped in front of him. Belladonna.

His blood boiled. She would pay for this. The faint heat of a threat pulsed across his chest, almost as if his talent were flickering out like a dying fire. That made his stomach lurch.

So did the fact that she held a whip. And that someone had removed his shirt.

Ryan loomed behind Belladonna, head lowered, glaring. He was a ghost of what he'd been. His eyes, typically so full of humor and charm, were lifeless.

Guards dressed in black with white shirts lined the walls, hiding in the shadows—armed and ox-huge—likely ready to do Belladonna's bidding. There had to be at least twenty.

Belladonna stepped toward the girls. "Jayden, I didn't expect the Mistress to have such a strong hold on your mind already. You must be weak."

"What do you want, Belladonna?" Serena asked.

"The Creator's power. I don't have much time to make you all mine before our common enemy shows up, so it's a good thing I enlisted help. Kara."

Kara stepped forward. She glanced at Ethan and smirked. "Soldier. Nice to see you again."

"Wish I could say the same," he bit out.

Belladonna's eyes met Ethan's. "Your strength belongs to me." She tugged thin air, and a ripping pain in his chest pulled forward, slamming him, hard into the pole.

"Serena's soul is already mine." Belladonna pulled out her dagger and sliced Serena's face, right under her left eye.

"Leave her alone!" Jayden fought against her bindings.

Ethan's talent begged him to save her, but how could he? He looked at his brother, pleading. "Ryan!"

Ryan's eyes narrowed slightly.

Belladonna nicked Serena's cheek again, and she spit in Belladonna's face.

"Stop healing yourself." Belladonna's voice was cool. Calm. And Serena's cut continued to drip blood.

Ethan's pulse raced. Belladonna could do that? He glanced at Ryan, who stared at Serena, the look on his face somewhere between pain and confusion. Hope ignited in Ethan. Did Ryan still have feelings for Serena? How far gone was he in truth?

Ethan braced for all the strength left inside of him and pulled at his bindings.

"Ryan's heart is mine." Belladonna walked over to him and stroked his jaw as if he were some pet, and he kissed her.

Ethan grimaced. "What are you doing? Snap out of it! Ryan! Look at me!"

Ryan's head turned slightly, and his cold, dull eyes met Ethan's. "Do I know you?"

"Y-yes! Ryan. It's me, Ethan. What has she done to you? Come back, brother. Don't let her—" A slight wave of warmth spread across Ethan's chest in a warning as Belladonna approached him. He didn't care. Let her hit him. It got her farther away from Ryan. Ethan kept talking. Trying to reach Ryan as he ignored Belladonna.

The back of her hand slammed into his face, and he tasted that familiar metallic tang. "He isn't yours anymore."

"Not mine?" Ethan looked at her like she was crazy—which she was. "Is that what you do? Wipe people's memories so you can claim them as your pets? Treat them worse than animals?"

"Shut him up!" She pointed to Ethan and four guards stepped forward.

Ethan's heart raced, but Belladonna held out her hand. "Wait. I have a better idea. Let's make her mine first." She approached Jayden, and Ethan pulled harder at the chains. Belladonna held out her hand. "Come, pet."

Ethan's heart slammed against his chest when Ryan followed her. Belladonna pulled back on Jayden's hair.

"Leave her alone!" Ethan's cries fell on deaf ears, and he yanked the chains with all his might.

She poured a dark liquid into Jayden's mouth while Serena shouted her protests and begged Ryan to help. Jayden struggled, but Belladonna held her in place with Ryan's help and forced Jayden to swallow.

Ethan pulled again, and this time his heart skipped as he felt some give. He just had to keep tugging.

Jayden stopped struggling. Her became lifeless like Ryan's. And Ethan's heart stilled. He looked at Serena, who wore the same look on her face that he felt. They'd come to save Ryan and instead had given Belladonna everything she needed to gain the Creator's power.

Belladonna showed Ethan a golden bracer on her arm. No. That was the weapon Connor had told them he needed. The one Morgan had seen. It was all coming true.

Serena gasped when she saw it. "What did you do to her?"

"I just made her into one of my black blood soldiers. Everyone had some but me. So I made my own. It was easy really. Spelled black lion venom turns their blood black. Another special potion stops the venom from taking over their hearts completely. And this lovely bracer gives me control over them. It's wonderful really."

Ethan tugged his bindings. "I. Will. Kill. You."

"Have you forgotten? You can't." Belladonna laughed. "When the Mistress gets here, she'll believe Ryan's heart and Jayden's mind are hers. She'll want Serena's soul and your strength. She'll think I delivered you to her. And then, I'll stab her in the back. Or the chest. I haven't really figured that part out." She leaned closer to Ethan. "Doesn't matter. You're going to give me what I want now."

He looked her in the eyes as realization hit him. "You don't have my strength."

A flicker of a patronizing smile stretched her lips. "I thought you might say that. We'll call this assurance then. Shall we?" She walked behind him, and his chest ignited. Her hand glided over his back, and he wanted to pull away. Then a thin, black weapon danced in his periphery. "You're about to become acquainted with my weapon of choice." Ethan had never felt a whip against his skin, but something inside him froze.

Serena started fighting against the ropes that bound her, but Jayden sat silent, and Ryan waited like a ghost of a man.

Ethan had to make them fight this evil, insane woman.

"Ryan." Belladonna held up the whip and he cringed. "Remember your training?"

He nodded.

"We need to train this one now. Would you like to do the honors?"

Of course she'd make Ryan torture him. Ethan's stomach flipped.

Ryan walked over to him, like a beaten dog who was too scared to disobey.

"Ryan, you don't have to do this." Ethan pulled at the chains again. He felt a surge of hope as one of them seemed to give. The anchor was in the wooden slats of the ceiling. Did he have enough strength left?

"Ryan, please. Don't." Serena trembled.

Ethan pulled harder, straining at the end of his chains. But he kept his face placid, stone. "Go ahead, whip me, Ryan, but if this is what she did to you, she doesn't love you."

"The torture was earned. Her healing was the act of love."

"Healing!" Serena screamed. Tears raced down her face as she struggled to get free. "Those scars she left on you? The way she treated you? Remember, Ryan! She doesn't love you! I—"

"That's quite enough." The sound of a slap silenced Serena, and Ethan bowed his head against the pole in front of him. Then Belladonna said, "What are you waiting for, pet? Break him."

Ryan stood in front of Ethan and showed him the whip. Then he smiled. This man looked nothing like Ryan anymore. All his kindness, all his caring bathed in humor was gone. He looked like one dining on wrath, and thriving.

"Ryan?" Ethan's voice trembled. "Hear me. You know me."

Ryan walked behind him, and the sound of the ends of the whip converging sent a shiver through Ethan. Ryan chuckled. "Scared?"

"I'm not scared." Ethan tried to put every ounce of his calm demeanor into his words.

"You should be."

"Not of you." He looked over his shoulder and met Ryan's dead stare.

Belladonna laughed. "He doesn't know you."

"Ryan, listen to me! Please?"

Ryan donned a smile that reminded Ethan of Belladonna. "You will break. They all break."

He looked away as Ryan swung the weapon. The whip slammed into him with more force than he'd anticipated. More sting than he'd thought possible. And the shock of pain stole his breath. "Like she broke you." His words strained as he yanked against the chains.

"She made me whole again." The whip lashed across Ethan's skin again, tearing his back open.

He caught his breath. "Torturing someone who can't fight back is weak."

"It makes me stronger!" Ryan slammed the whip against Ethan's back again, and Ethan screamed.

After each lash, he pulled the chains anew, but his strength was draining. "Fight me man-to-man, and we'll see who's stronger!"

"You are in no position to bargain." Another burn slapped across his back.

"Is this what she did to you?" Ethan asked, his voice wavering. "Is this how she *trained* you?"

Ryan's persistence with the weapon cut him off. Ethan pulled the shackles harder, but the ceiling was giving way. With one more yank, the wood splintered. A chain broke free. He turned around and stopped Ryan's incoming blow.

Ryan pushed back and drew his sword. A fire ignited in his hands and heated the weapon. Made the blade turn red. Ryan smirked, but there was no joy in it.

Ethan sank against the wooden beam, his back screaming, and faced Ryan the best he could with one arm still chained to the ceiling. "You don't hurt those you love."

Ryan paused. "She heals me." His voice wavered.

"No, Ryan. She hurts you. That's not love."

Ryan's sword barreled down toward Ethan's chained arm.

Serena screamed.

Ethan whirled toward the pole, and Ryan's sword slammed into the wall. His heart hammered. That was close. Ethan's foot hit something, and he glanced down. A sword? His pulse thundered. He looked up to see Kara slinking in the shadows behind the food crates. She pressed her finger to her lips. Ethan pulled with all his might and yanked his other arm free, then he scooped up the sword. The familiar weight of it told him it was his own sword.

As Ryan advanced, Ethan sprang up and kicked him hard in the chest, sending him sprawling into a beam.

"Come here!" Kara's whisper was harsh.

Ethan didn't know who to trust, but Kara hid behind the baskets in the old cell—not actively trying to kill him. He ducked back there, counting on his fading talent to mask the pain. It failed him and a lance of pain shot through him before dulling again. That was not good.

Kara held out a key.

"What are you—?"

"Do you always question your rescuers?"

Even as she unchained him, he glared at her.

Regret registered in her eyes. "I'll explain later. Just trust me."

"Fight me, coward!" Ryan's voice called to him.

Kara looked at Ethan's back. "How are you standing?"

Talents he wasn't as confident in. "Just give me the plan."

Kara nodded. "Leave Belladonna to me."

Half of him wanted to run her through, but she posed no threat. So he nodded. "I'll give you a distraction."

Ryan kicked over a stack of food baskets, and Ethan sneaked around another stack, bracing against them as another wave of pain got past his failing talent. As his strength returned, he jumped out of hiding and faced Ryan, sword ready.

Ryan sprouted a crooked smile. "I knew the fighter in you wasn't buried far." He advanced and swung his weapon. Ethan blocked the blow.

As metal scraped metal, Ryan started pushing Ethan. "Ryan, this isn't you. Fight her hold on you. Do you hear me?"

"You talk too much." He sliced his sword through the air, and Ethan jumped back. Ryan rounded on him and swung again. Ethan blocked blow after blow, his strength draining fast.

And he caught sight of Kara slinking out of the shadows.

Ethan didn't have a chance to worry about that—he was too busy dodging Ryan's attacks.

"You're not even trying!" Ryan's blade chopped toward him and sliced into Ethan's right shoulder. Ethan gasped and managed to get out of the way of the next blow, but Ryan was relentless.

"I don't want to hurt you!" He held the sword with two hands, his right arm trembling.

"That's your mistake!" Ryan slammed his sword against Ethan's. The blades shrieked, and Ryan kicked Ethan hard in the chest. He fell to the ground, every gash in his back screaming and Ryan struck again. Ethan blocked the blow, calling what was left of his strength, but Ryan had leverage now. And he pushed. Ethan's arms shook as he strained to keep Ryan's weapon from slicing his head off. His shoulder screamed. His back burned.

Ryan's weight pressed against it, and Ethan looked up into his eyes. The eyes of a madman.

"Ryan . . ." He pushed the words out through clenched teeth. "Please don't do this, brother."

At the word *brother*, Ryan flinched. Then he shook his head. "I don't have a brother."

"Yes . . . you . . . do . . ." Ethan's arms quivered, his right arm failing to support the weapon anymore. "You're *my* brother, Ryan. And I love you!"

Ryan's pressure wavered just enough that Ethan pushed him off and rolled out from under him. He struggled to his feet, sword in his left hand. There was no way he could keep this up. Everything hurt too much. His strength was fading. But Ryan knelt on the ground. He looked up, and something sparked in his eyes that wasn't heat or a threat. Recognition?

Ethan shivered as relief pulsed into him.

"Ethan?" Ryan shook his head. "Where?"

"Look out!" Serena shouted.

Ryan stood as Belladonna came at him.

Her eyes gleamed like dark sparks of cold, hard rock. "Men! Subdue them."

CHAPTER 61

BE READY

Ryan waited for the rush, but the guards against the wall did not move from the shadows.

"The guards are napping." Kara sauntered forward and held out her blow tube and wiggled it. "Tangle flower seed."

Ryan gasped. "You?"

Kara made eye contact with him. "I'll distract her, Charmer. You know what to do." She wiggled her fingers above her other hand.

Fire. She wanted him to kill Belladonna? His heart hammered. Kara raced toward Belladonna, dagger ready. She threw it.

Belladonna held up her hand and the dagger fell to the floor. "Stupid assassin."

Kara cocked her head. "I have more."

This was it. His moment. He could take her on and be rid of her. Why wouldn't his feet move?

Ethan charged after Belladonna, and she held out her hand to stop him. "I don't even need guards." She touched him, and Ethan fell to the ground screaming. Ryan stared at his brother in horror. He knew that feeling. She was pouring all of his previous injuries into him at once.

"Oh, isn't this interesting?" Belladonna's eyes went wide and she smiled. "You've died before?" She looked at Serena. "I can kill this one with a single touch. I just have to push. A little—"

Ethan's screams intensified.

"Stop it!" Ryan's voice cracked. "Don't hurt him!"

Belladonna looked at him and narrowed her eyes.

"Charmer!" Kara yelled. She raced toward Belladonna, a dagger in each hand. Belladonna reached her hand out in front of her, and Kara stopped mid-leap. She hung, suspended, gasping for air. Her daggers clattered to the ground as she pulled at something unseen around her throat. Then she swiped at Belladonna's face. Her hand caught the necklace Belladonna wore.

"Tramp!" Belladonna pushed Kara further away and she held tight to the necklace. It snapped apart, but she remained suspended, clawing at her own throat.

Ryan stepped in front of Belladonna, and her eyes widened. "You too, pet?"

He shook, lowering his weapon. "I'm sorry."

"No!" Serena's voice was desperate. "Ryan, no!"

But Belladonna smiled. "That's right pet." She took a step closer to him, holding out her hand as if she might touch him. He turned away from her, chest heaving.

"Don't be frightened," she said. And her words made him want to spit. She came closer, one arm still raised to keep Kara suspended. The other reaching for him.

He flinched away from her, and she paused. "I won't hurt you this time. I told you to obey me, though. I might have to"—she leaned closer, closed her eyes as if she was about to kiss him.

And Ryan straightened. This wasn't right. He looked down at Ethan's writhing, crumpled form on the floor. Ethan. His brother. This time Ethan was in need of rescuing. Ryan's heart clutched. Because this time it was all his own fault. He'd—he'd done this. He'd—no. He looked up at Belladonna and her seductive smile. "And I told you—" Ryan swung his sword with all his might. The blade sliced through her neck. Her eyes opened momentarily to reveal her surprise, and then her head tumbled to the floor and rolled across stone to sit at Jayden's feet.

"—not to hurt my brother." Ryan fell in a heap, leaning on his sword hilt. The bloody tip rested on the floor and blood, black as night, dripped off the blade and onto the cement. He'd done it.

He'd killed her.

His mind raced. Almost as if something inside of it clicked unlocked. She was dead? She was dead! His entire body started shaking.

Kara fell to the ground, and Ethan's cries of agony stopped.

"Ryan?" Ethan approached him and squeezed his shoulder, his voice hoarse from screaming, and his grip trembling as much as Ryan was. "You did it."

"I can't . . . I—"

"She's gone. She can't hurt you again."

Ryan bent one knee and rested his elbow on it, burying his head in his hand. His sword clattered against the ground. He'd done it. His shoulders shook as a rush of relief poured into him like a dam breaking.

"Ryan?" Serena's voice was closer. Both she and Jayden crowded around him. Kara must have set them free. He glanced up to see tears in their eyes. Jayden was the first to hug him close. Her arms wrapped around him as Serena pressed her hands against Ethan's back, healing him.

Ethan.

He'd . . . Ryan's memories flooded into him. The things he'd done. Fighting his own brother. "Ethan—"

"It wasn't you." Ethan stood and offered his hand. Ryan grabbed it, and Ethan pulled him up and into a tight embrace.

"I'm so sorry," Ryan whispered.

"You're forgiven. It's over. Done. You hear me?"

Ryan nodded. And then someone grabbed his hand. He'd know her touch anywhere. He turned and wrapped Serena in his arms.

"Glad to have you back." She looked up at him, eyes shimmering.

He breathed deep and squared his shoulders, clenching his jaw. "It's good to be back." Everything inside him felt stronger. Like he could take on the world now.

Ethan squeezed Ryan's shoulder again. "You ready for this?"

He nodded once. "Ready for anything now, brother." That last word choked him up a bit. "You came for me."

"Always will."

"Jayden?" Serena slipped her arms from Ryan and approached Jayden. She held her hand over her. "There's poison in you."

Her breaths shook. "I feel it. In my blood. It's fighting for control."

Serena grabbed Jayden's hands. "I can act as the white alor and absorb the poison from Jayden."

"You can't do that. You still have to fight the Mistress," Kara said.

Everyone turned to her. Ryan had nearly forgotten about her being there. "You!" He marched toward her.

She put up her hands in surrender and backed away from him. "Listen, you don't understand my motives, I know. And I don't really care. All I'm trying to do is save our lives." She motioned to all the sleeping soldiers around the room. "I have made sure every spot of danger you have gotten yourselves into hasn't ended badly for you."

"Not badly?" He pointed to Jayden. To Serena. To Ethan.

Kara held up a glass vial. "I found this neat recipe in Serena's counters book and thought I'd try it out."

Serena gasped. "You made the white alor potion?"

Kara shrugged. "Thea knew you'd be too late to tap into the white alor trees before they started dying. I took the page from the potion book and made it down here. I made enough to heal the black blood soldiers. It won't cure all of them, because some of them have been under the venom too long. But it should be enough to cure most of the Mistress's army." She looked at Ryan. "I'm sorry it won't work on you, Charmer. But let me give some to Jayden. As we speak, the Mistress's men are drinking their share." Kara handed Jayden a vial of white liquid. "It will cause quite the uproar for her when she realizes she has to replace half of her army. It will give the Wielder enough time to escape her clutches."

"She's telling the truth, but I don't know if you should trust her," Serena said. "Kara helps only herself."

"That hurts, Golden One." Kara folded her arms. "Let's just say I gave all the soldiers access to their drink of choice. The kegs were open. But it was a pity to waste all that alcohol. So they're all having a wonderful time in the camp awaiting the Mistress to call them to order. And she'll be here soon. We are under the base of the thrones. You'd better get out there if you want to defeat her."

"Aren't you just full of good news?" Ryan scoffed.

"What did you think I was doing when I told you I had my own plans? I helped Belladonna get you here. I made it so you could escape easily."

"You call that easy?" Ryan motioned toward Belladonna's severed head.

She spared him a look, then motioned to the vial Jayden held. "That's the last of the black blood antidote. Don't spill."

Jayden tipped her head back and drank. Ryan watched as she squeezed her eyes shut and then shook her head. She opened her eyes and grinned. "It doesn't taste that bad."

Kara almost smiled. Then motioned to the door. "Out there you'll find stairs leading up to ground."

"You're not coming?" Ethan asked.

"What's your plan now?" Serena asked.

"That I can't tell you. But rest assured, it'll be enough to change the course of the future." She handed Serena a folded-up handkerchief. "Take the keys and go up through the old staircase. The four thrones are cornerstones of this building. The Mistress will be here soon, and her army comes." Kara walked over to Belladonna's body and removed the bracer. She handed that to Ryan. "And give this to Wolf—I mean Connor. It's time to put that witch where she belongs." Kara pushed them through the door. "Talk to Wolf before Smoke gets here."

Seemed Thea had thought of everything. Ryan turned as everyone started through the doors, and Kara tugged Ryan's sleeve. He stopped as the others left. The haughtiness in her eyes disappeared. "The Mistress is bound to you. She chose you as her vessel."

"I know."

"You know that now more than half of your heart is compromised?"

He sighed, but he could feel it. His heart worked hard to push the darkness back. "I do."

"You two share a heart. If she dies, you die." Her eyes grew soft. "Serena won't want that to happen."

Ryan glanced up the stairs where his friends had gone. Then he faced Kara. "You want to kill me now? I won't stop you."

"I wouldn't do that. She'd just bond to a new vessel. Smoke has to die first. Are you ready for that?"

"I'm ready to save the world. Whatever it takes."

"Why save what's already lost?"

He smiled. "Hasn't Serena taught you anything? There's always hope. And hope is worth saving."

"My sister was right to have fallen for you." She touched his shoulder briefly.

"Thea?" Ryan thought back to their last meeting. Then he looked at Kara. "What else did she tell you?"

Kara shrugged, but she glanced away from him. "You will all hate me after what I've had to do. I know that." Her gaze pierced him. "But believe me when I say . . . I–I . . ." She stared at him as if telling him might make her more vulnerable than she was prepared to be. "Just go."

"Kara." He touched her arm, and she didn't pull away. Just stared at his hand for a heartbeat before she looked into his eyes. "I'll make sure they don't hate you, as long as you can prove to me that you're on our side."

Her eyes narrowed. "Don't tell the others?"

He shook his head.

She breathed deep. "I only save those I'd consider worthy comrades."

He crossed his arms, studying her. "Are you saying we're your friends?"

Her smile turned into a challenging grin. "I'm saying if you breathe a word of that to the others, I'll hunt you down myself."

"Your secret is safe with me."

She stopped him with a hand on his arm. "If you tell Serena that you'll die—"

"I won't."

"She's a unicorn. She'll know if you lie."

"I'm a dragon. I'll find a way."

CHAPTER 62

SMOKE ON THE HORIZON

Jayden pushed open the cellar door, and a sickly reddish light filtered in. That and the scent of a decaying forest. She peered up to see faces and weapons pointed at her, and relief filtered into her as they put their weapons down. The Feravolk had come.

Westwind bounded up to her and pressed his cold nose into Jayden's palm. She touched his head. "You're still here?"

He nodded and chuffed.

"I can't hear you." Tears filled her eyes.

Rebekah approached Jayden and touched her cheek. "I can't hear him, either. But he knew you'd be here. Your three-oath bond keeps him with us. That and I think he stays because he loves you."

Jayden looked down at him. "You are a true friend."

He flipped her hand over his head with his cool nose. She touched him. Scratched behind his ears. "I am honored to fight with you by my side, too."

Rebekah hugged Serena close. And Serena motioned to something behind Jayden. "Look."

Jayden faced the foundation of the ruins in front of her. Surely this couldn't be it? But then she saw four strange overgrown pillars. Moss and vines clung to them, distorting their shape, but they were indeed pillars. She touched one.

"I don't see any thrones," Ethan said.

"Or a castle, which I kind of expected." Ryan laughed as he joined them.

Jayden pulled vines away from one of the pillars and uncovered a stone, weathered and worn, but clearly the shape of a pegasus. Below the creature's head, on its neck, was a circle engraved into the stone.

A circle. "I think my key will fit in here."

The others crowded around her, and Serena touched the divot in the stone pegasus's chest. "I believe you're right."

Serena and the others rushed to the three remaining corners and uncovered worn pillars with stone busts representing the animals to which they had bonded. Each bust contained a hollowed-out circle perfect for the wooden tokens.

"Are we ready?" Serena asked as she pulled the handkerchief from her pocket.

Ryan shifted his weight and stared up at the sky. "Let's get this over with."

"Do you feel something?" Jayden asked him.

He nodded. "Smoke." His words, barely audible, sent a shiver though her core. Ryan's eyes bored into her. "We have to kill the dragon first. Or else we won't be able to kill the Mistress."

Serena gripped his shirt and faced him. "You—"

"I know. As soon as Smoke dies, I'm the only thing keeping her alive."

Jayden's heart clutched. "We'll make sure you have the Creator's power, Ryan. Connor said that could save you, right?"

"Yes." He looked at Serena. "If you don't kill the Mistress, she'll always have a hold on me. Always a link to get back. I refuse to be that link. As soon as she dies, I'll be free of her. Forever."

Serena nodded, eyes wide. "You can't be that link anymore. We'll kill her. You'll be free."

He touched her arm. "Thank you."

"Serena?" A small voice punctured the air, and Serena turned. Hundreds of women wearing Feravolk cloaks over white dresses melted into view as they moved through the trees, closer. One young woman with long brown hair stepped to the front of them.

Serena placed her hand over her heart. "Rochelle?"

Rochelle raced up to Serena and hugged her as the Healers, most dressed in Feravolk cloaks, followed, melting into view. They joined the Feravolk. "I brought as many as I could find."

"You're all Healers?" Rebekah stared.

"Our powers are waning," Rochelle said. "The Mistress's darkness taints everything. All of us have already watched our unicorns fade away, but we've come to fight alongside our people. Just as you sent Tessa to tell us." Rochelle shook her head and seemed to stare into a memory. "It's time. The Forest of Legends is the beginning of all. Life springs from it. Grows from it. Flows in it. The Creator's own heart beats in rhythm with it. If the Mistress wanted to kill all of creation she would merely have to stop the heart from beating. The prophecies are coming to pass. Through blazing fire and torrent of rain the Forest shall fall and rise again."

"Rise again. That's good news, right?" Jayden asked.

"It really depends on who it's rising under, I'd say," Ryan said.

"It's time to unlock the power." Serena unrolled the handkerchief. Four wooden circles sprinkled into her palm and she gasped. "These"—she held up the tokens—"aren't the keys." She buckled over, eyes wide. "She betrayed us again!"

"Kara?" Jayden peered into Serena's hand, willing this to be a mistake.

"They're circles of wood." Ryan plucked one from her hand and threw it into the woods. "Now what?"

Jayden's heart crumbled.

Ethan grabbed the rest from Serena's hand and hurled the tokens into the forest. "Where is that no-good assassin! I'll kill her myself!"

Jayden stared at Ethan and her chest ached. "Are we too late?" she whispered. Her knees were water.

"No," Serena faced her, fists clenched. "Kara has them. She has to. Or, maybe they're on Belladonna's body. We'll get them."

Jayden breathed in, hoping she could hold on to her dwindling talents long enough to kill the Mistress of Shadows the way she'd killed Idla and Franco.

With lightning. She clutched her dagger tight.

Cliffdiver approached, and Jayden looked at Ethan. "He's talking to you?"

He nodded, eyes wide. "The Mistress has Connor and Quinn."

"Not anymore." Connor's voice made Jayden turn. He carried Quinn toward them.

Serena rushed to his side. "How did you get free?"

"Long story involving the Mistress's army running off and my becoming a mouse, and then a gryphon. But can you help Quinn?"

"What's wrong?" Serena reached for her.

"I'm dying." Quinn's voice was raspy and weak.

Serena gasped. "This isn't something I can heal."

Connor's voice cracked.. "If we defeat the Mistress, we can save her."

"We don't have the keys!" Jayden touched Quinn's face. She felt unusually cold.

Ryan handed Connor the bracer. "I think you'll need this."

Connor stared at it until Rebekah took the bracer from him, fastened it on his good arm, and touched the side of his face.

Jayden felt the love blossom in Rebekah's heart. It melted into hers.

"Thank you." Connor mouthed the words to his mother, then he looked up at all those gathered around him. "You—you all know that half of those who fight will die as soon as I use my power?"

Everyone nodded. Rebekah touched his shoulder. "We will all die if you don't."

He breathed a shaky breath. "Cliffdiver will take Serena and Ryan to kill Smoke."

"You're still bonded?" Jayden asked.

"He's been bonded to three Wielders before me. His bond is old. But I'm not sure how much longer it will last." He looked into Jayden's eyes. "As soon as Smoke is dead, strike the Mistress with everything you have left. Ethan, Quinn, and I will open the door. You send her through with your wind. Got it? The rest of the Feravolk will keep as many of the remaining Black Blood Army from us as they can."

"Remaining?" Serena asked.

Connor faced her. "Half of them ran off. It was as if her hold on them vanished, but some remained. Enough to be a problem."

"Kara said that would be a possibility," Ryan said.

"And the keys?" Rebekah asked.

Connor touched her arm. "Will you help us find them?"

"I will."

"Check downstairs first." Serena motioned toward the way they'd exited. Rebekah hurried down the steps.

Jayden touched Connor and risked pulsing the feeling of calm strength into him. His eyebrows rose, and he placed his hand over hers against his shoulder and squeezed. "The Creator's blessing on all of you." He looked up at the sky.

The red moon on the horizon climbed higher into the sky. A massive, black dragon rose up in front of the sun.

"Smoke." Ryan's whisper chilled Jayden to the bone.

Smoke's laugh scraped through the sky.

"Look," Jayden whispered, echoing the feeling in her soul. Dark and tall, slender and cold, a cloud coasted toward them from the horizon, skimming over the ground.

Ethan clenched his jaw. "A storm. Yours?"

A shiver raced through her. Creator help her. The pain of loss speared her soul and her knees weakened. She pressed her hand against her tightening throat and shook her head. "I can't feel the storm."

Ethan glanced at her, and his eyes filled with so much emotion. But her sense of his feelings was gone. Everything Jayden had come to embrace and rely on . . . just gone. Not a hole. At least that would be something. It was just an absence of so much that she'd shared with Ethan. "My talents are gone."

The base of the cloud opened like a black drape, and the Mistress stepped out from the dark abyss. Her eyes had turned black, like a starless night, and her skin, which had once been a pale yellow, was white. She was death come to claim them.

What remained of the Black Blood Army, trailed after her, and hope bloomed in Jayden. The Feravolk gathered here could take them. Maybe they could beat her.

"How does it feel to be in my prison?" the Mistress's voice boomed as if it echoed itself. "You chosen ones, Feravolk. The Creator's most prized guardians. And where are you now? Powerless. Soleden is mine. You have nothing. This army of yours doesn't compare to what I've brought here. You destroyed many of my Black Blood Army, but I have creatures whose blood runs blacker than even those you've seen. The power is mine now. To create. To destroy. To kill. And to bring to life." She held her hand out toward the funnel cloud behind her. "Behold! My army!"

Deformed and distorted creatures with colors not before seen in this world poured out of the cloud like a torrent of debris scattering in the wind.

One creature stepped up to the Mistress's side—as large as Zephyr and twice as wide. Its fur stood out in black clumps, and white teeth extended past its lips. Flames made up its eyes. Jayden knew the canine-like creature all too well. The barghest, Gnarg. Her heart crumpled. How would they fight this?

The Mistress ran her fingers along the beast's fur. "Kill the Whisperer. And since the Wielder has chosen not to be my groom, destroy him." She tipped her head to the black shadow above her. "Smoke, bring the Deliverers to me. The rest of you, demolish."

Jayden clutched her daggers, but the fear choking her would not dissipate. This time, fear and hopelessness tugged inside of her, and those emotions belonged to her alone. Nothing from Ethan. Nothing from the storm. She looked at Serena, but no warmth of hope emanated from her. Jayden had never felt so utterly alone. Alone with her fear.

And it was crushing.

Logan's last direction filled her heart: *You have to stick together. You have to work together. Never stop believing that together you can beat her.*

Connor commanded them, and all the Feravolk shot forward with cries for Soleden. They clashed with the creatures of darkness, and Jayden stood beside Ethan and faced the Mistress as Smoke dove toward them.

CHAPTER 63

FIRE WITH FIRE

Ryan stared at the full moon. It shone hot and red. Like dragon's breath. And as the Mistress descended and called her monsters forward, her commands tugged at his heart. She didn't own half. She owned more. Much more. There was no hiding from Smoke now.

As Jayden stared wide-eyed at the approaching clouds flickering with lightning and mourned the loss of her power, fire crackled in Ryan's hands. The strongest, hottest flames he'd ever felt.

Serena touched his arm, her mouth open. "You still have your power?"

He curled his fingers into fists. "I'm one of them. Her taint fuels my power. And it's strong."

Two hands, dry and brittle as a tree devoid of water, wrapped around his hands, and he looked into Quinn's eyes. "Ryan. Fire. Fire hurts."

He looked at the scars on her arms and bowed his head. "The part of my heart that belongs to me, you don't need to fear it."

"I know." She tilted her head so he couldn't avoid her innocent eye contact. "Fire also heals."

"It's not mine. It's hers. It's—"

"No. It's yours." She touched his chest over his heart. "You fight her, and she knows it. You aren't hers to claim."

Ryan stilled the flame in his palms and placed his hand over Quinn's. Kara was right; he was about to die. So he only had to fight her for a little longer. He could do that. And die himself. Not her pawn. "Thank you."

"She's right." Connor's voice grew urgent as he spoke, his eyes wide. "Remember? It's the prophecy. 'A sorceress will come with power to destroy all the Creator has built. She'll break the land and the people's hearts and bring death to those who'd oppose her. But hope will be found when the Deliverers rise through fire, through ash, and heal the heart of the land.'"

Ryan looked at his hands. "I don't understand."

Connor swept his arm out, pointing at all the dying Forest of Legends. "Burn it. Burn everything."

"He's right," Quinn said. "The land can't grow again unless the evil is destroyed. Only fire destroys her evil. True fire. The kind from the Creator. Your fire."

Ryan glanced out at the once majestic trees. They were kindling now. He could easily—*I feel your heart.* Smoke's voice filled his mind, and Ryan looked up in time to see the dragon headed straight toward them. "Connor. Look out!"

Cliffdiver dropped in front of Ryan and Serena, who grabbed his arm. "Let's go. Spread your fire. I'll kill a dragon." She pulled him, and he mounted the gryphon behind her. As Smoke's head descended, Cliffdiver took flight.

"You can't run from me."

"I'm not running anymore." Ryan called the fire deep within him, and it surged through his veins, filling his very being. Heating him from the inside. As Cliffdiver swooped closer to the tops of the trees, Ryan held out his arms and sent a stream of fire from his hands. It slammed into each tree they passed, and the poison inside of them caused them to ignite.

Cliffdiver took them closer to the darker creatures, and they shrieked and writhed as his fire hit them.

And the more Ryan used, the more the tainted part of his heart thrashed.

He felt it wheezing inside of him. It resembled the day Serena had helped him break the bond with Smoke. This time, his heart was too tainted to survive on its own. And as the forest burned, the piece of him tied to the venom that pulsed through him began to writhe.

Smoke laughed.

The Mistress turned her thoughts onto him, and he felt her voice claw into his head. *"You'll die. But I will live on. Once I have the Creator's power, I won't need a vessel."*

"I will die. And you with me."

His fire crackled. Trees seemed to reach for his flame. The more he used, the stronger he felt. The freer. This *was* his power. It fought the taint. But it wouldn't be enough to reverse the effects.

Serena touched his arm. "Your fire is killing the poison. The plants are dying, but the heart is beating stronger with every poisoned tree that perishes, Ryan. The forest is getting healthier because of you."

"How can you be so sure?"

She placed her hand on her chest. "I feel its heart. Or Dash's heart inside of me feels it." She looked at him. "Can you hear Smoke?"

"Y-yes."

"Good. Get me close enough."

He touched Cliffdiver. "Okay, buddy, get us close to that dragon."

Smoke's amber eyes locked onto Ryan. *"You cannot kill me. If you do, you'll be killing yourself."*

"We are not the same."

"No. But we are linked to her. Killing the forest only takes power from yourself."

Ryan blocked the voice out. "Cliffdiver, take me to the ground, to the base of that white alor tree. I'll keep Smoke's attention, and you take Serena right to the beast's heart. Can you do that?"

The gryphon glanced over his shoulder, the look in his eye much more animal than before. He hoped the creature heard him. But Cliffdiver headed for the ground.

Smoke targeted him. *"I will take you to her. And you will give her the Creator's power."*

"Come and get me." Ryan shot fire at the dragon's face, and as Cliffdiver descended, he jumped off and rolled to the ground. He stood and pulled out his sword. Cliffdiver took flight beneath Smoke's answering roar of flame.

The Mistress's voice penetrated his mind, stronger now. *"Stand with me. You could live forever. You could be one of the black blood. You could be mine and fill the place the Wielder won't. You would be my right hand. Not some pet. You would be powerful. Never helpless. Never helpless again.*

"No one could hurt you.

"No one would need to heal you.

"The Creator's power would be yours.

"All yours."

Ryan shot her a half-smile and tapped into the link he'd been ignoring for so long. *"I already have all the power I need. I'm not helpless."* And, for once, he believed it.

He touched the white alor tree in his bare hands and ignited its core. His flames spread into the bark. Deep, deep inside.

Fire crackled and popped all around him and burst out from the tree, scattering bark and twigs in an explosion that didn't touch him. Black smoke filled the red sky.

The Mistress screeched at him with her eyes wild. "You will not beat me. You are too late!"

And she headed for him.

Ryan clutched his sword. It was made for him. The heat conducted into it but didn't soften the metal. It made it stronger. Harder. As if dragon's fire had forged this blade and dragon's fire powered it. He looked at the Mistress and smirked.

Today he'd die. But not in vain.

CHAPTER 64

BRITTLE

Connor gripped Quinn's arm and tugged her farther from the moving and consuming flames and out into the area where fire had already burned the forest. He had a direct view of the Mistress of Shadows from here, but the flames wouldn't come back this way. They were following Ryan's warpath. Still, he needed to get closer to the Mistress. Her army raced out of the fire and into the waiting weapons of the Feravolk army. Connor was mere yards from them, traveling the outskirts so he could get behind the army unseen and closer to the Mistress.

Quinn nearly fell, and he stopped to help her back to her feet. Her hands clutched him. They felt like dry, brittle wood.

"Quinn, we need to get closer to the Mistress so I can open the door. I'm too weak now to do it from here." He tugged her arm again, but she wouldn't budge. "Quinn?" He looked at her and her tearful eyes.

"I'm sorry."

"Sorry? No. We still have time. We're still alive, that means the heart still beats."

She pulled up the hem of her torn dress, and Connor gasped. Her legs had turned into a tree trunk. "I–I can't move from here."

A tremor shot through his body, and he dropped to his knees in front of her. "No." The word came out a whisper, but it echoed from the deepest part of him. How would he save half of them now? How would he save Quinn?

He stood up and cupped her face in his hand. She would die with the forest. "Can you hang on? I need you." He couldn't save anyone without her. He couldn't cause that much death. He—his knees weakened.

She grabbed his arm. "You can still do this. Your power is you."

"No. It isn't. I–I need you to be able to wield my power."

"I'll do anything I can for you." She touched the sides of his face, and her hands were like a plant devoid of water.

Heat.

Skin.

Heat.

Fur.

No.

No, no, no. His wolf form started to take over.

"Connor?"

"Stay with me." His heart ached. His eyes burned. And he couldn't hold on. This wasn't him. He wasn't changing himself. Nothing anchored him in this human form anymore. The Forest of Legends was dying and his power with it. "No!" The word came out in a howl as he lost control and his body shifted into wolf form.

Instead of full color, everything dulled as if he saw with the eyes of a natural wolf, not a bonded one. He tried to shift back but it was like hitting a wall. He was stuck in this form. No sword. Nothing.

Quinn's frantic eyes locked onto him. "Do you still have your power?"

"I'm wearing the bracer. I think it has enough in it for one shot."

A tear fell from her eye. "That's all we need. It's all you need."

"No! Quinn!"

Her skin and clothes turned to bark, and a look of determination crossed her face. "Never give up. Never lose hope. Take this." She tipped her head back, as if trying to breathe air above the surface of the water. Her arms spread and fingers splayed as she turned into a tree. A white alor tree. Leaves sprouted on her branches, and wind ripped them loose. They headed for Connor. He tore at the clothes clinging to him, freed himself and headed for Quinn's leaves. He had to finish what he'd come here for before he was lost to his wolf side forever.

As he raced for Quinn's parting gift, he swallowed his grief. And he looked to see Cliffdiver. The gryphon still stayed loyal, taking Serena toward Smoke's heart.

If he had Quinn's leaves, would that be enough to stop him from killing all of them?

He stopped just outside the battle. The din of clashing swords and shouts and screams rang in his ears, and he braced himself for the leaves to swirl around him.

Serena held tight to Cliffdiver's feathers as he flew straight toward the dragon's chest. This was up to her. Heat and char rode on the wind, and not just from Smoke's constant barrage of fireballs. Ryan's flames were saving the Forest of Legends. Now it was up to her to save him. She pulled out her dagger. Heat from Smoke's breath sailed over top of her, stinging her lungs, blistering her skin. And she didn't heal. She clenched her hands into fists around her daggers, gritted her teeth for what she was about to do, and prayed Ryan would be all right.

The dragon dove at them.

Thick, black scales drew closer.

Closer.

A heart beat beneath, dark as coal and as hard. She waited one moment more, urging Cliffdiver closer to the beast's chest. There it was. She held her dagger tighter and slashed open his scales as Smoke flew past.

Smoke roared.

He whirled his body around.

Her cut hadn't been deep enough, but blood, black as pitch stained the blade.

"Once more. We have to get closer."

Cliffdiver buffeted wind as Smoke's tail crashed toward them, strong and spiked. Serena clutched the gryphon tight, but he jolted beneath her as Smoke's tail slammed into him. Serena plummeted forward, freefalling.

The black dragon swooped below her. She braced herself for a landing on his armored head. A spine ripped into her thigh, and she cried out. Fell hard against his head. She wrapped her arms around one spike as he shook his head.

Pain stabbed her, nothing would quell it. Her powers weren't working.

She clutched the horn tight as one dagger plummeted to the earth. Then she let herself fall toward the side of his head. If she could just get a hold of the huge curved horn that curled out of the side of his head, she might be able to angle herself right to jump straight for his chest.

Smoke rose higher and higher as he flew straight up. The wind beat against her as he picked up speed. If she jumped now, while he was nearly vertical to the ground, she might be able to land on his chest. Might be able to puncture his heart.

It had to be now. This moment. Her hand grabbed the curved horn, and she held on as she dangled from it and slid to the edge. His huge, amber eye watched her. *"Stupid Healer. If you fall, you die."*

She swung toward his scaled chest and let go.

For a moment she remained, suspended in the air as his long neck glided past her. Then she fell. Fast. Faster. Dagger out, she slammed into the dragon's chest, blade first.

Her weapon sunk deep into the scales.

Smoke roared.

Fire shot out from his throat. The scales heated beneath her touch. And she pushed harder, gripping the hilt tight.

His wings stilled.

Then she hung in the air, going neither up nor down, and then, like a falling stone, he plummeted.

She held her weapon, anchoring herself to the beast, and braced for impact. Connor had said two Deliverers might die. This could be her final moment.

Smoke split the earth and sank beneath the depths. And she lay across his broken body. Blood still pumping from her. Cracked bones groaned. But she'd slain the dragon.

CHAPTER 65

BARREN

Fire spread, crackled, and streaked through the forest. Everything blazed. Ethan faced the beasts in front of him—the only thing standing in his way. He had to get to Ryan and Jayden, to fight beside them and do his best to protect them. But he had no speed and no strength, only his skill with a sword. He lunged and pushed the blade through an animal then pulled it out and whirled to face another enemy. His arm burned. His muscles quivered, and he didn't know if Jayden still lived.

Something slammed into him from behind, and he whirled around to face a black lion. Furry wings flapped as it swiped him with blood-red claws. They sliced into his arm, and it felt so different than before. This cut burned. Like a fire in his veins.

The poison.

He was no longer immune.

That meant he didn't have much time. Serena and Connor had better hurry.

He swung his sword at the beast. *C'mon, Ethan. You're stronger than this.* But for the first time, he wasn't sure. What was he without his talents?

A laugh sounded behind him, and he turned, putting him face to face with a ghost.

He blinked several times, certain he was seeing things. Surely this wasn't Belladonna.

He shook his head. It had to be the poison. She was dead. Ryan had killed her himself.

A smile snaked across her lips. "Surprised to see me?"

That wasn't the word he'd use. Ethan clutched his sword and willed himself to regain his lost speed as he raced at her. Before he could make it, someone cut him off, and clashed her sword against his. Ethan jolted to a halt, and his heart slammed into his ribs. "Kara?"

She kicked him and he stumbled back.

"You die today!" He tried to scramble to his feet, but a black lion smacked into him and pressed him to the ground.

He stared around the beast and met Kara's gaze. The Black Blood Army clustered around them. "How could you?" Every limb shook with the boiling anger inside of him.

"Means to an end, soldier." She shrugged. "Thea gave me a resurrection spell and instructed me to use it on Belladonna. So I did."

"You monster!" Ethan pushed against the lion.

It felt heavier, and its purr vibrated through him.

"Nothing personal." Kara tilted her head, bringing her weapon closer to his neck.

"It is to me." Belladonna stepped forward. "I have Ryan's heart, Serena's will, Jayden's mind, and finally I'll have your strength."

The lion purred against his chest, and its claws slashed into him deeper this time. Heavens, it stung. Kara placed her sword against his throat.

Ethan stared up at her, every ounce of hope leaking out of him.

Belladonna pushed a vial of black liquid to his lips. "Drink and be mine."

"Never."

Kara pressed her blade harder. "Sorry, soldier. You're going to have to do this one."

Belladonna poured the mixture down his throat and forced him to swallow. He choked, trying to spit and cough, but she held his mouth and nose closed until finally it trickled down his throat. "Now your blood will be black."

She let go; the lion let him up, and he gasped for air. Then Belladonna held up a ring and motioned for Kara to remove her blade from Ethan's throat. He stood and grabbed his sword.

"Drop the sword," Belladonna said.

Against everything that screamed within him, Ethan's hand opened and his weapon fell. He stared at her as a shiver buzzed in his bones.

"Your strength is mine." She pulled a handkerchief from her pocket and unfolded the material to reveal the four tokens. The actual keys. They'd been with her all along. She tossed Kara the ring. "The army is yours now. Consider yourself rewarded. Keep the fight out of here until I can complete this."

She headed behind him, toward the pillars. Ethan bent to pick up his sword. This would end now, with Belladonna's head burned in the fire.

"Stop, soldier." Kara's voice was quiet, but Ethan halted. All of his muscles quivered as he tried to defy her orders. He didn't move. His body wouldn't obey him. With a fire in his eyes, he glared at Kara.

She shook her head. "I know you don't understand. The only way to control those marked by the blood moon with compulsion was to develop this poison."

"You didn't cure them!"

"I did. But Thea knew it wouldn't work on all of them."

"Curse Thea!"

"No." Kara shook her head. "This isn't easy for me."

"Looks easy from here." Ethan tightened his grip on his weapon as Belladonna got closer to the pillars. "She'll get the Creator's power!"

"I know." Kara's eyes met his. "No one wants to be the traitor, Ethan. It's a thankless job. Thea knew *I* could handle it."

"You're not making sense."

"Belladonna needs to be alive for this. Enemy of my enemy."

Everything inside strained to fight Kara, but her command still anchored him to his spot. He glanced over his shoulder to where Ryan and Jayden still fought, and a hollow ache spread through his chest. The Mistress! She was headed right toward his brother. He had to get to them. Again, he tried to move, but the black lion poison inside of him surged. His blood was on fire. He fell to his knees, gasping.

"What's wrong with you? Oh."

He spoke through clenched teeth. "Give me the antidote."

Her eyes held panic. "I didn't know you'd need it. Nothing in Thea's note told me to save you some."

"Kara—"

She stepped closer to him. "You believe I'm on your side?"

Did he? "I believe you can be, if you choose to be."

"Then trust me."

He motioned to where Ryan and Jayden fought the Mistress side by side. "Then let me protect them!"

Kara's gaze swept the pandemonium around her, then landed on Ethan. She nodded once. "Go. Protect them. And kill the Mistress."

CHAPTER 66

THE POWER UNLEASHED

Jayden breathed deep, and a trickle of her powers filtered back into her. It was working. Ryan's fire was killing the poison! If she could get enough power back, she could stop the Mistress. Ethan would send her through Connor's door.

She pulled at the power filling her, wishing it could be more, and scanned for the woman. There. She strode past fighters, shoulders squared and on a mission. Jayden's eyes followed the Mistress's path and her stomach jumped. Ryan. She headed right for Ryan!

Clutching her daggers tight and focusing on her returning power, Jayden fled to her brother's aid.

Ryan stood, shaking, as the comforting heat of his spreading fire warmed his back. The Mistress walked toward him, burning coals for eyes.

Someone in a Feravolk cloak raced at her, and she swiped her arm to the side, not even glancing at her attacker. She didn't even lay a hand on the Feravolk warrior. Her power lifted the attacker from the ground and slammed the warrior into a tree. All the while, the Mistress still continued charging toward Ryan.

His eyes widened. How could he hope to defeat that?

His knees rattled. But he stood his ground.

She stopped in front of him. "You are weak."

That might be true, but it didn't matter. What mattered was what he chose to do right now. This moment. He glared. Let a half-smile tug at his lips. And raised his hand. "And you don't own me." Fire spouted from his open palm and slammed into her chest.

He created more flames. Hotter flames. They turned blue, then white. He roared as his power coursed through him like thunder and pushed into her in a steady stream that made her stagger backward.

There was no way he could hold her forever. The stream stopped, and he tried to catch his breath. Her gaze turned to him, her white skin cracking like an overcooked clay pot. And then Jayden raced into view. She threw her dagger, and it sailed toward the Mistress's chest.

But the dagger didn't pierce her.

It fell at her feet.

The Mistress lifted both of her arms and flicked her wrist. Jayden flew backward and into a tree.

"No!" Ryan lunged for her, but a force slammed into him hard and thrust him off his feet. He sailed backward and rammed hard into an unforgiving surface that cracked like snapping wood. He slumped to the ground, his vision wavering as he blinked a few times to refocus.

The Mistress was closer. "And now you'll pay for that mistake."

Ethan's heart nearly stalled as Ryan's stream of fire stopped and the Mistress sent him and Jayden flying. He tried to push himself faster. The black lion venom inside him wanted to pull him to his knees, but suddenly new speed coursed through his veins. His speed was returning? His talents! *Good job, Ryan! Please be okay!*

If he had power again, could he access his shield? He tried to pull it to himself, closer now, as the Mistress stood over Ryan.

She raised her hand.

No! Ethan tried to create a wind shield, but he wasn't close enough. Almost there! *Come on, Ethan! Faster.*

A flash of yellow light lit the entire sky and a crack—the sound of stone splitting—filled the air. Ethan flinched, ducking down, and spun around to see Belladonna standing on the foundation where the thrones were. Green light bathed her. She was taking the Creator's power.

Everything inside of him felt heavy. Hopeless. They were too late?

He faced his brother—he might be close enough to shield Ryan now. He was, but the Mistress's head had jerked up, staring at Belladonna. She glided toward the thrones as Ethan raced to his brother and Jayden.

"What happened?" Ryan stood.

Jayden didn't.

Kara skidded to a halt next to Jayden. Ethan pushed her away and knelt. Red leaked out from Jayden's hairline. His heart plummeted. "If that witch killed her—"

"She didn't," Kara said. "But in a moment, after Belladonna claims this power, the Mistress won't care anymore if you live or die." She touched Jayden's head, and her eyes fluttered open.

Ethan pulled her into him. "Are you all right?" A burn shot across his chest. Such a familiar sensation. His talents. His need to protect Jayden fueled him, and he dove for his sword and stood, weapon in hand. The burn of the poison leeched mercifully from his body.

With inhuman speed, he let go of Jayden and pressed his sword to Kara's throat. Shaking, he looked into her eyes. "Tell your army to fight the Mistress's creatures."

She looked over her shoulder at the soldiers. "You heard him. Fight the Mistress's army. Keep them away from Belladonna."

Belladonna's laughter shot forth into the sky, and she rose above them on the top of a funnel cloud that fanned the flames all around her. "Now the power is mine!"

Ethan stared.

Jayden's quiet "no" drained all the hope from him. A slight nudge from his talent told him to turn, and he did. His sword flew up to protect him faster than he thought necessary. He stabbed an abysshound through its skull and looked up.

Belladonna didn't come for him or Jayden or Ryan. She headed right for the Mistress. "I have your power now."

"You have nothing!" The Mistress glared back at her.

Ethan's heart raced. He scanned for Connor. Did he know? His talent told him to get closer to the Mistress.

"Ethan, do you have your powers?" Kara asked.

He nodded.

"Good. Go now. Kill Belladonna before the Mistress takes her powers. Softheart." She touched Jayden's shoulder. "Call your storm. This ends now."

Ethan took off running, his returned speed a welcome friend. He raced through the battlefield, eyes on Belladonna and her funnel cloud. How was he supposed to kill her? What did he have besides a sword?

She looked down at him, a crazed glint in her eyes, and he put up his shield. A torrent of wind slammed into him. Too strong. He crashed to the ground, blowing farther away from her. When he stopped rolling, he scrambled to his feet. She still charged after him, but she'd left her back open to the Mistress.

Ethan covered his eyes and formed his shield as a bolt of lightning crackled from the Mistress's fingers and zapped into Belladonna. A boom rocked the earth. The Mistress used the sparks of lightning to hold Belladonna in place and bring her to the ground. Then she thrust her hand into Belladonna's chest and ripped out her heart.

Belladonna crumpled.

The Mistress laughed as she crushed the heart. "I have the power now!" A bright light filled her. Cracked her skin. Tiny holes and fissures spread throughout her body as if the power inside her ripped her at the seams.

"No!" Kara screamed.

The sky crackled again. Heat exploded in Ethan's chest. The Mistress looked at Jayden. She'd kill Jayden.

Ethan scanned the battlefield for Connor. There. A three-legged, brown wolf launched itself at Gnarg.

"Connor! Now!"

CHAPTER 67

CALM THE STORM

Jayden stared at the form of the Mistress as she rose above the smoldering forest on a funnel cloud just like Belladonna had done.

But the Mistress's was stronger. Larger.

Ryan touched Jayden's shoulder. "You ready for this?"

"My power is back, thanks to you." She strode forward, toward her enemy, and called the storm. The roar of thunder coursed into her, and her power surged through her like a long-lost friend. She embraced every part of it. Whipping her hair and pulsing through her being. It burned with heat lightning.

The Mistress turned her face to the sky, basking in the stolen Creator's power, and it seemed to tear her from the inside. Too pure and bright for her to hold.

And as Jayden's storm rolled in, the Mistress turned her attention to Jayden. The Mistress's eyes had become sickly red. Like dried blood. "You cannot best me!" She raised her hands. "Behold my power!" A storm rumbled in the opposite direction of Jayden's.

She felt it. And it felt sick. But she reached out to it, and clouds parted around her probing talents. She smiled. The Mistress wouldn't sense someone else's lightning hiding in the storm she called. Jayden locked eyes with her enemy.

As the lightning sparked, wind whirled. Ash, from Ryan's spreading fire, rained down around Jayden like snow.

Snow.

White that choked her. Burned her lungs. Ripped through her chest like a broken heart.

She would fulfill her purpose. And she would die here.

Her eyes found Ethan, fighting off monsters that raced toward her, dust and ash and blood covering him. He was protecting her for this moment. As a surge of love for him swept through her, lightning cracked in the heavens. No doubting his love. Not now. This was her purpose. He'd been born to protect her so she could save everyone.

As Ryan joined Ethan, sword spearing through an abysshound, Jayden opened her arms and let the storm take all of her energy. She felt the Mistress shoot a bolt of her power out across the land.

That would be her last.

Jayden opened her eyes. Looked at the Mistress. "That power doesn't belong to you." Then she pulsed her lightning at the Mistress. Straight from the sky. No redirection. No dagger. Just a bolt to the heart.

As the green leaves from Quinn's tree headed toward Connor, he braced for their touch. Braced himself to open the door of death and claim the Mistress before she could hurt anyone. But the Creator's power unleashed. He felt every bit of it in his fur. His bones. Power that was meant to create and to heal and to protect. Twisted inside something evil, it tried to break free.

A wind that bit like rock and fire spread out across the whole army, sweeping the leaves into a stream in the air. Gnarg stood at the opening of the airstream and opened his mouth wider than any natural animal could. And he swallowed every leaf.

Connor's hope died.

Gnarg closed his jaws and his voice, like rock grating against rock, filled Connor's head. *"They call me the devourer of life. And now I shall devour you, Wielder!"*

Gnarg leapt. He pinned Connor to the ground, and razor teeth bit into Connor's neck.

"Now, Connor!"

Ethan's voice preceded a crack of thunder, and Connor sank his teeth into Gnarg's neck. Dust and maggots filled his mouth, and he ripped. Dead skin peeled from the Barghest, and it jumped off of him. Laughing, it paced in front of him. "You can't kill me. I'm death."

The Mistress's voice surrounded him. "Oh, Wielder. If you had used your power for me, you could have been so powerful. Now look at you. You're a dog. A creature of the light. Look around. The darkness is coming in."

She sent a bolt of lightning at him, and it hit hard. Stunned him. He flew backward. His spine slammed into a tree and snapped. Ribs cracked. His lungs tried to get air. Every part of him screamed in agony.

"You can't stop me now."

He tried to stand, but his body disobeyed. Sound began to mute, except for the screams. Dark spots started to overtake his vision.

He was dying.

It had to be now. He had to hold on long enough. Long enough to keep the door open.

The bracer would fuel him. And it would kill him. Quinn wouldn't be left behind to heal the damage he'd inflict. All of the Deliverers would die. All those who fought with them. Like the burning forest, they would perish in order to give new life a chance. His eyes filled with tears. This was his power. For this purpose. Meant to destroy this hideous evil. Maybe no one would forgive him for sacrificing so many lives, but they'd all come willingly.

Connor called on everything he could summon and opened the door.

His power bathed him in light as he lay at the base of the tree. Tore through him like a tempest. And he let it. It burned and cooled. It stretched his skin and made him feel as though a scream scratched his throat. And it shot through every dying vein unfettered, igniting him with life one last time.

Darkness, like the absence of anything light, filled the sky. Pulled at the evil creatures. They screamed as the door sucked them in. Black blood leeched up from the earth, and it groaned as the door extracted blood from its dying sands.

"You think you can open the door and order me in?" The Mistress laughed. "I have the Creator's power now. You cannot order me to do anything."

And lightning snapped from the sky.

Jayden's lightning bolt sailed true and hit the Mistress in the heart. And the Mistress screamed. Turned toward Jayden. Hate ignited in her eyes. Hate so strong, it fought to push Jayden to her knees. She held her ground as more lightning built in the heavens, coursed into her waiting hands, and then zapped into the Mistress.

And the door.

Behind the Mistress, a door had opened. Pulling. Killing. Taking.

An arrow of pure fire and light flew toward Jayden. She'd be powerless to stop it.

Ethan's chest burned. He looked up to see a gaping hole in the sky. Black like a tornado. And it looked just as angry. And the urging in his talent told him to protect Ryan, who fought by his side.

He turned to see Ryan clinging to a tree branch as so many were torn and pulled into the angry tunnel in the sky. Ryan's hands slipped, and Ethan threw his shield at his brother. The evil wind buffeted him, pulled at Ryan, but Ethan sank to his knees and held tight.

Hold on.

A voice flowed from the forest, surrounding Connor, and he held on to life for a little longer. He only hoped it would be long enough.

Where two had fought, one screamed and clawed at the ground. And death followed. Gnarg became ash and smoke in the wind, sucked into the door. So many screams filled the air as animals and people flew though the opening. But nothing pulled at him. He wasn't one of the ones being torn from this world. Why not?

What did he have left to live for but the knowledge that he'd destroyed everything? His Quinn had been turned into a tree. She'd

burned like everything else in this wood. His tears had dried out li
his heart. Like Quinn.

Hopefully Ethan would have enough power to push the Mistress
through.

Maybe the pain would end.

The Mistress swirled like ash in the wind, and Ethan's power swept
her form through the door.

It was done.

They'd done it.

Connor closed the door.

And then he closed his eyes.

His body trembled. He couldn't even move. Looked like he was
going to die after all. It was better this way. If only he could trade his
life for the Deliverers. *Creator, if you would see fit, spare the Deliverers.
Take me, but spare them.*

Ethan dropped his shield. Wind died away, leaving behind an eerie
calm. The hole in the sky closed, rendering sunlight so devoid of red,
the brightness seemed foreign. Rays spread across the battlefield, bath-
ing the aftermath in a quiet light. So out of place. All around him,
men and women stood and stared in silence. Healers rushed through
the masses of people, searching for those to heal. He needed to find
Jayden, Serena, and Ryan.

He whirled around to make sure the shield had worked. "Ryan!"

Ryan was there. Ethan raced over to him and threw his arms
around his brother. "Are you hurt?"

"You saved me."

"You saved all of us."

Serena ran over to them, dried blood all over her clothes. "We
did it!"

Ryan caught her and wrapped her in a hug. "You killed the dragon."

"You healed the forest." She wiped away a tear and turned to Ethan.
"Where's Jayden?"

"Sh-she—" Ethan scanned the landscape and his insides crumbled.

r just stopped, Ethan." Tears welled in Serena's eyes.
hirt sleeves. "I felt her pain. Then nothing."

rain had stopped.

Only ash fell from the sky.

Ash. Like snow.

He scanned the ground where he'd seen her last, while his heart screamed for him to find her. "Jayden!"

There. On the ground, still and silent. Ethan ran to her side and fell to his knees next to her. A black hole covered her middle. Her eyes stared into nothing. He cupped her head in his hands. "Jayden!" He pulled her still form into his chest, and a sob clawed its way out of him. "No! Don't go where I can't! Please."

Serena slid to a halt where Ethan sat. She touched Jayden's arm. "No. It's too late. It's—I'm going back for her."

Ethan looked up at her, tears choking him. "Serena, you—"

"I'm going!" She looked at Ryan. "Find Tessa or Rochelle. I'll need one of them once I bring Jayden back." She grabbed Jayden's hand and fell limp beside her.

CHAPTER 68

DEATH TOLLS

"Connor?" Something soft brushed his head and comforted him. He'd had a pack. A family. That made every sacrifice worth it.

Connor squeezed his eyes shut as the wave of pain ate through his body again. He opened them, the world hazier than before.

The dark-haired woman stepped out from the trees. Blood dripped beneath her eye. She wiped away the stain and no new blood took its place. Strange. She stared at Connor then turned to the woman next to her. "I have my powers back. I'll heal this one. Find another."

She knelt beside him. "Can you hear me?"

He nodded. At least, he thought he nodded.

"Here." She spread a cloak over him. Was he human again?

She pressed her hands against him and bowed her head as all the pain seeped away from his body.

His vision cleared, and he could see her now. "Madison?"

Tears dripped out of her eyes, and she wrapped him in a smothering hug. He hugged her back. "I–I was supposed to die."

She laughed. "No. You're going to be fine."

"Quinn wasn't touching me. She was the only person who could have saved me from the effect of the bracer." And it would have killed her.

"I *was* touching you."

Connor spun around at the sound of that voice. Her beautiful voice. "Quinn?" His heart swelled. "How? You were—"

She smiled that innocent smile and touched his face. "I was a tree."

hand to make sure she was real. To touch her. She
. "I'm also bonded to a phoenix. When Ryan burned
grew again."

The tree. The tree he'd landed into, lain at the base of, was Quinn.
"You regrew?"

She nodded and knelt beside him. He wrapped her in his arms as
his body shook. She was alive. And real. This was real.

"Are you okay?" Her small voice seemed concerned.

He laughed. "Okay? Quinn, you're alive. . . ." He let her go. "How
many?"

"More than half died when you opened the door, Connor. All the
Mistress's creatures."

"The Mistr—only the . . ." He couldn't breathe. Something welled
inside of him. Something joyful. "You mean . . ."

"Yes." She touched his face. "We won. And look."

He looked around him at the wood. Charred tree trunks were
scattered amidst young, green saplings. The once-scorched earth was
thriving. "How—you." He faced her. "You did this?"

She squeezed his hand. "*We* did this."

He pulled her close to him and kissed her. "You knew." He kissed
her again. "You believed when I didn't believe." He kissed one corner of
her mouth, behind her ear, on her adorable smile. "You complete me."

Her lips parted as she stared at him. Then she smiled, slowly. "And
you me, Wielder."

CHAPTER 69

NOBLE LIGHT

Air rushed into Jayden's lungs. She coughed, and the hole in her stomach screamed.

"Jayden?" a soft whisper touched her ear. A tear dripped onto her cheek.

"Ethan?" His name barely made it past her lips. Serena had brought her back from the dead—for Ethan.

"You're going to be all right. Tessa is here." His voice was shaky.

Tessa's hand pressed against her chest. It was so numb and so painful all at once. Then a familiar heat and cooling coursed through her. And she was whole. She grabbed Tessa's hand. "Thank you."

Tessa just smiled. "I am going to help the others." She touched Ethan's arm before she left.

Ethan.

He stared at Jayden. "I almost lost—"

"You didn't." She sat up, opened her arms, and crashed into him. His strong arms gripped her like he never wanted to let her go, and she breathed in this moment. Right here. She never wanted to forget how loved she felt. She found Serena's hand and squeezed. "Thank you for bringing me back for him," she whispered.

"Thank you for coming with me." Serena touched Jayden's cheek.

She hugged them both and then told Jayden she was going to tend to the wounded. But Ethan still wasn't letting go. He pressed his face into the crook of Jayden's neck. "I'm sorry she had to bring you back."

" She moved so she could look into his eyes.

ꜰly smile tugged on his mouth. "Not for me."

ꜰched his cheek. "Don't be sorry for me. I'm not. This is where I want to be. With you. Always."

His eyebrows lifted, but how could he be surprised? Her following laughter was half choked by emotion. "Oh, Ethan." She tipped his head so he'd look at her, teary eyes and all. "Are you doubting my love?"

It was his turn for a startled laugh. The kind that found joy in a sad moment and broke though. "Doubting your—no."

She smiled as he blinked away any coating of wetness, and then she kissed him. The way he held her, as if he never wanted this moment to end, as if he was memorizing the feel of her hair, her lips, her hands on his neck, made her forget everything else.

And when it finished, she looked into those brown eyes and said, "The correct answer is 'never.'"

And the crooked smile that her words pulled from him melted her heart.

"Jayden!" The voice made her stand up and turn in time to catch Luc in a tight embrace. "You're okay!" He squeezed her. Then stepped back to look at her. "That storm was you?"

She nodded. "I didn't know you were here."

"I fought with the Healers and Feravolk. Madison brought me to the Healers. Ryan, you're okay, too!" Luc kept one arm on Jayden and held out his hand to shake Ryan's.

Ryan complied, but something about him felt off. Sad in a strange way. Jayden was about to ask him, but Luc started talking to him about the fire.

Someone rubbed Jayden's back and she leaned into Ethan. She took a deep, calming breath and looked around. The Healers were tending to the wounded, and Quinn stood in the center of the meadow, arms raised above her head, growing new trees, with Connor beside her.

"I'm going to find Madison." Luc touched her shoulder. Then he nodded to Ethan and the two of them shook hands.

Now that Ryan was free, Jayden approached. She wanted to fling her arms around him, but his sadness choked her. Something was very wrong. His face had grown gaunt, his skin pale. Just like the day she'd returned to Anna's with the plant. "You're hurt?"

He shook his head but dropped to his knees.

"He's dying!" Serena raced back to them and knelt beside him. "You—you're poisoned."

"What?" Jayden clutched his sleeves.

"You lied to me." Serena stared at him, arms curled around her middle. "You said once the Mistress died, you'd be free."

Ryan's emotions crashed into Jayden, and they carried so much sorrow and peace all at once. "Free of her."

Tears flooded Serena's eyes. "Ryan! You deceived me on purpose."

He touched the side of her face. "You needed to defeat the Mistress."

Ethan knelt beside them, his sadness wrapping around Jayden's heart. "Is it true, Ry?"

"She claimed more than half of my heart. It's too late for me." He touched Ethan's arm. "But thank you for saving me from the door. For giving me a chance to say good-bye."

"I will not say good-bye to you." Serena backed up, eyes red-rimmed and brimming.

Serena stared at Ryan. Her insides quivered. Was this what Ethan had felt when he knew Jayden was gone? Because as she sat here, she could feel Ryan slipping away from her. From this world. He'd done it on purpose to save all of them. He'd known he would die, and yet he fought with them. It wasn't fair. Someone with such a pure heart should not be forced to carry around a heart tainted with so much darkness.

There had to be something she could do for him.

That was her purpose, wasn't it? To heal them. If she couldn't keep all of her family safe, why was she here? A sob welled in her chest and it ached. But she held it in. She had to figure this out. There had to be a way to do something. Now. Here. She couldn't go back for him.

Ryan touched her shoulder. She wanted to punch him and hug

him. "You lied to me," she whispered, every word making her throat hurt.

"Serena, you told me there was good in my heart. You told me to embrace my powers. You told me to hope. I chose to do that. I knew if I told you it would be the end of me, the three of you wouldn't have been able to defeat her today."

"It wasn't just us. You—"

"I know." He took her hand and kissed the back. "I never thought I was worthy to be a Deliverer. You did." He looked up at Ethan and Jayden, too. "You all did. You all accepted me even though I thought she'd claimed me. So I know it feels like you've lost, but really you saved me." He cupped Serena's neck in his hand and looked deep into her eyes. "You saved me. Remember that, always."

She hunched over and the tears came. Everything hurt. Why had she not seen this coming?

Ryan pulled her into his arms, and she wanted to scream. "Serena—"

"I'm sorry," she whispered. "Connor said two of us would die—and I could only go back for one."

If only Dash were here. If only there was a Healer strong enough. But only Madison and Tessa were, and they'd both already done this. She needed Dash right now. She—her eyes snapped up to meet Ryan's, and she wiped her tears away. She could not let him die tainted. "Ryan, do you trust me?"

His heart was completely open to her, she could feel it—the one piece of good that he clung to. He looked right into her eyes. "Of course I do."

"I can't let you die like this." She couldn't stop the shake in her voice. "You are not her pawn."

"But my heart is still dark. Tainted. I feel it. It will send me to the afterworld with her. Won't it?" He touched his chest.

"Not if I can help it." She pulled her dagger from her boot. "Hold still?"

He stared at the blade and then looked at her and nodded once. "Do it."

"Serena!" Ethan grabbed her arm. "What are you doing?"

"The Mistress has a hold of his heart now. I can't let him die with a tainted heart, Ethan. As a prisoner of the Mistress. He'd go to the afterworld with her. Wouldn't he? That's not him." Tears streamed down her face.

"It's okay, Ethan." Ryan gently removed Ethan's grip from her arm. Then he looked at Serena. "The Mistress said the only way to be free of her was to cut out my heart. She was telling the truth, wasn't she?"

"Yes." Serena could barely say the word.

"This is madness." Ethan grabbed Serena's shoulder. "You can't— Ryan, you could still have time. You—"

"I don't." He clasped Ethan's hand, stood, and pulled him in for a hug.

"Listen to me, Ryan. You are a hero. Don't—don't forget that." Ethan choked on his words.

Then Jayden wrapped her arms around him. "Don't you dare say good-bye to me."

"Then until we meet again." He kissed the top of her head and turned to Serena. Stared right into her eyes. "I trust you. I'm ready." He knelt and she with him.

She didn't even try to hold back tears now. Her chin trembled and her voice shook. "I love you." She thrust her dagger into Ryan's heart.

He cried out. She breathed deep. If Dash was right, she'd be able to see his heart. There. It beat so slowly, bathed in a strange, bright-but-dark light. She pushed the dagger against his flesh and the hole widened. She reached in and tore the heart from his chest. Easily it came, bathed in the noble light. She tossed the broken heart to the ground and reached inside her own chest. The heart there, that Dash had given her, beat strong and fierce. Full of light and love. As Dash had done for her, she pulled it out. The pain ripped into her, but the peace she felt, the love, covered it so quickly. Then she pushed the heart into Ryan's chest. The light that bathed him turned white and sparkled. She could almost hear Dash's voice telling her, *Well done.*

Then she recentered the dagger and thought of healing him as she pulled it out. Her energy was draining fast. But if Dash was right, she could do what a unicorn could. She could heal him.

White light suddenly bathed her eyes. She lost sight of him. Of everything.

No. She had to keep it together. She had to make sure he was healed.

But her head hit the ground.

CHAPTER 70

SCARS

Sunlight poured onto Serena's face and beckoned her to open her eyes. Above her, a candelabra sparkled. She lay on white sheets like those in a Healer's home. In fact, this looked strangely like her own home in the Valley of the Hidden Ones. She sat up.

Where was—"Ryan?" The relief that flooded her tingled in every part of her being. An overwhelming happiness. She clung to it. Breathed it in.

He stood by the window, smiling that charming smile she'd missed. "Morning, beautiful."

He neared her, a playful gleam in his eyes. "You were starting to worry me."

Truth. "You—you're alive? Right? Or am I dead?"

He chuckled and sat on the edge of her bed. "I've been awake for two days."

She scooted near him and placed her hand over his heart.

"It's beating," he said. "Thanks to you."

"Thanks to Dash."

"And you." He nuzzled her neck, and warmth spread through her whole being.

He was alive.

She sat back and marveled at how pure his heart felt. The same as before, only minus the taint. "I thought I'd lost you."

"I thought you had, too." His smile melted her insides. "I have to admit, I thought you were giving me a noble death. I never imagined you'd save me like that." He touched the side of her face.

"I hoped it would work. But I wasn't sure."

"Either way, what you did was to save me."

"Yes."

His gaze traced her face and he pulled her close. His lips pressed against hers tenderly. She tugged him closer, and he laid her against the bed. Kissed her again. Then looked into her eyes. He rubbed his chest where she'd stabbed him. That charming smile covered his face. "But you didn't even leave me a scar."

A shocked laugh escaped her throat. "A scar?"

His playful look returned, making his eyes practically sparkle. "When I tell the story to our children and have no scar to show for it, what will they think?"

"Our . . . children?"

His eyes grew wide, and he backed away from her. "Well, yeah. I thought—"

She sat up, pulled him closer, and found his jawbone with her lips. She kissed him again, inching closer to his mouth. "But you haven't asked me to marry you yet."

He chuckled. "Serena, will you—"

"Yes."

His fingers ran through her hair as he tucked her body into him. "Thank you."

○

Jayden followed Westwind as he loped through the Forest of Legends. Even this part, five days' journey from the heart of the forest, had been touched by Ryan's fire. Ethan, Ryan, Serena, Connor, and Quinn followed behind her, insisting that they'd all walk with her even though between their returned bonded animals—Blaze, Cliffdiver, and Zephyr—they could have been carried. Even Enya, Quinn's phoenix, had returned.

But not Stormcloud. Jayden's heart ached at the loss of her friend. She still didn't know what had happened to her.

"I hope we make it before the storm breaks." She nudged the wolf with her words.

"Not much farther." Westwind looked back at her and winked.

She glanced back at the others and shrugged. "He still won't tell me where we're going."

"This looks familiar," Ethan said.

Westwind splashed across a river. The other side held more green. Not so much fire damage over here.

"Oh. This place is amazing." Quinn stopped. She twirled in a circle, her eyes closed, and a huge smile on her face. "I feel it. Deep roots grow here. Old trees. So many memories. So much love."

Jayden spun to face Westwind. The creek. The trees. Any long grass had withered and fallen, but now that she looked at it and replaced dead and burned trees with living ones in the picture her mind created, she knew this place. "It's Anna's cottage." Her voice came out a whisper.

Westwind loped ahead, and Jayden ran after him, pulse racing. She stepped into the clearing and gasped. The cottage still sat in the middle of a tree grove. It housed different kinds of trees, a pond, a meadow perfect for raising chickens and goats. Joy bubbled inside of her.

Quinn touched the solid beams that constructed the cabin. "A Whisperer lived here."

Jayden dropped to her knees and hugged Westwind. "I love it."

Ethan breathed deep and looked over the property. "It's plenty big enough for a couple more cabins, don't you think?"

Ryan grinned. "I do. As long as my neighbors wouldn't mind a dragon sleeping by the pond."

Jayden smiled. "Of course not."

"May I see the house?" Quinn ventured toward it as if she were a pegasus and it was a bolt of lightning.

"We may all want to go inside." Jayden looked up at the darkening sky. "The storm is above us."

They all entered Anna's home. Though dusty with a few tipped-over chairs, it looked very similar to the day they'd left nearly a year ago. It felt more like ages. Jayden stood in the doorway and smiled. This would make a good house. And she'd fill it with laughter again.

S.D. GRIMM

Quinn touched the wooden beams, and the house groaned as it shifted. "I think it's welcoming us."

"Well, that settles it," Jayden said. "You and Connor will have to help the rest of us build our cabins."

Quinn's eyes glittered. "You mean it?"

She nodded.

Thunder rumbled, and she turned to the open door to feel the stormy air on her face. She caught sight of Ethan, leaning against the porch railing, and she joined him. Then the rain came. Hard and fast and strong. Drenching rain that covered everything. It made the new trees grow.

The Forest of Legends needed this now. Thanks to Quinn, they grew faster. Soon the Forest of Legends would be filled with towering trees again. Everything was rebuilding. Starting fresh.

Ethan moved behind her. He placed his hands on her shoulders and bowed his head close to hers. "Hey. What's wrong? I thought you'd be happy."

She turned around in his arms and laid her head on his chest. "I am. And I'm not."

He held her. "It's hard to be back?"

"No. That's not it."

"It's hard to come back."

Jayden looked up at him, but he was staring out at the rain. He was right, more right than he even knew. A pang squeezed her heart as she recalled how wonderful she'd felt when she was in the afterworld. She'd wanted to stay until Serena had reminded her that she'd be leaving Ethan behind. She couldn't leave him. She'd heard him speaking to her at that moment: *Don't go where I can't go with you. Please.* And those words had made her want to return to him.

The pang in her heart mended. This second chance to be with him was worth it. She'd make the same choice again. In a heartbeat. But how could she explain that to someone who had never been in the Creator's presence? Who had never . . . "Oh." Her mouth dropped open. She touched Ethan's stomach where the old scar was that he'd never told her about—the one Serena had felt in the house of wisdom. "Ethan, you died?"

He nodded.

"What brought you back?"

"Tessa grabbed my hand and brought me back. I didn't choose it. But the Creator wanted her to bring me back. He said I still had something to do. It's why I knew I had to protect you and the others."

"And you did."

He looked at her and smiled. "Anything for you."

Those words warmed her heart. Ethan's declaration of love. The rain churned. It would become a stronger storm if she pushed it.

"Come here." He motioned toward the porch steps.

"You want to go out in the rain?"

He smiled that boyish grin and nodded. Thunder pealed. She grabbed his hand and let him lead her into the rain.

"I wanted to show you something." He nodded toward the side of the house. Thunder rumbled again, like a growl that seemed somehow outside of the storm. "Someone."

Jayden peered around the side of the house, curious as to who would be there. Perhaps he'd told Luc or Rebekah where they were going. Maybe—her heart pounded as she stared at the black pegasus standing in the rain. And her name came out in a breath. "Stormcloud."

She raced to Jayden, wings extended, and nuzzled into her. *"I'm sorry I stayed away."*

And Jayden felt the bond reconnect. The hole inside of her filled. She stroked Stormcloud's nose and pressed her face against the pegasus. *"I'm just glad you came back."*

"I—well, would you get Serena?"

Jayden looked at her friend. *"Do you have a message for her?"*

Stormcloud dipped her head in what looked like an enthusiastic nod. But Serena and Ryan had already exited the front door. They met Jayden by her pegasus.

"You came back!" Serena pet Stormcloud's nose.

Stormcloud whickered and flipped her head. A tiny white pegasus stepped around the side of the house, seeming to melt into view as it moved, a little unsteady on its feet. The small nub of a horn grew from the top of his head.

Serena's hands flew to her mouth, and she remained rooted where she stood. "Is that . . . ?"

"I named him Dash, after his father."

The little pegasus pressed his nose into Serena's hand and closed his eyes. She pulled his face close and leaned her forehead against his. "His bond structure is for Healers."

"You bonded to him?" Stormcloud asked.

Serena nodded, not taking her attention from the winged unicorn.

Tears sprung into Jayden's eyes, and she hugged Stormcloud's neck. "He's beautiful."

"He is." Serena kissed his nose.

Lightning sparked across Stormcloud's coat. Dash whinnied and tossed his head. His fur shimmered like sparkling snow. The two of them took flight in the rain, and Serena stood there, waving after the small winged creature.

Jayden watched them, her heart full.

Ryan shivered. "How can you stand in the rain?" He tugged Serena, and she walked back with him to the house.

Jayden turned to Ethan. "You want to go in?"

"No. I want to stay with you."

Lightning lit the sky like fireworks, and she hugged Ethan close, basking in his contentment. "When I was . . . dead, I still loved you. It's what brought me back."

His breath hitched.

"I saw so many people I loved. Logan. My parents. My birth parents. My brothers. And they all encouraged me to leave with Serena. But I didn't want to go."

"Oh. Jayden, I'm sorry."

She grabbed his hand. "No. Stop being sorry. When I felt the pull of love for you, I was ready to come back. I wanted to." She paused to look into his brown eyes and make sure he felt her words. "Even in death, I loved you."

She slid her hand behind his neck and pulled him into her. His lips met hers and the rain splashed harder. Stronger. Drowning out everything else. Lightning cracked, and he lifted her into his arms. She pulled him as close as she could. Wrapped arms and legs around him. Felt every splash of rain roll along her skin. Tasted the electricity in their kiss. Felt it in his strength. The storm pulsed through both of them, she felt it alive and wild. Pure and strong.

When she opened her eyes, the kiss still on her lips, she smiled. "I'd do anything for you, Ethan. Anything."

EPILOGUE

Seven years later

Jayden breathed in the humid evening air and leaned against the back porch's railing as she looked out over the forest surrounding her house. The sun touched the horizon, sinking lower every second. Gold pierced through the old, charred trees of the Forest of Legends and bathed the new, rich, leafy forest in warmth. It looked so beautiful now with the young trees reaching toward the sky, growing into the gaps left by the burned trees. Light that hadn't shown there in years now punctured through and made the forest thrive.

That was what Serena said every time they walked there together. She'd look up at the sky and spin in a circle and muse that the forest was thriving again.

Five silhouettes stepped out from the massive trees and into the old grove beyond the pond. Westwind and Aurora loped. Ethan, Ryan, and Connor each carried a string of rabbits. Their deep laughter rode on the wind.

Someone tugged on her apron, and Jayden turned to see her son's big blue eyes staring up at her. She crouched down to his level and felt his pulse of worry. "What's wrong, dear one?"

"Auntie Serena says you'll kiss it, even if she already healed it."

Jayden smiled. "What happened?"

"I scraped my elbow climbing down from the tree."

Jayden kissed the spot, though no scrape remained.

Serena, her own little girl on her hip, appeared in the doorway holding Quinn's daughter's hand. Smiling, she joined Jayden on the porch. "I sent them to the river to wash up for supper. Your oldest seemed to think climbing trees the better idea." She winked at Jayden's boy. "Quinn is helping the other two finish washing—they needed more than just their hands cleaned." Her laugh swirled in the wind like a chime. Then she caught sight of the men returning and kissed her daughter. "Wave to Daddy."

Jayden's son whirled around. "Is my daddy coming, too?" His face brightened. "Daddy!" He rushed to greet them.

Quinn's daughter followed, tripping only once on the uneven grass. The goats and chickens frolicked after her, Enya flying above them. Blaze and Zephyr lifted their heads, seeming to want to join them, but lay back down, basking in the rays of sun instead. Stormcloud and her son, Dash, continued grazing. Jayden folded her arms and leaned against the railing, her eyes glued to Ethan as he patted their son's head.

"Well, the children seem excited," Serena said. "Perhaps we should send our husbands out to catch dinner more often."

Jayden laughed. "I wonder who won the bet."

"I'm guessing Aurora."

"I just hope the rabbits are already skinned."

Another soft laugh sounded behind Jayden, and she turned to see Rebekah slowly stepping onto the porch, careful not to wake Jayden's sleeping daughter in her arms.

Jayden held out her hands. "Would you like me to take her?"

"Nonsense." Rebekah smiled and rubbed the baby's back. "She's comfortable here."

Jayden smiled. "Then I suppose I should make sure the cookfire is still hot."

"Oh, Ryan will take care of that," Serena said as Ryan stepped up onto the porch. He wrapped his arm around her and pulled her close. "Did you win?" she asked.

His lopsided smile filled his face. "I think the wolves cheated."

Cliffdiver landed in the field and Jayden's children rushed off the porch. "Uncle Percy and Aunt Estelle are here!"

Jayden pressed her hand against her chest and looked at Ethan then Ryan. "Uncle Percy? Aunt Estelle? Which one of you—" she stopped as they both grinned.

Then she joined the running children as they raced out to greet her aunt and uncle. Uncle Percy—or as Ryan's kids called him, Uncle One Eye—was already passing out carved wooden animals. And Aunt Estelle was telling each of them loudly how much they'd grown since last time.

As the children seemed enraptured, a glowing, white unicorn stepped into the clearing. Wren jumped off its back as children rushed to great her. Jayden marveled at how Ryan's littlest sister had grown.

Just as she thought her heart couldn't get happier, another shadow-crossed over them, and Jayden looked up. A red dragon descended, and Jayden recognized Kara's Ember.

The dragon landed, and all the kids shouted, "They're here! They're here!"

Jayden's heart swelled as Luc slid off the dragon and helped his pregnant wife to the ground. Connor rushed over to greet them and Jayden followed, enveloping her brother and Madison in a huge hug. "You came."

"Wouldn't be anywhere else." Luc pulled her close again.

Kara even let Jayden hug her. "Thank you for inviting me, Softheart."

Jayden smiled. "As I've said before, you're always welcome here. We're your family."

Kara rolled her eyes, but the sense of joy pulsing through her coursed into Jayden's heart.

Rounds of hugs and laughter filled the meadow as everyone greeted one another, and gradually they all made their way inside, where children's voices—exuberant from the day's coming excitement—echoed in the house.

Rebekah touched Jayden's shoulder. "I'm going to calm those little ones. You take your time." She held her hand out, motioning for Jayden's boy to follow.

Jayden blinked as she watched Rebekah go inside. Did she know what day it was? Did they all? Was that why nearly her whole family had insisted on joining her for supper tonight? Why Ethan had orchestrated this whole party?

Ethan stopped in front of her and touched her arm, drawing her attention back to him.

The sun sank ever lower.

Westwind paused next to Jayden and looked up at her. Her son scratched behind his ears, and the wolf smiled.

Jayden's fingers brushed his coat. "If I didn't know any better, I'd think you liked that, Westwind."

He chuckled. *"Your son looks like his father."*

She looked up at Ethan's soft smile. "He does."

"He's got his mother's eyes though."

Jayden nodded. "It makes him look so much like his grandfather."

"He's got the same bond structure, too."

Jayden snapped her gaze to Westwind. "You've bonded to my son?"

He smiled. *"I have."*

She dropped to her knees. "I can't think of a better friend." She looked at her son. "Logan, you've bonded?"

He nodded, a huge grin on his face. "Westwind says his mate caught the most rabbits."

She laughed and hugged him close. Then she let go and watched the wolves follow her son inside. She stood and faced Ethan. "Did you know about the bond?"

He shook his head.

She wrapped her arms around him and laced her fingers together.

He hugged her back. "Hey, what's wrong? What do you need?"

She shook her head and leaned against his chest. But tears stung her eyes. They weren't sad tears. Well, some of them were. Eight years ago marked the day the queen had stolen her family from her. Burned her home and tried to rob her of the one thing that had kept her going through all the heartache: love. But most of these tears coated her eyes because happiness filled her to the brim. She'd lost so much, but she'd also gained so much. Learned so much.

She'd been given a chance to have more family. More life. More love.

She could think of nothing stronger than love.

Like the Forest of Legends regrew, so new growth, new life, and new love flourished, even in her bruised and broken heart. She'd persevered because of family she'd lost and family she'd gained. And the love they gave her in return strengthened her. Made her thrive. Made her believe it was possible to return home—she'd just needed to build a new one. One that would embrace her past, one that accepted her for who she was, and one she could grow old with. She would be at home when all of that came together to keep her whole. Keep her thriving.

Ethan kissed the top of her head. "Jayden? What do you need?" he repeated. He held her closer. Strong and gentle at the same time.

She breathed in and cuddled as close to him as she could. "Just this." She closed her eyes and pressed her ear against his chest, listening to his heartbeat. The sound that told her she was home.

S.D. Grimm's first love in writing is young adult fantasy and science fiction. That's to be expected from someone who looks up to heroes like Captain America and Wonder Woman, has been sorted into Gryffindor, and isn't much taller than a hobbit. Her patronus is a Red Voltron Lion, her spirit animal is Toothless, and her lightsaber is blue. She has been known to write anywhere she can curl up with her laptop and at least one large dog. She has also been caught brandishing a wooden spoon in the kitchen while simultaneously cooking dinner and "head-writing" a fight scene.

She believes that with a little faith, a lot of love, and an untamed imagination, every adventure is possible. That's why she writes. Her debut novel was *Scarlet Moon*, the first book in the Children of the Blood Moon series. Learn more about her books at *www.sdgrimm.com*.

Facebook: *www.facebook.com/SDGrimm*
Twitter: *www.twitter.com/SDGrimmAuthor*
Instagram: *www.instagram.com/s.d.grimm*
Pinterest: *www.pinterest.com/SDGrimmAuthor*